THE MALLEN SECRET

Catherine Cookson's classic family lives on...

Each and every generation of the Mallen family has been beset by unhappiness and tragedy – it is said that they are cursed by the dramatic white streak in their jet-black hair. Now, the horror of World War One has finally come to an end and, as with so many other families, the Mallen family has been devastated by loss, injury and memories that are almost too terrible to bear. As they struggle to rebuild their lives in the aftermath of war, secrets and lies from generations past will come to light – causing destruction of a different kind...

THE MALLEN SECRET

by

Rosie Goodwin writing as
Catherine Cookson

Magna Large Print Books
Long Preston, North Yorkshire,
BD23 4ND, England.

British Library Cataloguing in Publication Data.

Goodwin, Rosie, writing as Cookson, Catherine
    The Mallen secret.

    A catalogue record of this book is
    available from the British Library

    ISBN   978-0-7505-2895-5

First published in Great Britain 2007 by Headline Publishing Group

Copyright © 2007 The Catherine Cookson Charitable Trust

Jacket illustration © Bridgeman Art Library
Airplane © Mary Evans' Picture Library

Published in Large Print 2008 by arrangement with
Headline Publishing Group Ltd.

Magna Large Print is an imprint of Library Magna Books Ltd.

Printed and bound in Great Britain by
T.J. (International) Ltd., Cornwall, PL28 8RW

Contents

Part One

The Secret

Chapter One

11 November 1919

'Eh, there were times that I never thought I'd see this day dawn, sir.' Nurse Byng raised her hand to swipe the happy tears from her cheeks as Ben Bensham nodded in agreement. The air was alive with the sound of church bells that were ringing to herald the first anniversary of the ending of the war.

'Now all we have to do is count the cost of all the lives that were lost, and hope that life can return to some sort of normality,' Ben said sombrely, but even as the words were uttered, he knew that this would be easier said than done.

For the last fifteen months he had known happiness in the cottage that he and his new wife, Hannah, had made their home. Or at least happiness of a kind, for the nightmares were never far away and still had the habit of coming upon him when he least expected them to. Many a night, Hannah would wake him and hold his sweating body to her as he shivered and sobbed in her arms.

'Don't forget how far you have come,' she would remind him, and he had to admit that he had come a long way since his time in 'the bunker' at High Banks Hall. The Hall had been given over to the military to use as a hospital for the duration of the war. The bunker, as it was termed, was the room where the officers who came here were first placed whilst they recovered from the terrible ordeals they had been forced to endure on the battlefield. Once they were over the worst, they would then be transferred to E Dormitory, which they would share with other officers while working their way through D, C and B wings until finally they were well enough to return to their units or their homes.

Even now, Ben shuddered as he recalled the time he had spent there in that damn room. It had been all at the same time a sanctuary yet a prison, and at one point he had thought that he would never recover from the atrocities he had seen. But that was before Petty, as his nurse was affectionately known, had taken him in hand and yanked him back from the edge of the dark pit he had almost fallen into. Now she was his wife, and every single day he thanked God for her, for had it not been for her, he was well aware that he might have lost his mind altogether. But still, today was a day for rejoicing, and his handsome face now lit in a smile as an officer hurried towards him with what looked like a generous glass of port in his hand.

'Ben, man!' His face was glowing as he thumped Ben affably on the shoulder. 'Get yourself along to the day room. Nurse Conway is allowing us all a drink by way of celebration. Just think of it. When we leave here, we'll be going home.'

Ben grinned back at him. 'Then that's all the more reason to hurry and get well, eh?'

The officer nodded before speeding on his way, sipping at his drink as he went.

'So – are you going to share in the celebrations

or what then, sir?' Nurse Byng asked as Ben headed off towards the staircase that led to what had once been the nursery quarters of High Banks Hall. This was where Mrs Bensham, formerly Miss Brigmore, the governess of the children who had once lived here, now resided.

'Perhaps later,' Ben told her across his shoulder, 'when I have seen Brigie. How is she today, Byng?'

Her face became straight now as she slowly shook her head. 'Not good, sir. I would be a liar to say otherwise; though no doubt the good news will act as well as any tonic.'

Ben made no reply but now took the stairs two at a time. Hardly a day passed when he didn't call in to see Brigie, as he affectionately called her, for she had been the one who had shown him fondness when his own mother had denied it him.

He was breathless by the time he reached the bedroom door and there he paused to straighten his waistcoat and smooth his hair, which had 'the Mallen streak' as it was known, running all through the left side of it. As his fingers patted it flat he briefly wondered if he would be the last to bear it. There was every possibility, unless Hannah presented him with a son. If this should be so, then he could only pray that the child would not be cursed with the streak, for it was acknowledged by one and all that any Mallen bearing the streak died a tragic death and rarely knew happiness. Many a time, Ben had wished that he could tear the streak from his scalp, but he never had. What would have been the point? The way he saw it, it would have only grown back again. But now was not the time to worry about it, and so he gently

11

knocked on the door before throwing it open without waiting for anyone to bid him enter.

As always, he had the sense of stepping back in time, for Mrs Bensham was not one for change, as the staff at the Hall had soon found out. China figurines and fine Worcester vases were dotted along a large marble mantelshelf above a roaring coal fire, which Brigie insisted was kept burning throughout the day and night. A large brass bed stood in the centre of one wall and next to it was a finely carved mahogany bedside cabinet that matched the wardrobe and chests of drawers that were placed about the room. Persian carpets were scattered here and there, and a huge marble washstand, with a pretty china jug and matching bowl, was placed at the other side of the bed. A dressing-table, on which lay a silver hairbrush and comb, dominated the wall opposite the bed, and the looking-glass in the centre of it reflected the eerie grey light that was struggling through an enormous bay window.

Brigie was propped up on pillows, and a young nurse was walking towards the door with an empty tea tray in her hands.

'Ah, Mr Ben.' Her eyes were twinkling. 'Wonderful news, eh?'

'It is indeed, Nurse. But how is she today?'

'I'm quite capable of answering that question for myself, young man,' came a sharp retort from the bed and at that, Ben and the nurse both laughed as he held the door open for her and she disappeared into the corridor. Once he had closed it behind her he crossed to the bed and smiled down on the tiny woman lying there. Brigie seemed to

12

have shrunk over the last months, though her eyes were still bright and alert as she smiled back at him and patted the bed at her side. She had always been a great one for following proprieties and knew that the nurse frowned on anyone sitting on the bed when there was a perfectly acceptable chair to the side, but for Ben – and his father, Dan, if it came to that – she would make exceptions.

'So ... the war is finally over then?'

He nodded. 'Yes, Brigie, it's over, and not a day too soon from where I'm standing.'

He took her wrinkled hand in his, and now as her eyes moved to the window, she asked, 'And how is Hannah?'

'In a word – blooming. Just this morning I told her that if she's only halfway through this pregnancy, at the rate her waistline is growing she'll burst before the child gets the chance to put in an appearance. She's going to try and get over to see you later – if Lawrie will let her out of his sight, that is.'

Brigie's eyes moved back to him. 'He is settling at the cottage?' she wanted to know.

'Oh yes, he's as happy as a sand-boy. As you suggested, we have turned the outhouse into a place where he can whittle his wooden animals to his heart's content. In fact, I have an idea to put to you about that.'

'Oh – and what would that be then?'

'Well, as you are aware, Lawrie has a great gift in that direction and Hannah and I were wondering if we could perhaps get a shop in Newcastle to start selling some of his carvings? We could put the money they made into a bank account for him.

13

Not that Aunt Katie left him short, of course, but it might give him a sense of independence.'

She nodded her approval. 'I think that is an excellent idea, Ben. You can have no idea how much easier I feel, knowing that Lawrie has you and Hannah to keep an eye out for him.'

Lawrence, or Lawrie as he was affectionately known, had been a cause of great concern to Brigie since his mother's demise, for although his body was now that of a man, his mind remained that of a child. But for all that, he was much loved by those who knew him, and Brigie was pleased to see him settled following the death of his mother.

However, her thoughts swiftly moved on from Lawrence, and she suddenly asked, 'Will you do something for me, Ben?'

'Of course – name it.'

'Would you tell your father that I would like to see him at his earliest convenience?'

Seeing the concern on her face, he stroked her hand and murmured, 'There is nothing wrong, is there, Brigie?'

She, paused before answering. 'Not wrong exactly, but there is something I need to discuss with him. I have a feeling that I won't be long for this life now and there is something that has been weighing heavily on my mind.'

'Nonsense!' The denial burst from him before he could stop it. The thought of life without Brigie was unthinkable. 'We've always said that we'd have to shoot you, Brigie. You'll live to be a hundred at least. But, this matter that is concerning you, is it anything that I can help you with?'

'No, Ben... But thank you for your kindness.'

14

He gently squeezed the frail hand resting in his own. Brigie was now ninety-eight years old, and for the first time he noticed the blue tinge around her lips and the weary look in her eyes.

The sound of the church bells covered the brief silence that fell between them until Brigie then enquired, 'Have you heard how Constance is faring?'

A frown settled across Ben's face. 'We have every reason to believe that she and Sarah are well,' he said. 'Hannah still goes across there from time to time, when it is necessary.'

'Good, good. And what will you do with High Banks Hall, now that the war is over? Will you and Hannah be coming to take up residence here? It is, after all, yours – once I am gone.'

He stood now and began to pace the room as he shrugged, 'I haven't given it much thought as yet, to be honest. I certainly wouldn't want to reclaim it until all the officers here were well enough to be discharged, and long after they are, I hope that you will still be around. Sadly, although peace has been declared for a year now, I think there will be a need for this place for some considerable time to come.'

She nodded and a cold hand closed around his heart as for the first time he realised that Brigie was fading. He had imagined that she would somehow live for ever, but now he was forced to admit that this was not going to happen.

She was plucking at the eiderdown, seemingly in a state of agitation. Now that he came to think of it, she had seemed very nervy for the last couple of visits. However, he had no chance to question her, for at that moment the door

15

opened and the nurse re-entered the room with a broad smile on her face.

'There is a party going on down there,' she informed them. 'The men are taking full advantage of the fact that they are being allowed a drink. The way they're carrying on, they'll all be in bed and fast asleep for lunchtime.' Crossing to the bed, she smoothed down the top cover as she eyed Mrs Bensham, who was looking tired.

Ben meantime was moving towards the door. 'Well, I'll be off now then, Brigie.' His tone was jocular. 'It's time for you to have your mid-morning nap and I don't want Nurse here throwing me out. I'll come back about the same time tomorrow, shall I?'

The old woman in the bed inclined her head as, with a final wave, Ben stepped out onto the landing and looked around him. As a child, both his father and his mother had been tutored in these very rooms by Miss Brigmore. The thought of his late mother brought his face into a frown and, hurrying now, he propelled himself forward and descended the stairs, pushing the unpleasant memories away.

Just as the nurse had said, the atmosphere downstairs was so charged with joy that he felt that he could almost have reached out and touched it. He briefly considered joining the officers for a drink in the day room, but then, deciding against it, he slipped out of the double oak doors and paused on the terrace that fronted the house to admire the view. The terrace was bordered by an open balustrade. Stone balls festooned it, and the steps that led down to the drive below were flanked by two large pillars on which perched a pair of stone cupids that had stood the test of time, since Thomas Wigmore Mallen had had the Hall built in 1767. They were stained with age now but still pleasing on the eye nonetheless. As he looked back at the impressive front doors his eyes came to rest on the inscription above them and his face became sad. *Man is compassionate because he gave God a mother*, it read. Ben could have argued that point, for he had craved his mother's love since the day he drew breath until the day she died – without success.

His eyes moved back to the view, of which he knew he could never grow tired. The hills in the distance were covered in snow and reached up into the sky from the vast barren plains laid out before them, and as always, the sight of all that space made Ben Bensham feel as free as a bird.

He glanced back towards the top-floor windows. What was it Brigie had said? *Will you and Hannah be coming to take up residence here?*

He had never given it much thought before, but soon he might be forced to, for his grandfather, Harry Bensham – Brigie's late husband – had bequeathed the Hall to him on her death. It was a sobering thought, and as he descended the steps and made his way towards the gates, his mind was preoccupied.

As Ben approached the cottage which had once belonged to Brigie, his gloveless hands were blue with cold and his nose was bright pink. Lawrie was waiting for him at the gate.

'Cousin Ben, can you hear the bells?' Lawrie's

childlike voice was full of excitement. 'Hannah says they are ringing to remind us again that the war is over. That's good, isn't it?'

'Yes, Lawrie, it is very good.' Ben reached up to ruffle Lawrie's hair as they made their way indoors together, Lawrie gambolling along like a spring lamb at the side of him.

'Nancy is doing us some roast pork for dinner,' he chattered on. 'I like the crackling. Do you, Cousin Ben?'

Ben smiled as he told him, 'Oh yes, I like it very much indeed, Lawrie. Now why don't you go into the kitchen and keep Nancy company while I have a quick word with Hannah?'

The man scampered away, his long legs flying in all directions as Ben took off his coat and hung it on the rack at the side of the door. He then smoothed his hair down, straightened his jacket and moved towards the small lounge where he found Hannah reading the newspaper with her feet resting on a stool. When she raised her face to his for a kiss he felt his heart lift. Not so long ago, when he was convalescing at the Hall, he had wished himself dead on more than one occasion, but now he had everything to live for. Hannah had been his saviour and these days, he could not contemplate life without her.

'How is Brigie?' she asked as she motioned towards a tray that was placed on a small occasional table. 'The tea is still hot.'

Lifting the teapot and pouring himself a cup, he frowned. 'Not so good, to be honest,' he replied. 'She doesn't look at all well and she's asked me to get Father to call in and see her. There's something she says she needs to discuss with him.'

'How strange.' As Ben carried his drink to a chair facing her and sat down in it she asked him, 'What do you think it's about?'

'I have no idea,' he admitted. 'But I thought I might go and see Father this afternoon and pass on the message. Would you like to come with me?'

She glanced doubtfully towards the window, then back at Ben, thinking how much better he looked, now that he had put a little weight back on. He was tall, dark and handsome, and she could never look at him without her heartbeat quickening. 'I think I might stay here,' she said eventually. 'It looks like it's going to snow again, and I'm not as nippy on my feet as I used to be, now I'm carrying this little lot about.'

His eyes rested proudly on the mound of her stomach. Because Hannah was so thin, her bump seemed even more pronounced than it would have done, had she been more rounded. Brigie had once described Hannah as having an 'interesting' face, for she had somehow just missed being pretty, but now, with the bloom of pregnancy on her, she was positively radiant. Initially, when she had informed Ben that they were going to have a child, he had been shocked. Strangely, it was something that they had never discussed, but now as the pregnancy progressed, he could hardly wait to hold his firstborn in his arms. And this child, he silently vowed, would be loved as he himself had never been.

At that moment there was a tap on the door and a plump woman with thick curly dark hair and a wide smile on her face stepped into the room. 'Dinner will be served in half an hour, sir,' she addressed Ben.

'Thank you, Nancy,' he said, smiling back. 'I shall be ready for it – the walk has given me an appetite. I could eat a scabby horse and its rider along with it.'

'Eeh, Mr Ben, you're a one you are,' she giggled, and then with a grin at the mistress, as she insisted on calling Hannah, she backed from the room.

Turning to his wife, Ben asked, 'Are you feeling a little happier about having Nancy here now?'

Hannah liked to think of herself as a modern woman and had for some time put up resistance when Ben suggested they have a live-in servant. Now, however, she sometimes wondered what she would do without Nancy, for as well as being hard-working and loyal she adored Lawrie, who in turn adored her back.

'I dare say she'll do.' There was a twinkle in his wife's eye now. In truth, she had come to think of Nancy as one of the family. Before she had come to them, the woman had nursed her elderly mother until she died, which Hannah thought was sad, for Nancy had had little or no life of her own, the way she saw it. Not that Nancy seemed to mind. She was now approaching her thirtieth birthday and seemed quite content with her spinster status.

As Ben looked into his wife's happy face he found himself thinking of Brigie again. On the rare occasions when Brigie was dressed now, she still insisted on wearing a dress that would cover her from neck to ankle. The first time Hannah had visited her with her shining new bob hairdo, and wearing a calf-length dress that revealed her ankles, Brigie had been appalled.

'Why, it's ... it's nothing short of being *immoral,*' she had gasped, and Hannah and Ben had fallen together laughing.

Thoughts of Brigie made him recall what they had discussed that morning. 'Brigie was wondering if you and I would be going to live in the Hall, now that the war is over,' he told his wife. 'After she is gone, of course.'

'*Us* ... live in the Hall?' Hannah's eyebrows rose into her neatly cut fringe. 'Whyever would we want to do that? We have everything we need right here.' Her eyes swept the small lounge, which in the time they had lived there, they had totally transformed. The antimacassars and bobbled mantel covers were gone, as were the aspidistra pots and all the other fussy Victorian ornaments that had cluttered the room. The dark velvet curtains that Hannah insisted must have housed at least a million moths had been torn down and replaced with lighter flowered ones that now allowed more light to flood through the small leaded windows.

Ben sighed. 'Well, it's something that we're going to have to think of eventually,' he told her with a note of regret. 'Grandfather did leave it to me in his will, and if we decide that we don't want to live there, we shall have to discuss what we're going to do with the place.'

'Huh! I can just imagine how my mother and grandmother would react if we were to move in there,' Hannah said gloomily. 'It's bad enough to them that you and I came together, but if we were

21

to move into the Hall, that would be the final insult.'

Ben knew that she was right. His Aunt Constance had never forgiven him for marrying Hannah, and still somehow thought that she had more rights to the Hall than he did, possibly because she had spent her early childhood there with her Uncle Thomas, who had been Miss Brigmore's lover for over twelve years. It was strange how things had turned out, now that he came to think of it, for after the Hall had been repossessed by bailiffs when Thomas got into debt, the latter had been forced to come and live here in this very cottage with Miss Brigmore, Mary Peel, her devoted servant, and Constance and Barbara, his nieces.

Ben's thoughts were interrupted when Lawrie lumbered into the room, excitedly holding out his latest offering to Hannah.

'Look, Petty,' he cried, using his usual endearment for her. 'Lawrie made a pig.'

As Ben watched her admire it, a cold finger traced its way down his spine. If he could have wished for anything in the world at that moment he would have wished that things could stay just as they were right now, but knowing that he had Mallen blood flowing through his veins he also knew that the chances of any lasting happiness for him were unlikely, for it was widely known that the Mallens were cursed – and it had been proven to be true, time and time again.

Chapter Two

'It's amazing that a year has already passed since peace was declared, isn't it, Father?'

'Yes, Ben. It is indeed.' Dan Bensham watched Betty divest his son of his coat and then side-by-side the two men stepped into the drawing room where Dan lifted a decanter of whisky.

'How about a drop of this? It will warm you up and we can drink a toast to peace at the same time.'

Ben nodded as he held his hands out to the roaring fire and his father filled two cut-glass tumblers with the sparkling amber liquid. Passing one to Ben he ushered him to a chair and when they were both seated he asked, 'So, how are things with you?'

'Couldn't be better.' Ben took a gulp of the fiery liquid, revelling in its heat as it burned its way down before going on, 'There is one thing, though. I was up at the Hall this morning and Brigie asked me to pass on a message. She wants to see you as soon as it is convenient.'

'Oh really, and why is that?'

'I have no idea,' Ben told him truthfully. 'She said there was something that she needed to discuss with you. I have to say she wasn't looking too grand... In fact, she said that she didn't think she'd be long for this world now.'

'I see.' His father's brows drew together in a

frown. He too had noticed a change in Brigie during his last couple of visits and was concerned for her.

'And how is Hannah?' he went on.

'Blossoming.' The smile was back on Ben's face now. 'Though I have to say I see trouble ahead when the baby is born. She's adamant about going back to nursing, particularly since Elizabeth Garrett-Anderson became the first qualified woman doctor in the country.'

'Well, that's what you get for marrying a modern woman,' Dan chuckled. 'Hannah's got a mind of her own and isn't going to conform to old-fashioned ideas. Mary Ann is much the same. Ruth is almost despairing of her ever settling down. Did I tell you she's been driving trams for a living? I ask you – whoever heard of a woman doing such a job? But it is commonplace now, from what I can see of it. The world is changing. Throughout the war, women have been forced to do jobs that beforehand only men did, and I wonder now if they'll ever be able to go back to being what a woman was expected to be.'

Mary Ann was Dan's illegitimate child to Ruth Foggety, who had once been Ben's and his dead brothers' nursery nurse. Ben, Jonathan and Harry were triplets; all three had gone to war, but only Ben had survived. Dan had established Ruth in a small two-up-and-two-down house on the corner of Linton Street on the outskirts of Jesmond Dene whilst she had been carrying Mary Ann, and there she had stayed ever since. Dan still visited both her and their daughter regularly. Ruth never tired of her little house – or of Dan, if it came to that. The house had a tiny self-contained yard with its own water tap, and gas had been piped into all the rooms both up and down. It was commonly known within a very short time of her moving there that she was a kept woman, but as people came to know her, they accepted her and liked her – for as they said, it would have been hard not to like Ruth.

A fresh peal of bells could be heard, and both men looked at each other, feeling deeply moved.

'To peace, and long may it reign...'

Father and son chinked glasses and took long swallows of their drinks.

As Dan pushed open the door to Ruth's house that evening, he shouted, 'Ruthie, it's me!'

When Ruth's portly figure bustled into the hall to meet him, he stamped the snow from his boots and passed her his coat.

'Eeh, you look perished!' she exclaimed. 'Come on in an' I'll make you a nice warming drink.'

As always, Dan experienced a feeling of coming home, and as he followed her into a small parlour, he saw a young woman sitting at a table smoking a cigarette in a long holder.

'Hello, Father,' she greeted him.

Crossing to her, he planted a kiss on her cheek. 'Weather put you off going out, has it, Mary Ann?' Pulling a chair out, he joined her at the table.

'Not likely. I'm off to a dance with my friend in half an hour or so,' she informed him. 'It would take more than a bit of snow to keep me in.'

Dan took in her short bobbed hair and her straight day dress with a grin. Mary Ann was a strong-willed young woman, but likeable with it – and though she often brought Ruth to the verge of despair he found her amusing and usually ended up siding with her.

'And how is your love-life nowadays?' he enquired mischievously.

'Huh! I've just broken off my fifth engagement so that should give you some idea,' she quipped. As she said it, Ruth was entering the room with a loaded tray, which she placed on the table before raising her eyebrows.

'I give up with her, I really do,' she said sorrowfully. 'There ain't a man born yet as could tame this one.' To which Mary Ann and Dan threw back their heads and laughed aloud as Ruth tutted indignantly.

'It's all very well for you to laugh,' she scolded Dan. '*You* don't have to live with the little imp.'

Many a man in Dan's position would have taken the remark as an insult, but knowing Ruthie as he did, Dan was aware that none was intended. That was the wonderful thing about Ruth, as he had discovered over the years. She had taken him and given him comfort when his wife, Barbara, had started an affair with Michael Radlet, the farmer, and then, and in all the years since, she had never expected more of him than he could give. It was just as well, for whilst he had a great fondness for Ruth, they had both always known that no more would ever come of it – and with that she had been content. Dan knew that he could never wholly love again. Barbara had been the love of his life, and since her passing he had not felt the urge to find another. No, the urge that was on him

26

was to travel, as he had always yearned to do since his youth. He broached the subject to Ruth when, some time later, they were sitting side-by-side in the glow from the fire.

'I er ... I've been thinking that I might take a little holiday. Do some travelling,' he told her cautiously.

'Oh yes, an' where were you thinkin' of goin'?'

Dan sighed as his mind raced ahead. 'I'm not sure really. I thought perhaps Rome; Spain and Italy too. I would also like to return to Paris. Barbara and I lived there briefly when we were first married, if you recall. In fact, the triplets were born in Paris. I had a little bookshop there.'

'Aye, so you once told me,' she replied softly, but there was no condemnation in her voice. Where Dan was concerned, her love for him was such that she was glad of any time he could spare for her. Not that he had ever done wrong by her. Oh no, quite the contrary from where she was standing, for she had never had to worry about paying her bills or putting food on her table, as some of those hereabouts did.

'So when were you thinking of going?'

He pursed his lips. 'I hadn't thought that far ahead, to be truthful. But don't worry, when I do decide you'll be the first to know.'

'That's good enough then, lad.' She now brought her lips down onto his and whispered softly, 'Will you be staying the night?'

He glanced towards the window, where the snow was coming down with a vengeance, before replying. 'Yes, Ruth, I think I will – if you don't mind.'

She smiled with satisfaction as her eyes played across his handsome face. Time had been kind to Dan Bensham. He had never been tall of stature, but he had retained his slim build, and although his dark hair was now streaked with grey, it only made him look distinguished.

'Good, then you stay there an' keep warm while I go an' pop a couple o' stone hot water bottles in us bed, eh?'

He nodded contentedly as he pushed his feet towards the fire and dreamed of the places he would shortly be visiting.

The following morning, after a good night's sleep and a hearty breakfast, Dan began to pull his boots on. Ruth fetched his coat from the hall and warmed it in front of the fire before holding it out to him. Mary Ann had gone off to work and there were just the two of them in the house.

'I thought I'd call in and see Brigie before I go home,' he told her, and knowing him as she did, Ruthie picked up on the note of concern in his voice. 'She sent word with Ben yesterday that she wanted to see me and it's been playing on my mind.'

'Well, have a care on the way, lad. The roads are going to be treacherous,' she warned him.

Guilt wrapped itself around him like a cloak as she fussed over him. If only he could love Ruth as she deserved. There was none better than she, and yet despite this, he could never envisage living out his days with her. As if reading his mind, she said softly, 'Get off wi' you then. I'll look forward to seein' you again when you have a mind to call.'

'Oh, Ruthie.' There was a catch in his voice now and his eyes were moist, but she paid him no heed as she gently propelled him out onto the snow-covered step. Standing on tiptoe, she planted a loving kiss on his lips then closed the door between them. Only then did she lean with her back against it and screw her eyes up tight. She knew that lately, since Barbara had died, Dan was feeling that he should offer her his name and, oh, how she would have loved to be Mrs Dan Bensham. But there was no chance of that now.

Wearily she crossed to a dresser that took up almost a whole wall in the small kitchen, and taking a small glass bottle from a drawer she hastily shook a tablet into her hand and then swallowed it down. Eeh, she found herself thinking, life can be a rare bitch at times. It was only a matter of weeks since the doctor had told her of her severe heart condition. 'You could go on for a matter of years. But then again, you could go just like that,' he had told her with a snap of his fingers. But what of Mary Ann – not to mention Dan? How would they cope without her when she went? She knew that she should have told them of her condition but if she did, Dan might offer to marry her for all the wrong reasons and Mary Ann would go into a flap and start to treat her like an invalid. No, it would be better if neither of them knew. Heaving a sigh, she began to load the dirty pots onto the wooden draining board.

When the automobile that Dan had hired drew up at the steps of High Banks Hall he clambered out and, after paying the driver, took the steps two at a time. In the hallway, he almost collided with Nurse Conway.

'Well, you've certainly brought the weather with you,' she said as she nodded towards the window. 'If it carries on like this, we'll be snowed in for Christmas.'

'You could be right.' Taking off his coat and muffler, he slung them across the bottom of the banisters before asking, 'Is it all right if I go straight up?'

'Of course. To be honest with you, I'm pleased you've come. Mrs Bensham hasn't seemed quite herself for the last few days and a visit from you might be just the tonic she needs.'

His face solemn now, he headed towards the stairs. At Brigie's quarters, he paused to knock before entering. She was sitting in a chair to the side of the window, gazing out, across the snowy landscape, and just as Ben had done, he found himself thinking, She seems to have shrunk. The old lady was warmly wrapped in a thick dressing-gown, and her snow-white hair was lying across her frail shoulder in a long plait.

A nurse was in the process of folding fresh linen before placing it into a cupboard, but at sight of Dan, Brigie flapped her hand at her.

'Nurse, would you kindly leave us, please? Perhaps you could have a tray of tea sent up? I'm sure that Mr Bensham would welcome it on a cold day like this.'

'Of course, ma'am.' The nurse nodded at Dan and then slipped through the door, closing it softly behind her.

Dan crossed the room and, taking Brigie's thin hands in his, he shook them gently up and down before asking, 'How are you, Brigie, dear?'

'Never mind about that for now. I am so glad you have come, Dan. Did Ben pass on my message?'

'Yes, he did – and it caused me some concern. Is something troubling you, Brigie?'

'Yes, dear boy.' It was funny, she thought, that she still saw him as a boy when he was now a man in his fifties. 'There *is* something I need to talk about before it is too late, and you are the only one I can trust.'

'I see.' Realising that it must be something of importance to her, he carried a chair over and placed it at the side of the bed. Once he was seated within an arm's length of her, he asked, 'Would you like to begin?'

For one of the few times in his life, he saw that there were tears trembling on her lashes and suddenly they burst from her like water from a dam and poured down her wrinkled cheeks unchecked.

Shock kept him silent. Eventually, with a great effort, she managed to compose herself and falteringly she began, 'What I have to tell you, Dan, may change the way you look at me for ever, for I have done a terrible, *terrible* thing.'

'No, Brigie. Surely not you! There is *nothing* you could tell me that would change the way I think of you. You have been my rock for as far back as I can remember. And I am sure that if John and Katie were here, they would say the same thing too.'

She thought briefly of Katie, Dan's late sister; and John, his brother. The siblings had been

31

close during their childhood and their affection for one another had continued into their adulthood, but Katie was dead now and Brigie knew that Dan still missed her desperately. However, her own concerns were weighing heavily on her and so she pushed this from her mind and continued, 'Please reserve your opinion until you have heard me out.' Now a flash of the governess he had come to know and love was present again as she sat straight in the chair and folded her hands primly in her lap.

'There was only one other person in the world who knew what I am about to tell you,' she confided, 'and that was my dear servant and companion of many years, Mary Peel. When Thomas Mallen was declared bankrupt and we were forced to move to the cottage, we had nothing more than Barbara and Constance's two hundred pounds a year to live on. But that is another story... And as you are no doubt aware, for many years after taking up residence there, Thomas and I lived as man and wife. I know it was wrong in the eyes of God, to live in sin as it is classed, but ... I loved him, Dan. With all my heart I loved him – and you should understand this, for your love for Barbara was as ill-fated as was mine for Thomas.'

The old lady's hands became still in her lap and her eyes were dreamy now as she allowed herself to drift back in time. 'It came about in 1862 that I developed a severe cold, which then developed into influenza. I was very weak and became confined to bed for some months. Mary Peel saw to my every need as well as to the running of the cottage, but Thomas... Well, let us just say that it came to my attention that he was having an association with a certain woman from the village who was working at High Banks Hall. It was round about then that I made another discovery too, for I found that I was pregnant. I was forty-one years old and about to have my first child, and I was elated. At last Thomas would do right by me and make an honest woman of me, or so I thought. But before I had the chance to tell him about the child he ... he arranged to meet this woman one evening in the barn at the back of the cottage. It was a wild, dark night...'

Brigie gulped deeply as the full horror of that night came back to her. Then she forced herself to go on. 'If I close my eyes, I can see it as clearly now as if it were yesterday,' she whispered. 'It just so happened that my dear Barbara had been out that evening too, and as she was returning home, Thomas mistook her for Aggie Moorhead, the woman he had agreed to meet, and dragged her into the barn where he ... he raped her. When he realised what he had done, he could not live with himself. Thomas had many faults but he loved Barbara and Constance as his own, you see? He had brought Barbara up as his own child, and whilst in the depths of despair, he took his own life. That was not the worst of it though.'

The old lady closed her eyes and shuddered. 'Shortly afterwards we discovered that my beloved Barbara was pregnant, and to this day I swear it was the shame of it that killed her! As you can imagine, I was beside myself with grief. It was Mary Peel who suggested that I might get rid of *my* child once it was born. After all, as she pointed out,

Barbara was going to need constant attention – and how would I cope with the shame of bringing up yet *another* Mallen bastard? And so, God forgive me, I did as she suggested. But now I need to find my daughter, Dan. Can you understand that?'

For long moments that seemed to stretch into an eternity, Dan was silent as he tried to absorb what Brigie was telling him. Finally he asked, 'But why, Brigie? *Why* – after all these years?'

Brigie chewed on her lip as she rapidly tried to blink her tears away. Then, composing herself with a great effort, she pointed a shaking finger towards the tall mahogany wardrobe on the opposite wall.

'In there you will find a box,' she told him falteringly. 'Bring it to me and I will try to explain.'

Dan now rose and followed her pointing finger, and just as she had said, there in the bottom of the wardrobe was a large wooden box, which was secured with a small padlock. After placing it down on a side table, he watched as Brigie took a little key from the pocket of her gown and unlocked it.

'Soon after that terrible night,' she went on, 'Mary read an advert in a newspaper out to me. It was this one here.' With shaking fingers she withdrew a folded newspaper that was brittle with age and handed it to him. It was the *Christian*, and he saw at a glance that it was dated 1862 before his eyes fell on an advert that had been circled in ink.

It read: *ADOPTION – A person wishing for a lasting and comfortable home for a child of either sex will find this a good opportunity. Advertisers having no children of their own are about to proceed to America. Premium, Fifteen Pounds. Apply Mrs*

Stirling, 10 Myrtle Cottages, Bow.

'Oh, my dear God, Brigie – you didn't respond to this, did you?' Dan was horrified as he stared at her aghast, and now the tears flowed faster as she nodded miserably.

'What choice did I have? Shortly afterwards, I gave birth to a beautiful baby girl. Mary Peel delivered her and within hours she had drawn out all her savings to reply to this advert, God bless her soul. She took my baby away soon after she was born, and from that day to this, as God is my witness, not a mention of her has ever passed my lips. You see, I convinced myself that she had never been born – and when, some months later, my poor Barbara died giving birth to your dear late wife, all the love I felt for my own child was poured into her... But then in 1896 I read in the newspapers of Mrs Dyer, who had run a baby farm for years, and I could ignore what I had done no longer. This wicked woman had placed adverts such as the one Mary replied to, and then murdered many of her poor innocent charges within hours of the little mites coming into her care. The investigation started when two bargemen on the River Thames found a parcel, which had been weighed down but disturbed by their barge-pole. Inside was the body of a baby, but the paper that the child was wrapped in led the police to the "respectable" Mrs Dyer of Reading who was known to have a pronounced fondness for babies of all descriptions. When the police started to drag the river, more little bodies were found, each of them wrapped in newspaper and weighed down with a brick. Young women who had entrusted their babies to her care began to come forward, and it soon became obvious that the said Mrs Dyer had advertised under many aliases and had run a profitable baby farm for many years. Two of the infants were even identified as being the bodies of Doris Harmon and Harry Simmons. Sergeant Richard Relf of the Metropolitan Police linked at least eighteen dead babies to Mrs Dyer during his investigation, and this led to her execution in 1896. It was from the moment that I read that report that I could ignore what I'd done no longer.

'*If* my daughter is still alive, she will be almost fifty-seven years old now, Dan. But what if I submitted her to an untimely death before she had even known life? What if the woman that Mary took her to was one of these wicked baby farmers?' Brigie drew in a long, shuddering breath and rocked herself to and fro.

'Oh Dan, I have lived in hell for so long, and now that my time is drawing near to leave this earth I have to somehow make amends, if it is not too late, for the wicked thing I have done.'

For a long moment in time Dan sat motionless as he tried to digest what she had told him. Thankfully, the nurse came in just then with a tea tray and seeing at a glance that Mrs Bensham was visibly upset she hastily placed it down on a small table at the side of the fire and backed from the room.

Dan rose from his seat and, for want of something to do, began to strain the tea into two cups. He was so shocked at Brigie's disclosure that for a time he had been rendered speechless, but now as he handed the cup and saucer into

36

the old woman's trembling hand he asked her, 'What do you intend to do?'

'Ah ... now that is what I wanted to talk to you about,' she told him brokenly. 'I am past looking for her myself – but I wondered, would you consider trying to find out what happened to her for me? I know it is a lot to ask but I have a fair amount of good quality jewellery that my dearest Harry bought for me, and if the woman is alive I would like her to have it, with my apologies for the way I abandoned her. Often now I think to myself ... for what? So that I could maintain my good name and pour all the love that I should have given to my own child into Barbara, who ended up hating me just as her mother and her aunt had before her? Oh Dan, I have been *such* a fool! If only I could have my time over again, I would *never* have parted with her.'

Suddenly the cup and saucer slid from her hands and the tea lay in a pool on the fine Persian carpet beneath her feet as Brigie buried her face in her hands and began to sob brokenheartedly.

Dan had her wrapped in his arms in a second as his heart went out to her. How she must have suffered over the years, and as she'd said, had Barbara been worth it? Deep inside, the answer screamed at him: *No, she wasn't – for didn't she break your heart too?* But then some of the blame for that must be placed at Brigie's door, for Barbara had been cosseted and spoiled from the second she was born. Only now did he realise why. In Brigie's mind, Barbara had become the child she had given up. And now, all these years on, Brigie was asking him to try and find what had become of her. It would no doubt be like looking for a needle in a haystack to locate her after all these years, but what choice did he have but to try? Brigie had always been good to him and he owed her that at least. Glancing back at the address in the newspaper he noted the area was Bow in East London.

'Please don't cry, my dear,' he whispered into her hair. 'I think I can understand why you did what you did, and rest assured, if I can find out what became of your daughter for you, I will, though I don't envisage it being easy.'

Dan had arrived at the Hall feeling happier than he had been for some long time, with the prospect of the places he would visit, to look forward to. But now, once again, it seemed that his urge to travel would have to be put to one side. It was funny, now he came to think of it, the things that life could throw at you. Beyond the enormous bay window, people the length and breadth of Britain were celebrating. The newspapers were full of the first anniversary to mark the end of the war, and street parties were going on everywhere despite the severity of the weather, and yet here, in this room, this one old woman's war raged on.

Chapter Three

'Are you keeping well?'

'Yes, I am very well, thank you, Mam.' Hannah took the heavy mug her mother, Sarah, was handing her across the scrubbed oak table and an uncomfortable silence settled between them as they sipped at their drinks. Constance Radlet, Hannah's grandmother, was dozing in a chair at the side of the kitchen fire, her feet held out to the flames.

'And how is Grandma?' the young woman asked.

'Oh, you know – up and down.' Taking her crutch from where it was leaning against the side of the table, Sarah slipped it beneath her arm and limped towards the large walk-in pantry. 'I'll get you a shive of fruitcake to go with your tea,' she told her daughter, as Hannah looked around the room. It was exactly as she remembered it from when she had lived here as a child, as if time had stood still. The walls were still lime-washed and dippy rugs were thrown down here and there to break the coldness of the stone floor. Not that the same could be said for her mother and grandmother. Oh no, Hannah thought. If anything, time has made them even more bitter towards the world. She supposed she could understand it; after all, they were both more than aware that Brook Farm was hers by rights, for her late father, Michael, had left it to her in his will, and they were only allowed to stay there under her conditions. Not that her conditions had made much impact on either of them. Since the day she had laid down the law and told them where they stood, neither of them did much about the place. If it wasn't for Jim Waite and his family, who lived in a nearby cottage, she had no doubt that the whole place would have crumbled by now. Still, she was prepared to turn a blind eye. As she saw it, neither of them could have much time left, particularly her grandma, so if they wanted to spend the rest of their days pretending to be ladies then that was up to them.

Sometimes she dreaded her monthly visits to them so much that she had to force herself to come, for the atmosphere had become even more strained since they had learned of her pregnancy. She supposed it was to be expected, for marrying Ben had incensed both the women. 'It's unholy!' Sarah had cried when she learned of their love for each other. The fact that Hannah's father, Michael, and Ben's mother, Barbara, had been having an affair for years before dying together had almost caused Sarah to lose her mind with jealousy. Added to that, it was Ben's mother who had been the cause of Sarah losing her leg when she was naught but a girl.

Time and time again, Hannah had tried to point out that nothing that had happened in the past was anything to do with her or Ben, but her words fell on deaf ears, and now whenever she came to Wolfbur Farm, there was an unspoken pact that his name would not be mentioned. As far as Sarah and Constance were concerned, Ben was a Mallen through and through, the son of the bitch who had stolen Sarah's husband, and as Constance was fond of pointing out, no good could come of the association, for it was a proven fact that the Mallens and all those close to them were cursed.

Today looked set to be no different, for when Sarah came back to the table and placed a large fruitcake down, knowing her mother as well as she did, the girl sensed that there was trouble brewing. She didn't have to wait long for it, for as Sarah sliced into the cake she looked disdainfully towards her swollen stomach and remarked, 'Looks like the new Mallen is growin' well.'

Hannah bristled but her voice was as calm as a millpond when she replied, 'In case you'd forgotten, Mam, my name is Bensham, as the baby's will be.'

'Huh! It'll still have Mallen blood flowin' through its veins though, won't it, whichever way you look at it. Its other grandma was the Mallen bitch, so how could it be otherwise? Let's just hope as it ain't a lad, else it'll be another that will bear the Mallen streak.'

Hannah was trembling, and rising abruptly now, she pulled her chair away so quickly from the table that it almost overbalanced. 'I think it's time I was going before one of us says something that we might regret.' She marched towards the coat-stand and snatched down her coat.

'But ... but you haven't touched your cake!'

'No – well, perhaps you should have thought of that before you started having a go at me, eh?'

At that moment, old Constance roused and, seeing the cake on the table, she asked, 'Is there any of that for me?'

'You can have mine, Grandma,' Hannah snapped. 'I'm just leaving.'

She was storming towards the door now and she could hear her mother's crutch dragging across the stone floor as she followed her. As if nothing untoward had happened, Sarah asked, 'Come in the dog-trap, did you?'

'Yes. I put the horse in the barn when I arrived,

out of the snow.'

'Wouldn't have thought *he'd* let you come out in this weather,' Sarah remarked sarcastically.

'I assure you the main roads are clear, but even if they hadn't been, Ben doesn't tell me what I can or cannot do. He respects me too much for that.'

Sarah opened her mouth to reply with yet another sarcastic remark but then clamped it shut again. She knew she had pushed Hannah as far as she dared for one day.

At the side of the fireplace, Constance watched the open hostility between mother and daughter. She and Sarah had always been close, ever since the day many years ago when she had come to live on the farm with her uncle, Jim Waite and his family. It was Constance and Brigie who had pushed Michael, Hannah's father, to marry Sarah, when deep inside they had both known that it was Barbara he loved. And look at the outcome. Years and years of hate and unhappiness, so many lives ruined. Right at this very moment, Brigie, as Constance and her sister Barbara had called their governess, was lying waiting for death up at High Banks Hall, where the two sisters had spent their early years. Sometimes, Constance longed to go to her and make things right between them, for once, Brigie had been the centre of her universe. But it was too late now. What was done was done and now they must all live with the consequences.

Fred Burton, who had come to live in the rooms above the small stables shortly after Hannah's marriage to Ben, was waiting for her at the back of the cottage when she drew the trap to a halt

42

following a hazardous journey across the fells. Normally, Hannah had all the time in the world for Fred, for he was a kind, gentle man approaching middle age. Tall and lanky, with flame-red hair, Ted was not afraid to turn his hand to anything that needed doing about the cottage, as well as tending to the horses and the gardens, and in the time he had been with them he had become invaluable. Hannah had always found it strange that some woman hadn't snapped him up, and the only reason she could think of why this had not happened was the fact that Fred was a very shy man who had a tendency to blush the colour of a beetroot if you so much as looked at him. Today, however, she could think of nothing but getting back into the warm, and so all she said to him now was: 'Ah Fred, there you are. Would you mind seeing to the horse for me?'

He helped her down and nodded as she added, 'He'll need a good rub down after being out in this.'

'No trouble at all, missus. You get yourself away in now,' Fred replied good-naturedly.

The snow was coming down so thick and fast that she could barely see a hand in front of her as she stamped into the cottage, slamming the door behind her.

Ben, who was just passing through the hallway, moved towards her with a wry smile on his face, but she, snapped, 'Don't you dare start!'

Instantly her shoulders sagged as he put his arm about her and moved her towards the fireside chair. 'Come and sit down,' he said gently. 'Nancy has got a bowl of nice hot soup ready for you. We thought you might need warming up.'

At that very moment Nancy bustled into the room and placed a tray on Hannah's lap. 'Eeh, it's right glad I am to see you back safe and sound, missus,' she clucked. 'Master Ben here has been pacing up and down the room like a caged animal. It's a wonder he hasn't worn a hole in the carpet.'

'I'm quite capable of getting myself about, Nancy. I'm only pregnant, not *ill.*'

'Even if you weren't, it's fit for neither man nor beast to be out in this weather,' Nancy declared with a shudder. Then with a wink at Master Ben she headed towards the door. 'Right then. Master Lawrie is waiting for his bedtime drink an' if it's late in comin' he'll raise the roof. You know what a stickler he is for routine.'

'Oh Nancy, could you get Fred a warm drink too, please?' Hannah was feeling guilty now for the way she had been so abrupt with him. 'He's settling the horse in the stable for me and I'm sure he'll be glad of one.'

Nancy's head bobbed, then with a last cheery grin she left the room.

Ben turned to his wife. 'Those two give you a bad time again, did they?' he asked.

'Well, Mam did,' she replied. 'But in fairness, Grandma was asleep at the side of the fire for most of the time I was there. Oh Ben ... I'm so *tired* of all this bad feeling. Why can't they just let the past go? None of what happened back then has anything to do with us. Mam is so bitter that sometimes she's frightening. She's like a powder keg waiting to explode. I tell you, if she doesn't soften a bit soon I shall stop going over there altogether.

She even had a go at the baby today. And this innocent mite will be her first grandchild.' As her hand dropped to stroke the precious mound that was growing inside her, Ben lifted the tray from her lap and sank onto his knees before her.

'We both knew when we came together that it wasn't going to be easy,' he murmured. 'But never lose sight of the fact that no matter what anyone says, we have each other – and soon we'll have this little one too. That is enough for me.'

'Oh Ben, I can hardly wait.' Her voice was heavy with longing but then her face brightened as she teased, 'I still intend to go back to nursing though, when the baby is old enough to be left.'

Ben grinned, 'We'll see. If I have my way, before then you'll be pregnant again ... and again...'

'Oh, you–' She was stayed from saying any more when his lips came down on hers, and once more she told herself what an extremely lucky woman she was.

He was lying in bed at the side of her, soothed by her gentle snores. Yet sleep eluded him. Over the last couple of years he had gained back some of the weight that had dropped from his bones whilst he had been at war, and he was stronger in all ways. And yet, still he sometimes had to force himself to put one foot in front of the other, for a gaping hole would suddenly open up in front of him and once again he would be back in 'the Bunker' at the Hall, or back on the battlefield, screaming like a raving lunatic in his mind. The fear could come upon him at the most unexpected of times – when he was walking the hills, for example, or shopping in Newcastle. Lately, the times it had happened had lessened and he took that as a good sign, for as the Matron and the doctor up at the Hall had told him, 'These things do not just disappear overnight. You must be patient and fight it.'

He did fight it, every second of every day. It was funny though, now he came to think of it. The hole never appeared when Hannah was at his side.

He turned now and slung his arm loosely across her stomach. The child was still tonight, as it had been the night before. All last week it had been so active that he had lain awake long after Hannah was asleep as it kicked against his hand when he rested it on her stomach.

It's probably sleeping like its mother, he thought, and then his breathing slowed and soon he too was fast asleep.

He and Hannah were at breakfast in the dining room the next morning when Nancy tapped at the door and poked her head round it. 'Message for you, Master Ben.' She held out an envelope to him. 'Someone from the Hall brought it but they've gone now. They wouldn't wait for a reply.'

'Thank you, Nancy.' Ben wiped his mouth on a napkin and Nancy quietly left the room. 'I wonder what this could be about?'

'Oh dear, I do hope Brigie hasn't taken a turn for the worse,' Hannah remarked as he slit the envelope open. Then, as she saw his eyes scanning the page, 'What is it? It isn't Brigie, is it?'

'No, dear, it isn't Brigie. Apparently, Matron

has had a new arrival and she thinks it may be someone I know. They're in the Bunker so whoever it is must be in a bad way. She's asking if I'll call over there.'

'Then of course you must go.' Hannah's eyes were troubled. Perhaps it would be someone whom Ben had known on the battlefield.

'Can I come too, Cousin Ben?' Lawrie asked eagerly, but Ben shook his head.

'Not this time, Lawrie. The weather is awful so you stay here and keep Hannah company for me, eh? I need someone I can trust to keep an eye on her for me and look after her until I get back.'

Feeling very important, Lawrie's smile broadened. 'I'll look after her, Cousin Ben, don't you worry.'

'Good man.' Ben ruffled his hair as he rose from the table, and looking back at Hannah he asked, 'Would you mind very much if I went over there now? A walk would do me good and I feel like a bit of fresh air.'

'Then let me get your coat for you.' She disappeared into the hall and fetched his coat from the cupboard. He noticed that she looked a little pale, and as she held his coat for him he asked, 'Feeling all right, are you, love? If you're not, while I'm over there I could always ask the doctor to pop in and have a look at you.'

'I'm perfectly all right.' She watched as he slid his feet into sturdy walking boots. 'Now you just get off and see what's going on. Lawrie and I will be fine. Take as long as you like.'

He kissed her before slipping through the door onto the snow-covered front path. The drifts were

47

so deep in places that in no time at all, the snow had risen above his boots and his feet were frozen through. The road was deserted, and only the smoke that rose into the grey sky from the chimneys of the Hall, which was about a mile away, told of anyone else existing in the world other than himself.

He was shocked on entering the Hall to see his father there, speaking in hushed tones to the Matron.

'Ah, Ben.' Dan shook his son's hand warmly, then taking him by the elbow, he led him into the day room, which luckily for now was empty.

'What are you doing here so early?' Ben asked, now that they were alone.

'Same thing as you are.' His father's face was strained. 'I got a message to come as soon as possible, so here I am. Seems they think the chap that was admitted late yesterday could be someone to do with us.'

'But that's *impossible*. The only other people whom we both knew were Harry and Jonathan, and God rest their souls, they have both been long gone.'

'That's what we were led to believe,' his father said solemnly, 'but apparently, the poor fellow up there just keeps saying the name Bensham. Seems he's been in a hospital abroad since the war ended and had a complete breakdown. He was transferred here yesterday in an ambulance with a few more patients. You ... you don't think it could possibly be Harry or Jonathan, do you?'

Ignoring the tremor in his father's voice, Ben said grimly, 'There's only one way to find out.'

48

A nurse met them at the door of the room in which Ben himself had spent so many months, and she slipped out onto the landing to have a few words with them.

'Thank you both for coming so promptly,' she said, before addressing Dan. 'The gentleman I have asked you to come and see is in a poor way. The only word, or name he has uttered is Bensham, and we thought... Well, we have reason to believe that this officer is from the regiment that your other two sons were in, so perhaps by some miracle... I have no wish to falsely raise your hopes, sir, but...'

'Come along, Nurse.' Dan's voice was harsh with tension. 'Let's just go in and see the poor soul, eh?'

'Of course.' Without further ado she turned and opened the door, and Dan and Ben followed her into the room. There was a man huddled in a chair gazing out of the window, but as his back was to them they were forced to approach him so that they could see his face. When they did so, Dan's shock was so great, that had Ben's arm not come out to steady him, he would likely have slid to the floor. And then one word broke from his lips as tears also exploded from his eyes.

'*Johnny...*' And it was Johnny. By some miracle, this beloved son who had been presumed dead was really here, and he was alive.

The nurse's hand flew to her mouth. She had no need to ask if they knew the unfortunate soul, for Mr Bensham's reaction spoke volumes. For what seemed a lifetime, silence reigned as Ben supported his father, but then the man almost sprang from his side and in seconds he was on his hunkers, staring up into the young man's face.

'Johnny, Jonathan… It's me, your father.'

The patient stared unseeingly ahead as if he had not heard him, and now as the shock subsided a little, the joy was wiped from Dan's face, to be replaced by a look of deep sorrow. The man in front of him *was* his son, there was no doubt about that, and yet in no way did he resemble the handsome young man who had gone away to war. His eyes were sunk deep into his pallid face and he was so thin that he appeared to be almost skeletal. His hands convulsively picked at the material of the dressing-gown he was wearing that seemed to bury him as he rocked gently back and forth, and Dan's heart felt as if it were breaking all over again. Jonathan's eyes were empty, bleak, and it hit his father that his beloved son had lost the will to live. Ben meanwhile stood by, with tears wet on his own cheeks as he tried to take in this miraculous occurrence. His brother was *really* here – back from the dead to all intents and purposes – and it took some sinking in. He and this man had lain side by side in their mother's womb, along with their other brother, Harry, who had also been lost in the war. Ben was the oldest of the triplets by minutes, and had used to joke with them that it was he who had been pushed from their mother's womb first to make way for them. Not that his mother had ever had time for him. All her love or at least the small amount that was not reserved for her lover, had been poured into Jonathan and Harry. Ben had never held it against them. After all, it was hardly their fault. And strangely, he had

50

been close to his brothers and it had almost broken him when news reached the family that the boys had both been killed in battle.

His feelings at that moment were indescribable: shock, joy and grief all vying for first position. The nurse turned on her heel and ran from the room in her excitement, leaving the door to swing behind her in her haste. Minutes later, she was back with the doctor and Matron close on her heels.

'Well, there's a turn-up for the books,' the doctor beamed. 'Who would ever have believed it, eh?'

Dan's face when he turned to speak to him looked suddenly old. 'He will come through this, won't he, Doctor?'

'God willing.' The man addressed Ben, who was still too shocked to utter so much as a single word. 'You of all people should believe, Captain Bensham, for if *you* could come back from the brink, then so can he. But as we all know, these things take time. Nothing is going to happen overnight. The main thing is that your brother is alive. The rest will come: have faith.'

Ben nodded numbly. His life had never run smoothly and he had thought that it had thrown all it could at him. And then for this to happen... But this was something to rejoice at, he told himself, for it wasn't every day that a brother you had been told was dead was returned to you, was it?

'I ... I'm going to tell Brigie the good news, Father.' He had to get out of this room and for more reasons than one. The memories of the time he had spent there were pouring back, and

51

although his heart was racing with joy at the sight of Jonathan, yet still he ached for him, for he better than anyone knew of the dark, cold place his brother was floundering in. He placed his hand briefly on the man's shoulder then hurried from the room, and what he was thinking was, life is a funny thing. Oh yes, it was that all right. And you just never knew what it had waiting up its sleeve for you...

Chapter Four

'What are these for, Mam?' When Mary Ann turned to her mother with the small glass bottle of pills in her hand, Ruth flushed.

'Oh, I er ... I got them from the doctor for me indigestion.' Ruth avoided her daughter's eyes as she stacked the clean pots back on the dresser. 'Me own fault,' she continued lightly. 'You know what I'm like with me food. If I weren't so greedy and I didn't gobble it down so fast, happen I wouldn't need them.'

Mary Ann slowly lowered the bottle back into the drawer but there was a feeling of unease on her that she couldn't explain. Her mother had never been good at telling lies, and right now every instinct she had, screamed at her that the woman was lying. She certainly didn't believe that the tablets were for indigestion. In the past, if Ruth had suffered from indigestion she would simply have taken a spoonful of bicarbonate of soda in water. She was a great believer in home cures and had never been one for going to the doctor's. It was strange that she hadn't mentioned it, either. Now that Mary Ann came to think of it, her mother hadn't seemed quite herself for a few months past now, not that she had complained of feeling unwell. Oh no, Ruth had always been a great believer in getting on with things, but... Mary Ann eyed her thoughtfully. She looked a little pale and didn't seem quite as chirpy as she normally was.

As if reading her thoughts, Ruth turned on her and wagged a finger. 'Now don't you get reading things when there's nowt to read,' she warned her. 'I'm as fit as a butcher's dog. And ain't it time you were getting ready to go out? Your father will be here soon and no doubt he'll be full of it – young Johnny being alive, that is. Eeh! It makes your heart sing, don't it? There's been so much bad goin' on in the world with the damn war, and then for something wonderful like this to come out of the blue. Bless him; he's like a cat with two tails. Mind you, from what he's told me, poor Master Johnny's in a bad way. Don't know his arse from his elbow at present, by all accounts – but then it's wonderful what they can do with medicine nowadays. Take Ben ... he weren't no better when he first arrived at the Hall, but look at him now. You'd hardly think he were the same chap as he was two years ago, an' about to become a father into the bargain. It does your heart good to think of it, don't it?'

'Oh Mam, you're a hopeless romantic.' Mary Ann chuckled but deep down she felt a great sense of sadness. Of course, it was wonderful that Jonathan was alive. And it was wonderful that Ben had finally found happiness with Hannah. But what about her mother's happiness? Mary Ann loved her father with all her heart, but lately she had begun to feel a little resentful towards him. Neither her mother, nor her father for that matter, had ever lied to her, and she had grown up accepting that her father was married to someone else and had another family. He had called around on the same days a week as regular as clockwork for as far back as she could remember, and she had never wanted for a thing, least of all his love. But now... Well, the way she saw it, he was a free man now, so why didn't he make an honest woman of her mother? It was as plain as the nose on your face that Ruth worshipped the very ground he walked on. And her affection seemed to be returned, so why didn't he just marry her and have done with it?

As if her thoughts had conjured him up from thin air there was the sound of a key in the lock, and there he was, stamping the snow from his feet with a broad smile on his face. Since they had discovered that Jonathan was alive Dan seemed to be brighter, and tonight looked set to be no different, for he crossed first to her and then to Ruth and gave them both a resounding kiss on the cheek.

Sniffing at the air, he asked, 'Is that beef stew I can smell?'

'It certainly is,' Ruth told him, stirring a large pan on the stove that was emitting delicious odours. 'Mary Ann has already eaten because she's going out, but I thought I'd wait and have mine with you.'

Mary Ann tactfully made towards the stairs door. 'I'll leave you to it while I go to get ready then.' She smiled, but once the stairs door was closed between them a frown settled across her face as she thought of the pills she had found. Perhaps it was time she had a little chat with the doctor.

'When can I come and see Cousin Jonathan, Cousin Ben?'

'As soon as the doctor feels he's up to it,' Ben assured him as he fingered the latest carving Lawrence had done. It was of a donkey and once again he was awed at the detail of it. At present, Lawrie was carving a crib for the new baby in the outhouse they had given over to him. In there, with a good fire on the go to keep him warm, he could whittle away to his heart's content and he never seemed to tire of it. The crib was the biggest thing he had ever attempted, and sometimes he was so excited about it that Ben was sure he was going to blab it out to Hannah rather than let it be the surprise they had agreed on. Lawrie had never been very good at keeping secrets and Ben was surprised that he had lasted this long. Earlier in the day, Ben had gone to the outhouse to see how it was progressing, and the sight of it had rendered him temporarily speechless, for the carving was so fine that it would have done a carpenter proud. Now Lawrie leaned towards him in the kitchen and whispered conspiratorially, 'I reckon the crib will be done in another couple of days, Cousin Ben. Can I give it to Hannah then?'

'Of course you can.' Ben squeezed his hand and Lawrie beamed good-naturedly. He loved living with Cousin Ben and Hannah, although he still missed his mother, of course... Thoughts of her brought tears stinging to his eyes and instantly, Ben's arms went around him and he cradled Lawrie's head against his chest. It had been hard for Ben when Lawrie first came to live in the cottage, for he had a child's mind trapped in a man's body. But now, whenever he looked at him he saw the child, as Katie, Lawrie's mother had done, and because he accepted Lawrie as he was, he was able to treat him as such.

'Where is Hannah?' Ben asked now, and wiping his sleeve across the tears that were dripping from the end of his nose, Lawrie answered, 'She said she was goin' for a lie-down. The baby will be here soon, won't it, Cousin Ben? Will it be here for Christmas?'

'No, I'm afraid not,' Ben chuckled. 'You're going to have to be patient for just a few more months. But still, we have Christmas to look forward to, don't we?'

Lawrie was bright again now as he nodded eagerly. 'Yes, we do. Nancy is making a pudding with brandy in it. And she said we're going to have a big turkey and stuffing.'

'There you are then. We'll look forward to that first, eh? The baby will be here before you know it, once we've got that over with.'

Lawrie scampered away in the direction of the outhouse and Ben went towards the stairs door. Hannah had taken to having a lie-down in the afternoon over the last couple of weeks but he had never known her to rest in the morning. He found her lying on the bed on her side and thought how pale she looked, but he kept his voice light as he asked, 'Little devil keep you awake in the night, did he?' He stroked her stomach as she smiled up at him.

'Actually, he's been remarkably quiet, this last few days. Up until last week I felt as if he was kicking a football around inside me, but I think he must have run out of room.'

Ben chuckled as he sat down beside her on the edge of the bed. 'Is there anything I can get you?'

'A waistline would be nice,' she grinned. 'I feel like a beached whale. I've forgotten what it's like to be slim.'

'Well, you'd better get used to it because I intend to have this house crowded with children,' Ben warned her teasingly, and then as he remembered something, he became serious. 'Uncle John and Jenny are coming from Manchester tomorrow to see Jonathan at the Hall and I invited them here for dinner. Is that all right?'

Hannah was very fond of John and Jenny. John reminded her a great deal of Dan, Ben's father, but then as he was Dan's older brother she supposed this was hardly surprising.

'Of course it is,' she assured him. 'I'll have a word with Nancy and I'm sure she'll come up with something nice for them. Uncle John is rather partial to roast lamb, if I remember correctly, and Lawrie will be happy to have company. But how was Jonathan today?'

'The same, but then as the doctor warned us,

57

it's not going to happen overnight so we just have to be patient. He's heavily sedated most of the time at present. You know Matron's saying, sleep is a great healer!'

'I'll second that, and now if you don't mind, I'd rather like to have a nap myself.'

He stood up and tenderly tucked the blanket up under her chin before quietly leaving the room. When he got downstairs, he found Lawrie and Nancy arranging bunches of holly with bright red berries shining amongst their green leaves in vases.

Lawrie turned to him with a look of excitement on his face. 'Nancy says as we can start decorating the cottage ready for Christmas, Cousin Ben. It's only three weeks to go now, you know.'

Ben winked at Nancy before replying, 'Is it really, Lawrie? Goodness me, I shall have to be thinking of taking you shopping for some Christmas presents soon then, shan't I?'

'Could we go into Newcastle?' Lawrie was hopping from foot to foot. 'I like it in Newcastle at Christmas-time. All the shops are pretty and all lit up. I have lots of presents I need to buy. One for you, one for Hannah, one for the new baby, one for Nancy, one for Cousin Jonathan, one for–'

'Whoa!' Ben laughed. 'Slow down. There will be nothing left in the shops at the rate you're going.' Anyone hearing the conversation would never have guessed that the two men were almost of the same age, for Ben was addressing Lawrie as one would a child, which mentally, Lawrie still was, just as Ben's Aunt Katie and his Uncle Pat had done when they were alive. They had loved him unconditionally, refusing to lock him away in a garret or have him sent to some terrible institution, as was the fate of so many unfortunate children who were born with mental deficiencies or deformities.

But the mood of jollity was broken now when Nancy sighed, 'Come along then, Lawrie, there's me fine lad. Off to the kitchen with you, and get yourself a glass of milk now. I need to have a word to Ben. Fred's in there and no doubt he'll keep you company.'

Without argument, Lawrie lumbered clumsily away and once they were alone, Nancy turned to Ben and asked him, straight out, 'How did you find the mistress, sir?'

'Tired,' Ben replied. 'I left her to have a nap. Why ... is there something amiss?'

Nancy chewed on her lip. 'In all honesty there's nothing I can quite put me finger on. But I have to say, she don't seem herself somehow. A bit quiet like, an' not as patient with young Lawrie as she usually is.'

'Well, isn't that to be expected?' Ben rejoined. 'She is pregnant, Nancy, so she is hardly going to be at her best, is she? However, if you have genuine concerns I could always get the doctor to call in and have a look at her.'

'Eeh, don't be doin' that, she'd have me guts for garters for talkin' out of school,' the woman fretted as she placed a large bowl of holly on one end of the mantelpiece. 'Happen you're right anyway. You should know me be now, sir. If there's owt to worry about I'll find it. And now, I'll away and get your dinners on the go. It's chicken today an' carrots an' roast potatoes. That should keep

Lawrie quiet for a while. He might be lacking in certain areas, God bless him, but there's certainly nothing wrong with his appetite.'

Ben nodded and flashed her a smile as she hurried from the room, but once she was gone he crossed to the fire and, leaning on the mantelpiece, he stared down into the flames with a look of deep concern on his face. Despite what he had told Nancy, he too was worried about Hannah. As Nancy had said, she didn't seem quite herself. Aw well, that could soon be remedied, he decided. When he popped over to the Hall to see Brigie tomorrow he would ask the doctor to call in and have a look at her, just to be on the safe side.

At that very moment up at the Hall, Dan was sitting at the side of Brigie's bed sipping at a cup of tea that the nurse had just brought in for him. He had come from spending an hour with Jonathan in his room and was feeling mildly depressed that his son had shown no recognition of him. It had been bad enough going through this with Ben, but doing it a second time was even more gruelling. However, his Johnny was alive – *alive!* –and that was all that mattered.

Outside, the snow had started to fall again and as he turned to Brigie, he noticed that she was looking at it, too. The nurse had informed him on his arrival that the old lady had had a bad night, and today she had chosen to stay in bed, which he knew went against the grain with Brigie, for she had always possessed an energy that astounded him at times.

She suddenly turned her head to ask, 'And how

is Jonathan doing, Dan?'

He placed his cup and saucer on a small table before replying, 'Still the same. But as we all know from Ben's experience here, time is a great healer. Time – and peace and quiet. He'll come out of it, no doubt, but these things cannot be rushed. It breaks my heart to see him so, yet still I thank God that he is alive.'

'Quite.' She paused, and then said tentatively, 'Dan, I must appear very unfeeling asking you this when Jonathan has so recently been returned to you but ... have you given any thought to what I asked you to do?'

'I have thought of little else, apart from Jonathan,' he reassured her. 'And I fully intend to fulfil my promise to you and go to London at the earliest opportunity. In fact, I would have already gone, had it not been for Jonathan coming home. It has certainly been a time for surprises. But have no fear, Brigie. Now that I know Johnny is all right I shall be making plans. I hope to leave within the next few days so that I can be home for Christmas.'

'Thank you, Dan. I can think of no one else in whom I could have confided, which is strange when I come to think of it, for I openly admit that when you were a child I found you the most difficult of the three at times. Katie and John were angels, and yet ... you took Barbara and never stopped caring for her when many would have left her, given the circumstances.'

'I'm a firm believer that our lives are mapped out for us, Brigie, and I think I loved Barbara from the very moment I set eyes on her when you first brought her to High Banks Hall to join Katie, John and myself in the nursery. I told her when I married her that I loved her enough for the two of us. In fairness to her, she never pretended to love me. Oh, I admit that I hoped that in time she would come to do so, but there was only ever one man for Barbara, and so I have to say that I deserved all I got.' He had crossed to the fire and stood now with his back to her, and yet Brigie could feel the sadness coming from him in waves.

'Have you thought what you want me to do, should I succeed in finding your daughter?' he now asked suddenly, and the old lady's hand came to her breast as she tried to still the wild thundering of her fragile heart. For so many years she had blocked all thoughts of her child from her mind; forced herself to believe that her womb had always been barren, until she had read the article on the evil Mrs Dyer, that was, and then she had found that she could live with herself no longer without at least trying to find out what had become of the child.

What would she look like? she found herself wondering. Would she resemble her, or be a Mallen, like her father, Thomas, with hair as black as pitch? Had she been a male, it would no doubt have made the quest Dan was about to embark on much easier for him, for it was generally known that very few Mallen men missed having the distinctive white streak running through their hair. But the girls normally had hair as black as a raven's wing, as her poor dear Barbara had had before her death.

Pulling her thoughts back to the present she

answered tremulously, 'I have not dared to think that far ahead, Dan, for there is a strong possibility that the child did not survive. If she did, then it will be enough for me to know that she will have something of me to keep in the way of my jewellery. She will probably resent me and condemn me for giving her up, and in truth I could not blame her for that. I just pray that if she did survive, she has been treated kindly and has not suffered hardship.'

'Well, I can make you no promise other than this, Brigie. If your daughter is still alive I will do my utmost to find her: on that you have my word.'

'Thank you, I can ask for no more.' Brigie shrank against the pillows and seeing that she was becoming tired, Dan went to her and he kissed the parchment-like skin on her cheek.

'Goodbye, my dear. I'm going to see Jonathan again now, but rest assured I shall call in before I leave for London.'

A faint smile that hid the turmoil she was feeling was his only answer as he quietly left the room. It was as he closed the door behind him that he saw Florrie Harper walking down the landing. A woman from the little West Allan village of Whitfield, Florrie had recently been appointed as a cleaner at the Hall. The woman was carrying an armful of dirty linen, and she turned to greet him before disappearing down the narrow staircase that led to the first floor. Could he have known the thoughts that were passing through her mind, Daniel Bensham would not have gone on his way with such an easy mind.

Chapter Five

It was not purely by chance that Florrie Harper happened to call in at Wolfbur Farm on her next day off. Florrie was known to be something of a gossip and she knew that the particular piece of gossip she was about to pass on would cause a stir there, to say the very least. It just so happened that Florrie was a friend of Lily Waite, the daughter of Daisy and Jim, who had helped Constance and Sarah to see to the running of the farm since Sarah's husband Michael's untimely death. Knowing Lily as she did, she had gleaned over the years just how much animosity was directed at Mrs Bensham, or Brigie as they tended to refer to her. And so, on this particularly cold and snowy Saturday, not even the prospect of a seven-mile walk from the village where she lived was enough to put her off her visit.

By the time she arrived in the farmyard she was blue with cold and breathless. It was only mid-afternoon but the lamps were already lit in the farmhouse as she hurried by it to the cottage that Constance had had built for the Waite family, some years before. The door was opened on her first knock, and as Daisy peered out into the snow she exclaimed, 'Why, Florrie! Whatever brings you out in this weather? You must have more sense than feelin', lass. Come away in afore you catch your death o' cold.'

Florrie obediently stepped into the small kitchen and the warmth wrapped itself around her like a blanket as Daisy helped her take her coat off.

'Get over by the fire,' Daisy commanded. 'There's only me and Lily in at present. Harry and Jim have gone up to the top field to try and get some of the sheep down. We lost two last week with the weather, but enough of that. How are you and what's happening up at the Hall?'

Since the day Florrie had started to work there she had kept the Waite family up to date with everything that was going on, but she considered this juicy piece of information too good to blab out and had every intention of savouring it, so she simply said, 'Oh, I'll tell you all about the goin's-on in a minute, once I've got somethin' warm inside me.'

Taking the hint, Daisy flushed. 'Oh, I'm sorry. Whatever am I thinkin' of? Of course you must have a drink. I'll put the kettle on while you get warmed through.' As she bustled away, Florrie turned her attention to Lily, who was hanging her snow-covered coat over a large wooden clotheshorse that stood to one side of the fire. 'So how you doin', Lily?'

Lily shrugged. She had recently lost her husband, Bill Twigg, to a bad bout of influenza, and had temporarily returned to live with her parents. 'Oh, you know. Up an' down. Just taking each day as it comes at the minute. But how are things with you?'

'They could be worse, I suppose, though I have to say the Matron over at the Hall would have been better placed as a Sergeant bloody Major.

65

Talk about crack the whip! By, that woman hardly gives you time to draw breath when you've finished a job afore she's barkin' at you to start another. She's a right bloody old slave-driver. Still, I dare say I shouldn't complain. The money I earn keeps the wolf from the door, an' now my Sid can't work no more, someone has to, don't they?'

Lily smiled politely; she had visited Florrie's home on more than one occasion, and judging by the state of it, she found it hard to believe that anyone would ever get a hard day's work out of her. Even so, she was a friendly sort and there seemed no harm in her – and so they had formed a friendship of sorts. Lily was kneading dough at the large table that took up the centre of the room and now she clapped the flour from her hands and after expertly flipping the ball of dough into a large dish, she covered it with a damp cloth and joined Florrie at the side of the fire. Within minutes, Daisy carried two steaming mugs of tea over to them and then, pulling on her boots she told them, 'I'm just nippin' over to the farmhouse to check on the missus and Sarah. You two have a rest an' a bit of a natter while' I'm gone, eh?'

'Thanks, Mam.' Lily watched her mother un-hook a heavy shawl from the back of the door and after she had flung it across her head and shoulders and disappeared into the fast-darken-ing afternoon, she turned her attention back to Florrie. 'So, what's to do, then?' she asked. 'An' don't say nothin' 'cos you wouldn't have come out in this weather if there weren't somethin' as you were breakin' your neck to tell me.'

Florrie took a long slurp from her mug and

chuckled. 'Actually, there is somethin' I picked up as I reckon you'll find of interest, though it's so unbelievable that I admit it took some time for it to sink in, even for me – an' *I* heard it first-hand.'

'Oh aye?'

Florrie saw at a glance that she had Lily's undivided attention and so now she went on, 'Well, the thing is, it just so happened that the Matron sent me up to the top floor o' the Hall some days back to fetch some dirty linen down. The top floor, as you probably know, used to be the nursery quarters but Mrs Bensham lives up there now. Rarely ventures out of it neither. They reckon as she's on her last legs. Anyway, that's by the by. I were collectin' the linen from the basket outside her room when I hears her an' Mr Dan talkin'. I weren't earwiggin', o' course, but I couldn't help but hear what were bein' said – an' you'd never believe the way the conversation went, not in a million years.'

She stopped at this point to take another drink of her tea, and impatient now, Lily urged her, 'Well ... go on then.'

Florrie settled herself more comfortably into the chair. She was thoroughly enjoying herself now and had no wish to rush it.

'Well, the first part o' the conversation I heard was aimed at Jonathan. Poor lamb, they reckon he's mad as a March hare. But then ... well, I heard the old woman ask Dan if he had thought any more about what they had talked about. So, o' course, at that me ears pricked up. An' it were then I got the biggest shock o' me life, 'cos from what I could glean it seems that Brigie had a daughter many years ago that she gave up for adoption. An' the long an' the short of it is, she's asked Mr Dan if he'll try to track her down.'

'*Never in this world!*' Lily's eyes were almost starting from her head in shock, to such an extent that the tea in her mug slopped over the rim and burned her hand, which had her cursing as she hastily dabbed it dry with her apron. 'You ... you must have it wrong,' she stuttered eventually when she had managed to compose herself a little, but Florrie shook her head.

'I'm tellin' you it's true, as sure as eggs is eggs. Seems old Miss Starchy Pants weren't *quite* as starchy as we all thought. But then it's common knowledge that she lived wi' Thomas Mallen for years wi'out a ring on her finger, an' that were *before* she tricked Mr Bensham into marryin' her. Stands to reason that she'd end up wi' a bellyful at some time or another, don't it? If you were to ask me, I'd lay odds the child belonged to *him*, Thomas Mallen – which means if the woman's still alive there's yet another Mallen somewhere who just might have some sort o' claim on the Hall. It could be that Mr Ben an' Miss Hannah won't, get their hands on it as easy as they think when Brigie snuffs it – iffen Mr Dan finds her daughter, that is.'

'Good Lord.' Lily could hardly take it in. So Brigie had once given up a child? Now that she came to think of it, it went some way to explaining her obsession with Barbara, for it was a well-known fact that from the second Barbara's mother had died giving birth to her, Brigie had treated the child as her own. No doubt she had

68

poured all the love that should have gone to her own child into Barbara, not that it had done her much good, for Barbara had never returned the love. If anything, before her death, she had ended up resenting Brigie's interference in her life, seeing her as the one who had kept her from marrying Michael, the love of her life.

'So what do you think the missus will make o' this little snippet then, eh?' Florrie demanded, and it was all Lily could do to drag her thoughts back to the woman who was sitting smiling smugly at her. She had no doubt that by 'the missus' Florrie was referring to Constance Radlet, and for a while she was at a loss as to how to answer her. How would Aunt Constance, as Lily had always referred to her, take it indeed? No doubt it would shock her to the core, to say the very least.

'I have no idea,' she said eventually. 'But if you don't mind, Florrie, I would like to be the one to tell her when the opportunity arises. Aunt Constance has been unwell for some time and a shock like this could do her harm if it isn't approached properly. Leave it with me, would you? I'll have a word to Mam and see what she thinks we should do about it.'

Florrie sniffed indignantly. Huh! She had imagined that Lily would have gone racing over to Wolfbur Farm to tell the missus the gossip. Just went to show, she thought to herself, that she didn't know Lily quite as well as she thought she did. And to think that she'd walked all this way just to pass the news on, on her day off an' all!

Draining her mug, she rose stiffly from her seat. It seemed that she had no sooner got there than

69

it was time to set off for home again, and it would have to be soon, for she didn't want to get caught out on the fells in the dark.

At almost that exact moment, Dan was entering his home, Brook House, so named because of the stream that ran through the two-acre garden at the back of it. It was a solid red-brick building, set well back from the road on the outskirts of Gosforth, on the road that led to Morpeth. He and Barbara had moved into the house many years ago on their return from Paris when the triplets, Ben, Jonathan and Harry were small, and Dan had continued to live there following Barbara's death. It was a spacious house boasting a large hall, three reception rooms leading off from one side of it and a kitchen, dining room and a morning room from the other. Since his wife's death few of the rooms were ever used now. In fact, Dan had often been heard to say that the house was much too large for him, but despite his complaints he had never offered to put it up for sale, and so it remained as a shrine to his late wife, for not so much as a stick of furniture had been changed since her passing.

Long before her death, Dan had chosen to sleep in a room across the first-floor landing from the bedroom they had once shared, and there he had remained ever since. Betty Rowe, who saw to the cleaning and the running of the place, and Ada Howlett, who did the cooking, had been devoted servants and still remained loyal to him. Both lived in, though they were getting on in years now. In truth, one person would have been sufficient to keep the house running smoothly and to see to his needs, which were few, but he hadn't the heart to retire either of them. Besides, it was always nice to come home to their welcoming faces. It gave him a sense of belonging somehow.

Now as he pushed the front door open, Betty came hobbling from the direction of the kitchen and instantly began to fuss over him like a mother hen. 'By, lad.' She might have been addressing a child as her plump arms came up to help him off with his coat. 'Just look at the state of you – you're white over, so you are. You'll catch your death one o' these days, venturin' out in weather such as this.'

'It would take more than an inch or so of snow to see me off, Betty,' he replied jovially, and then, 'What's that lovely smell coming from the kitchen?'

She chuckled. 'Ada had an inklin' that you'd be back today so she's done a pan of your favourite beef stew an' dumplin's. Then to follow that, there's an iced puddin'. But before I away to see to it for you, how is Master Johnny?'

The smile slid from his face and his head slowly wagged from side-to-side. 'Bearing up, Betty, which I dare say is the best we can hope for, given the circumstances. The war may be over, but for many the battle goes on. There have been another three admissions up at the Hall besides Jonathan this week, and the poor souls are all at the end of their tether. To see them now you would never believe that any of them could ever lead normal lives again. War is a terrible thing, Betty.'

'Aye lad, it is that. It's over a year since it fini-

71

shed, yet still the casualties are filtering through. But you get yourself away to the fire now. I'll bring you your meal on a tray, shall I? Then you can eat it in the warm.'

'You spoil me,' he told her with a wink, and a flush of pleasure spread across her homely old face.

'Get away with you. You know flattery will get you everywhere.' With that she turned and hurried back in the direction of the kitchen, whilst Dan made his way into the drawing room and poured himself a stiff measure of whisky from the cut-glass decanter placed on a small table to the side of the settee. He had barely finished drinking it when Betty bustled in with a laden tray in her hands.

'Is there anything else I can do for you?' she asked as Dan lifted the lid from the soup and sniffed at it appreciatively.

'There is actually, Betty. I shall be leaving for London in the morning. I shall probably only be gone for a few days, but I wondered if you could throw some clothes into a case for me? You're so much better at that sort of thing than I am.'

'No trouble at all, lad. Is it business or pleasure that is takin' you there?'

Dan avoided her eyes as he settled himself into the fireside chair and lifted the tray onto his knees. 'It's pleasure,' he lied. 'I thought I'd book myself into the Ritz and do a bit of sightseeing. There is also an exhibition of modern French art including works by Matisse and Derain that I would like to see.'

Her face lit up with approval. 'Then it's right

glad I am to hear it,' she told him sincerely. 'Though I have a feeling you'll find London much altered since the end of the war. Times are changin' in all ways, from what I can see of it. Why, only recently I read in the newspaper that Lady Astor had taken her seat at the House of Commons. Who would ever have thought we'd see a lady MP, eh? Still, you don't get out and about half as much as you should, and a change of scenery will do you the power of good. I'll put one of your good suits in, just in case you should decide to go and see a show an' all.'

'Thank you, Betty.' He watched her walk from the room and once alone again, his eyes strayed to the flames licking up the chimney. He hated lying, but what choice had he had? He had promised Brigie that he would tell no one of the secret she had entrusted to him. Sighing, he lifted his spoon and began to eat.

The house was silent when sometime later he made his way up to bed. Ada and Betty had long since retired, but when he opened his bedroom door he saw an open case neatly packed with everything he might need for a few days away from home. He wondered where his search would lead him and what he would say if he should manage to find Brigie's daughter. But it was no use worrying about it for now. He would cross that bridge when he came to it.

For no reason that he could explain, he began to pace restlessly up and down the room. The fire was blazing in the grate and the room was warm and inviting. Betty had drawn the heavy velvet curtains against the cold night, but now he crossed to them and twitched them aside to stand staring out across the snowy landscape. The grounds of Brook House and the woodland beyond looked beautiful in the moonlight, and as he stood there the memories flooded back. The snow was suddenly gone and in his mind's eye he could see his children racing across the emerald-green lawns with a much younger Ruthie in hot pursuit of them, and Ben as always leading the way. The house had rung with the sound of the triplets' laughter back then, and yet it had never been a truly happy house, for Barbara had never settled there. Of their own will his feet suddenly turned from the scene and he found himself out on the landing, then he was opening the door to the room that he had once shared with his wife – and he had the sense of stepping back in time.

Closing the door softly behind him, he lit the oil lamp with the matches that Betty always kept to the side of it, and a warm glow soon enveloped the room. It was cold in here, for fires were only kept lit in the rooms that were in use.

Barbara's silver-backed hairbrush and comb still lay on the mahogany dressing-table from when she had last used them, and as he gazed at them he was shocked to see a few strands of her jet-black hair trapped amongst the bristles; funny that he had never noticed them before. Crossing to the wardrobe, he carefully opened the door and there were her dresses, just as she had left them. He fingered them reverently before burying his face in one of them. The smell of her still lingered and he felt tears smarting at the back of his eyes. *Oh Barbara, why couldn't you love me?*

The answer instantly came back at him. *Because I only ever loved one man and that was Michael Radlet, but Brigie kept us apart.*

Barbara had always believed that Anna Bensham had been the cause of her never coming together with Michael – and if it were true, then Brigie had also been the cause of his own life being ruined, for whilst he had adored the ground Barbara walked on, her love for Michael had stayed true. And now Brigie was asking him to go off on some wild-goose chase to try to find the child that she had once borne to Thomas Mallen, who had been the source of all the trouble in the first place. Dan was aware that many men in his position would have refused, and yet... A picture of Brigie's tortured face floated in front of his eyes and he knew that he would try, although he had very little hope of his quest being successful.

He left for London early the next morning with Betty's words ringing in his ears. 'Mind how you go now. Though why you couldn't wait till the weather's a bit better I'll never know. It will be a miracle if you ever get there! Why, there's every chance the train will be de-railed with the snow comin' down as it is.'

Lifting his case, he smiled at her before he strode away down the path. 'Never fear, Betty,' he reassured her. 'I'll get there. You just keep this place going for me whilst I'm gone, and get Ada to prepare some of her delicious Christmas puddings because I shall definitely be back for Christmas, no doubt with an appetite like a donkey's.'

Chapter Six

Newcastle was alive with shoppers, and it was all Hannah could do to contain Lawrie's excitement as they passed the brightly lit shop windows. Lawrie had already managed to choose many of the gifts he wanted to buy with Hannah's help, and now they were heading towards the market-place, where she had promised to get him a tray of faggots and peas, which was one of his favourite treats. Ben had hoped to come with them but had been called away to Manchester to deal with a problem at the mill, which he now jointly owned with his Uncle John. John's health had been giving them all cause for concern for some time now, for he had recently suffered his third stroke. It had been a severe one this time, and now he was bedridden, which left a lot more responsibility for the running of the mill on Ben's shoulders. Normally, Ben would not have minded, but this time he had fretted about leaving Hannah.

'I shall be perfectly all right,' she had assured him when he had expressed his concerns. 'Both you and Nancy are treating me like an invalid when I am merely pregnant. Now go off and do what needs to be done.'

'But I had promised Lawrie that *I* would take him into Newcastle to do his Christmas shopping,' Ben pointed out and Hannah had laughed.

'Well, I'm sure I am quite capable of doing

that,' she had retorted. 'Now will you *please* just go and stop fretting? The sooner you go, the sooner you'll be back, which will be no bad thing because I think Lawrie may burst with excitement long before the big day dawns, the way things are going.'

And so, somewhat reluctantly, Ben had gone and now here she was, loaded down with bags and longing for the day to end. Not that she didn't enjoy her outings with Lawrie, for he was the only person she knew who had a permanent smile on their face, with never a bad word to say about anyone. No, it was nothing to do with him – it was just this persistent ache that she had had in her back for some time now. Today it seemed worse, but then she supposed this was due to the fact that Lawrie had almost dragged her from one end of Newcastle to the other in his search for gifts. Still, she consoled herself, we are almost finished now. Then we can go home and I can put my feet up.

'There's the pie-man – look, Hannah!' Lawrie yelled suddenly, and she fumbled in her handbag for some change as he hopped from foot to foot in anticipation.

It was as Lawrie was standing with his tray of faggots and peas clutched in his hand that a child who was walking amongst the stalls caught his attention. He looked to be about four or five years old and was poorly dressed and painfully thin. The child was walking away from him and yet there was something about him even from the back view that Lawrie found vaguely familiar, which was strange, for Lawrie's world seemed to centre around the cottage and the Hall and the

77

very infrequent visits he made to Newcastle with Hannah or Ben.

Lawrie glanced at Hannah, but she was deep in conversation with the pie-man at the stall so he looked back towards the place where the child had been. He had disappeared as if by magic, and though Lawrie's eyes scanned the marketplace, there was now no sign of him. For no reason that Lawrie could explain, he experienced a sharp feeling of loss, but then as the appetising smell of his treat drifted up to him he forgot all about the little boy and turned his attention back to his meal.

By the time Lawrie and Hannah arrived home it was late afternoon and the sky was darkening. Fred took the pony and trap round to the stables and Nancy met them at the door, and before he had even taken his coat off, Lawrie was pulling his gifts from the various bags in his haste to show her.

'Look, Nancy. I got this for Aunt Constance. I wanted to buy her some leather gloves but Hannah said as she doesn't get out an' about any more that this would be more suitable. Do you think she'll like it?' He held up a fine lawn nightgown for her inspection and Nancy dutifully clucked her approval.

'Why, I think it's beautiful, Master Lawrie. I've no doubt she'll be over the moon with it.'

'An' I got this for Cousin Ben.' He produced a wallet made from soft black leather, which Nancy again admired, and so it went on until only two bags remained unopened. 'I can't show you these,' he bubbled. ''Cos one is for you an' one is for Hannah, an' if you see them then it won't be a surprise on Christmas Day, will it?'

'Quite right,' Nancy agreed and then, 'now come on, let's be havin' you. I've got you a nice bit o' brisket for your tea wi' crispy roast potatoes just the way you like 'em. Why don't you get yourself away an' wash your hands, eh? The meal will be ready in half an hour.'

When Lawrie scampered gleefully away, Nancy turned her attention to Hannah, who was tidying her hair in the ornate gilt mirror that hung above the console table in the hall.

'I gather the day was a success then?'

Hannah grinned ruefully. 'You could say that. I'm sure he's dragged me into almost every shop in Newcastle. My legs feel as if they're about to drop off, I don't mind telling you, and my back feels as if it's about to break.'

'Then come and take the weight off your feet while I get on with the dinner,' Nancy urged. On close inspection, Hannah looked peaky to say the least, but half an hour with her feet up and then a good warm meal inside her should put the colour back into her cheeks.

Hannah obediently made her way to the drawing room whilst Nancy bustled back to the kitchen. Settling into the cosy fireside chair that Ben always commandeered when he was home, she lifted her feet onto a small footstool and in no time at all had slipped into an exhausted sleep.

It was almost two hours later when the pain in her back woke her. She winced as she eased herself up in the chair and glanced at the clock on the mantelshelf. It was well after seven o'clock and she was shocked to find that she had slept right through dinner. Rising, she went hurriedly towards the kitchen where she found Nancy sitting in a chair with her feet held out to the fire and Fred sitting opposite her.

'Ah, you're awake,' she grinned. 'You went out like a light, so you did, and you looked so peaceful that I didn't like to disturb you. Don't worry though, Lawrie had his meal in here with me and yours is keeping warm in the oven. I just hope it hasn't dried up.'

'I'm sure it will be fine,' Hannah assured her, feeling more than a little guilty. 'I'm just sorry to put you to so much trouble.'

Nancy flapped a tea towel at her. 'Get away with you. 'Tain't no trouble at all. Now get yourself to the table an' while you're eatin' your dinner I'll make you a nice strong cup o' tea.'

As Hannah sat down at the table, Lawrie bounced back into the room.

'Nancy and Fred have been helpin' me wrap some o' me Christmas presents up,' he informed her gleefully, and then his face falling, he followed it with, 'When will Cousin Ben be back, Hannah? I miss him.'

'I do too, Lawrie. But don't worry, he should be back tomorrow.'

Happier again, he smiled and left the room, and for a time silence reigned as Hannah ate her meal.

Dan emerged from the doors of the Ritz Hotel in London, turned right and strolled along to Piccadilly Circus, enjoying the crisp night air. He was

80

heading for the Palace Theatre, Shaftesbury Avenue. *The Whirligig*, a revue devised by André Charlot, was playing there, and tonight Dan felt the need for some sort of light entertainment. Tomorrow would be soon enough to begin the search for Brigie's daughter, even though he feared he was on a fruitless mission. So many years had passed since Mary Peel had delivered the baby to the East End of London. There was every possibility that the woman who had taken her in was dead and buried by now. And even if she were still alive – assuming that she had been a genuine person who really did find homes for the unfortunate, abandoned children she took in – how could she be expected to remember one particular child from so very long ago?

Dan pulled his fine Melton coat closer about him as depression suddenly settled itself around him like a cloud. The last time he had come to London, his wife had accompanied him, and he had enjoyed showing her the sights. But tonight he was alone – no one to share it with. But then he thought – had he not always been alone? For even when Barbara had been at his side, she had never really been wholly with him. Her thoughts had always been firmly fixed on Michael Radlet. And then, on the other hand, there was Ruthie. Now *her* thoughts had always been firmly fixed on *him*, whilst his were fixed on Barbara. Dan shook his head and doubted if he would ever understand the complexities of human beings, even if he lived to be a very, very old man.

When he emerged from the theatre later that night he was shocked to find that he could barely see beyond a hand in front of him. A thick smog had settled and this, combined with the frozen snow on the ground, had turned the grimy pavements into a skating rink. As Dan had soon discovered, the snow here was nothing like that which fell at home. There it made everything appear clean and fresh, but within minutes of falling here it was turned to a filthy slush from the many feet trampling across it. He cautiously stepped to the edge of the pavement, suddenly longing for the peace and quiet of his luxurious suite of rooms at the Ritz, just a few minutes' walk away.

Couples were pouring out of the theatre behind him; beautifully dressed women laughing gaily up into the faces of their husbands and companions, and this further added to his deep sense of loneliness. He briefly considered going on to a club but then thought of the search that lay ahead of him the next day. A good night's sleep would do him far more good, he decided.

'*Well!* You could knock me down wi' a feather!' Daisy Waite declared when Lily had passed on Florrie's latest bit of tittle-tattle. 'You just wait till the missus an' our Sarah get their teeth into this.'

'Do you think it's a good idea to tell them?' Lily's voice was weighed with concern. After all, Brigie was now a very old lady and there was no knowing what those two over in the farmhouse might do if they were to learn of her illegitimate daughter, hating her as they did.

'Why *shouldn't* we tell them?' Daisy snapped indignantly. 'It were Miss Prim an' Proper Anna Brigmore who ruined our Sarah's life an' were the cause of her losin' her leg. Or at least it were that damn bitch, Barbara, who Brigie brought up as her own. Our Sarah would still be walkin' about on two legs if that cow hadn't pushed her down the incline.' She shuddered as she thought back to the fateful day when Barbara had attacked Sarah in a jealous rage over Michael. 'I'll never forget the sight o' that poor lass when they carried her home on a door wi' her leg all mangled beyond savin'. Barbara had pushed her down the rise onto all the old rustin' farm equipment. The poor lass never stood a chance an' she were such a sweet-natured little thing back in them days. Trouble was, Brigie gave the hellcat ideas above her station an' all the time there were a little Brigmore bastard floatin' about. You wouldn't give it credit, would you?'

'We can all make mistakes, Mam,' Lily pointed out. She knew how much her mother had thought of Sarah ever since the day they had taken her in following the death of Sarah's parents. It had seemed a natural thing to do, as Sarah's father had been Lily's uncle, her father's brother. And as Daisy had said at the time, families should stick together.

But Daisy was having none of it. 'What's done is done an' there's no turnin' the clock back,' she declared. 'But if I can give our Sarah a single second's satisfaction, then I shall. Oh, I can just imagine how she'll gloat when she knows that Brigie weren't whiter than white after all.' Before Lily could stop her, she had snatched up her shawl and almost tripped in her haste to get to the door.

'You're surely not going over *now*, Mam?' Lily gasped incredulously. 'They'll likely just be sittin' down to dinner.'

'Ain't no time like the present,' Daisy chortled gleefully, and throwing the door wide, she plunged out into the snowstorm that was fast blowing itself into a gale.

Once she had reached the farmhouse at Wolfbur Farm she staggered into the kitchen, and the blast of air that came with her sent the flames leaping up the chimney.

Just as Lily had predicted, Sarah was leaning against the table carving a small joint of lamb onto a serving plate. Constance was dozing in a chair at the side of the fire but on her entrance both pairs of eyes looked towards her and Sarah grunted, 'What you lookin' so pleased about then? You look like the cat that got the cream.'

'Oh, believe me, it's even better than that,' Daisy told them, and after throwing her shawl off she dropped into the chair opposite Constance and began to impart the news, her words tripping over each other in their haste to be told.

When she had finally finished, she looked expectantly towards Constance and was shocked to see that the woman had paled to the colour of bleached linen. Her wrinkled hand was tight across her mouth and was visibly trembling. Sarah also appeared to have been rendered totally speechless, and was looking from one to the other of them with a look of total confusion on her face. It was just too much to take in. Brigie with a child of her own? It was unthinkable!

Constance finally broke the silence. 'If what Florrie has told you is true,' she said quietly, 'then it is best left alone. It is in the past now and best forgotten.'

'Ah, but that's just it, ain't it? It *can't* be left alone, 'cos accordin' to Florrie, Brigie has asked Master Dan to try an' find her, an' he's gone harin' off to London to do just that.'

Constance's mind was reeling, for Brigie had been the closest thing to a mother that she had ever known. And even if they had been estranged for some years, it still tore at her heart to think of what it must have cost Brigie to give her child away. And for what – so that she could maintain her respectability? Oh yes, Brigie had always been a great one for playing the lady. She would never have borne the shame of admitting to having a child out of wedlock. Constance's thoughts now moved on. When Harry Bensham had died, he had left the Hall to Brigie for the duration of her life, with the request that it should then pass to Ben, who until Jonathan had reappeared from the dead, had been his only surviving grandchild. But if Dan were to find Brigie's long-lost child, who would inherit the Hall then? For surely Brigie, as Harry's widow, would be within her rights to change the will?

The same thought had just occurred to Sarah, and her hands clenched into fists. It was bad enough that she was forced to endure her only daughter being married to the son of the Mallen bitch Barbara, and faced with the prospect of seeing *him* become Lord of the Manor. But now, if Brigie's child were to crawl out of the woodwork, might things change?

Her hatred for Brigie and Ben was such that she would even be happy to deny her own daughter the inheritance if it meant getting revenge on the other two. 'Damn and blast that woman. I hope she rots in the fires of hell!' she ground out through gritted teeth.

Constance clutched at her throat. Sarah was so full of malice and spite lately that sometimes she frightened her. It was as if all the pain and indignity she had been forced to endure throughout her married life to Michael had come to a head, and now it was ready to burst ... like a great poisonous boil. A horrible sense of foreboding settled around Constance and she silently prayed that the quest Dan had embarked on might be in vain, for God help them all if he were to succeed.

Early the next morning, after a most substantial breakfast, Dan emerged onto Piccadilly. Again, as was normal until mid-morning, he found the wide street shrouded in fog. Wrapping his muffler more tightly about his throat, he waited as the doorman hailed a cab and climbed inside. The luxurious environs of London's West End were soon left behind, as the cabbie took him down the Strand to Fleet Street, and then on up Ludgate Hill, where the fog cleared enough for Dan to admire the dome of St Paul's Cathedral before they motored through the City, getting caught in heavy traffic near Tower Bridge. And then they were travelling up through the mean streets of Stepney and into the strange world of Limehouse, with its glimpses of Chinese seamen gathering on street corners... At last they were heading north up the Burdett Road into Mile End and Bow, to Myrtle Street.

Stepping down onto the dirty cobbles awash with freezing slush, Dan paid the cabbie and watched him drive off with a sense almost of abandonment. He looked around. Never had he imagined that such poverty still existed. Tiny cottages, their windows filthy or packed with rags or paper, lined the streets. In front of them, merely inches from their doors, were gutters swimming with excrement. Dan felt the bile rise in his throat and hastily taking a handkerchief from his pocket, he pressed it against his nose to stem the terrible smell. One cottage was missing its front door, and as he glanced in he saw six children huddled together in a corner of the room. Two more were fast asleep in front of them on a bare floor. There appeared to be not a stick of furniture in the room, and despite the bitterness of the weather, Dan saw that the children were all barefoot and painfully thin, dressed in what amounted to little more than bundles of rags. A woman of indeterminate age with a tiny baby sucking at her sagging breast was leaning against another wall, and as she looked out at Dan he saw that her eyes were without hope. He paused and after fumbling in his wallet, he produced a sovereign, which he laid on the doorstep. The woman's eyes fastened on it greedily as one of the children crawled forward to retrieve it. As the boy came from the shadows, Dan was shocked to see that his hair was alive with head lice that could be seen freely running across his dirty parting. The woman inclined her head by way of thanks, though not a word was spoken. Dan nodded back, but felt as if his heart was breaking. Such filth, such squalor: how could people survive in appalling conditions like that?

He took out the crumpled piece of paper on which the address he was seeking was written, and saw that it was Myrtle Cottages, not Myrtle Street, that he sought. As he stood there, an upstairs window suddenly opened above him and the contents of a chamber pot hurtled towards him. Just in time, he managed to step aside. As quickly as it had opened, the window then slammed shut, and keen to be on his way now, Dan moved on, thinking that he must surely have died and gone to hell.

''Ere, mister, are yer lost? I could 'elp yer find what yer were lookin' for. It wouldn't be any bovver, 'onest.'

Dan found himself looking down into a pair of deep brown eyes that belonged to a little boy who looked to be no older than seven or eight years old at most.

'I'll take yer wherever yer want to go fer a tanner. Can't say fairer than that, now can I?' The child was somewhat better clothed than the ones Dan had just seen in the door-less cottage, in as much as his feet were clad in wooden clogs and he was wearing a thin shirt and ragged trousers.

'I ... er ... I am looking for Myrtle Cottages. Number ten,' Dan told him. The child nodded, then beckoning, he urged Dan to follow him down yet another passage that, if possible, smelled even worse than the street he had just come from.

'That's number ten there, mister.'

Dan took a shiny shilling from his pocket and when he tossed it into the air, the boy expertly caught it and hastily tucked it into his pocket before going to stand against a wall. 'I'll wait 'ere fer yer, then if yer should get lost when you've done yer business I can show yer back to the main road,' he chirped cheekily.

'Thank you.' Dan cleared his throat, then, approaching the door the boy had pointed to, he hesitantly knocked. For some moments there was no reply, but then he heard footsteps shuffling towards it. The door opened and an old woman peered at him in astonishment. It wasn't often that anyone as well-dressed as this gentleman was seen around these parts.

'Yes?'

'I er ... Mrs Stirling?'

She shook her head and would have closed the door on him but he put out his hand to stay it before pleading, 'Spare me a minute, I beg you. I will make it worth your while. I wish you no harm, I assure you. I am merely trying to find someone.'

She cautiously inched the door open again. 'Mrs Stirling left 'ere some ten years back,' she informed him abruptly.

Dan's stomach sank into his shoes and yet he had not really held out any hope of finding her. 'Would you happen to know where she went?'

Again the woman shook her head, but when Dan produced another shilling from his coat pocket, she eyed it with glee and told him, 'Word 'ad it that they took 'er to Bow Institute. More than that I can't tell yer.'

'Thank you.' Dan placed the money in her hand and almost instantly the door was slammed in his face.

The boy now came to stand at his side. 'I can take yer to Bow Institute, mister,' he said importantly. 'I knows where it is as I live near there, but it'll cost yer another tanner.'

'Then lead the way, young man,' Dan instructed him. 'And it would be cheap at double the price.'

The boy set off at such a trot that Dan almost had to run to keep up with him. They seemed to walk forever and Dan began to tire as he realised that he was neither as young nor as fit as he had once been. At last they turned into Adderton Road and the boy pointed. 'The Institution is just up 'ere. Not far to go now, mister.'

Here the road was bordered with large Victorian townhouses that looked very grimy and neglected. 'I live in that one there wiv me ma an' me bruvvers,' the boy now told Dan conversationally as he pointed towards a rundown-looking house.

'Do you really? Then you must have lots of space,' Dan commented.

The boy, Pip, threw back his head and laughed in hearty amusement. 'We don't get to live in the *whole* house, mate. Each family has one room,' he explained. Cor, this toff didn't know much did he? 'Some o' these houses 'as as many as twenty families livin' in 'em, an' there's only one privy to serve the lot of us. It don't 'alf stink sometimes.'

'And where is your father?'

Pip sneered. 'Oh, *him*. He pissed off an' left us years ago. Went off wiv the barmaid from the Red Lion, 'e did. An' good riddance, that's what I say. At least me ma don't get knocked from pillar to post no more. We're better off wivout the drunken old sod.'

The boy then pointed again. 'That's Bow Institution,' he informed him solemnly. 'An' all I can say is, you'll be lucky to find who yer lookin' for if they've been long in that place. Once they get put in there it ain't often they come back out unless it's feet-first in a bleedin' box.'

Looking at the façade of the building, Dan could well believe it, for it was a bleak place with shutters up at the windows.

'Well, thank you, young man. You have been most helpful,' he told his young escort, and when he placed a half a crown in his hand, the child's face lit up brighter than the sunshine.

'Cor, ta, mister. God bless yer! I'll just 'ang around again till yer come out so's I can point yer in the direction of 'ome, shall I?'

Dan had a feeling that it would be useless to argue and so after nodding he moved towards the grim building on legs that suddenly seemed to have developed a mind of their own. Would he find the person he was seeking here? Deciding that there was only one way to find out, he raised his hand and tugged on the large bell-pull that hung to one side of the enormous oak door. The sound of footsteps echoing hollowly on the tiles within sent a chill up his spine. It was bad enough coming as a visitor to this god-forsaken place, but how must people feel, who were about to be locked away in here?

When the door creaked open he found himself confronted by a young girl with a face the colour of dough.

'Yes?'

She seemed so lifeless that Dan was reminded of a corpse.

'I would like to see the Matron of this establishment, if you please.'

'Do yer 'ave an appointment?'

'No, but I need to see her now on a matter of some urgency. Could you tell her that my name is Mr Daniel Bensham?'

'Matron don't see no one wivout an appointment.' The girl was in the process of closing the door in his face when Dan's arm shot out and stopped her. He was angry now, and it told in his voice.

'I have already informed you that I am here on important business, and I have no intention of leaving until I have seen the Matron, so kindly show me to her room!'

Shrugging her thin shoulders the girl stood aside and allowed him to enter. Dan found himself in a spacious hallway, but that, as he soon discovered, was all that it had in its favour, for it appeared more like a prison than an institution.

'Wait there,' the girl told him as she nodded indignantly towards a hard-backed chair. 'I'll go an' see if Matron is able to see yer.'

'Thank you.' Dan undid his coat and removed his hat, then after smoothing his hair down he perched uncomfortably on the edge of the wooden chair. Once the sounds of the girl's footsteps stopped echoing in the corridor a silence settled, broken now and then by a loud moan or groan that seemed to float down from the upstairs. He shuddered. This was the second shock he had received today, the first being the terrible squalor he had witnessed in the back streets. And then to discover that there were places like this where poor people who had no means of helping themselves could be incarcerated and forgotten... He tugged at his cravat, suddenly feeling the need for more air, but at that moment the young woman who'd admitted him came slopping towards him again.

'Matron will see you, but she can only spare you five minutes. Foller me, please.' She turned about and Dan hastily rose and followed her until they came to a door at the far end of a long corridor. Here she jerked her thumb at a door, then without another word, turned about and left.

He watched her depart before tapping at the door which, he noted, was painted the same dull brown as all the others.

'Enter!'

He swallowed before opening the door to be confronted by a huge Amazon of a woman who was sitting behind an equally enormous mahogany desk.

'I understand that you wish to see me on a matter of some urgency, Mr Bensham?' she said without preamble. The woman wore a drab brown dress that strained across her gigantic breasts, and a tiny lace cap that looked ridiculously out of place, was perched precariously on the top of her head.

'Yes, I er ... I'm rather hoping you may be able to help me.' Dan gulped deep in his throat, feeling like a schoolboy who had been called in front of the head teacher for some misdemeanour. 'I'm looking for a woman who I have cause to believe was admitted to this place about ten years ago.'

'Many people are admitted to this place.' Her eyes were like slits and he noted with horrified fascination that when she talked, her many chins wobbled.

'Does this person you are seeking have a name?' she went on.

'Yes, yes of course. Her name is Mrs Stirling and she lived in Myrtle Cottages in Bow before being admitted here.'

'I see, and is Mrs Stirling a relation of yours?'

'Well, no... I'm looking for her on behalf of someone else actually.'

'Then I'm sure you will understand that if you have no blood ties to this person, it would be very unethical of me to divulge her whereabouts.'

Dan sighed. He felt as if he had come up against a brick wall, but then he thought of Brigie and knew that he could not go away without putting up a fight. He produced his wallet and placed it on the desk in front of him.

'Surely there must be some sort of register in places such as this?'

Her eyes were fixed on the wallet as she slowly nodded. 'Well, yes, there are ... but even so, if you are no relation...'

He opened the wallet and withdrew a large, white five-pound note. 'It is of the utmost importance that I trace Mrs Stirling, Matron.'

The woman licked her lips and wiped her hands down the length of her skirt before muttering, 'Well ... I dare say a quick look in the register would do no harm. You do look like a respectable gentleman.' She rose from her seat and as Dan's heart began to thunder in his chest she crossed to a large metal filing cabinet that took up almost the width of one wall.

'Now let me see ... 1899 ... 1900 ... ah, here we are –1909.' She unhooked a large bunch of keys from her belt and after opening the drawer that contained the names of admissions for that year, she began to thumb through them. 'Silvers, Smith, Soloman, Stirling! This must be it.' She withdrew a file and began to read through it, then turned back to him.

'According to this, Lillian Stirling was only here for a short while. It seems that when she recovered, a niece by the name of Margaret Fellows took her to live with her.'

'And where does this Margaret Fellows live?' Dan asked abruptly, as all hope of meeting the woman slipped away.

'I have no idea.' The Matron slammed the file shut and replaced it in the drawer before carefully locking it again. 'It is not our policy to question relatives who choose to take their kin from our establishment. I'm afraid there is nothing more I can do to help you, Mr Bensham.'

'Thank you anyway for your time, Matron.' As Dan slid the five-pound note across the desk to her she snatched it up and pocketed it immediately.

'My pleasure, Mr Bensham. Don't hesitate to call again if I can be of further assistance to you.'

After inclining his head he left the room, and as he trailed miserably back along the corridor he was asking himself, Just how the hell am I supposed to find this Margaret Fellows?

Once outside, he found his little friend waiting for him, and seeing the dejected look on his face, the child asked, 'What's up then? Weren't the person you was lookin' for still there? 'Ad she snuffed it?'

'No, she hadn't snuffed it, as you put it. What's your name anyway?'

'Pip,' the child piped up. 'What's yours?'

'Mr Bensh ... Dan.' He extended his hand and the child solemnly shook it as they began to walk along together.

'So, what was the name of the person you was lookin' for?' Pip asked. 'I know loads of people 'ereabouts, an' them I don't know I can usually track down.'

'I was looking for a Mrs Stirling who used to live in the cottage that you first took me to. It seems that after being admitted to the Institution, a niece of hers then took her to live with her. Unfortunately, the niece left no forwarding address so I'm back to square one.'

'Mm.' Pip scratched furiously at his head before asking, 'An' what was the name of the woman's niece?'

'It was someone called Margaret Fellows. Do you know anyone of that name?'

'It don't ring any bells,' Pip told him regretfully. 'But give me a couple of days an' no doubt I'll be able to find sumfink out for you. Where can I reach you?'

'I'm staying at the Ritz,' Dan informed him, and a smile danced across his lips as he wondered what the doorman there would think of the child, should he care to put in an appearance.

'The problem is, I need to get home for Christmas,' he went on. 'But if you have no objections, I could return in the New Year, and now that you have shown me where you live, I could perhaps come and see if you had managed to find anything out for me?'

'Sounds all right to me,' Pip beamed, and when Dan took a shining sovereign from his pocket the child's eyes almost popped out of his head.

'This is for you and your family,' Dan told him. 'Can you see that they have a good Christmas with that?'

'Not 'arf. Thanks, Mr ... Dan. I'll see you in the New Year then, an' never fear – I'll be puttin' the feelers out fer this 'ere Margaret Fellows. Bye fer now.'

Dan found himself laughing despite himself as he watched Pip skipping across the slushy cobbles, then turning about he shoved his hands down into his coat pockets and headed back towards the Mile End Road, where he could pick up a cab to go back to the West End. A deep depression tempered with loneliness had settled about him. Brigie would be so disappointed when he told her of his efforts to find what had become of her daughter so far. But then, as Pip had quite rightly said, he wasn't finished yet. Not by a long shot. He would come back in the New Year and continue the search, and meantime he would do some Christmas shopping. There was sure to be something to please the women in Mayfair. And then he could perhaps visit Hamley's Toy Shop in Regent Street, which was just around the corner from the Ritz. He would

97

buy a nice teddy bear for when Hannah and Ben's baby arrived. That way it wouldn't matter if it were a boy or a girl. Yes, that's what he would do. He would soon be a grandfather!

The thought put a spring back in his step. After shopping, he would treat himself to a slap-up lunch. And tomorrow, he would go home. In a slightly happier frame of mind again, he hurried on his way.

Chapter Seven

A wild wind was whipping across the fells as Ben opened the gate to the cottage. He had just endured an eight-hour train ride from Manchester in a carriage that amounted to little more than a freezing box. Normally the journey would have taken less than four and a half hours, but the drifting snow on the tracks had slowed everything down. There had been seven stops along the way, the first being at Staleybridge; they had then gone on to Mossley, Greenfield, Huddersfield, Dewsbury, Batley and then on to his first change of trains at Leeds. He had had to change trains yet again in York before continuing on through Northallerton, yet another stop, then two more at Darlington and Durham before finally arriving in Newcastle, where he had hired a cab to bring him from the station to the cottage.

It was now late afternoon and a faint light shining from the outhouse window told him that

Lawrie was still inside, no doubt putting the finishing touches to the crib that he was carving for the new baby.

He smiled as he inserted his key in the lock, noting that here at least, all the paths were clear; Fred had obviously been hard at work. It was good to be home, and he hoped that would be the last visit he would have to make to the mill in Manchester until after Christmas.

Nancy appeared in the kitchen doorway when she heard him enter, and she smiled a welcome before saying, 'Did you manage to resolve the problems at the mill?'

'I did indeed,' he said cheerily as the warmth enveloped him. 'Now where is that lovely wife of mine?'

'She popped up to see Brigie and Jonathan at the Hall about an hour or so since. No doubt she'll be back any time now. I asked her not to go with the roads bein' as they are, but you know what she's like when she's set her mind to somethin'. Fred offered to take her in the trap an' all, but she were havin' none of it. She has a mind of her own, does Hannah.' She hung Ben's coat on a hanger. ''Twouldn't surprise me if we didn't get snowed in for Christmas, the way this lot is comin' down. Looks like you might get stuck with me after all, for word has it that some o' the roads are already impassable.'

Dan nodded in agreement. 'Well, we'll just have to wait and see, Nancy. Obviously, it would be nice if you could get to spend Christmas with your sister but if you can't, you are more than welcome here.'

'Aye, I know I am, lad,' she beamed, thinking that it had been a good day when she had come to work for the Benshams, for they were a kindly couple with not an air or a grace between them – unlike some she had worked for before who had treated her as little more than a skivvy. And there was another attraction here as well, in the form of Fred Burton. Eeh, he were a lovely man, there were no doubt about it. He too had been set on shortly after Ben and Hannah moved into the cottage, and although he was some years her senior she had an inkling that he had taken to her, though he hadn't said as much as yet. Still, she could always live in hope. Nancy was under no illusions. She was plump and she was plain, and now that she was approaching thirty there were those who had termed her an old maid. But who knew what the future might hold?

Her happy thoughts were interrupted when the door once again banged open and Lawrie almost fell into the room, his eyes alight with excitement. They stretched even wider at the sight of Ben and he flung himself into his cousin's arms as a child would have done.

'Cousin Ben, I didn't know you were back. I'm so glad... I've missed you.'

'Well, I've missed you too.' Ben held him at arm's length and looked into Lawrie's eyes, which were on a level with his own before asking, 'And how is this wonderful crib coming along then?'

'That's what I was coming to tell Nancy.' Lawrie's arms were flapping wildly now, as if he were a bird trying to take flight. 'It's done ... I've just finished it. Shall I bring it across?'

'No, no, don't do that. We'll keep it a surprise for tonight after dinner, shall we? It will be something to look forward to. I'm sure Hannah will be thrilled with it, then you can put it in the nursery until the baby comes and it will be all ready and waiting for it. How would that be?'

'Ooh, yes. I'll just go across and give it one final sanding down. We d ... don't want any sharp edges for the baby to cut itself on.' With that, Lawrie flung himself about and lumbered out into the snow again as Nancy and Ben watched him with indulgent smiles on their faces. Lawrie had the temperament of an angel; there was no disputing that.

It was an hour later when Hannah returned, looking as if she had walked ten miles instead of one. Ben hurried to greet her and, after kissing her soundly, he took her coat and led her into the warmth of the drawing room where he pressed her down into the fireside chair. 'How did you find Brigie and Jonathan?' he asked once she was comfortably settled.

Hannah frowned. 'Jonathan was as well as could be expected, but Brigie...' She paused. 'I don't know what to think, Ben. She seemed sort of agitated.'

'I see.' Ben stared into the fire. 'Did she say if there was anything worrying her?'

'No, but she did ask three or four times if we had heard anything from your father. I told her that he had gone to London for a few days *at least* three times – and then she would ask after him again.'

'How strange.' Ben took a seat beside his wife. 'Now you come to mention it, that was strange too

– the way Father just took off like that. I mean, he doesn't usually go haring off at the drop of a hat. Not that a short break won't do him the world of good, of course, but it's so unlike him, isn't it?'

'I suppose it is, now that you come to mention it.' They stared at each other for some moments until the sombre mood was broken when Ben suddenly wrapped his arms around her and muttered, 'I missed you, Mrs Bensham.'

'And *I* missed you, Mr Bensham.' And then their lips joined and for now their concerns were forgotten as they gave themselves up to the pleasure of being together again.

Dinner was a jovial affair. Lawrie chattered away, and when he could get a word in, Ben told them of how he had found Jenny and John. To-night, Nancy had cooked them a large cottage pie that made Lawrie's mouth water and a large dish of chopped buttered cabbage, which just happened to be another of Lawrie's favourites. In no time at all he had downed a record-size portion. It was as Nancy was carrying the pudding to the table, which was apple pie and custard, and one of Ben's favourites, that Hannah suddenly turned an awful ashen colour and clutched at her stomach.

'What is it, my dear?' Ben had thrown his napkin down and was round the table in a second, his face a mask of concern.

'I ... I don't know,' Hannah gasped. 'I just suddenly got this awful pain. But don't fuss, it's going now. I probably just overdid it today. I'll be fine in a minute.'

Ben reluctantly went back to his seat as Nancy sliced up the pie, keeping a watchful eye on her mistress at the same time. Lawrie might have been struck dumb, for he looked absolutely terrified. He loved Hannah and could not bear to think of her in pain.

Seeing his obvious distress, Hannah told him, 'I'm fine now, Lawrie, really I am. Eat your pudding up and then I'll read you a story, shall I?'

Brighter again at the prospect, Lawrie lifted his spoon and began to attack his pudding as if he hadn't eaten for a month. Ben, however, noticed that Hannah barely picked at hers and so his own appetite fled too.

As soon as the meal was over he suggested, 'Why don't you go upstairs and have a lie down for a while, my love? I can read to Lawrie, can't I, my good man?'

Lawrie nodded; his eyes huge in his frightened face. His mother had had a pain and then she had died, and now he feared that history was about to repeat itself with Hannah.

'I think I might just do that.' Hannah allowed Ben to lead her from the dining room, but they had barely reached the bottom of the stairs when yet another pain gripped her and she clutched at his arm as she bent almost double.

'*Nancy!* Come quickly!' Ben was unable to keep the panic from his voice as Nancy emerged from the kitchen, wiping her hands on her apron. Between them they managed to get Hannah to a hard-backed chair that stood to one side of the console table in the hall. Ben was nearly beside himself with fear, and realising that she would have to take control of the situation, Nancy snapped, 'As soon as this pain has passed, we need to get her upstairs. And you, Lawrie, get yourself off over to the outhouse and find yourself something to do, there's a good lad.'

Lawrie was standing in the doorway of the dining room, and he seemed to be shaking with terror from head to foot. For some seconds he stood as if he had been rooted to the spot, but then Nancy said again, 'Lawrie ... just *go*, will you?' This time her words had the desired effect, for he suddenly sprang forward and ran for the door as if his very life depended on it. Meanwhile, Hannah had raised her head and now she muttered, 'It's gone again. What's happening, Nancy? Am I losing the baby? It's far too soon for it to come. I have three months left to go yet.'

Nancy had no time to answer, for Ben had swept Hannah into his arms and was striding towards the stairs with her as if she weighed no more than a feather. Once upstairs, Nancy hastily turned back the covers on their bed and he gently laid his wife down. It was then that Nancy noticed the dark stain on Hannah's skirt and her heart sank. Keeping a firm grip on herself, she yanked Ben out onto the landing and said in a low voice, 'We need a doctor, Ben, and it's Fred's night off. You will have to fetch one. How long do you think it would take you to get into town?'

His lips pursed into a grim line as he looked out of the landing window. The snow was coming down thick and fast with no sign of ceasing. 'Too long,' he ground out, and his fear was so tangible that Nancy felt she might have been able to reach out and touch it. It was then that another low moan from the bedroom brought both pairs of eyes back to the bedroom door. Ben was almost beside himself. What should he do? He couldn't possibly get into town in the dog-trap, with the roads the way they were. And then it suddenly came to him and he was clattering away down the stairs.

'Where are you going?' Nancy's voice brought him to a shuddering halt halfway down.

'I'm going to the Hall to get a doctor.'

'But ... but will the doctors there know how to deliver a baby?'

'They're doctors, aren't they? Unless you have a better idea!'

She ignored his harsh tone, for, knowing him as she did, she knew that he was suffering just as much as the poor soul who was now writhing in agony on the bed. She would have said more but all she could see and hear now was the back of his black head and the sound of the door slamming resoundingly behind him.

Once out on the road, Ben had gone some way before his footsteps suddenly slowed. He had come out in such a rush that he had forgotten even to put a coat on, and now the chill wind and the driving snow were biting into him. He turned to look behind him. Already the lights of the cottage had been swallowed up by the storm and there was nothing to be seen either before or behind him. He might have been the only person left on earth. The old fear began to settle around him and his breath caught in his throat. He was back on the edge of the earth again and should he try to put a foot forward, he would topple over into the abyss.

It's a long way to Tipperary... He was on the

battlefield, flat on his stomach in stinking mud, and now despite the cold he was sweating and he could hear Murphy singing. But it *couldn't* be Murphy. He had watched Murphy be blown to pieces in front of his very eyes. Murphy was dead ... dead ... *swimming like a tadpole in the womb.* Hannah! Somehow he managed to bring his thoughts back to his wife. She was going to have his baby and it was too soon ... if he didn't get help he might lose them both – and he was the only person who could help them. There was no one else in this vast wilderness, only him. But the Hall was less than a mile up the road now. He had walked there and back so many times that he could have done the journey blindfold. Taking a deep breath, he lifted his eyes from his feet. If he didn't look he could take that step; he *had* to. His brain sent a message to his legs but they remained immobile as if they had been struck by some weird kind of paralysis.

It's a long way back home.

'Go away, Murphy. Do you hear me, man? You're dead but my wife and my child are alive and I have to help them. Get out of my head, damn you!'

Silence settled across the snowy landscape and now his foot was twitching into life; he could feel it lifting and he wasn't falling. That's it, he told himself. Now the next one ... and again ... and again... His walk progressed to a stumbling run, hampered by the drifting snow. His breath was ragged now, and when some lights appeared ahead of him he almost cried with relief. It was the Hall – he had nearly made it. Minutes later he dragged himself up the steps, threw one of the heavy oak doors open, and there he fell into a sprawling heap on the long Persian runner that stretched the length of the hallway.

'Eeh, Captain Bensham. Whatever is the matter?'

Nurse Conway was running towards him and then there were hands helping him to his feet as he struggled to get his breath.

'The doctor... I need the doctor,' he gasped incoherently.

The woman propelled him towards a chair, and once she had placed his head between his knees she disappeared, only to return seconds later with what looked to be a large tumblerful of whisky. 'Get some of that down you,' she ordered. 'And then you can tell me what's wrong.'

Ben's first instinct was to dash the glass from her hand, but then he saw the sense of what she said and so, as she held it to his lips he took a good long swallow, coughing and choking as the spirit burned its way down into his stomach.

'That's better.' The nurse might have been addressing a child. 'Now, can you tell me what has happened, sir?'

'I ... it's Hannah. I ... I think she might have gone into labour and it's too soon. I'd never get through to the town with the roads being so bad, but she needs a doctor ... *now*.'

'I see.' The nurse pressed the glass into his hand and then she walked swiftly away and up the impressive staircase.

When she reappeared, there was a silver-haired doctor in a white coat at her side and Ben was relieved to see that he was carrying a black bag.

107

The man squeezed Ben's shoulder before asking him, 'Are you up to the journey back to the cottage, sir?'

'Yes, yes – and there's not a moment to lose,' Ben assured him. A small crowd of officers had gathered about them now and each of them looked concerned as the nurse hurried away to return with two heavy overcoats.

'Put these on, gentlemen,' she ordered, and when they had done as they were told, she accompanied them to the door. She did not shut it behind them until the storm had swallowed them up, and what she was praying was, 'May God help them all.'

Her heart was heavy at this latest turn of events, for she herself had been one of the nurses who had cared for Ben Bensham when his poor shell-shocked body had been delivered to the Hall. There had been times back then when she had wondered if he would ever be well again, for he had been teetering on the brink of insanity. But Hannah, who had been his named nurse and was now his wife, had somehow reached out to him and pulled him back from madness. And now it looked as if they might lose the child they had both been looking forward to so much. She shook her head sadly at the injustice of it all. Why should certain people be made to suffer so very much? Her eyes moved to the staircase and she pictured Mrs Bensham, who had once been Ben's governess, lying upstairs. Rumour had it that for almost all of her life Brigie, as she was known, had had associations with the Mallens in one way or another. Rumour also had it that the Mallens, and all those that were close to them, were cursed. Particularly the Mallen men. At this very moment in time, Nurse Conway, who had always been known to be not the least bit superstitious, had cause to believe it.

'This is it.' Ben guided the elderly doctor through the gate and up to the door of the cottage. The first thing they heard as they stepped into the hallway was Hannah groaning in agony, and not even waiting to take his coat off, the doctor headed upstairs.

Nancy raised her head as the two men entered the room and exclaimed, 'Eeh, thank God! The poor lass is in agony.'

The doctor crossed to the bed and after gently moving Nancy aside, he began to run his cold hands across Hannah's heaving stomach. 'The baby is coming, all right,' he told them. 'Now – I shall need hot water, lots of it, and towels.'

'I'll see to it right away, sir.' Nancy lifted her skirts and scuttled away.

The doctor then addressed Ben. 'And you, sir – get yourself downstairs. It will be easier for me if I don't have two patients to worry about. I shall call you the second I have news. But I warn you, first babies have a habit of taking their time, so don't expect too much too soon.'

'Hannah is barely six months' pregnant. Does the baby have any chance of surviving?'

The doctor took a deep breath. 'I think at this moment in time we should be more concerned about saving your wife. Let's just take one step at a time, eh?'

Ben turned away, with tears starting in his eyes. Just a couple of hours ago he had been the happiest man on earth. For the first time in his life he had a woman who truly loved him, but now there was the chance that she might be snatched away from him and he knew that if she was, then he too would die, for life without Hannah was unthinkable.

Nancy found him standing in a trance-like state on the landing some minutes later when she staggered up the stairs with the first bowlful of hot water for the doctor. Her first instinct was to draw him to her and comfort him, but she knew that this was not what he needed. He needed to be kept occupied, to feel useful.

'Get yourself away to the kitchen and set the kettle on to boil again,' she barked. And anyone hearing her might have thought it was she who was the mistress and he the servant. But the way she saw it, now was not the time for observing niceties. The baby's life – and Miss Hannah's, if it came to that – were hanging in the balance.

Her words had the desired effect, for Ben sprang forward and nodded vigorously.

'Of course, I'll carry it up when it's ready and leave it outside the door, shall I?'

'Aye, lad, you do that ... an' keep it comin'. I've a feelin' on me that this is goin' to be a very long night.'

It was now almost two o'clock in the morning and Ben's eyes were gritty from lack of sleep as he paced up and down the drawing-room carpet. He had fetched in the coal and built up all the

110

fires. He had settled Lawrie down to sleep, although it had not been easy, for he was almost as upset as Ben was. He had carried one kettleful of boiling water up the stairs after another and he had made more cups of tea this very night than he had ever made in his entire lifetime before, but now there was nothing to do but wait.

In their room, the doctor's face was grave. Hannah's screams had now dulled to thin whimpers as one contraction followed another, and he knew that she was almost at the end of her tether, yet still the child showed no sign of being born. Nancy was standing at the head of the bed, bathing Hannah's forehead and whispering words of encouragement. Now as their eyes met over the young woman's head they each saw the fear reflected in them.

'She can't keep this up for much longer.' Nancy's voice was as flat as a pancake.

The doctor watched helplessly as yet another contraction arched the poor woman's body from the bed. He knew that Nancy was right, which left him with only one choice; he would have to help the child along. Crossing to his bag, he fumbled inside it for a moment before producing a wickedly sharp-looking scalpel.

'Wash that thoroughly for me in boiling water, would you please, Nancy?'

She nodded numbly as he proceeded to wash his hands again in a china bowl.

When they were once again positioned at the side of the bed he took the scalpel from her shaking hand and instructed her, 'Make sure she

111

keeps her legs well open and hold her down if you have to.'

'*I ... I can't.'* Panic had drained the colour from Nancy's cheeks but now his voice was stern as he said sharply, 'Would you rather see her die then? And make no bones about it, that is exactly what is going to happen if I don't deliver this child – and soon. But I cannot do it on my own... So, will you help me or not?'

Nancy took a deep breath, then crossing to the bed she caught Hannah's knees in a firm grip and thrust them as far apart as she could. 'Do it!' she said quietly.

The evil-looking scalpel glinted in the light from the oil lamp as the doctor bent across his patient and suddenly there was a scream that turned Nancy's blood to water followed by a silence that was so profound she was convinced she had lost her hearing.

She looked down just in time to see a perfectly formed but tiny body slither from her mistress onto the bed, and now she was crying as she whispered, 'Is it alive? And is it a lass or a lad?'

Hannah had slipped into unconsciousness as the doctor cut the cord that bound the baby to its mother. He then lifted the child and slapped it soundly on its backside. There was nothing save silence, so now he bent his head and began to blow breath into its rosebud mouth. Nothing! His hands began to pump the tiny chest and as Nancy watched, she saw that the child was a boy. A beautiful little boy. She began to silently pray as the doctor worked tirelessly on. Eventually, it was she who pulled his hands away and stared into his weary eyes.

'It's no good,' she told him softly. 'You could have done no more but the bairn is gone.'

His chin drooped to his chest as Nancy lifted the child from the bed and wrapped it in a towel before laying it aside.

'Come along. We must see to her now,' she urged. The doctor nodded before turning to deliver the afterbirth and to try and stem the life-blood that was flowing from the poor young woman on the bed.

An hour later, he raised his eyes to Nancy and nodded. 'I think she'll make it now,' he said, and there was all the weight of the world in his voice. 'She has lost a lot of blood and she will be very weak for some time, but I think she'll pull through.'

'May the Lord be praised.' Nancy slowly turned and made her way downstairs. Ben was sitting in the drawing room with his head bent and his hands dangling loosely between his knees, but as she entered the room he sprang up and turned to face her.

'*Well?*'

'She's had a bad time of it but she's going to pull through.'

Tears spurted from his eyes. 'Thank God. And ... the baby?'

Nancy could not speak for the tears that were swelling in her throat, but eventually she told him brokenly, 'It was a little boy ... but he didn't make it.' And then suddenly he was in her arms and they were both sobbing, and it was hard to tell who was comforting whom.

It was early the next morning when Lawrie pushed the cottage door ajar and struggled through it with the crib he had so lovingly carved in his arms. Unlike the others, he had slept like a log and was as bright as a button, for to Lawrie every day was a good day.

'Nancy!' His excited voice echoed around the cottage and seconds later the kitchen door opened and Nancy appeared. Lawrie saw at a glance that she had been crying, and the smile slowly slid from his face as he told her hesitantly, 'I brought this over for the baby. It's all finished an' I thought you an' me could put the blankets in it. Is the baby here yet, Nancy?'

She glanced fearfully towards the stairs before crossing to him. She then took his elbow and propelled him back towards the door. 'Best not bring that in just now, lad. It ain't goin' to be needed. Not this time at least.'

'But *why*, Nancy?' he asked innocently. 'Ain't Hannah havin' a baby after all?'

'Not any more,' Nancy told him. 'Now you just go an' put it safely away. I've no doubt it will get to be used one o' these days.'

Normally, Lawrie was very obedient but today he refused to be moved. '*Why* ain't she havin' a baby any more, Nancy? I know she *was*, so where has it gone?'

Seeing no alternative but to tell him, she whispered, 'The baby was born too soon, Lawrie, an' so it's gone to heaven.'

Instead of being upset as she had expected him

to be, his face lit up in a radiant smile. 'To *heaven*, did you say? Why, that's where my mama is ... an' my papa. I bet they're lookin' after it, so it will be quite all right.'

So saying, he shuffled back the way he had come as Nancy slowly shook her head in amazement, tears pouring down her face, and what she was thinking was, If only it could be so easy for everyone to accept.

Part Two

A Time for Tears

Chapter Eight

The second that Dan stepped through the door he knew that something was wrong, for the very atmosphere of the house seemed steeped in sadness. He was loaded down with shopping bags as well as the small valise that contained his clothes, and placing them down at the side of the door he shouted, 'Hello ... is anyone in?'

Ada shuffled from the kitchen, her eyes red-rimmed from weeping. 'Eeh, Mr Dan, you'll never guess what has happened.'

Dan's heart did a somersault in his chest. 'It's Jonathan, isn't it? Something has happened to him.'

'No, no, lad. Jonathan is the same as when you left. It's...' She drew her apron up to her face and swiped the tears away as they spurted from her eyes yet again. 'It's poor Master Ben an' Miss Hannah. She had the baby an' it was too early. A doctor from up at the Hall attended her, but there were nowt he could do. The poor little mite, it was dead when he delivered it, an' it were a little lad an' all.'

The colour drained from Dan's face as his eyes dropped to rest on the Hamley's bag that contained the teddy bear he had bought for his first grandchild. The child would never see it now. It was funny, but now that he came to think of it, he was forced to admit that deep down he had hoped for the child to be a boy. And it had been. *Had ... had.* The word churned around in his head.

Forcing his own shock and sorrow aside he asked Ada, 'How are Ben and Hannah coping?'

She sniffed before replying, 'Not so good, as you can imagine. Master Ben is distraught, by all accounts. Nancy stopped by to bring us the news an' I promised I'd tell you soonever as you got back. I'm so sorry, lad.'

'Thank you, Ada. So am I.' And he was. Oh, no one would ever know just how much. But now was not the time for thinking of himself. It was Ben who was his main concern. How must his poor lad be feeling?

He had promised himself that he would go and see Ruthie tonight, but now he felt torn. Making a hasty decision, he asked Ada, 'Do you think you could rustle me up something to eat and a warm drink? Just something light will do, and then I'd best get over there.'

'Aye, o' course I can, lad. I'll away and see to it right now. There's some nice hot soup on the stove an' I baked a fresh loaf today. You go an' get warm by the fire. I'll not be long.'

True to her word, Ada was back within minutes with a tray that she placed on a small table 'Now get that down you,' she ordered, and the words were said with a wealth of affection, for over the years she had become more than fond of Dan, who to her mind, had had a raw deal of it one way or another. In no time at all she was standing at the door with him.

'Will you be back tonight?' she asked respect-fully. 'I only ask 'cos if you are, then I'll make sure as Betty puts a nice stone hot water bottle in your bed.'

'Thank you, Ada. That's very kind of you but I think I might call round and see Ruth after I've been over to Ben's.'

'As you wish, lad.' Ada held his coat whilst he shrugged his arms into it, and as she watched him stride out into the bitterly cold evening her heart was heavy. As if the poor man hadn't suffered enough!

As the cab drew to a halt in front of Ben's cottage, Dan looked at the horse and trap that had been pulled into the small stable across the yard. It could only belong to one person, and that was Sarah, Hannah's mother. No doubt Jim Waite had driven her over from Wolfbur Farm. Sure enough, when he entered the cottage via the kitchen door, he found Jim sitting at the kitchen table with a steaming mug of tea in his hands.

Jim nodded respectfully as Dan passed through the room and as he entered the hallway he saw Nancy descending the stairs with an empty tray in her hands.

'Hello, Mr Dan. You'll find Master Ben in there.' She cocked her head towards the parlour door. 'Mrs Radlet is upstairs visitin' Hannah. Can I be gettin' you a drink?'

'No, thank you, Nancy.' He moved on towards the parlour, where Ben was standing at the window, staring out into the snowy night. There was no sign of Lawrence and Dan guessed that he had chosen to go to bed early as he was known to do when he was confused or upset.

'Ben.'

The man turned and a thousand emotions flitted across his face as he stared at his father.

'I'm so *very* sorry, son. I know how much this baby meant to you both.'

Ben nodded, but still he said not a word. And then suddenly his face contorted and he had the sensation of choking as the tears suddenly spurted from him. He was drowning, he was sure of it, for the tears were coming not only from his eyes but from his nose and his mouth also. It felt as if they were coming from every pore of him and he was powerless to stop them, and then he felt his father's arms about him and a gruff voice said, 'That's it, lad. Let it all go now. It will help to let it out ... and I should know.'

And so the two men stood clasped in each other's arms as the younger of them sobbed as if his heart would break.

Upstairs in the bedroom, Sarah was leaning heavily on her crutch as she stared down at her daughter, whose face was as white as a ghost's. The atmosphere was strained, for Sarah had never so much as set foot in the cottage before.

'So how are you?' Even to her own ears the words sounded ridiculous. How could she expect Hannah to be feeling, having just lost her first child? Not that it had surprised her, if she owned to the truth. After all, was Hannah not married to a Mallen – and wasn't it a known fact that sorrow followed them about?

Hannah's voice, however, surprised her when she answered calmly, 'I am feeling a little weak but that will pass as I get my strength back. It is to be expected; I lost a lot of blood.'

Sarah's lips came together in a straight line. There she went again, forever the nurse. Even at a time like this, Hannah could be calm. *When did we grow apart?* the woman asked herself, and the answer came straight back: *When Hannah and her father shut me out of their lives.* Well, Michael was dead and buried now, as was his whore, so why then were she and her daughter still acting like strangers towards one another? Even the death of her firstborn had not made Hannah seek her out. Sarah had come of her own choice when the news reached them.

Feeling that because of the circumstances, she should make an effort, Sarah asked quietly, 'What will you do now?'

Hannah stared back at her for a moment before replying, 'I shall get on with my life, Mother, and go back to work when I am well enough. Of course, Ben and I are greatly upset at the loss of our child, but as a nurse I have seen this happen dozens of times. It is a sad fact of life. Thankfully, we are both still young so we will try again when I am recovered.'

At a loss as to what to say, Sarah now told her, 'Your grandmother sends her condolences. The weather is too bad for her to venture out.'

'Of course.'

'She wondered if there was anything that you might need?'

'I have everything I need, Mother. But thank her for me.'

'In that case then, I er ... I ought to be starting for home. Jim had a right old game getting the trap across the rise with the drifts as they are.'

Their eyes locked, yet neither made a move towards the other and now Sarah turned and hobbled towards the door saying, 'I'll be going then.'

'Yes. Goodbye, Mother, and thank you for coming.'

As Sarah closed the door behind her, Hannah was ashamed to feel relief at her departure.

Sarah was almost at the bottom of the stairs when Dan came through from the parlour with an empty decanter in his hand. It had been many years since they had seen each other, and as Sarah looked at him she thought that the years had been kind to him, for though he was small of stature he was still a very presentable-looking man. He in turn was thinking quite the reverse, for bitterness had prematurely aged Sarah, and her face was deeply lined. In fact, she looked far older than her years, though Dan was far too much of a gentleman to ever have said it.

'How are you, Sarah?' he asked instead, and as she came to stand abreast of him, leaning heavily on her crutch, she shrugged.

'Not bad, I dare say... And you?'

'Very well, thank you. Though deeply saddened by all this.'

'Yes, yes, of course.'

Rage and hatred was beginning to swell in her. It was this man's whore of a wife who had stolen her husband, and word had it that he had known of their goings-on for years, yet rather than lose her altogether he had turned a blind eye to her adultery, with the result that she herself had

124

suffered. She was completely alone now because of this man, whilst he still had the comfort of that little slut of a nurserymaid who everyone knew he had kept in a house as his bit on the side for years. Turning about before she might say something that she would live to regret, she flung herself towards the kitchen.

'Goodnight, Sarah.'

Ignoring him, she entered the kitchen and closed the door firmly between them. God works in mysterious ways, she told herself, and if this were true then one day Daniel Bensham would get his comeuppance. And from where she was standing, it would not be a day too soon.

It was the day before Christmas Eve, and as Mary Ann made her way towards the house that had been her home since birth, she was smiling. She was loaded down with packages and was in a happy mood. She had managed to do all her Christmas shopping in a single afternoon and now all she had to do was wrap the presents up and deliver them.

'Somebody's been busy, by the look of it.'

Mary Ann turned and found herself looking into the face of Mrs Flynn, a portly woman who lived just across the road from them. She was carrying the largest turkey that Mary Ann had ever seen. Its neck was hanging slackly across one of her arms and as she came abreast of her and saw Mary Ann looking at it she laughed, a loud gurgling sound that told Mary Ann the woman had hit the bottle earlier than she normally did. It was a well-known fact that Mrs Flynn was

125

partial to the odd jug of ale. Not that Mary Ann had a problem with that. The way she saw it, the woman was entitled to some comfort. She had lost her husband in an accident down at the docks some years ago and since then she had been reliant on her four strapping sons to keep a roof over her head and food on the table. They had done her proud from what Mary Ann could see of it, for as her mother had once commented, *She's built like an all-in wrestler.*

Mary Ann's motto was live and let live, so now she smiled back at the woman as she told her, 'Yes, I've been doing my Christmas shopping, Mrs Flynn. I usually leave it all to the last minute on Christmas Eve so I thought I'd be good this year an' get it done early.'

'Huh! I wish I could say the same,' the woman snorted good-naturedly. 'I've no doubt I shall be dashin' round the shops like a blue-arsed fly, come tomorrow. Happen it'll take me all night to pluck this damn thing.'

They fell into step, picking their way carefully through the slush that had turned the cobbled street into an obstacle course, and once they reached the gate that led to Mary Ann's door the woman told her, 'Have a good Christmas then, pet. I'd best get in an' make a start pluckin' this monster. Wish yer mam a Merry Christmas for me, would yer? I hope she's feelin' a bit better.'

With her hand on the latch of the gate, Mary Ann paused to look her fully in the face. 'What do you mean, feeling better?' she asked.

'Well, when I saw the doctor leavin' earlier on I just assumed as she were under the weather,' Mrs

126

Flynn replied hesitantly, then shifting the bird into a more comfortable position she flashed Mary Ann a final toothless smile and picked her way across the street to her own front door.

Mary Ann hurried up the path and once inside the small entrance hall she gratefully dropped the bags onto the floor, unwound the scarf from around her throat and took off her coat. She could hear voices coming from the small parlour and when she pushed the door open she saw her mother and father sitting at either side of the fire.

Dan instantly rose to meet her and dropped an affectionate kiss on her cheek. 'Hello, Mary Ann. How are you, my dear?' he asked.

'I'm fine, Dad.' She returned his kiss and then hurrying to the fire, she held her hands out to the welcoming blaze as she peeped at her mother from the corner of her eye. 'And how are you, Mam?' she asked innocently.

'Fine as ninepence,' Ruth shot back. 'Me an' your dad have been waitin' on you gettin' in afore I set the dinner out. Get all your shoppin' done, did you, lass?'

Mary Ann nodded. If Mrs Flynn had been right and the doctor had called around today, it certainly didn't seem that her mam was going to admit to it.

Ruth was already out of her seat and heading towards the door, where she stopped to warn them, 'Dinner will be on the table in ten minutes. It's all ready to dish up, so don't get startin' a game of cards or anythin', now will you?'

Dan glanced at Mary Ann with a mischievous twinkle in his eye before replying solemnly, 'No,

127

ma'am. We'll behave, won't we, Mary Ann?'

'We'll try to,' the girl joked.

Ruth laughed and flapped her hands at them as she sidled out of the door, declaring, 'I don't know – I sometimes wonder what I'm to do wi' you pair.'

Once she had gone, the smile slid from Mary Ann's face as she asked her father quietly, 'Did Mam seem all right to you, Dad?'

'Why, yes. Shouldn't she be?'

The girl shrugged as she stared into the flames. 'I'm not sure.' She glanced towards the door before going on, 'I just met Mrs Flynn out in the street and she told me that she had seen the doctor leaving earlier. Has Mam said anything to you about him visiting her?'

'No ... no, she hasn't.' The smile had gone from his face too now, but then he told her, 'I shouldn't get worrying unnecessarily, my dear. Your mother is as tough as old boots, as well you know. I could count on one hand the number of times she's visited the doctor in all the years I've known her. It's probably Mrs Flynn got it wrong.'

'Happen you're right.' She had no wish to worry him so Mary Ann forced a brightness into her voice before saying gaily, 'Come on then. We'd best go and get the table laid. I reckon we've got roast lamb tonight and after shopping all afternoon, I'm ready for it.' They moved on to the small dining room side-by-side and soon they were tucking into one of Ruth's delicious roast dinners.

'So, will you be staying for Christmas then?' Mary Ann asked as she loaded a roast potato onto her fork.

Dan nodded. 'I certainly will. There's no one can cook a turkey like your mother.'

Mary Ann watched as warm colour flooded into her mother's cheeks and all at once a feeling of sadness descended on her. Her mother had never made any secret of the fact that she worshipped the very ground that Daniel Bensham walked on. In all fairness, he obviously had a great fondness for her too, but as Mary Ann had discovered, there was a wealth of difference between love and fondness, and all her father's love had been wasted on Barbara, his late wife. Sometimes it hurt the girl to see her mother so accepting. Especially now that Barbara was dead. Once she had dared to say as much to her face and Ruth had almost snapped her head off.

'I went into this relationship wi' me eyes wide open,' she had scolded her. 'An' never once has your dad let me down, so let's be hearin' no more on the subject, eh? I'm happy wi' me lot an' you should be an' all.'

'Oh, but I am,' Mary Ann had retaliated. 'It's just that I was hoping that now *she* was out of the way, me dad might marry you an' make an honest woman of you.'

'Huh! We have more of an honest relationship than he ever shared with the mistress. We both went into it knowin' exactly where we stood, an' let me tell you now, my girl, I've never for a minute regretted it. As far as I'm concerned we *are* married, all but for a piece o' paper an' a ring on me finger, so don't let me hear you raisin' the subject again, do you hear me?'

'Yes, Mam.' Mary Ann had heard loud and clear,

129

and she had done as she was asked and never spoken of it again, but all the same she knew that her mother's words were empty, and it made her question this thing called 'class'. At the present time the newspapers were full of Lady Dorothy Cavendish's engagement to Captain Harold Macmillan, and because she was the daughter of the Duke of Devonshire, much regret was being expressed that Captain Macmillan was a mere commoner. Mary Ann was sure that, had her mother been raised as a lady, her father would no doubt have married her by now, but seeing as she had been a servant when he met her, the best she could hope for was to be his mistress. For some years before Barbara had died, her father had taken to coming here for Christmas, but Mary Ann knew that it was only because his wife had usually sidled off to the cottage she and her lover rented for the occasions when they could spend some time together, and her father didn't want to be alone.

Even so, they had been happy times, and despite the fact that she was illegitimate, Mary Ann was wise enough to know that she was fortunate compared to many in her position, for her father had always ensured that she went without nothing. Now as she looked across the table at her parents she was determined to put her unhappy thoughts away until after Christmas.

At that moment, her mother asked, 'How is Hannah, Dan?'

'Oh, bearing up. In fact, I'd have to say she's taken the loss of the baby much better than Ben has.'

Ruth sighed heavily. 'And Brigie?'

'Not so good.' He shook his head regretfully and in that moment he longed to tell her of the secret that Brigie had entrusted to him. Knowing that he had been enrolled to find her daughter was weighing heavily on him and sometimes he wished that she had never confided in him. But still, just as Mary Ann had done only moments before, he pushed the thought to the back of his mind. It was almost Christmas and he owed it to Mary Ann and Ruth to make it as happy as he could for them.

The roast lamb was followed by a steamed pudding with bottled plums and a jug full of piping hot custard. They were almost halfway through it when Dan said casually, 'I shall be going back to London again, the day after Boxing Day.'

'Oh?' When Ruth looked at him questioningly he kept his eyes firmly fixed on the dish in front of him.

'Just a bit of business to finish up,' he told her.

'I see, an' will you be back to see the New Year in with us?'

'I shall certainly do my best.'

Ruth nodded and rose from the seat, and in that moment he longed to confide in her. Why had Brigie had to tell him her secret, he wondered? And how would Brigie take it, if he failed to find out what had become of her long-lost daughter?

It was Mary Ann who broke his chain of thought when she asked, 'Do you remember that year when we had a New Year's Eve party here with all the boys? They were all back from school and Jonathan got tiddly on the wine me mam had kept for the occasion in the pantry.'

'Yes, I do,' Dan grinned. 'Though I'd have hardly called it tiddly. If I remember rightly, it took Harry and Ben all their time to get him up to bed, and he was as sick as a dog for days afterwards. Happen that was what made him have such an aversion to alcohol from then on.'

Ruth's smile was tinged with sadness as her mind went back in time. Eeh, that had been a grand party with all of them together. It was funny, now she came to think of it, the way Dan's sons had accepted her and always been regular visitors to the house. She had been particularly close to Ben, right from the time when she had been his nursery nurse and he was still in short trousers, for even then, his mother had ignored him whilst showing open affection to Jonathan and Harry. And now Ben was mourning the death of his firstborn, Jonathan was stuck up in the Hall not knowing what time of the day it was, and poor Harry was dead and gone, cut down in his prime on some stinking battlefield. It hardly bore thinking about.

She looked across the table at the two faces that were so very dear to her, and inside she was crying, for following the doctor's visit today she had a strange feeling that this might be the last Christmas she would spend with them. Thankfully, she had no worries about how Mary Ann would manage; she knew Dan would never see his daughter go short. And Dan... Well, Dan had never professed to love her. Oh, she knew that he thought fondly of her, and with that she had always been content. Even so, she was determined to make this a good Christmas.

'Fetch the port for your father, would you, pet?' she said to Mary Ann. 'An' how about you an' me having a drop o' sherry? It is almost Christmas Eve, after all.'

Mary Ann hurried away to do as she was told whilst Dan patted his stomach contentedly. 'I have to say, love, that was a dinner fit for a king. Thank you, my dear.'

Ruth smiled at him with all the love she felt for him shining in her eyes, and in that moment she thought, If the Good Lord should decide to take me tomorrow, then I have had a charmed life.

Chapter Nine

Lawrie squealed with delight as a child might have done as he lifted the fine patterned waistcoat Ben had bought him from its wrappings. It was silk and the front of it was heavily embroidered in gold and burgundy thread.

'I'll wear this today for Christmas dinner, shall I, Cousin Ben?'

'Yes, Lawrie, you do that,' Ben told him affectionately, but then Hannah was passing him another present and the waistcoat was thrown to one side as Lawrie fell on it in his excitement. This parcel contained a bright woollen scarf and gloves that again had Lawrie gasping. And so it went on until they had all opened their presents.

Ben had bought Hannah a string of finely

133

matched pearls and she had presented him with a pair of gold cufflinks that he immediately told her would be kept for special occasions.

They could hear Nancy clattering about in the kitchen as she chatted to Fred and prepared breakfast, and now Lawrie scuttled away to give them the presents he had bought for them as Ben sat beside Hannah in front of the fire.

'So how are you feeling?' he asked, and a look of annoyance flitted across her face.

'I'm perfectly all right, Ben.' She struggled to keep the irritation from her voice but then, seeing the hurt look in his eye, she said softly, 'We have to stop thinking about the baby now, dear. In a few weeks we can try again and hope that, next time, all will go well.'

'Yes, yes of course. I'm sorry, it's just–'

'Will you be going up to the Hall to see Jonathan and Brigie this morning?' Hannah now interrupted, deliberately changing the subject, as much for herself as Ben, for she was suddenly thinking of how Christmas Day should have been, with her child still safely growing inside her. 'It's stopped snowing for now, so if you are, you could perhaps take Lawrie with you? Or Fred could take you both in the trap, if you preferred.'

'No, I don't want to drag Fred out on Christmas Day,' Ben replied. 'We'll walk. It will do us both good. After breakfast I'll get Lawrie to wrap up warmly and I'll take him out from under your feet for an hour. Brigie will be pleased to see him, I'm sure, though I doubt Jonathan will recognise either of us. I believe my father is calling at the Hall today too.'

134

'Well, you can tell him he's welcome to come back with you and have dinner with us if he's a mind to,' Hannah offered, but Ben shook his head.

'It's a kind thought but I've no doubt he'll be having dinner with Ruth and Mary Ann. Thanks all the same.'

'It's quite all right. Just so long as he's not spending Christmas Day on his own. I've got some presents for Brigie and Jonathan so you could perhaps take them with you?'

'Of course.'

The door now flew open and Lawrie told them breathlessly, 'You're both to come to the table. Nancy's done us all a lovely breakfast. Kidneys an' bacon an' everything.'

'Then we mustn't let it get cold if she's gone to all that trouble,' Ben told him, and hoisting Hannah to her feet, he pulled her arm through his and side-by-side they strolled along the hallway to the dining room.

Once the savoury meal was finished, Lawrie scuttled away to get his outdoor clothes on as Hannah handed the presents she had bought for Brigie and Jonathan over to Ben. She then told them to be careful, and as they struggled into their boots she made her way upstairs. She had intended to go to her room for a lie-down, for she still tired easily following her ordeal, but as she passed the room they had prepared for the nursery she hesitated before slowly pushing the door open.

Ever since the day she had lost their child she had forced herself to be brave for Ben. He had gone through so very much and she could not bear to cause him yet more hurt and so she had remained optimistic and calm when in his presence. But now ... her eyes settled on a pile of tiny matinée coats that Nancy had knitted in readiness for when the baby arrived and it hit her full force that they would never be worn now. As a sob rose in her throat, she stifled it. If Nancy came across her she would no doubt tell Ben, and the way Hannah saw it, he was hurting enough already without having to worry about her. Her eyes moved on to the tiny animals placed in a regimental line across the windowsill; Lawrie had lovingly carved them for the baby he had been so looking forward to. She lifted a little pig, amazed at the detail of it. Lawrie had rubbed it until it was as smooth as silk so that the baby would be able to play with it without fear of getting splinters in its fingers. But they wouldn't have to worry about that now. Suddenly she could stand it no more and she fled from the room and into her own where she collapsed on the bed and sobbed as if her heart would break.

In no time at all, Ben and Lawrie were well on their way. The snow had stopped falling for now, but the sky was eerie and grey, and here and there the drifts on the road to the Hall were so deep that Ben had to take Lawrie's arm and steer him past them. It was a mile-long walk, and by the time the Hall came into sight, both men were puffing with exertion.

They clambered up the steps leading to the enormous oak doors, and once inside the hallway they stamped the snow from their boots and began to take off their coats. It was then that Matron bore down on them with a wide smile on her face.

'Ah, Captain Bensham. I was just saying to Nurse Byng here that I thought you might drop by today. The other officers are in the day room. Would you like to join them? I could bring you a hot drink – or possibly something a little stronger? It is Christmas Day, after all.'

'Perhaps later, Matron, thank you. I think I'll just pop up and see Brigie and my brother first. How is he, by the way?'

She chewed on her lip for a second before telling him, 'I don't wish to raise your hopes, but I think there has been a slight improvement. Yesterday he knocked the dish of soup Nurse Byng was feeding him out of her hand and told her quite clearly, NO! That's the first coherent word he's uttered since being admitted, so we're hoping that this will be the first step towards his recovery.'

Ben's face lit up in a smile before he said teasingly, 'Well, he hasn't lost his courage then. Nurse Byng must weigh at least fifteen stone and I'm not sure that I'd be brave enough to say no to her.'

The Matron playfully slapped at his hand whilst thinking what a handsome young man he was before blushing like a schoolgirl. Really, she scolded herself, I should never have let the officers talk me into having that small glass of sherry. She needn't have worried though, for Ben was striding towards the staircase with a great grin on his face whilst Lawrie stood at the side of her watching her expectantly.

She smiled at him before asking, 'Would you like me to take you up to see Mrs Bensham?'

'Yes, please, ma'am.'

137

She straightened her starched white apron and moved towards the lift that would take them up to what had once been the nursery floor, with Lawrie close on her heels.

As Sarah wrapped a heavy shawl over her warm coat, Constance glanced up from her seat at the side of the fire to ask, 'Where are you thinking of going?'

'I thought I might get Jim to run me over the hills to see our Hannah.'

'Are you mad!' Constance exclaimed. 'You'd be lucky to get over there on foot, let alone in the trap. The drifts will be so deep up on the fells by now that you could get lost in them. And by the looks of that sky, there's more to come.'

Angry colour flooded into Sarah's cheeks as she snatched her crutch and tucked it beneath her arm. Deep down she knew that her mother-in-law was right, but since the day she had learned of Anna Bensham's illegitimate daughter, the knowledge had been eating away at her like a canker. She needed to see Hannah – to pass on the news and see what her daughter thought of Mrs Prim and Proper Bensham then!

The smell of roasting turkey was heavy on the air and now her shoulders sagged as she was forced to see the sense of what the older woman was saying.

'Take your coat off,' Constance urged. 'Everyone will be busy going about their business today, entertaining their families and visiting and such.' She knew that Sarah was only wanting to go in order to pass on the gossip she had heard from Florrie Harper, rather than to see her daughter, and as she looked at her now, Constance could hardly believe that this was the same sweet-natured girl she had encouraged her son Michael to marry. Most women in Sarah's position would have been appalled to find that there might be someone who had more of a claim to High Banks Hall than their own flesh and blood, but Sarah was so bitter about Hannah marrying a man with Mallen blood in his veins that she would have no qualms about taking her own daughter down if it meant she could take Ben with her. Constance shuddered, and it had nothing to do with the cold. She too had suffered at the hands of the Mallens, but now as old age claimed her she found that she was growing tired of feeling bitter. What had bitterness ever done for her but eat her away and make her old before her time? Her thoughts turned to Anna Bensham, or Brigie as she had always called her. She was lying up at the Hall right this minute, and from what Constance had heard, the time she had left to her was short. So why then did Sarah still hate her so? Surely it was time to let the past rest.

A movement behind her brought her thoughts sharply back to the present and, turning slightly in her seat, she saw Sarah fling first her shawl then her coat over the back of a chair.

'Happen you're right,' she muttered sullenly. 'I'll wait till the weather picks up then make my way over there.'

Constance let out a sigh of relief even as her wrinkled face settled into a frown, and in that moment she prayed that the snow would con-tinue to fall for some time to come.

Ben entered his brother's room just in time to see a fresh-faced young nurse settling a blanket across Johnny's knees. He was sitting in an arm-chair in the deep bay window.

'Hello, sir. Happy Christmas!' The nurse flashed him a friendly smile. 'I was just telling your brother that he's going to have turkey for dinner today. But I'll go and leave you two alone for a while now, shall I? Just ring the bell over there when you're ready to leave and I'll come back.'

'Thank you.' Ben watched her go, then lifting a straight-backed chair that was standing to one side of the bed, he carried it over to Jonathan and sat down beside him.

Placing Hannah's parcel on his brother's knee, he told him, 'Hannah thought you might like this, Johnny.'

When the sick man continued to stare blankly out of the window, Ben tore the parcel open and lifted a fine music book in front of his eyes. 'Look, it's got all the latest tunes in,' he told him, as he stifled the urge to cry. 'Remember how good you used to be on the piano? When you start to feel more yourself, you could have a tinkle again. The piano is down in the day room now, and no doubt the other men would love a bit of entertainment.'

Still the stare and silence, but he forced himself to go on. 'You were always the best at that sort of thing. Whereas Harry and I... Well, we never seemed to have a flair for music.' The thought of the brother he had lost caused tears to clog in his throat and he had to compose himself before going on. He of all people knew what Jonathan

140

was going through. After all, it wasn't so long since he himself had been shut away in this room, the Bunker, locked in his own private hell. Hannah had helped him escape from that place, and for that alone he would always love her.

His eyes strayed to the snowy scene outside. A wind had come up and was swirling the snow across the terrace, and the topiary trees were swaying as if they were engaged in some sort of macabre dance. He chatted on and on about anything he could think of, but not once did Jonathan so much as blink until finally Ben laid the music book across his lap and slowly rose.

'Right, I'd better get up to see Brigie then. I'll be by to see you again very soon. Merry Christmas, old chap.'

Jonathan's head moved very slowly to the side and just for a second he raised his eyes to look into those of his brother. For the briefest instant, Ben could have sworn he saw a glimpse of recognition there. But then the shutters came down again and once more he was staring out of the window. Crossing heavily to the bell, Ben rang it and waited for the nurse to return.

The mood lifted slightly when Ben reached Anna's room, for Lawrie was still excitedly telling her of the special breakfast Nancy had cooked for them and of the presents he had received. Anna was propped up against her pillows listening with an indulgent smile on her face, and when Ben entered, he caught a fleeting vision of the woman she had once been. It was funny, now he came to think of it. Brigie's body had aged yet her eyes

141

still had the brightness and intelligence of a much younger woman.

'Ben.' She held a gnarled hand out to him and crossing to her, he lifted it and gently pressed his lips against the paper-thin skin. 'Lawrie here has been telling me about what a splendid Christmas you are having.'

'Oh quite. And there's more to come when we get home. According to Hannah, the turkey Nancy is cooking is large enough to feed a regiment.'

The old lady's face became solemn now as lowering her voice she said, 'I was so sorry to hear about the baby, Ben. How is Hannah now?'

He gave an imperceptible shrug, though pain briefly lit his eyes. 'Oh, you know ... not too bad. It was a blow, I won't deny it, but she says we can try again in a month or so. You know Hannah – she's a great one for putting a brave face on things. She doesn't seem to realise that I can see straight through her.'

'Then God willing all will go to plan next time.' She squeezed his hand and for a time they watched Lawrie wandering around the room, lifting first one thing then another to examine it until Ben asked him, 'Have you given Brigie her present yet?'

'Oh no, I'd forgotten all about it.' Lawrie began to fumble in his coat pocket until his hand came to rest on a small crudely-wrapped parcel, which he held out towards her.

'I didn't know what to get you,' he apologised, 'so Cousin Ben said I should make you something. He said that people like presents that other people have taken the trouble to make.' He now hopped from foot to foot as Brigie carefully unwrapped it, then watched with excitement as her mouth fell into a gape. Lawrie had carved a tiny eagle in flight for her and the workmanship was so fine that for a moment she was speechless.

'Do you like it?' he asked eventually, and now her eyes were full as she looked back at him.

'I think it's one of the most beautiful gifts I have ever received, and I shall treasure it,' she assured him.

He beamed from ear to ear, then remembered the crib and told her, 'I carved a crib for the new baby too, but Cousin Ben says we won't need it now 'cos the baby has gone to live with Mamma in heaven. It would be nice if we could visit heaven, wouldn't it, Brigie? I could go to see my mamma and the baby then whenever I liked. I would have especially liked to see them today because it's Christmas Day, but Cousin Ben says we're not allowed to. Is that right, Brigie?'

'Yes, dear. But we all go to live in heaven eventually so you will see them again one day. Though I hope you won't be going there for a very long time to come.'

Her eyes were sad as she looked at this child who was trapped in a man's body, and thought of Katie, his mother. Poor Katie, she had been devastated when she had discovered that Lawrence was 'backwards', as the doctors had termed him. But to her credit, she had refused to have him locked away and institutionalised, and slowly Lawrie had become the centre of her universe...

It was at that moment that a tap came on the

door and when it was inched open, Anna saw Dan pop his head round it.

Lawrie lumbered awkwardly across to him and Dan gave him an affectionate cuddle. Lawrie was almost a head taller than him but nonetheless he hugged him as he might have a child.

'Why, Lawrie. I'm sure you grow an inch every time I see you,' Dan told him as he held him at arm's length and smiled into his eyes. He then looked towards Anna and told her, 'Merry Christmas, Brigie. And how are you feeling? I was hoping to see you up and about today.'

Ben rose from his seat and beckoned to Lawrie. 'Come on, young man,' he said. 'I think we'd better be starting for home. If we're late for our dinner, Nancy will skin us alive after all the trouble she's gone to, preparing it. I have a horrible suspicion we're going to be eating turkey for the next week at least.'

Lawrie skipped towards the bed and planted a sloppy kiss first on Anna's cheek and then on Dan's before joining Ben at the door.

'Will you be calling into the cottage for a drink on your way home, Father?' Ben enquired as he looked back at him.

'Thanks for the offer, son, but no, I won't if you don't mind. Ruth is hard at it in the kitchen too and you know what women can be like if we're late.'

'Oh, I know,' Ben assured him and then he and Lawrie flashed Anna a last friendly wave before slipping away.

Once alone, Anna asked eagerly, 'Did you go to the address I gave you, Dan?'

'Yes, I did, but I'm afraid I discovered that Mrs Stirling was admitted to Bow Institution a number of years ago.'

'And is she still there?'

'No. It seems that shortly after she was admitted, a niece of hers turned up and took her away to live with her. I shall be returning to London next week and I can assure you, I shall be doing all I can to track her down. As it happens, I met a little chap there who is going to help me. His name is Pip and he was a right little cockney sparrow.' He went on to tell her all about his meeting with Pip, and by the time he had done so, the morning was slipping away. Taking out his pocket watch he glanced at it and told her regretfully, 'I really should be going now, Brigie. I just wanted to stop by and tell you the news, and to give you this. And to wish you a Merry Christmas, of course.' From his pocket he produced a small, gaily-wrapped parcel which contained some scented toilet water, and after he had laid it on the cover at the side of her he smiled down and said, 'I shall be back sometime towards the end of next week, and hope to have some news for you – but try not to fret in the meantime.'

She inclined her head as her eyes followed him to the door. When she was alone, once again she tried to picture what her daughter might look like. Would she resemble her, or her father, Thomas Mallen? Would she be plain, as she had always considered herself to be, or would she have the Mallen dark good looks as Barbara had done?

Barbara. Her heart broke afresh as she thought back to the girl into whom she had poured all her

145

affections – the affections that should have been channelled towards her own flesh and blood.

How would she feel if Dan managed to find her lost girl? Her emotions were so mixed that she had no way of knowing. She only knew that time was running out, for lately she had been feeling more and more tired with each day that passed. Sometimes she was so weary that she would have welcomed death, and only the possibility of seeing the daughter she had once so callously abandoned kept her struggling to stay alive. Only last night she had woken in the early hours with a curious pain in her heart. The room had been in darkness, save for the dim glow of the night light that the nurse always kept burning, and she could have sworn for just a second that she saw Thomas standing in the corner, just as once, Barbara had sworn she had done. Rather than be afraid, the image had comforted her, for deep down he had always been the love of her life. Oh, she had loved Harry Bensham with all of her heart, for he had put a ring on her finger and allowed her to wear the cloak of respectability that she had always craved. But Thomas ... just the thought of him could still make her pulses race, even now after all these years. Poor misjudged Thomas. No one had ever understood him as she had.

Biting down on her lip, she turned her head towards the window. It had started to snow again and now she prayed as she had so many times before of late: *Dear Lord, allow me just a little more time. Just enough to know if my daughter is still alive somewhere...*

Chapter Ten

'Your room is ready, Mr Bensham. I'll get the porter to take your luggage up for you, sir.'

Dan thanked the portly gentleman with a handlebar moustache behind the desk, then followed a spotty-faced youth in the hotel uniform to the lift that was set to one side of the luxurious foyer of the Ritz.

The lift rose to the second floor, and after the youth had shown him into his room and placed his bag on the table provided for luggage, Dan tipped him generously and went to the window that overlooked the bustling panorama of Piccadilly below.

It seemed a million miles away from Brook House and the quietness that surrounded it. Just for a moment Dan felt a pang of homesickness as he thought of Ruth and Mary Ann. The three of them had spent a wonderful Christmas together. He had considered asking Ruth to come with him to London as a short break, and had he been here for any other reason he would have done so, but his vow to Anna Bensham had made him decide against it. After all, what excuse could he have made for leaving her alone, while he went off on his investigations? Not that she would have pestered him. That was the wonderful thing about Ruth. She always accepted what he was able to give and never asked for more.

A frown settled across Dan's face as he thought

of her. She had not seemed quite herself over Christmas – not that she hadn't made an effort to be cheerful. Oh, Ruth always went out of her way to pander to him, there was no doubt about it. But she had seemed ... he searched his mind for the right word and suddenly it came to him – pensive. Yes, she had seemed to be in somewhat of a reflective mood, now that he came to think of it, and she had looked rather pale. This, added to what Mary Ann had told him of the doctor visiting, made him pace the room but then he pushed his anxiety away. They were in deep winter, so everyone was pale, were they not? And Mary Ann had probably been mistaken about the doctor calling.

Dan decided that he would go down to the dining room, have a spot of lunch and then go in search of Pip. Yes, that's what he would do. Perhaps this time his mission would be successful and then he could return home to the bosom of his family. In a happier frame of mind he straightened his cravat and strode purposefully from the room.

'Come along, Lawrie. Don't dawdle, there's a good fellow. It's enough to cut you in two out here, and I for one will be pleased to get home and into the warm again.'

Lawrie reluctantly pulled his attention from the shop window he had been gazing into. It *was* cold, he was forced to admit, but he could never resist a shopping trip into Newcastle with Hannah. Today had turned out to be somewhat of a disappointment, for being the week in between Christmas and the New Year, the market was nowhere near as busy as it had been the week before, when everyone had been bustling to buy their Christmas fare. As he trudged through the slush towards her, Hannah's face softened and she suggested, 'How about we visit the candy shop before we head for home? I could get you some gobstoppers and some sugared mice, if you like?'

Instantly he was brighter, and followed her down the cobbled street with alacrity. The bell above the candy-shop door tinkled merrily as they entered and Lawrie gazed around in awe. There were shelves full of big glass jars containing every kind of sweet he could imagine, and his mouth watered.

A large man appeared through a door behind the counter and smiled at them pleasantly. Hannah often came to the shop when Lawrie was with her and he had come to know them.

'Good day, Mrs Bensham. An' how are you today, Lawrie, me lad?'

'I'm fine, Mr Green, thank you.'

'That's good then. An' what can I be gettin' you?'

'I ... I'll have some sugared mice an' a quarter of gobstoppers, please.'

'And you'd better give us some liquorice sticks too,' Hannah added, and now Lawrie's grin stretched from ear to ear.

As the shopkeeper started to weigh the sweets and chat to Hannah, Lawrie wandered off to gaze from the window, and it was as he was standing there that a small boy across the street caught his eye. Suddenly he remembered back to the week before when he had seen the boy briefly in the market, and now it struck him like a blow between the eyes what it was that had seemed so familiar about him.

'Ha ... Hannah, come quick.'

Hannah turned from the counter to stare at him. 'Why, Lawrie? What is it?'

'*Please,*' he implored her.

Sensing that something was troubling him, she hurried to his side. He jabbed his finger towards the street. 'Look, Hannah! The boy over ... there...'

He stopped abruptly, for the boy was now no longer in sight. He had vanished.

'What boy, Lawrie? There's no one there.'

'But there was,' he told her insistently. 'And he had a white streak here.' He now ran his hand across one side of his head in agitation. 'Black hair and a streak, I tell you, just like Cousin Ben's.'

Her teeth nipped down on her lip with shock before she told him, 'It was probably a trick of the light, Lawrie.'

But Lawrie's head wagged from side-to-side as he insisted, '*No!* I'm telling you, he had a streak – I saw it quite clearly.'

'Well, there's no point in worrying about it now, dear.' Taking his hand she drew him back to the counter with her and hastily paid for his treats as he looked back towards the window. Once outside, it was all she could do to haul him along beside her, for his head went constantly this way and that as he looked for a sight of the boy. It was a relief when they finally arrived home to find Ben waiting for them.

'Had a good time then, have you?' he asked Lawrie, but the young man merely nodded distractedly before trooping towards the kitchen and Nancy.

'So what's wrong with him then?' As Ben helped Hannah out of her coat she shrugged.

'We were in the candy shop in Newcastle when he insisted that he saw a young boy with a streak in his hair like yours.' Her eyes twinkled as she asked him, 'There isn't something that you haven't told me, is there?'

'Certainly not!' he stated indignantly, and then seeing that she was teasing, his face softened. 'It was probably just a mistake.'

She nodded in agreement and arm-in-arm they entered the sitting room, and for now the boy with the streak was forgotten.

Thick fog was settling across the streets and darkness was falling when Dan eventually turned into Adderton Road. He eyed the rows of houses until he came to the one that Pip had pointed out. This was it – at least, he hoped it was. They all looked much the same in the fading light. Still, he thought to himself, nothing ventured nothing gained, and crossing to the front door he was about to knock on it when it was flung open and a wizened old woman, wrapped in a shawl of indeterminate colour, appeared.

'Oh, I'm so sorry,' Dan apologised as he stood aside to let her pass. 'Would you happen to know if a little boy called Pip lives here?'

She stared at him suspiciously as she hugged her shawl more tightly about her before asking, 'An' who wants ter know?'

'I met Pip a short time ago and he's helping me to find someone,' Dan explained. 'I assure you I mean the boy no harm.'

151

'An' he ain't in no sort o' bovver?'

'Not that I am aware of.'

She continued to stare at him for some moments, and then deciding that he appeared harmless, she told him, 'In that case, you'll find Pip an' 'is family up on the third landin'. Up them stairs there.' As she cocked her finger towards a staircase that stood at the end of a long hallway he smiled his thanks and stepped inside. The smell hit him like a blow in the face. A group of barefoot children were playing at the foot of the stairs with a tin can that they were pushing along with sticks, but the second that Dan entered they stopped and gawped at him.

'Can yer spare a penny, mister?' one of them asked and Dan's heart sank when the child extended his hand. It was covered with sores and was so thin that he appeared to be nothing more than a bag of bones.

The second that Dan put his hand into his pocket the children were around him like a swarm of flies, and they didn't disperse until each of them had a coin in his or her hand. They then scuttled away as if they had the Crown Jewels in their possession and Dan found himself alone, apart from the noise that seemed to be coming from each and every doorway he passed.

Taking a deep breath, he moved up the staircase. The wooden stairs were bare and his footsteps echoed hollowly off the grubby lime-washed walls as he climbed. It was as he was crossing the second-floor landing that an enormous rat suddenly scuttled from the shadows and almost leaped across his shoe. With a look of horror on his face, Dan pressed himself back against the wall as a door opened and two small children emerged.

'What's up, mister?'

Dan found himself looking into the eyes of a little girl who appeared to be no more than nine or ten years old.

'I er... There was a rat,' he explained and now the girl grinned, exposing a set of rotten teeth that would have looked more in place in the mouth of an old, old woman.

'Yer get used to 'em in 'ere,' she told him nonchalantly, then taking the hand of the small boy at her side, she pottered away down the stairs.

Pulling himself away from the wall, Dan continued on his way and soon he found himself on the third-floor landing from which led a number of doors. He hesitated; the noise of family life was coming from each one, and the sound of children squabbling and babies crying hung on the air. As he had no idea which one Pip might live in, he approached the first one he came to and rapped on it loudly. The sounds from within ceased instantly. Seconds later, the door was inched open and a woman of indeterminable age peered out at him warily.

'Ah, good afternoon, madam.' Dan cleared his throat. 'I was wondering if you could tell me where a little boy called Pip lives. He pointed the house out to me but unfortunately he did not tell me which room he and his family lived in.'

She sniffed, before stepping out onto the landing to join him. 'You'll find the Beddows lot in that room there, last on yer right.'

Dan opened his mouth to thank her, but before

he could do so, she had disappeared back the way she had come, and the noise from within had resumed. Shivering, he made for the door she had indicated. The whole house was freezing cold and his breath hung on the air in front of him. He knocked on the door and once again a silence settled on the room beyond and then he heard footsteps approaching. This time a young boy with a pinched face and enormous brown eyes stared out at him; Dan knew instantly that the child was related to Pip, for the resemblance was uncanny.

'Hello, young man. Is your brother Pip at home, by any chance?' Dan flashed the child a disarming smile, but the boy stared back expressionlessly.

'Wot if he is? An' who are you, mister?'

The conversation was stopped from going any further when the very person Dan was seeking appeared over the boy's shoulder.

'*Mr Dan.*' Pip's face lit up at the sight of him. Roughly elbowing the other boy aside, he grabbed Dan by the elbow and hauled him into a small passageway.

'Did yer have a good Christmas?' he asked, but before Dan could answer he went on, 'We did. Wiv that sovereign yer gave us I got us a turkey an' some coal an' loads o' treats. But come on, I've told me ma all about yer an' she'd like to meet yer. She's just through here.'

Dan followed the boy into a room that seemed to be packed with bodies everywhere he looked, all boys ranging in age from about five years old. There appeared to be two younger than Pip whilst the other four looked considerably older. Seven boys in all, he found when he had quickly counted them. On one wall was an enormous brass bed and Dan was shocked to see a woman who looked extremely ill lying in the centre of it. A small fire was burning in the grate on which bubbled a pot of what appeared to be some sort of thin vegetable gruel. But even with the fire burning the room was still cold, and there was an air of dampness that seemed to permeate through Dan's thick woollen coat. The children, who were dressed in little more than rags, seemed to be oblivious to it and stared at him from dull eyes.

Taking off his hat, Dan quickly introduced himself, 'How do you do, Mrs Beddows?'

'Pleased to meet yer, sir, I'm sure. An' I'm not doin' too badly, thanks.' The words had barely left the woman's lips when a paroxysm of coughing seized her and she raised a strip of rag to her mouth as she doubled over. Dan was distressed to see the stain of blood on it when the bout eased off but felt powerless as to know what to do. She now smiled apologetically before telling Pip, 'Get the kettle on the fire, son. Where's yer manners? I've no doubt our visitor could do wiv a cuppa.'

'Oh no, no. Please don't go to any trouble on my account,' Dan said immediately. 'I was just hoping to have a quick word with Pip, if you have no objections?'

'None at all,' she assured him. Her smile was sweet, and even in the throes of her disease, there was a trace of prettiness in her face and her soft, dark-brown eyes. The bed was covered in a motley assortment of threadbare blankets and coats, and the pillows she was resting on were without covers and looked grimy, to say the very

155

least. Even so, Dan saw at a glance that she had done her best with what she had, for the bare wooden floorboards were swept and the mantel-shelf had been dusted. His heart went out to her and again he wondered why it was that people should still be forced to live in such conditions.

Now that the introductions to his mother were out of the way, Pip nodded towards his brothers. 'That's Steven,' he informed Dan, pointing to the tallest of the brood. 'An' that there is Simon, then that's David, Luke, Willy an' Matthew.' The smaller two, Simon and David, peeped shyly at Dan as they clung onto Pip's hands.

'Good afternoon to you all,' Dan said. The room was so bleak, he thought, as they went back to their various pursuits. Thin curtains hung at the window and two mismatched chairs stood to either side of the fireplace. A door led off into what Dan assumed must be the boys' bedroom. Against the side of the window was a sink that leaned drunkenly to one side, with a rickety table and two more hard-backed chairs next to it. Above that was a long wooden shelf, on which stood an array of crockery and some cooking pots, and surprisingly, a small selection of books. Other than that, the room was empty with no trace of comfort what-soever.

Seeing his visitor looking around, Pip told him defensively, 'It ain't exactly the Ritz, what you're used to, but at least we all stick together, an' as long as we've got each other we're all right.'

'I can see that,' Dan told him, having no wish to cause offence. 'But ... well, I hope you won't mind me asking, but how do you manage?'

'We get by.' Pip's chin jutted proudly. 'Me an' me brothers do any odd jobs that we can, an' that usually amounts to enough to pay the rent an' keep some grub on the table. We go into the parks an' pick up fallen wood to keep the fire goin' through the winter, if we can't afford any coal, an' each night when the market is over we go around an' collect up the vegetables that have fallen off the stalls. We even manage to find odd bits of bruised fruit sometimes. I like me ma to have a bit o' fruit 'cos she ain't been too well lately, have yer, Ma?'

His mother's pallid face beamed with pride as she looked back at him. 'There's not much wrong with me, Pip. It's only this blooming cough. I daresay it'll right itself when the weather turns warmer again.'

Pip now turned his attention back to Dan and told him jubilantly, 'That address yer was after. Well – I reckon I've found it. I made a few enquiries about that Mrs Stirling you was lookin' for who went off wiv 'er niece called Mrs Margaret Fellows, an' I was told they lived over Clapham way. Mrs Fellows was married to a tailor who had his own shop, by all accounts. They lived by the common in Forthbridge Road, though I can't promise she'll still be there, mind. River House, the address is. Do yer reckon we should go an' 'ave a butcher's – see if she's still there?'

'I certainly do,' Dan told him with a broad smile. 'You've done really well, Pip. I doubt I would ever have found this information on my own. But I think it's a little late to be heading there this evening. How about we meet up and go over there first thing tomorrow?'

'Perfick.' Pip beamed at him and now Dan began to feel about in his overcoat pocket. When he produced a sovereign and held it out to the child, Pip frowned. 'I don't reckon that what I've done up to now warrants all that,' he said soberly. 'And it ain't Christmas no more. P'raps yer should slip me a couple of bob when we've found her?'

Dan waved his objections aside. 'As I said, I would never have found the address without you. Take this and go and get a bag of coal, there's a good lad. And while you're at it, call in at the butcher's and get some meat for your evening meal and some decent vegetables to go with it.'

He pressed the coin into Pip's hand and now the child's face lit up in a radiant smile that brightened the dismal room. 'Ta very much. I'll come out wiv yer then, if yer sure, an' go an' see to it straight away, shall I?'

Dan nodded, and after saying goodbye to Mrs Beddows, he and Pip left the room to begin the long descent to the ground floor. Once outside, the fog was still thick, making everything seem mysterious and alien.

As they walked slowly along the pavement, Pip asked him, 'So, 'ow long are yer plannin' on stayin' this time?'

Dan shrugged. 'No longer than a couple of days. I'd like to get home for the New Year. But of course, it will all depend on what we find out tomorrow. If this Mrs Fellows has moved, we may have to begin looking for her all over again.'

Pip nodded in agreement, and for a time they moved on in silence. Once they reached the corner of the street, Pip pointed in the direction that Dan needed to take. 'If you walk to the end there, yer should get a tram that'll take yer as near as dammit back to Piccadilly,' he told him helpfully.

Dan reached out to tousle his hair, only to stop himself just in time as he thought back to the head lice he had seen rampaging about the local children's scalps.

'Right, Pip. I'll see you bright and early tomorrow morning then. Do you think you could find your way to the entrance to the Ritz? I could meet you outside at – shall we say, ten o'clock?'

'Sounds all right to me,' Pip assured him, and then with a final friendly wave he turned and was soon swallowed up by the all-pervading smog.

Dan felt pleased with his progress so far. The boy had done well to discover the address of the woman he was hoping to speak to. All he could do now was cross his fingers and hope that tomorrow would bring him closer to discovering what had become of Anna's child. In a somewhat happier frame of mind, he climbed on to the tram. Luckily, he still had some coppers left to pay for his fare

Chapter Eleven

'Mam ... what is it? Are you ill?'

Mary Ann had just entered the kitchen to find her mother bent almost double as she leaned across the sink with her fist pressed hard into her chest. Ruth raised her other hand to wipe the spittle from her pursed lips as she tried to raise a smile. 'I'll be fine in a minute, lass,' she gasped. 'Just get me one of those tablets out o' that there drawer, would you?'

With fumbling fingers, Mary Ann shook one of the small tablets from the bottle and pressed it into her mother's hand, then quickly filling a glass with water, she held it to Ruth's lips as she swallowed it.

Within seconds, a little colour began to flood back into her mother's ashen cheeks and she stumbled across to a chair and sank heavily down onto it.

'That's better,' she told Mary Ann, who was now almost as pale as she was. 'It's that damn indigestion again. I really shall have to stop bein' such a pig at mealtimes. Don't get frettin'. I'm fine now ... look.'

'You are *not* fine,' Mary Ann said anxiously, and her voice was heavy with concern. 'Don't you think it's about time you told me what's going on?'

'There's *nothin'* goin' on,' Ruth snapped back and then instantly contrite, her voice softened as she assured her, 'I'm fine, hinny, really I am. It's just a bit o' indigestion, so don't get readin' no more into it than what there is.'

Mary Ann took the glass from her mother's hand and poured the water into the sink without saying any more, but her face was troubled and, this time, she decided she would get to the bottom of things. With or without her mother knowing, if she had to.

The opportunity to do so arose later that same morning as she went to collect the milk from the doorstep, for there was the doctor just leaving the house three doors down with his black bag clutched tightly in his leather-gloved hand.

'Morning, Mary Ann, and a Happy New Year to you,' he shouted, then thumbing across his shoulder, he confided, 'I doubt it's going to be much of a happy time for Mrs Blakemore. Got three of her brood down with measles she has, poor little things. You can barely put a pin where there isn't a spot on them. They're covered from head to toe, and poorly with it too.'

'Oh dear, I'm sorry to hear that.' Mary Ann glanced furtively around, then, despite the fact that she was in her house shoes, she hurried through the snow to the gate and beckoned him to her. Once they were face to face she asked him, 'Is there any chance of you popping in to have a look at my mam, Doctor Williams? She had a funny turn this morning and I'm a little worried about her.'

'Did she now? Been overdoing it again, has she? I told her she must take it easy.'

Pushing the gate across the hard-packed snow, he walked back down the path with Mary Ann. Once they had entered the hallway together, Ruth appeared at the kitchen door and exclaimed, 'Why, Doctor, whatever brings you out in this weather!'

'I actually came out to see three of Mrs Blakemore's brood,' he told her truthfully. 'But as I was leaving, Mary Ann here told me that you hadn't been too well this morning so I thought I'd better pop in and see what you've been up to.'

Ruth now flushed to the roots of her hair as she looked guiltily from the doctor to her daughter

161

and wrung her hands together. Deciding to try and bluster it out she told him, 'Eeh, that girl o' mine has always been a one fer flappin,' as you well know. There's nothin' wrong wi' me other than a bit o' indigestion, and those tablets you gave me have shifted it now.'

'Mmm, well, all the same I think I'll be the best judge of that, so let's have a look at you, shall we?'

When Ruth opened her mouth to protest he looked at her sternly and snapped his bag open. 'There's no point in arguing, Ruth. Now sit down here and unbutton your blouse, please. I shan't be going anywhere until I've examined you, even if I have to stay here all day, so you may as well make your mind up to it.'

She pursed her lips in annoyance but obediently took a seat and slowly began to unbutton her blouse.

After taking his stethoscope from his bag, the doctor listened to her heart for some minutes before frowning at her. 'It isn't good, Ruth. Didn't I tell you quite clearly that you had to slow down?'

Mary Ann was now bordering on panic as she stared into his face. '*What* isn't good? And *why* should she slow down?'

The doctor sighed. 'Your mother's heart is in a very bad way, Mary Ann, as I told her some time ago. She could go like *that* – if she doesn't do as she's told.' He clicked his fingers to add emphasis to his words before going on, 'But you know how stubborn she is.'

Mary Ann clutched at the back of a chair for support and now it was she who was pale as she tried to digest what the doctor had just told her.

Eventually she pulled herself together enough to ask, 'Is there nothing that can be done?'

'I'm afraid not, my dear. The tablets I've given her should help to thin the blood, if she takes them regularly, but other than that there is nothing anyone can do.'

Throughout this exchange, Ruth had kept her eyes downcast but now she raised them to her daughter to ask imploringly, 'You won't mention this to your father, will you, Mary Ann? You know what a worrier he is.'

Her eyes bright with unshed tears, Mary Ann turned and walked away without so much as another word.

As Dan emerged from the hotel the next morning, he saw that the streets were once again teeming with people. He had just eaten a magnificent British breakfast, washed down with copious amounts of strong tea from a silver teapot, and now he felt ready to face anything. The doorman tipped his cap respectfully as Dan passed through the large glass doors and once outside he paused to look around for a sight of Pip. He saw him almost immediately, standing in his wooden clogs and blowing into his hands to try and warm them, and Dan's kind heart was saddened. The poor child must be frozen, for a cold wind was whipping across the pavements. Even so, his face lit up when he saw Dan.

'Mornin', Mr Dan. Sleep well, did yer?'

'I certainly did,' Dan assured him as he turned northwards, in the direction of Bond Street.

'This ain't the way to Clapham Common,' Pip

objected as his wooden clogs clattered on the pavement.

'I'm quite aware of that, young man. But before we set off, there's a little shopping I'd like to do.'

'Huh! They won't let *me* in the posh shops wiv yer, not lookin' like this,' 'Pip informed him grumpily.

'Oh, I think you'll find they will,' Dan told him with a grin and so they walked on. Eventually they came to a large clothes shop that specialised in men's and boy's clothing, and Dan ushered Pip before him into the warmth. The boy's nose began to run as the heat wrapped itself around him, and he swiped his shirt-sleeve across it, much to the amusement of a friendly assistant who had hurried forward to meet them.

The woman was dressed in a smart navy-blue dress that was simple yet elegant, and had a tape measure slung around her neck. 'May I help you, gentlemen?' she asked.

'Yes, I think you can,' Dan told her imperiously. 'I'd like to see what you have in the way of coats to fit this young man. And perhaps some stout shoes too? Do you sell shoes here?'

'Well, no, actually we don't, sir. But there is an excellent shoe-shop right next door, where I'm sure you'll find something to suit your needs. But first I'll look at what we have in the way of overcoats to suit the young gentleman.'

The assistant measured Pip's chest as the boy stood there with his mouth gaping in amazement. She then hurried away as Dan winked at him and advised, 'I should close your mouth if I were you, Pip. They could drive a tram in there.'

164

The boy hastily clamped his mouth shut before hissing, ''Ere – what you playin' at? I ain't never owned a proper coat in the whole o' me life.'

'Then it's high time you did,' Dan answered. There was no time for further conversation because the assistant was now bearing down on them with a selection of overcoats slung across her arm that had Pip's eyes almost popping out of his head.

'May I suggest that sir tries this one on?' the woman smiled.

Pip tried it on but instantly shook his head. 'Ner, I want one a bit bigger if yer don't mind.'

'But sir, it's a perfect fit,' the assistant assured him, and Pip nodded in agreement.

'I know it is, but if I 'ave one bigger it'll fit me older brothers an' all, an' that way we can all get to wear it,' he said disingenuously.

Dan stifled a grin as the assistant smothered a smile and swept away again. In no time at all she was back, this time with the next size, which reached almost to Pip's ankles.

'Cor, that's just the ticket,' Pip told her as he swayed this way and that in front of a long cheval mirror.

'Well, if sir is quite sure. Would sir like it wrapped?'

'Not on your nelly. I'm keepin' it on,' Pip informed her, and with that Dan could hold his amusement back no longer and he laughed aloud.

'In that case, perhaps you would like to come to the counter and pay for it, sir?' the assistant said to Dan, who followed her to the ornate brass till that stood on the shop counter.

Once the coat was paid for, they visited the shoe shop next door. Dan treated young Pip to a pair of leather boots, again a size too large so that they would also fit his brothers. He also bought him three pairs of long warm woollen socks, which almost had Pip swooning with delight.

Back outside on the pavement again, Pip swaggered along like Burlington Bertie as Dan watched him with a twinkle in his eye.

'Thanks, Mr Dan. All me new fings are smashin',' Pip told him gleefully.

'Think nothing of it. It was my pleasure,' Dan replied and then, 'So, shall we get on? You should be a little warmer now with your new togs on.'

They caught a tram at the end of Oxford Street and eventually the red-faced conductor shouted, 'All alight fer Clapham Common!'

Pip and Dan climbed down and looked about them. It was nowhere near as busy here as it had been in Central London, but it was still busy nevertheless.

'A cabbie told me that Forthbridge Road is this way – second to the left after that pub called The Highwayman, next to the Common,' Pip told him.

Once there, the lad said self-importantly, 'Right, we're lookin' fer River House now.' And he set off at such a rate that Dan had a job to keep up with him.

'Good job I can read, ain't it?' Pip chuckled as he looked at the house names and numbers. 'Me ma makes sure that all of us know our letters. She reads to us every night before we go to bed.' He would have said more, but suddenly came to an abrupt halt and jerked his thumb at a house to the left of them.

'Looks like this is it. Do yer want me to come in wiv yer?'

Dan shook his head. The building was nowhere near as big as the house in which Pip lived, though it was quite substantial. Three concrete steps led up from the pavement to a front door that was painted red, whilst other steps dropped away to one side down to what looked like a basement room beneath pavement level.

'No, it might be as well if I go in alone for now,' Dan answered. 'But look – there's a pie stall on the edge of the Common there. Why don't you go and get yourself something warm to eat while I try my luck?'

After giving Pip a shiny sixpence, he watched as the child skipped merrily away in his overlong coat with a smile on his face that stretched from ear to ear. Grinning, Dan then climbed the steps and, grasping a shiny brass knocker in the shape of a lion's head, he rapped on the door. A young girl dressed in an ankle-length, plain grey dress answered it.

'Yes, sir. May I help you?' she enquired politely.

'I'm hoping so, my dear,' Dan replied. 'I'm looking for a Mrs Margaret Fellows and I was told she lived here. Do I have the right address?'

'Yes, sir, you do. But I'm afraid that Mrs Fellows ain't in right now. She's at her shop in Town durin' the day. Would you like to leave a message? I could pass it on when she gets 'ome.'

'Thank you, but no. I wish to see her about something of a personal nature – unless Mrs Stirling is in, of course? If she is, I could perhaps

167

have a word with her instead?'

The girl shook her head. 'I'm afraid Mrs Stirling passed away some years back,' she informed him gravely.

'Oh, I see.' Dan had half-expected this, but even so he could not help but be disappointed. 'Then could you tell me what time Mrs Fellows will be back?' he now asked. 'I could perhaps call around to see her then?'

'It varies, to be 'onest. But she's never in no later than five o'clock, so perhaps you could call around this evening?'

'Thank you. I'll do that.' Dan doffed his hat then slowly descended the steps as the little maid quietly closed the door. He was wise enough to know that all was not lost, and at least she was still at the address he had been given, which was a bonus as far as he was concerned.

Pip, who had been watching from across the street, hurried over to join him and asked through a mouthful of pie, 'Does she still live there then, or wot?'

'Yes, Pip, I'm pleased to say that she does, though unfortunately I was informed she has a shop in Town and is there most days.'

'That'll be the tailor's shop her 'usband owns, I bet,' Pip said wisely. 'Though what a woman would be doin' workin' in a tailor's is beyond me. I mean, ask yerself, if you was to go in fer a fittin', yer'd hardly want a woman measurin' yer inside leg, now would yer? Though come to think of it, it was a woman that served us wiv me coat, weren't it? An' she was a bit of all right an' all, wasn't she?'

Dan swallowed his amusement as he looked

down at Pip. If anything, the coat he had bought him looked totally out of place on the child. But at least he knew he was warmly wrapped now, which was a small blessing at least. There was something about this boy that he found strangely endearing. Perhaps it was his fierce loyalty towards his mother and his family? Or perhaps it was simply his sunny personality that appealed. Whatever it was, Dan felt that he owed the child a great debt of gratitude for making his search for Mrs Stirling's relation so easy for him. He had no doubt at all that without Pip he could have been searching for weeks – months even, with no success at all.

They had now reached the tram stop and as they were waiting, Pip asked, 'So, what are yer goin' to do now then?'

'I shall come back again this evening and hope to have more luck,' Dan informed him.

'So, will yer want me to come back wiv yer then?'

Detecting the note of hope in the child's voice, Dan shook his head. 'No, Pip. I don't want to drag you out at night unnecessarily in this inclement weather. But depending on what I discover – if I discover anything at all, that is – I may need your help again. Would it be all right to call on you?'

'Not 'arf,' Pip answered enthusiastically, and as the tram trundled to a stop they climbed aboard side-by-side, and once seated they lapsed into a compatible silence as the tram wound its way back towards the city centre.

It was mid-afternoon when the nurse tucked Anna into a bathchair and wheeled her along the corridor towards the lift. Anna had spent a sleepless

169

night wondering how Dan was getting on with his search in London, and now she was determined to make the effort to go to 'the Bunker' and see Jonathan.

From the news that she got from the nurse, the poor lad was still in a very bad way, and the need was on her to see him.

When the bathchair was finally wheeled into his room, she saw him sitting staring out of the window, and deep inside she started to cry although her eyes were dry as she instructed the young nurse, 'Wheel me closer to him, Nurse, would you?'

'Of course, Mrs Bensham.' The nurse wheeled the chair as close to the man as she could get it before asking, 'How about I go and get you and Mr Bensham a nice cup of tea and a slice of Christmas cake? The cook made so many, I think we'll be eating it for weeks.'

'That would be lovely. Thank you.'

The nurse discreetly took her leave, and now that they were alone, a silence settled over the room until Anna broke it when she said softly, 'Oh, my dear ... to see you so. What you must have gone through. What terrible sights you must have seen.' The man she was looking at was merely a shell of the handsome young man she had waved away to war, but in her mind's eye she saw him as the mischievous child he had once been, so easily led by Ben, as his brother Harry had been too. Harry – the name brought the tears stinging to her eyes now, for she knew that she would never look on Harry again. He was gone, cut down in his prime. But Jonathan at least had survived ...

after a fashion. She took his limp hand gently in her own and held it to her cheek as she told him, 'You must *fight*, my dear. You have all your life in front of you just waiting to be lived.'

When he continued to stare blankly ahead she went on, 'Life is so short, Jonathan. Mine is almost at an end. There is only one thing that is keeping me alive now and that is the thought that your father may discover the whereabouts of my daughter. You didn't know I had a daughter, did you, Jonathan? No one knew apart from Mary Peel, may God rest her soul. But I did, as sure as God is my witness, and I gave her away, for I could not endure the shame of bearing a child out of wedlock. It's odd when you come to think of it, isn't it? I lived with a man for years as his wife, and yet when I achieved the one thing I had always longed for, which was to have a child of my very own, I gave her away for fear of what people would say. And then what did I do but pour all my affections into your mother, only to have her end up hating me. If only we could turn back the clock, eh? Then I would have kept my child and you might never have gone away to war. Harry would still be here and I would have let your mother marry Michael, the one true love of her life. But then if I had done that, neither you, Harry or Ben would ever have been born, would you? Oh my dear, life is so complicated and I am so tired of it.' She wiped her hand across her weary eyes and then with nothing but the popping of the logs to bear witness to her distress, she lowered her head and did what she had rarely done in her life before. She sobbed as if her poor old heart would break.

Chapter Twelve

Taking his watch from his waistcoat pocket, Dan glanced at it. It was almost seven o'clock and time to begin his journey back to Clapham Common. He had just enjoyed a cigar and a glass of port following a sumptuous meal in the hotel dining room, and would have liked nothing better now than to go to his room and rest. But he was aware that time was of the essence if he was to get back to Ruth and Mary Ann to see the New Year in with them, and so he forced himself from his seat and headed towards the hotel foyer.

Smog had once more settled across the streets and an icy wind could do nothing to dispatch it as he strode along with his coat collar turned up. He briefly thought of catching a tram as he had earlier in the day with Pip, but it was so cold that he decided to be frivolous and hailed a cab. Once he was settled into his seat, he told the driver. 'Clapham Common if you would, my good man.'

'Aye, aye, guv.'

Dan settled back in his seat and for the first time, thought of what he might say to this Mrs Fellows if she should happen to be in. He had not really given it much consideration before. She would probably think he was a raving madman to turn up out of the blue like this, asking if she happened to know the whereabouts of a child who had been given into her aunt's care some fifty odd years ago.

A voice from the front of the cab sliced into his thoughts when the driver informed him, 'We're comin' up to Clapham Common any minute now, guv. Is there anywhere in particular that you'd like droppin' off?'

'Forthbridge Road, if you please,' Dan informed him, and several minutes later, the cab drew to a halt. Dan quickly climbed out and after handing some coins through the window, he then turned in the direction of River House. He was rewarded by the sight of a light shining through curtains that had been drawn tightly across a downstairs window. Climbing the steps, he rapped at the door and once again the little maid he had spoken to earlier in the day answered it.

'Good evenin', sir,' she said respectfully. 'Was it the mistress you was hopin' to see?'

'Yes. I wonder if you would give her my card and ask her if she could perhaps spare me a few moments?' Dan took off his gloves and after feeling in his pocket he handed a small card to the girl who now told him, 'Please come in, sir. I'll just go an' see if it's convenient fer the mistress to see yer.'

Dan stepped past her into a hallway that was simply but elegantly furnished. A large gilt mirror reflected the light from a small crystal chandelier that was suspended from the high ceiling, and a small chair that looked to be a Chippendale stood next to a marble-topped table on which was placed a vase of winter greenery.

He was still admiring his surroundings when the girl reappeared from a doorway further along the hall and beckoned him to join her.

'Mrs Fellows will see yer now, sir,' she told him. 'Would yer like me to take your coat?'

'No, that won't be necessary, thank you. I have no intention of taking up too much of Mrs Fellows's time.'

'Very well, sir.' The girl held the door open and he stepped past her into a compact but comfortable sitting room. As he entered, a woman who had been sitting in a leather chair to the side of the fire rose to greet him, and instantly Dan had the feeling that he had met her somewhere before. She looked to be in her early forties, and as she held out her hand to him he noticed that she was very attractive. Her blond hair had been pulled into a sophisticated chignon on the back of her head, and her dress, like the surroundings he found himself in, was simple but elegant. The only pieces of jewellery he could see were a plain gold wedding band on her left hand and a strand of pearls about her slim throat.

'Good evening, Mr...' she glanced down at the card in her hand ... 'Mr Bensham. Sally informs me that you called earlier to see me. In what way may I help you?'

Dan suddenly felt very foolish as he wrung his hat in his hands and shuffled from foot to foot. 'The truth of it is, I hardly know where to begin now that I'm here, Mrs Fellows.'

'Well, I usually find that the best place to begin is at the beginning.' Dan thought he could detect a note of amusement in her voice as she motioned him gracefully towards a chair. 'Won't you take a seat?'

'Thank you.' He sank down into the chair at the

other side of the fireplace and tugged uncomfortably at his collar as the warmth of the room settled around him like a blanket.

She was looking at him enquiringly, and realising that he would have to begin somewhere, he stuttered, 'I'm afraid that the story I am about to tell you will sound very strange, but my stepmother, Mrs Anna Bensham, is the owner of High Banks Hall near Newcastle. She was married to my late father for some years before his death, and before that, she was the governess to my siblings and myself. Before *that* she er ... lived for some time with a man by the name of Thomas Mallen, who owned the Hall before my father. Anna, or Brigie as we have always affectionately called her, is now well into her nineties and she has always been, what can I say ... a rather prim and proper person. Not that you would think so, from what I have just told you. But that is why the confession she made to me a short while ago was so shocking, for she revealed that back in 1862 she gave birth to an illegitimate child by Thomas Mallen.' He withdrew the newspaper that Brigie had kept hidden all these years and handed it to Mrs Fellows.

'It is this that has led me to you. You see, Brigie felt that she could not keep the child and so her faithful companion Mary Peel took the newborn baby to this address.'

Mrs Fellows dragged her eyes away from his to read the advert he had handed to her, and as the words leaped off the page at her, the colour drained from her face.

Adoption – A person wishing for a lasting and comfortable home for a child of either sex will find this

175

a good opportunity. Advertisers having no children of their own are about to proceed to America. Premium, Fifteen Pounds. Apply, Mrs Stirling, Myrtle Cottage, Bow.

'Oh, dear God. This is my aunt's address!' she gasped in horror.

'Quite,' he said softly. 'Were you aware that she ran a baby farm?'

'Well, I hardly think what she did would amount to a baby farm,' Mrs Fellows told him, and there was an edge to her voice now. 'I know that my aunt helped to find a home for certain babies who were unwanted but I can assure you, she was a genuinely kind person. My mother told me that the babies that were left in her sister's care all went to good, loving homes.'

'Oh, I'm quite sure that they did,' Dan assured her hastily.

'However,' she went on, 'I'm afraid that my aunt passed away some years ago, so if you have come to discover the whereabouts of this particular baby, I'm afraid I am not going to be able to help you.'

Dan's shoulders visibly sagged and suddenly the woman found herself feeling sorry for him and also for the woman who had sent him.

'Well, to be truthful I had an idea I would be embarking on a fruitless quest when Brigie first asked me to come here,' Dan confided as he slowly rose from his chair. 'But thank you for your patience and your time, Mrs Fellows.'

It was as he was walking towards the door that her voice suddenly slowed his steps when she said, 'Wait a moment. Now that I come to think of it, I believe my aunt kept some sort of ledgers about where the children were placed.'

Hardly daring to believe his luck, Dan looked back at her with hope shining from his eyes. 'Would you happen to know where these ledgers are now?'

She chewed on her lip for a time as she thought and then suddenly she told him, 'I seem to have some recollection of my husband, George, putting them up in the attic after Aunt Lillian's death. I could look for you, if you like, but I'm afraid it won't be until after the New Year now. I am leaving to spend the holiday with relatives on the Isle of Wight tomorrow, but I could always look to see if they are still there on my return, if you would like me to?'

'Oh yes. Yes, please!' he told her breathlessly. 'At least that way I can return to my own home with a glimmer of hope for Brigie.'

'Then consider it done,' she told him with a twinkle in her eye and he found himself thinking what a lovely woman she was. It was as he was pumping her hand up and down that it suddenly came to him where he had seen her before, and he laughed aloud now as he exclaimed, 'Why, *you* are the lady who served Pip and me earlier in the day when I took him into a menswear shop to buy him a new overcoat!'

'Of *course!* I remember you too now,' she laughed. 'Goodness me, what an amazing coincidence! And how is the child?'

'Fine, I hope,' he told her and then he admitted sheepishly, 'You'll probably think me a complete fool, but I only met Pip a short while ago. He has been showing me around London. He comes from ... shall I say, a very modest home, and I felt so sorry for the poor little chap that I felt I'd to treat him to some suitable clothing for the weather.'

The woman glanced towards the door before leaning towards him conspiratorially and whispering, 'I don't think you are a fool at all, Mr Bensham. That's how I came to have my little maid, Sally. I felt so sorry for her that I took her in off the streets. Not that I have any regrets. She is such a loyal girl.'

They were openly smiling at each other now and Dan almost regretted the fact that he had to leave. But he had no wish to outstay his welcome so as he followed her to the door he asked, 'Was it your husband's shop you were working in?'

'Yes, it was. But now let me see... I shall be home the day after New Year's Day, so shall we say you can call again a week after that? That will give me time to go up and have a forage around in the attics for the ledgers.'

'That would be wonderful. Thank you.'

Dan shook her hand again and wished her a very Happy New Year before slipping outside onto the cold dark pavement. The street-lights were casting an eerie glow across the cobblestones, but strangely there was a spring in his step now as he made his way back to the hotel. He would catch the train from King's Cross first thing in the morning, he decided, and on that happy thought he hurried on his way.

The following morning, he called in at Fortnum & Mason's, a grand store a stone's throw from the Ritz, and asked one of the uniformed assistants, 'Could you have a hamper made up and delivered for me?'

'Certainly, sir,' the man assured him smoothly. 'What would you like in it?'

Dan thought hard. What would the Beddows family appreciate most? 'I'll have some vegetables and some fruit, of course. And what about meat?'

'We had some chickens come in only this morning that are as fat as butter,' the man told him cheerily. 'Fresh from the countryside.'

'Excellent, then put two of those in as well, with some bacon and sausages too. Also, a nice fruit cake and some mince pies and a big tin of biscuits, I think.' On and on he went until he felt satisfied. Standing back, he scribbled down Pip's address and handed it to the assistant. 'Have it delivered there, please – the last room on the right, on the third-floor landing.' Ignoring the look on the man's face, he said, 'Now what do I owe you?'

After paying a substantial sum, Dan lifted his valise and went on his way with a smile on his face that lasted throughout the whole of his six-and-a-half-hour journey home.

The smile was wiped away the second he set foot through the door, when Betty ran to meet him with tears streaming from her eyes. 'Eeh, Mr Dan. Thank the Lord you're back,' she gabbled as she wiped her apron around her tear-drenched face. 'We had Miss Mary Ann here last night an' she were right upset, I don't mind tellin' yer.'

'All right, Betty. Calm down and tell me what's happened.'

Taking her arm, he gently pressed her onto a chair that stood in the hallway and now Betty tried to compose herself as she told him, 'It seems that Ruth is poorly. Somethin' to do wi' her heart, so Mary Ann was sayin'. She wanted to know when you would be home, but all I could tell her was that you'd said you'd be back to see the New Year in.'

'Well, I am back now, so try to stay calm.' Dan's own heart was hammering. So many things made sense now. The way Ruth seemed to have slowed down of late. The pallor of her skin … the bluish tinge he had sometimes detected about her lips – and yet she hadn't breathed so much as a word to him. But then, that was Ruth. She had never been one to complain about anything, looking back over the years.

Dropping his valise onto the floor, he turned back towards the door. 'I'm going over there right now,' he told the blotched-faced Betty. 'I shall be staying there to see the New Year in with Ruth and Mary Ann, so you and Ada can have a little rest.'

'Bless you, Mr Dan,' she told him as he slipped back out of the door. 'Give Ruth our love and best wishes, won't you?'

He nodded solemnly and after closing the door quietly behind him he strode away down the path.

Ruth was standing washing dishes at the sink when he arrived and she flashed him a smile. That was one of the things he had always loved about this dear woman. She had never asked for more than he was able to give, and each time he appeared she accepted it as if he had never been away. There were no complaints or recriminations, and today was no different as she told him, 'I thought I'd do us a nice fish pie for dinner today. Would that suit you? Mary Ann is off out with her friends tonight. They're goin' dancin'. Between you an' me, she's been a bit starry-eyed lately, an' I just wonder if there ain't another chap in the picture. Not that I'm holdin' out much hope of anythin' comin' of it, even if there is! After five broken engagements I'm beginnin' to wonder if there'll ever be one to keep her in line. She's a mind of our own, has our Mary Ann.'

'Well, she wouldn't be much good without one,' Dan joked as she took his coat off. For the first time in his life he found that he was feeling vaguely uncomfortable in Ruth's presence and wondered if he should ask her about what Mary Ann had disclosed to Betty. As he carried his coat to the coat-rack that stood to one side of the front door he decided to wait until he had spoken to Mary Ann.

Ruth looked quite well, so could it be that Betty had got it wrong? He was just crossing back to the kitchen when Mary Ann came clattering down the stairs. When she saw him, her face lit up and she hurried across to give him an affectionate cuddle.

'Hello, Dad. Just got back, have you?'

'Yes, dear, I have and I've decided to stay until after the New Year – if that's all right with you?'

Mary Ann looked slightly confused. Her father had never told her when he would be coming or going before. As she looked into his face, she saw the concern there and knew that he had been back to his own house, and that Betty had spoken

181

to him of her visit.

Taking his elbow, she glanced towards the open kitchen door before drawing him into the parlour, where she softly closed the door behind her.

'Betty's spoken to you, hasn't she?' she whispered urgently.

'Yes, she has, and I have to say, what she told me was most distressing. Do you want to tell me all about it?'

'Of course. Mam tried to make me promise that I wouldn't say anything to you, but I think you have a right to know But we can't talk here – Mam will be in any minute. How about we go for a walk after dinner?'

He nodded his agreement and side-by-side they went back into the kitchen together to join Ruth.

Late that night, as Dan lay at Ruth's side in her comfortable feather bed, sleep eluded him. They had all spent a pleasant day together and now it suddenly struck him that Ruth and Mary Ann were his family. Looking back, they had always been his family, even when his wife had been alive, for Barbara had never professed to love him as Ruth did. Turning his head slightly on the pillow he gazed into her slumbering face.

Ruth had never been what anyone could term a beauty. She was short and plump, and yet there was a freshness and honesty about her that made people look beyond her appearance. She was gentle and sincere, and Dan had never had a doubt that she loved him with all her heart, even though she had always known that he had

182

nothing but affection left to give her. Barbara had seen to that, for she had sucked all the love out of him like a leech and given nothing in return.

His thoughts returned to the conversation he had had with Mary Ann that afternoon. It seemed that Ruth was living on borrowed time. It could happen today, or next week – or there again, she could go on for a few years, the doctor had said. Dan tried to visualise his life without her and it was a shock when he realised how painful it would be. She had given him so very much whilst he was ashamed now to admit that he had given very little. Oh, he had always made sure that she had no financial worries, but he had come and gone as he pleased and she, being the kindly individual that she was, had accepted it without complaint.

As he stared up at the ceiling he searched his mind for a way to make it up to her. There was one thing he could do, he knew. He could make an honest woman of her. But would she allow it now, or would her pride tell her that he was only doing it because her time was short?

There was only one way to find out and he determined to do it at the first opportunity.

Chapter Thirteen

On the morning of New Year's Eve it started to snow again and this time with a vengeance. Dan had stayed the night with Ben and Hannah, after promising Ruth that he would be back the next

183

day. Already the roads to Nine Banks Peels and the West Allan village of Whitfield were impassable, but Dan was determined to keep his promise even if it meant he had to walk every step of the way. First though, he needed to see Anna and inform her of what was happening regarding her daughter. He was preparing to go to High Banks Hall and do just that right now, with Lawrie protesting loudly in his ear.

'But *why* can't I come with you, Uncle Dan?' he pleaded. *'I* want to see Brigie and Jonathan too.'

'You can go when the weather improves and your cold is better,' Hannah told him firmly as she helped Ben into his coat. He was going to accompany his father to the Hall.

Lawrie pouted as a child might have done but Hannah would not be swayed from her decision. 'Look at you,' she said. 'Your nose is streaming already and that's an awful cough you have. You need to stay here with Nancy and me. If you go out in this, you're likely to catch pneumonia.'

'She's right, Lawrie,' Dan told him placatingly. 'You'd do much better to stay here in the warm. But don't worry, I'll pass on your best wishes to Brigie and Jonathan, and I'll tell them that you'll be over to see them as soon as you're better.'

Lawrie sighed resignedly before skulking away to the parlour as the men headed towards the door. Ben paused to plant a kiss on his wife's cheek and then they were out in the snow and could barely see a hand in front of them.

'Good Lord!' Dan exclaimed as he pulled his scarf up around his ears. 'It could freeze the hairs off a brass monkey out here.'

Ben chuckled as he nodded in agreement and for a time they fell silent until Dan suddenly told him, 'There's something I'd like to talk to you about, Ben. And I dare say that now is as good a time as any.'

With his head still bent, Ben turned to peer at his father through the snow. 'It sounds important. So, fire away then.'

'Well, the thing is...' Dan suddenly felt as if he was the child as he told his son, 'The thing is, we've just found out that Ruth is ill. Very ill, I'm afraid. It's her heart. According to the doctor, she may not have long left.'

The shock of his father's words brought Ben to an abrupt halt. He stood as if turned to stone as his father faced him and said, 'It got me to thinking, I don't mind telling you. Ruth has been a part of our lives for so long that I never envisaged a time when we might have to be without her, but now... Well, it got me to wondering if I shouldn't ask her to marry me. What do you think, son?'

Ben chewed pensively on his lip as he stared across the snowy mountains, then looking back at his father, he asked, 'Do you want to marry her?'

Dan sighed deeply. 'I'm ashamed to admit that I'd never considered it before, but... I want to make her last days happy,' he ended lamely.

'Then do it with my blessing,' Ben told him. 'Ruth was always more of a mother to me than my birth one. She loved me, whereas my mother hated me because of this.' He now tugged at the streak in his hair and his voice was loaded with bitterness when he said, 'All I ever wanted was for her to love me, Father. Did you know that?

185

But she never did. I can remember back to when I was a child and Ruth was our nurse. Mother would come up to the nursery to say goodnight to us and she would kiss Harry and Jonathan and stroke their hair. But *never* mine, even though I waited every single night for a kind word from her. And then, when she was gone, I would cry and Ruth would take me on her lap and give me the love and cuddles that I needed from my mother. So, as I said, marry Ruth if it will make her happy, and don't concern yourself with what people will say. Grandfather married Brigie, did he not, and she was at one time a governess.'

Dan nodded and both men fell silent, occupied with their thoughts, as they strode on through the storm.

The second they entered the Hall, the Matron hurried towards them with a broad smile on her face.

'Oh, Mr Bensham, I'm so glad you've come!' she exclaimed. 'I think we've had a breakthrough with Officer Bensham. Nurse Byng was just giving him his mid-morning tea when he told her quite clearly, "Too sweet." Now I know that might not sound much, but it's yet another step in the right direction, don't you agree?'

Ben let out a sigh of relief. He hated to think of Jonathan in the Bunker, locked away in a world where no one could reach him. This, as the Matron had said, could well be another step towards his recovery. Ben was under no illusions, for he knew that the way ahead would be hard – terrifying at times – but they would be there to help Johnny and do whatever it took to restore him to the young man he had once been.

'Why, that's excellent news, Matron. The best New Year gift you could have given me,' Dan said warmly, as he and Ben handed their coats to Florrie. Upstairs, Ben went straight off to Jonathan's room, while Dan headed towards Brigie on the nursery floor.

To his surprise, he found her dressed and sitting in a chair, and his face expressed his delight as he hurried over to kiss her cheek. 'Why, it's nice to see you out of bed,' he said. 'Are you feeling a little better?'

The old Miss Brigmore was very much in evidence when she replied curtly, 'I am not ill, Dan. I am merely old, and old age takes its toll on one. But now ... have you any news for me? I was hoping you would come today.'

'As it happens I have,' he told her, and when her tightly clenched fist pressed into her breast and the colour drained from her cheeks, he hurried on, 'It's only a minor advance, Brigie, so don't go getting yourself all worked up. Look ... this is what happened. I managed to track down Mrs Stirling's niece – a delightful woman by the name of Mrs Margaret Fellows. She lives in River House, Forthbridge Road, Clapham Common...'

Slowly he related what had happened in London whilst Brigie listened avidly, her unblinking eyes never once leaving his face. When he was finally done she took a deep breath and said, 'So the ledgers this Margaret Fellows has might well tell us the whereabouts of my daughter?'

'Yes, they might. But I don't want you getting too excited just yet. If the child was adopted by

187

Americans, as I learned that some of the children were, then that'll only complicate things further.'

'I am fully aware of that,' she retorted primly. 'But it will be a different matter, will it not, if she is still somewhere in this country?'

'Of course,' he conceded. 'Then there is much more chance of us finding out what became of her.'

'Then I shall pray that it is so.'

Dan now told Brigie, as he had told Ben, of his plans concerning Ruth and he watched as conflicting emotions flitted across her face.

'But Dan, I thought you said you would never marry Ruth?'

'I did,' he admitted. 'But that was before...'

When his voice trailed away she asked him softly, 'Do you love her, Dan?'

His eyes were full of pain as he replied, 'I have only ever loved one woman, and you know who that was. But what I can truthfully say is, I have a great affection for Ruth and do not know how I would have survived without her.'

Outside the door, Florrie Harper pulled herself into an upright position as she removed her ear from the door panel, and now over and over in her mind she began to recite the address she had heard: *Mrs Margaret Fellows, River House, Forthbridge Road, Clapham Common. Mrs Margaret Fellows, River House, Forthbridge Road, Clapham Common.* And what about Ruth Foggety bein' ready to peg it an' Mr Dan plannin' to make an honest woman of her, eh? With a gleeful smile on her plain face she crept along the landing. Eeh, this would be a nice bit o' gossip to pass on to Lily

Waite the next time she saw her and no mistake!

'Happy New Year, Ruth, and to you, my dear! May 1920 bring you both everything you hoped for.'

Dan held up his glass but Ruth surprised him when she said softly, 'I already have everything I ever wished for right in this room.' Her eyes, as they locked across the table with his, were full of love and contentment and Dan knew a moment's shame.

Mary Ann meantime was refilling their glasses and it was she who now proposed a toast: 'To 1920!'

'Hear, hear!' There was a chink of glasses and then they all tucked into the delicious dinner that Ruth had cooked for them. They had almost finished the treacle tart that followed, when Mary Ann suddenly asked them, 'You don't mind if I go out for a while this afternoon, do you?'

Noticing the slight blush on her cheeks, Ruth teased her, 'This outing wouldn't be sommat to do with a young man, by any chance, would it?'

'Well, as it happens I *am* meeting someone,' Mary Ann admitted, and Ruth surprised her when she threw back her head and said, 'Well, I wondered when yer were goin' to tell us about him. You've been wanderin' round like a lovesick cow fer weeks now. I know the signs – I've had enough experience, ain't I?'

'Oh, *Mam*.'

Ruth playfully flapped her hand at her as she waved her away from the table. 'Go on, get yerself off an' enjoy yerself. I'll see to the pots.'

'Not on your own, you won't,' Dan told her. 'You know the saying, many hands make light work, so we'll do them together and then we'll put our feet up in front of the fire.'

Ruth looked slightly embarrassed, for in all the years that Dan had been staying in the house in Linton Street he had never before so much as lifted a pot. Still, she supposed it was all to do with modern life, for women were still doing jobs that had been allocated to men before the war. The way she saw it, the days when a woman's place was chained to the kitchen sink were long past. It was more to do with equality now. Her Mary Ann was a shining example. Being an old-fashioned sort, Ruth wasn't altogether sure that she approved of it. The only thing she *was* sure of was the fact that there wasn't a thing she could do about it, so she may as well get used to it. *If* she was about long enough, that was. The thought spoiled what had been an otherwise carefree meal and now as she stacked the dirty dishes and carried them to the sink, her ailing heart was heavy.

The fire was crackling in the grate and the only sound to be heard was the ticking of the clock on the mantelshelf when Dan cleared his throat and said, 'There's something I've been meaning to ask you, Ruth.'

'Oh aye, an' what would that be then?' They were sitting at either side of the fireplace and now her knitting needles became still as she looked at Dan inquisitively.

'Well...' Dan wasn't quite sure how to broach the subject and it was some seconds before he

190

said, 'The thing is, now that Barbara is ... gone... What I'm trying to say is, it seems silly for us still to be living apart and keeping two houses on the go, so I was wondering – how about if you were to marry me and move into Brook House?'

Dan had been uncertain what reaction he would get, but it certainly wasn't the one he got now when she told him, 'Thank you for the offer, Dan. I really appreciate it ... but I don't think that would be such a good idea.'

'*What?* You mean you don't *want* to marry me?'

'I didn't say that, did I? I'd be a liar if I said that I hadn't always dreamed of being your wife. But the thing is ... well, Mary Ann and I are happy here. This is our home, an' I can't somehow see meself as the mistress o' Brook House wi' servants at me beck an' call.'

'Oh!' Somewhat deflated, Dan now said, 'So would you consider marrying me and staying here then?'

'It all depends on why yer were askin' me,' Ruth told him truthfully, and her voice was sad now as she went on, 'I've no doubt our Mary Ann has told yer of ... me condition. Are yer sure yer not just askin' 'cos yer feel obliged to make whatever time I have left happy?'

Dan thought on her words before replying sincerely, 'I admit that it was learning of your illness that made me first think of asking you. But I've had time to think on it now, and I've come to realise how much you mean to me, Ruth. If it wasn't for you, I don't know how I would have survived these last years, and that's the truth of it. So I ask again and for the right reasons ... will you marry me, Ruth? Because, you see, I've realised over the last few days that ... I can't bear to think of life without you!'

There was a big lump in her throat that seemed to be swelling by the second, and somehow no words would come past it as she looked back at him. And then suddenly the lump exploded and tears were spurting from her eyes. So many tears that she thought she might drown in them.

Dropping to his knees in front of her, he asked. 'Is that a yes or a no then?'

Now she gulped deeply before saying, 'It ... it's a yes.'

And then they were in each other's arms and Ruth felt as if she might burst with joy. It didn't matter any more that the time they had left together might be short. She would die as Mrs Dan Bensham. It was all she had ever dreamed of, and her dream was about to come true. But oh, if only he could have told her that he loved her too, it would have been perfect.

In the first week of January the snow stopped falling and a thaw set in. In no time at all, parts of the country were flooded, Allendale being the worst affected, for word had it that some of the cottages there were two foot under water. The occupants of the cottages were being housed in the village church hall, and the rest of the villagers had rallied round to help them with clothes and food until such a time as their homes might be habitable again.

The mood in Ruth's home, however, was one of excitement as she prepared for her wedding, which was to take place in the first week in February. She and Dan had decided that there was no point in waiting, and already their banns were being read out at St Matthew's, which was a short walk from Ruth's house in Jesmond Dene. She had insisted on a small affair, for as she had loudly proclaimed, 'What do I want with a load o' fuss an' palaver at my age?'

And so now she, Mary Ann and Hannah were shopping in Newcastle for her wedding outfit and Ruth's eyes were shining with happiness as the young women dragged her from one dress shop to another.

'I'm not havin' nothin' too fussy,' she continuously warned them. 'I want somethin' simple but elegant that I can wear again.'

The two girls raised their eyebrows as they exchanged grins and held up various outfits for her perusal.

In no time at all it was approaching lunchtime and they had come no nearer to finding something that met with Ruth's approval.

'Look, how about we go and have a bite to eat in the Dog and Hedgehog?' Mary Ann suggested. 'I could kill for a cup of tea and we'll all feel more like starting again after having a break.'

The others agreed that this was a good idea and they had just started through the marketplace when Hannah saw a little boy with a white streak running through his black hair coming towards them. So Lawrie had been right then, she thought. There really *was* a child with the Mallen streak living hereabouts. But who could he belong to? As far as she knew, Ben was the last of the line of men who bore the streak, so could that mean...? Her heart began to hammer in her chest. The child looked to be about four or five years old. Could it be that Ben had had an affair with someone before going away to war that had resulted in this child being born? She had heard rumours that Ben had been having a light-hearted association with a certain Miss Felicity Cartwright at one time, but from what she had heard of her, she certainly hadn't been the sort of young lady who would have had a child out of wedlock. She had come from a very good family, by all accounts. So who *could* the child belong to?

Glancing towards Ruth and Mary Ann, she saw that they were deep in conversation and had not noticed the little boy. She looked back but he had gone now as if he had never been, even though her eyes swept back and forth along the length of the street.

'Come on, Hannah. Me stomach thinks me throat's cut!'

Ruth's voice brought her thoughts sharply back to the present, and pushing the child to the back of her mind she hastened to catch them up.

Soon they were in the warm, smoky atmos-phere of the Dog and Hedgehog where they ordered a meal before retiring to a table set at the side of a roaring log fire.

'Ah, that's better.' Ruth sighed with ecstasy as she wriggled her shoes off under the table and held her hands out towards the flames. 'It might have stopped snowin' but it's still damn cold out there.' Seeing that Hannah seemed preoccupied she asked, 'Is everything all right, pet? Yer seem

194

to be off wi' the fairies.'

'What...? Oh yes, yes of course it is. I was just wondering if we are ever going to find an outfit to suit you, that's all.'

'Happen I am bein' a bit picky,' Ruth admitted. 'But the truth of it is, I can't say as I'm keen on some o' the latest fashions. It don't seem right to be flashin' yer ankles to all an' sundry, somehow.'

'Oh Mam, you're living in the Dark Ages,' Mary Ann teased her.

Ruth sniffed indignantly as she crossed her arms beneath her ample breasts and hitched them up. 'Then so be it. I like what I like an' that's it. I'm too old to be thinkin' o' changin' me ways at my age. I'll be wed in what I feel comfortable in, an' that's an end to it.'

The two younger women roared with laughter and by the time their meal arrived the atmosphere was light again, although in the back of Hannah's mind was the picture of a little boy with jet-black hair streaked with white, and eyes that could have charmed the ducks off the water.

They eventually found just what Ruth was looking for, later in the afternoon. By then the sky was dull and overcast, and a drizzle had begun to fall. They had visited almost every ladies' dress shop in Newcastle town centre when Ruth pointed to a smart navy and white suit in a window and declared, 'I like that.' After it had been duly tried on and declared to be just perfect by both Hannah and Mary Ann, they then bought a white hat, white shoes and a pair of pretty white lace gloves to go with it. As an after-thought, Hannah

195

also purchased a string of luminous white pearls from a jeweller's shop. She had loved her own necklace from Ben, and wore them nearly every day. She intended to give these to Ruth on her wedding day as her bridal gift to her, so for now they were hidden in the bottom of her bag.

It was a merry party that finally made its way home on the tram, and they all laughed aloud when Ruth declared, 'Well, I don't know about you two but *I'm* worn out. I'm almost glad Dan has gone off to London again fer a couple o' days. At least I won't have to worry about cooking his dinner tonight.'

'Charming!' Hannah teased her. 'That is your future husband you're talking about.'

'Well, he's been me husband in all but name fer almost as long as I can remember, so I can't see as a bit o' paper is going to make that much difference.'

Hannah and Mary Ann exchanged an amused glance, for despite her words they both knew that Ruth was delighted that at last she was about to become Dan's legal wife. And from where they were standing, it couldn't come a day too soon.

Chapter Fourteen

The sound of raised voices reached Hannah the second she set foot through the door of her cottage, and looking towards Nancy, who was wringing her hands in the hallway, she raised her eyebrows questioningly.

'Whatever is going on in there?' she asked, but Nancy had no chance to answer, for the parlour door was suddenly flung open and Sarah hobbled from the room on her crutch with a face like thunder.

'*Mother!*'

Sarah glared at her before snatching her coat up from the hall chair where she had left it. 'You want to teach that husband of yours some manners, my girl,' she spat furiously, and then without another word she sailed from the house, slamming the door resoundingly after her.

'I'll go an' put the kettle on, shall I?' Nancy muttered, and without waiting for an answer she turned about and scurried away to the kitchen.

Hannah took off her coat and then, after tidying her hair in the hall mirror, she approached the parlour where she found Ben pacing up and down like a caged animal.

'I don't know, I can't leave you for a minute without you're getting into bother, can I?' She had been hoping to lighten the atmosphere but knew instantly that she had failed, for Ben looked absolutely furious.

'I know she's your mother, Hannah, and I probably shouldn't say it – but she's a bitter, twisted old *cow!*'

'*Ben!*' Never once in all the time she had known him had Hannah ever seen him so angry, and now she sank onto a chair as she waited for him to tell her what was wrong.

Eventually he stopped his pacing and, standing in front of her, he said, 'Your mother came

197

because she felt that there was something we ought to know.'

'Yes?'

'It seems that someone who works up at the Hall overheard a conversation between Brigie and my father, and the long and the short of it is ... they heard Brigie confessing to having a child some years ago to Thomas Mallen, and then giving it up for adoption soon after its birth. She has asked my father to try and trace the child, which was a girl who would now be in her fifties. That might explain why Father has been shooting off to London so much lately. Anyway, as your mother went to great pains to point out, *should* this woman be found, Brigie could well change her will and leave the Hall to her daughter instead of us.'

Hannah was so shocked that for a time she was rendered speechless, but eventually she pulled herself together enough to ask, 'Is it the thought of losing the Hall that is upsetting you so?'

'Is it hell!' Ben stormed. 'You of all people should know that after what I went through in the war, material things mean nothing to me. It's the *malice* that I object to. This must be very painful for Brigie and yet your mother seems to be out to try and destroy her. Once this becomes common gossip, as I have no doubt it will, now your mother has got her teeth into it, Brigie will die of shame. You know how she has always tried to be exemplary in her behaviour.'

Hannah's head bobbed in agreement, and as she thought of the pain it must have caused Brigie to give away her only child, her heart flooded with sadness. It was only a short time

198

since she had lost her own child so she could well imagine the heartache Brigie must have suffered over the years.

'Ben, we shall have to ask my mother – appeal to her better nature – to keep this quiet.'

'Huh! I fear we would be flogging a dead horse,' Dan retaliated. 'I don't think your mother *has* a better nature. This is aimed as much at me as at Brigie; she has never forgiven me for marrying you, and she would rather see the devil himself residing in the Hall than me. I sometimes wonder how she ever managed to give birth to such a sensitive person as you.'

'I like to think I take after my father in nature,' Hannah told him quietly, 'though even he had his faults, for he was weak. It was all those years when he deceived my mother with yours that has made her as she is. Oh Ben ... I'm so sorry!'

Gathering her hands into his, he gently shook them up and down. 'You need never apologise to me, my love. You cannot be held responsible for your mother's actions. But what we have to do now is think about how we can minimise the impact this will have on Brigie.'

Hannah nodded slowly, but did not hold out much hope, for she better than anyone knew just how inflexible her mother could be.

Dan was standing as usual at his hotel window, looking down into the hustle and bustle of Piccadilly below, when an idea occurred to him. He had arrived in London earlier that morning after travelling on the night train, and was counting the hours until he could call on Mrs Fellows again and see if she had managed to find her aunt's ledger. But now he realised that there was no need to wait, for he could call at her shop and ask if it would be convenient to visit her later that evening. Now that he'd a purpose, he quickly took his coat from the wardrobe and put it on. While he was at the shop he might even treat himself to a new suit, he decided; he'd need one for the wedding.

The day was dismal. There was a light rain falling and by the time Dan reached the shop, his shoes were squelching. He shook his brolly and then entered, and almost at once he saw Margaret Fellows. She was serving someone at the counter, but when she saw him she flashed him a special smile that set his heart racing before she turned her attention back to the customer.

While she was busy he began to look around at the suits that were displayed on mannequins at intervals about the shop. It was amazing to see how the styles were changing and Dan began to wonder if he might not end up having to buy himself a whole new wardrobe. Mary Ann was forever telling him how old-fashioned he was, and now he was beginning to understand why. He noticed that the jackets of the lounge suits on display were decidedly longer than the ones that had been so popular at the turn of the century. And morning coats seemed to have replaced the frock coats of which he had always been so fond. Dan had always worn a tweed Norfolk jacket and knickerbockers for the odd game of golf or for shooting, but even they seemed dated now as he looked at the sports jackets and breeches that were so obviously in fashion.

'So, is there anything that's taken your fancy?' The melodic voice at his elbow made him start, and as he looked into Margaret Fellows's laughing blue eyes he found himself blushing like a schoolboy.

'Actually, I was just thinking how outdated my wardrobe is,' he admitted. 'My daughter has been telling me for some time that I should treat myself to some new clothes, and I'm beginning to think that she may be right.'

'Oh dear, a daughter. Between her and your wife, you'll be quite outnumbered.'

'My wife died some time ago,' he told her quietly and she immediately said, 'I'm so very sorry. Trust me to go and put my foot in it.'

'It's quite all right. You weren't to know.' He pointed towards a smart morning suit that was in the shop window. 'I was just admiring that suit there. Would you happen to know if it's in my size?'

'Even if it isn't we can have it altered or a new one made up for you,' she assured him, and then calling a male assistant to her she asked him, 'Henry, could you see what size the morning suit in the window is, please?'

'Of course.' With a friendly smile the man clambered into the window display and after a moment he shouted back, 'It's a forty-two chest and thirty-six-inch waist.'

'That's fortunate because that just happens to be my size,' Dan told him. In no time at all the man had carried the suit from the window and escorted Dan to a fitting room where he tried the suit on. When he emerged, Mrs Fellows remarked, 'Why – apart from the length of the trousers it might have been made for you, Mr Bensham. When were you needing it for?'

'Actually, I'm ... I'm going to a wedding in three weeks' time, and I'm not sure that I'll be coming back into London again for a while after I leave in a couple of days.'

'In that case, if you like it I shall see that it is altered by tomorrow morning,' Mrs Fellows said immediately.

Dan wondered why he had not told her that it was his own wedding he was going to, but then scolded himself. Why should he tell her? He hardly knew the woman!

He shuffled back to the fitting room, where the man took his leg measurement, and soon re-emerged dressed in his own clothes again, whilst the assistant scuttled away through a door in the back of the shop with his new suit folded neatly across his arm.

Now that they were alone, Dan asked, 'Did you have time to look for your aunt's ledger, Mrs Fellows?'

'Yes, I did. And just as I had thought, I found it up in the attic where my husband had put it.'

Dan's face lit up. 'Why, that's wonderful! So would it be all right if I called around this evening to have a look at it?'

'It would be perfectly all right,' she assured him, and they shook hands.

Dan left the shop with a wide smile on his face. He could hardly believe how easy it had been, although he was aware that it was mainly down to Pip. Without him, he would never have been able to track Mrs Stirling's niece down. And now she had the ledger in her possession – and for all he knew, he might be just a step away from finding Anna's daughter for her. Whistling merrily, he went on his way.

'So, you told him then?'

'Yes, I told him, and why *shouldn't* I? After all that family have done to me and mine, why should I care about their feelings? Least of all that stuck-up bloody Brigadier!' Sarah flung her shawl across the back of a chair as her eyes flashed defiance at Constance.

Her mother-in-law sighed deeply. Sarah had been bitter and twisted ever since the day she had discovered that Michael was having an affair with Barbara, the girl whom Anna Bensham had brought up as her own. But since learning that Anna had an illegitimate daughter somewhere, Sarah had been like someone possessed. Thankfully, the heavy snow that had fallen over Christmas had kept her a virtual prisoner at Wolfbur Farm for a time, but she had taken the first opportunity she could to cross the hills when the thaw set in – and now, no doubt, all hell would break loose.

'Did you see Hannah?' she asked and Sarah's lips slid back from her teeth in a snarl.

'No, I *didn't* see Hannah!' she spat. 'She was out shopping for a wedding outfit – *for Ruth*, can you believe? Dan Bensham is actually going to marry her, after all this time of keeping her as his bit on the side! But I did see the Mallen bastard. Oh, you should have seen the look on his face when I

203

told him that his precious Brigie had had a bastard of her own. It was priceless, I'm telling you. I bet he won't keep her on a pedestal now, eh?'

'Oh Sarah, what have you done? And what has happened to you? I sometimes feel that I don't know you any more and yet once I looked upon you as my own flesh and blood.'

Sarah stared back at her scathingly. 'You must be going soft in your old age. Have you forgotten what Brigie did to you? She made you come here and marry a man you didn't love rather than face the scandal that you might be carrying the child of the man you *did* love!'

'That is all in the past now.' Constance's voice was loaded with regret. 'Looking back, I realise that she only made me do what she thought was right for me.'

'Huh! Believe that if you will, but I'm telling you now, if I can do *anything* at all to stop that bitch ever meeting her daughter, then I will do it. You just mark my words. I admit at first that I liked the idea of the Mallen bastard my daughter is married to never owning the Hall, but now all I want is for Brigie to die never knowing what became of her daughter – and may she rot in hell!' With that, Sarah shoved the crutch beneath her arm and thundered out of the kitchen as Constance buried her face in her hands and wept.

Dan stood outside River House and after shaking the raindrops from his brolly he rapped at the door. The sound echoed hollowly along the deserted street and within seconds he heard footsteps coming towards the door. The same little maid who had admitted him on his first visit greeted him with a smile as she told him, 'Come in, sir. The missus is expecting you.'

Dan returned her smile and once he had stepped into the hall and the door was closed against the elements he took off his coat and handed it to her. She then led him towards a door and told him, 'You'll find the missus in there, sir. Just go in.'

She hurried away as he tapped at the door and then entered. The lamps that were scattered on occasional tables about the room cast a warm glow on Margaret Fellows, who he saw was leaning across a large ledger that she had spread out on a small table in front of her. And in that moment he might have believed that her hair was spun gold.

'Ah, Mr Bensham. Do come in. As you can see, I have already started to look through my aunt's ledger. I can assure you, it makes heartbreaking reading. Can you imagine how *awful* it must have been for these poor young women to have to leave their babies like that, knowing full well that they might never see them again?'

'In truth, I cannot,' he admitted, and then he asked, 'Do you have any children, Mrs Fellows?'

A look of regret briefly flitted across her face as she shook her head and told him, 'No. Sadly, my husband, George, and I were never blessed.'

'Oh, I'm sorry.' It was Dan's turn to feel embarrassed.

But she did not seem to have taken offence. Instead, she said, 'Won't you come and sit down? It seems that my aunt recorded each child she took in, though I have to say that her handwriting is really most appalling.'

Dan perched uncomfortably on the small settee at the side of her as she asked, 'What year did you say the child you are looking for was born?'

'Eighteen sixty-two.'

She began to turn the pages of the book and said eventually, 'Ah, here we are – this is the right year. Unfortunately, it appears that my aunt never wrote down which month the babies came to her. So let me see ... altogether there are seven babies recorded for that year.'

Dan was curious now and leaning towards the book, he gazed at the page she was pointing to.

'See?' she said. 'The first one was a boy baby so we can discount that one, and the second was a girl, but it appears that she was adopted by an American couple who took her back to the United States with them. The third...' Her fingers moved down the page. 'Ah, it looks as if that was another boy, so again that one would be of no interest to you.'

Seeing the tension on Dan's face, she assured him: 'My aunt was a good woman, I can promise you. Each and every child she took in went to a very good home, and she always told the adoptive parents where they had come from. The way she saw it, it was better for the babies to be left with her than be pushed away and forgotten in some orphanage somewhere. I've known her to keep some of the little ones for months until a good home could be found, and whilst they were with her she doted on them and shed many a tear when they left her.'

Dan remained silent and after a time she turned her attention back to the ledger. 'The fourth baby was a girl... According to this, she was adopted by a couple in the Midlands. It gives an address in Hartshill, which apparently is a village on the outskirts of a small market town called Nuneaton. Unfortunately, there is no surname, only the initial G, but as I said, there is an address.' She went on to the next entry. 'The fifth was a girl too, and she went to a family in Southend. Again, there is no name – only the initial R. The sixth was a boy, and the seventh and final entry for that year was a little girl who went to a couple in Manchester with the initial W.'

'That is really most helpful,' Dan told her. 'Would you mind if I wrote down the address of the first girl who went to live in the Midlands? I think I will try there first and if I have no luck, I hope you won't mind me coming back again? I rather dread having to trek to America if it was Anna's child that went there, so I think I will try the ones in this country first.'

'Of course.' She wrote down the address and her eyes were sympathetic as she told him, 'You do realise that you might not find this woman, don't you? She would be fifty-eight years old now.'

A pain passed through his heart as he realised that Brigie's daughter would be the same age as Barbara would have been, had she still been alive. He pushed it firmly away as he told her, 'Yes, I do realise that – but for Brigie's sake I have to make an effort to find her. I have given her my word.'

'Then I wish you every success with your search but now, would you care to stay for a cup of tea? I was just about to have one, but of course, if you have to rush off...?'

'No, no,' he assured her. 'Tea would be lovely, thank you.'

She rang a small hand bell that stood on the end of the mantelshelf and now the maid Sally appeared in the doorway and bobbed her knee.

'Yes, ma'am?'

'Ah, Sally. Would you mind making us a tray of tea, dear?'

'Of course.' Sally respectfully bobbed her knee again and once she had disappeared back the way she had come, Margaret Fellows confided, 'I really don't know what I would do without that girl sometimes. She is so very good to me.'

'Will er ... your husband be joining us?' Dan asked politely, and Mrs Fellows looked away as she answered, 'No. George won't be joining us.'

Dan felt himself blush. What did he have to go and ask that for? Suddenly he blurted out, 'Actually, I am getting married again in three weeks' time. Hence the suit I ordered from your shop today.'

'Then may I offer my congratulations? I shall have to make sure that the suit is just right for you.'

For no reason that he could explain, Dan felt very foolish and it was a relief when Sally returned seconds later with their tea. As Mrs Fellows poured it she asked, 'Will you be staying in London for long, Mr Bensham?'

'No. I thought I might call to see Pip and his family in the morning before picking my suit up, and then I shall head for home before travelling to Nuneaton to follow up this address.'

'Will you let me know how you get on?'

'Yes, of course I will. That's the least I can do after you've been so helpful, Mrs Fellows.'

She suddenly giggled, and peeping at him out of the corner of her eye she said, 'Why don't you call me Meg? Mrs Fellows is so formal, isn't it? And I have a feeling we are going to be seeing quite a bit of each other whilst all this searching is going on.'

Dan felt himself relaxing again as he returned her smile. 'Very well then. But only if you will call me Dan.'

'It's a bargain.' She passed him his tea and soon they were chatting away like old friends. When Dan looked at the ornate clock on her mantel-shelf some time later he was shocked to see that it was almost ten o'clock.

'Meg, I'm so sorry,' he said, and rose hastily from his chair. 'I didn't realise how late it had got.'

'Neither did I.' She smiled. 'It's been nice to have someone to talk to. It can be lonely, living on your own. But then that won't be a problem for you for very much longer, will it? If you're getting married again, I mean.'

'No, I don't suppose it will.' He wondered what she had meant by living alone. Where was her husband? Had they perhaps separated? He dismissed that idea almost immediately, for when Meg had spoken of her husband, her tone had been affectionate. Perhaps he was just forced to be away from home a great deal on business? Of course, Dan was too polite to ask outright, so instead he extended his hand and she shook it warmly as he told her, 'I'll say goodnight then. Thank you for the information and the hospitality, and I'll see you in the morning.'

She inclined her head, and as he left the room he found himself thinking what a charming woman she was – which was strange, for he had not given another woman so much as the time of day since Barbara had died – apart from Ruth, that was. But then, Ruth was Ruth. And Meg Fellows, despite the strange comment about living alone, appeared to be a very happily married woman.

Chapter Fifteen

'So where are you going, so early in the morning? I thought you had work to do in the dairy today.'

Sarah shrugged nonchalantly. 'I thought I might go into Newcastle and do a bit of shopping. Lily can handle whatever needs to be done here. Jim has to go in for some feed for the beasts so I thought I'd get a lift with him.'

'Oh.' Constance frowned. For all Sarah's faults, and lately they were many, she did not normally venture far. But then at least she was being civil today, which was something to be grateful for, and Constance supposed that she did deserve a day off now and again, so she told her, 'In that case I hope you have a good time. Why don't you treat yourself to something new to wear?'

'I might just do that.' As Sarah shrugged her arms into the coat that she kept for special occasions and put her hat on, a wave of sympathy suddenly washed over the older woman. Sarah had not had it easy being married to Michael, and Constance knew that this was what had made her so bitter and had prematurely aged her.

As Sarah moved towards the door she asked her mother-in-law, 'Is there anything that I can get for you while I'm there?'

'No, I don't think so, but thanks for asking.'

They exchanged a smile and then Sarah left the room to find Jim waiting for her on the trap outside. Thankfully it was dry today but there was a bitterly cold wind blowing and she shuddered as Jim helped her up onto the hard wooden seat.

'I hope you're well wrapped up,' he said as he clambered up beside her. ''Twill be blowin' a gale up on the fells.'

'I shall be fine,' Sarah assured him, and so with their heads bent against the wind they began their journey.

When they reached the town, they parted company with promises of meeting back up at the Farriers, where Jim was leaving the horse and trap, in two hours' time.

Jim set off in the direction of the market and once he was out of sight, Sarah took an address from the depths of her strong wicker basket and looked at it.

Private Detectives, Wolfe & Peale, 39 Dock Street it read. Sarah set off in the general direction of where she believed it to be, and sure enough, after five minutes of manoeuvring her crutch across the slippery cobblestones, she came to Dock Street. She saw at a glance that it was not the most salubrious of areas. Many of the doors she passed were boarded up whilst others hung off their hinges. Sarah did not much care. As long as the gentlemen she intended to hire could do what she requested, then she didn't care if their office was in the middle of a field.

When she came to number 39 she saw an open doorway with an arrow pointing to the first floor and the names, *Wolfe & Peale*. Cursing softly, she began to climb, swinging her crutch from step to step as she heaved herself up the steep staircase. By the time she reached the first-floor landing she was breathless, but her discomfort was forgotten when a door opened and a man dressed in a frock coat and breeches appeared. He was so tall that Sarah was forced to look up at him, and so thin that he was almost skeletal. His appearance was made yet more bizarre by the fact that the top of his head was shiny and bald, whereas the biggest waxed ginger handlebar moustache that Sarah had ever seen trembled on his top lip as if it had a life of its own.

'Good afternoon, madam.'

Sarah noted that the tone of his voice was quite refined.

'Were you looking for the services of my colleague and myself?'

'If you're Mr Wolfe or Mr Peale, then yes, I was.'

'Excellent, then perhaps you would care to step into the office?'

Sarah moved past him, and once inside the room she saw another man, who was slouched in a chair cleaning his nails, sitting at a scratched mahogany desk. The moment she entered, he sat upright and flashed her a smile that made her stomach churn, for his teeth were nothing more than blackened stumps.

'Afternoon, madam,' he said whilst his partner ushered Sarah to a chair.

Once she had regained her breath she told them, 'I have a job for you, if you're interested. It involves finding someone. Do you undertake that sort of work?'

'Oh yes, madam,' the tall man assured her, and then looking towards the man sitting at the desk he told him, 'Herbert, put the kettle on, would you? I'm sure our charming visitor would like a cup of tea.'

When the second man rose from his seat it was all Sarah could do to stop herself from laughing aloud, for whilst the first man was tall and thin, his partner barely reached her shoulder and was almost as round as he was high. It crossed her mind what an odd-looking pair they made, but then looks were unimportant if they could do what she wanted them to. She glanced around the room. Two large filing cabinets stood at the side of a bare window, and in the centre of the room was the desk and two chairs. A door led off into what Sarah presumed must be some sort of kitchenette, but apart from that the room was empty and cold.

Leaning across the desk, the tall, thin man extended his hand.

'Quentin Wolfe at your service, madam.'

Sarah again had to stifle the urge to laugh as she shook his hand, but then as she remembered the reason she was there, she became solemn once more. Taking a deep breath, she told him of Anna Brigmore's daughter and of the fact that Anna had asked Dan Bensham to find her.

'So you are asking us to follow this Dan Bensham then, and should he be successful in his search, you wish us to inform you?' Mr Wolfe stated when she had done.

'That's about the long and the short of it,' Sarah agreed.

Herbert Peale now reappeared and placed a chipped cup and saucer in front of her and after nodding her thanks she looked back at Mr Wolfe.

'Mm.' He steepled his fingers under his chin and stared at her thoughtfully. 'The way I see it, this would involve us following Mr Bensham then.' When Sarah nodded, he said smoothly, 'You do understand, do you not, dear lady, that this could prove to be quite expensive? My colleague or I would have to keep a very watchful eye on him and follow him wherever he went, for possibly some time to come.'

'You can follow him for however long it takes and to the end of the earth, as far as I'm concerned,' Sarah told him shortly. 'And don't worry, I have the money to pay you. In fact, I could pay you something now, if you liked? I could also give you the address of a certain Margaret Fellows who I have reason to believe is helping Mr Bensham in his search.'

'Now that would be *most* helpful,' he simpered as he played with the ends of his moustache.

When Sarah leaned across the desk towards him, he quickly scribbled down the address she gave him as a cold smile played across his lips.

'I er … I had some visitors yesterday,' Ruth told Dan tentatively. He was sitting at the side of the

214

fire reading the newspaper but now he raised his head and looked at her inquisitively as she laid down the magazine she had been reading. It was *Vanity Fair* and one of the very few extravagances she allowed herself.

'Oh yes, and who was that then?'

Ruth seemed nervy and on edge, which was unusual for her. 'It was Ben and Hannah.'

'So? They often pop in to see you, don't they?'

'Oh yes – yes, they do – but the thing is... Well, I lay awake all night wondering if I should tell you this, but they were both deeply distressed. You see, Sarah had been to see them full of some cock and bull story about Brigie having once had an illegitimate child that she is supposedly now trying to find. I told them that it was probably nothing more than malicious tittle-tattle, but they were upset, all the same.'

Dan now surprised her, for on hearing this, his chin drooped to his chest and he screwed his eyes tight shut as the newspaper crumpled in his lap.

'Dan, what is it?' Crossing to him, she lifted his chin and when she saw the raw misery in his eyes she had the urge to cry. 'Tell me, please. What is it that's troubling you?'

'Well, I feel terribly guilty now but I have to admit to knowing about this already. The thing is, Brigie told me about her illegitimate child just before Christmas and begged me to find her. That's why I've been going backwards and for-wards to London. I *wanted* to tell you, Ruth, really I did – but Brigie made me swear that I would tell no one. You know what she's like. Even though she is an old woman now, she is still fiercely proud

215

and I dread to think what effect this will have on her if she finds out it has become common knowledge. But how did Sarah hear about it? And how have Ben and Hannah taken the news?'

'Not well,' Ruth told him sadly. 'Apparently it was someone who works up at the Hall who told Lily Waite about Brigie's child; the Waites then passed the news on to Sarah.'

'Damn and blast!' Dan thumped the arm of the chair in his frustration as Ruth draped her arm about his shoulders.

'There's no point in thrashin' yourself about it,' she told him sensibly. 'The word is out now, an' no doubt it will spread like wildfire. These bits o' gossip usually do. The only good thing is, Brigie rarely leaves her room now so perhaps she'll never know that it's common knowledge.'

Dan nodded miserably in agreement, yet felt somehow as if he had let her down as he racked his brain to try and think of who might have overheard them talking. It came to him in a flash. The last time he had left Brigie's room following a visit, he had almost collided with Florrie Harper, who had had her arms full of dirty laundry on the landing. Could it be that she had listened in to their conversation at the door? Dan had no way of knowing for sure, but every instinct he had told him that it was her. Not that he could prove it, but he'd be damn sure she wasn't within earshot the next time he paid Brigie a visit.

Suddenly feeling very guilty, he drew Ruth's portly little figure onto his lap. 'I'm sorry I didn't confide in you, my dear. But let's try not to think of it, eh? We don't want to spoil the lead-up to the wedding. Is everything organised now?'

'There wasn't that much to organise,' she told him, and the smile was back on her face now. 'It's hardly going to be a big posh affair, an' I thought we'd just come back here for a bite to eat afterwards.'

'But then that means you will have to do all the work,' Dan objected. 'Why don't you let me book a nice room in a hotel and let someone wait on you for a change?'

There was a twinkle in her eye now as she told him, 'Why change the habits of a lifetime? You can't teach an old dog new tricks, you know. Besides, I'd feel more comfortable havin' it here. This is me home an' where I'm happiest.'

Guilt washed over him again as he stared up into her smiling face. Ruth asked for so little and yet she gave so much in return. She had been his lifeline throughout all the years he had been forced to stand by and watch his wife loving another man. She had cradled his head against her chest when he cried and given herself freely. So why then couldn't he love her as she deserved, he wondered. It was 1920 now and class was not as important as it had once been. Oh, he did love her in his own way, but he saw Ruth as more of a port in a storm than a lover. She had never been able to make his pulses race as Barbara had ... *and Meg!* A picture of her face popped into his mind unbidden and gently he now put Ruth from his lap and rose from the chair as guilt brought a flush to his cheeks.

'Right, I think I'll go up for an early night, if you don't mind. I'm feeling a little tired.' He yawned to add emphasis to his words and she

217

patted the cushion he had been leaning on back into place as she told him, 'Aye, you go on up, hinny. I'll join you in a while when Mary Ann gets in. She's off dancin' again. The Charleston seems to be the latest craze. Did I mention she brought her new chap in to meet me last night?'

Pausing at the door, he looked back at her to say, 'No, you didn't. What is he like?'

Ruth chuckled. 'He seems a nice sort actually. Quieter than the type she usually goes for, but I have to say she seems smitten. Not that I'm placin' a lot o' store on it. We've seen our Mary Ann smitten afore but it's never lasted for long, has it, so I won't hold me breath.'

Dan returned her smile before slowly making his way up to the double bed they shared in the front bedroom. His heart was heavy. Had Florrie Harper been there, he could happily have strangled her. But then, there was nothing he could do. The cat was well and truly out of the bag now and all he could do was pray that Brigie never discovered that others were aware of her secret. He had a terrible feeling that if she were to find out, the shame would kill her.

It was a cold wet Saturday morning late in January as Hannah wandered through the marketplace in Newcastle. In truth, she had very little shopping to do but somehow since the day she'd seen the child with the streak in his hair she had been able to think of little else, so today she had come hoping to catch another glimpse of him, rather than for any great need to shop. Already she'd walked the length of the market three times, but as yet there

218

had been no sign of him, so wearily she turned her feet in the direction of the teashop. She would buy herself a nice hot cup of tea and then, after treating Lawrie and Nancy to a cake from the cake shop, she would make her way home. As she thought of Lawrie now, she frowned. He had still not managed to shake off his heavy cold, and she decided that if he was no better by the next day, she would get the doctor to call in and take a look at him.

Ben and Dan had gone to visit John and the mill in Manchester, and suddenly the day stretched endlessly in front of her. Over the last couple of weeks she had been feeling physically recovered from her stillbirth. So much so that the doctor had now informed her that she and Ben could start trying for another child if they had a wish to. In the meantime she had decided to approach the Matron up at the Hall and ask her if there was any chance of having her old job back for a while. Hannah had never been very good at sitting about and was keen to get back to her nursing, and for more reasons than one, for although her body was healing, her heart still ached when she remembered the glimpse of the tiny baby that had slithered out of her.

The bell above the door tinkled as Hannah entered the teashop, and after ordering a hot buttered scone and a pot of tea she took a seat at a table in the window. For as far as she could see beyond it were brightly covered market stalls, sporting everything from fruit and vegetables to pots and pans, but the cold weather had kept most people indoors and today the market was almost deserted.

She took off her hat and gloves and smiled warmly at the little waitress in the crisp white apron before pouring out her tea and stirring it slowly as she stared pensively from the window. Who *was* the child with the Mallen streak? Was he really anything to do with Ben? Time and again she had just managed to stop herself from mentioning him, but the more she thought of the child, the more curious she became. The Mallen streak was so distinctive that only someone with Mallen blood in their veins could have sired him. And that, as far as she knew, only left Ben.

Sighing deeply, she sipped at her tea.

Chapter Sixteen

'I now pronounce you man and wife...'

As Ruth stared up at Dan there was a huge lump in her throat and a look of wonder on her homely face. It was done ... they were truly married in the eyes of God.

Dan leaned forward to plant a gentle kiss on her lips and she had the sensation of floating and knew that if she should die, right there at that very minute, she would die a happy woman.

Dan was smiling, every one of the small congregation was smiling, and as she stared down at the plain gold band on the third finger of her left hand, she wondered if she *had* already died and gone to heaven. Dan was urging her forward now and the vicar was handing her a pen to sign the register. She wrote clearly and precisely. She was Mrs Daniel Bensham now. *Mrs Bensham.* The name was echoing in her head and everything suddenly took on an air of unreality. This man, this wonderful, kind, gentle man whom she had adored since the second she had clapped eyes on him, was really hers at last.

Dan was signing the register now, and people were surging forward to shake the happy couple's hands and congratulate them.

There was Ben, Hannah and Lawrie. Ada and Betty and Nancy and Fred had come too. Mary Ann was beaming and her new boyfriend, Tom Butterworth, who was standing close beside her, was smiling too.

Not many people really, when she came to count them, but everyone she needed and loved was right there in that very room.

Dan looked at her in wonder; he had never considered Ruth to be beautiful, yet today there was a glow about her that had transformed her. She looked positively radiant, and he knew in that moment that he had done the right thing in marrying her.

'Congratulations, Mr and Mrs Bensham! May you spend many, many happy years together!' The vicar was pumping Dan's hand up and down and just for an instant, Ruth felt a great sadness. They would not spend many happy years together, for her days were numbered. But she wouldn't think about that for now. She would just take each moment of this wonderful day and lock it away in her memory.

Once outside the church, someone shouted,

'Throw the bouquet then! Don't keep it all to yerself!'

The bouquet had been a surprise present from Dan that morning, and when it had been delivered she had burst into tears of joy. It was made up of cream roses and gypsophilia and she was loath to part with it. But then, deciding that it'd be mean not to, she turned her back on the small party and tossed it high in the air. When she turned around, she saw that Mary Ann was holding it. Her face was as red as a beetroot and she grinned shyly at everyone as they slapped her on the back.

'Happen it'll be you next then, lass,' Betty said jovially and if it was possible, Mary Ann turned even redder as she avoided Tom's eyes. He, on the other hand, was grinning like a Cheshire cat.

'You know,' he whispered, leaning towards her, 'that really doesn't sound like such a bad idea to me.'

'*Tom!*' Mary Ann was so shocked that she was rendered temporarily speechless, but then they were all heading toward the lych-gate and everyone was showering Dan and Ruth with confetti and laughing aloud.

There were three automobiles waiting at the gate, another surprise from Dan. He and Ruth climbed into the back seat of the first one, and the rest of the wedding party piled into the ones behind.

'Are you happy, Mrs Bensham?' he asked softly as he slid his arm across Ruth's shoulders, and when she looked back at him, although she said not a word, her eyes said it all.

The merry mood continued when they arrived

back at the house. Ruth had been cooking for days, and the dining-room table was sagging beneath the weight of food. There were pies and pastries and pickles as well as fresh-baked bread and a whole roast pig that took up the entire centre of the table. A smaller table that had been pushed against it was loaded with drinks, and although Ruth had never been much of a drinker, today she allowed Dan to fill her glass with sherry as he proposed a toast.

'To my wife!'

Everyone duly raised their glasses and once more, Ruth had to pinch herself to believe that this was really happening.

'So, will you be moving to Brook House now then?' Ada asked Ruth after a while, and when Ruth grinned and shook her head, Ada's mouth fell open. 'What – you mean to tell me Mr Dan is going to move in here with you then?'

'That's the general idea,' Ruth laughed. 'Though things will probably go on much as before. He'll still have to go to Brook House occasionally to make sure that things are running smoothly.'

'*What?* You mean to say he's going to still keep *two* houses on the go?'

Ruth nodded. 'Of course. Brook House has been Dan's home for many years. I am happy here and Dan is happy there, so I see no reason for things to change.'

'Well, stone the crows. Whatever are things comin' to if a man an' wife can't live together under the same roof? It's a sign o' the times, so it is!'

The sherry was now having an effect and Ruth giggled like a girl as she told her, 'It's worked well

223

enough so far, so why mend what isn't broken? I can think of a few couples who would see mine and Dan's relationship as being perfect.'

'Well, there *is* that in it,' Ada admitted and now she too laughed, before turning to attack the delicious spread.

Only then did the smile slip from Ruth's face as she thought of what the woman had said. She supposed that it would look strange to outsiders, the fact that Dan was keeping Brook House on, but then they could not know what the house had once meant to him. It was there that he had lived with Barbara, his first wife, whom he had openly adored. And it was there that he had first turned to Ruth in despair when Barbara had repeatedly rejected him for her lover, Michael Radlet. After Barbara had killed both herself and her lover in desperation, when she had thought she might be losing him, Ruth had thought for a time that Dan would go mad. But he had come through it, and now here they were, man and wife, which only went to show you, life could be a funny old thing at times.

At that moment, Dan suddenly took her elbow and her thoughts jerked swiftly back to the present. Today was her wedding day, a day she had thought she'd never see. It was not a day for being sad, and she determined to make the most of every single minute of it, for it would never come again.

Mary Ann and Tom had been absent from the room for some time but they reappeared just as Ruth and Dan were about to cut the elaborate wedding cake that Ben and Hannah had bought them.

Ruth fingered the lovely strand of pearls about her neck. 'There was no need for you to go to all this expense, lass,' she scolded Hannah. 'These pearls alone were more than enough.'

'Nonsense,' Hannah retorted. 'The pearls were a present for *you*. I can hardly see Dan wearing them. And the cake is a present for you both, though I'm not sure what you're going to do with the top tier – unless you're planning on surprising us all. I believe the tradition is to keep the top tier for a christening cake?'

'Huh! In that case I shall save it for you an' Ben,' Ruth quipped. 'Believe me, I reckon my childbearin' days are long past. At least, I hope they are. I'm a bit long in the tooth to be startin' wi' any more bairns at my age.'

As she looked across at Mary Ann and Tom, who were standing as close together as it was possible to get, she noticed the sparkle in her daughter's eyes and asked, 'An' what are you lookin' so pleased about then, miss?'

Mary Ann glanced at Tom and when he gave an almost imperceptible nod she answered, 'Well, actually, Tom here has just asked me to marry him and I've just said yes.'

'*Well* ... I'll be. Happen we'd better fill us glasses again, in that case. Congratulations to the pair of you.'

Dan hurried forward to shake Tom's hand and once again that wonderful feeling of unreality stole over Ruth. What a day this was turning out to be! Oh, she had seen Mary Ann in love before, but somehow she thought that she might have found the right one this time, for her eyes grew

225

starry every time she looked at the handsome young man at her side. Eeh, it would be nice to think that her daughter had someone to care for her, apart from her father when she went. There I go again, she scolded herself. I won't think sad thoughts today. As her eyes came to rest on a large box that was placed to the side of the door she asked, 'What is that?'

'Ah, I almost forgot.' Ben hurried forward to lift it. 'It's a wedding present from Brigie. She asked me to bring it for you.'

Ruth fumbled with the strings that were tying it to reveal a shining mahogany box, which turned out to be the most stunning canteen of solid silver cutlery she had ever seen, for it would have graced the table of a palace.

'She apologised for not being able to be here,' Ben told her now, 'but she said to tell you that she would be here in spirit.'

As Ruth lifted a silver fork to the light she shook her head in disbelief. Eeh, it was amazing how kind people could be, and that was a fact.

Whilst the wedding party were celebrating, a certain Mr Wolfe was just stepping down from the train in Trent Valley railway station in Nuneaton in Warwickshire. His journey had started very early that morning and had involved four changes of train – at York, Leeds, Derby and Leicester – as well as stopping at six other stations along the way. It had taken over nine and a half hours, and now he was stiff and glad to be out in the open air again as he looked curiously around him. It was a small station and he hesitated on the platform

226

until he spotted the exit.

Once outside, he breathed deeply. The air seemed to be so much cleaner here than in Newcastle. He meandered along and soon came to the entrance of what appeared to be a cattle market. There were pens and cages full of chickens, geese, goats, pigs, sheep, cows and every sort of farm animal he could think of, for as far as his eye could see. Many of them were protesting loudly and the sound they were making vied with red-faced farmers who were haggling for the best bargains.

Approaching a policeman who was standing at the edge of the crowd he asked him, 'Could you possibly direct me to Hartshill, please? I believe it is a village on the outskirts of the town.'

'It is that, but if you were thinkin' o' walkin' it then you have a fair old hike ahead of you,' the officer informed him solemnly. 'There's two ways you could take. You could either go through Stockingford, or you could get there via Tuttle Hill. Personally, I'd head fer the bus station an' wait for a bus. You'll find it back there in Bond Gate beyond the market.'

'Thank you kindly, Officer.' Mr Wolfe touched the brim of his hat and walked away in the direction the policeman had pointed.

It was almost an hour later when he alighted from the bus in Victoria Road in Hartshill and fingered the address in his hand: 28 School Hill, and the initial G. Deciding to get it over with, Mr Wolfe walked on, and when he came to the end of the road he found himself at a crossroads. The road running downhill was School Hill. Greatly encouraged at how easy his task had been up to now, he began the steep descent until he came to number 28. It was a terraced house and looked neat and tidy. White lace curtains were draped at the window and the doorstep had been painted red and polished until he could see his face in it.

He tapped at the door and waited but there was no reply, so after a while he tapped again. It was then that the door of the next house opened and a middle-aged woman who was wrapped in a voluminous white apron peered out at him.

'Was it Mrs Gallimore you were after?'

So that was what the initial G had stood for. He smiled charmingly before answering, 'Yes, madam. It was.'

'Well, you'll not catch her in fer at least another couple of hours,' the neighbour informed him. 'She goes to market on a Saturday an' I doubt she'll be back till mid-afternoon at the earliest.'

'I see. In that case, could you perhaps direct me to an establishment where I might be able to get a meal?'

'Happen you might get sommat up at the Royal Oak,' she told him. 'Just follow the road back up the hill until you come to Oldbury Road on yer left an' you'll find it along there a way. Oldbury Road is just afore you get to the Holy Trinity Church. Yer can't miss it.'

'Thank you, you have been most helpful.' As she disappeared back into the house Mr Wolfe turned about and began the climb back up the hill. After a few minutes the road levelled out and up ahead he saw the church. Looking to his left, he spotted Oldbury Road and in no time at all he was settled in the pub with a jug of ale in front of him and a pile of cheese sandwiches that would have served as doorsteps.

It was mid-afternoon by the time he left and the day had already lost its brightness. The sky was leaden and overcast and he shivered as he retraced his steps to the house in School Hill. This time as he approached he was heartened to see a light shining beyond the heavy lace curtains. Once again he rapped on the door and almost instantly an old woman who looked to be somewhere in her mid-seventies answered it.

'Yes?'

'Mrs Gallimore, is it, madam?'

'Who's askin'?'

'Well, er ... perhaps if you would permit me to come in for a few moments I could explain?'

She glared at him suspiciously but then, deciding that he looked respectable enough, she held the door wide for him to step past her.

Twenty minutes later he doffed his hat and stepped back out onto the pavement. Well, that was the first on the list ruled out. There was no doubt at all that the woman who had just been described to him was not Anna Brigmore's daughter. According to the old dear who had adopted her, she had been the illegitimate child of a street girl in London, and like mother like daughter, the girl had finally ended up back there herself. He would report his findings to Mrs Radlet and then perhaps try the address in Southend next. He quite fancied a day at the seaside. But not too soon, of course. If Mrs Radlet had money to burn then it wouldn't hurt her to wait a while. He would tell her that the search was proving to be far more difficult than he had thought and keep the cash flowing in for a while. Twiddling his moustache, the tall man hurried on his way.

They had now been married for a week and it was almost as if the ring on her finger had given Ruth a new lease of life, for she never seemed to be without a smile on her face. Even so, she had noticed that for the last couple of days, Dan had lapsed into a somewhat subdued mood and she rightly guessed it was because he was worrying about when he could get back to fulfilling his promise to Brigie. She dared to broach the subject that evening over tea. Mary Ann had gone to meet Tom's mother and father, and seeing as she and Dan had the house to themselves it seemed to be the perfect opportunity.

'So, now all the fuss an' palaver of the weddin' is over, I've no doubt you'll be anxious to resume your search for Anna's daughter?'

'What – you mean you wouldn't mind?'

She grinned at him. 'O' course I wouldn't mind. Just 'cos we're wed now doesn't mean you have shackles on, lad. You are still free to come an' go as you please. In fact, I wouldn't have it any other way.' There was a smile in her eyes as she slid a slice of homemade sponge sandwich across the table to him as she spoke.

For a moment he was silent, but then when he raised his face to hers he said quietly, 'I really don't deserve you, Ruth.'

'Get away wi' you.' She now pushed a cup and saucer towards him. 'Why don't you get off in the mornin' an' start the search again? Brigie ain't well, from what I'm hearin', an' you'd never forgive yourself if anythin' were to happen to her before you'd at least tried to find her daughter.'

Reaching across the chenille tablecloth, he gently squeezed her hand. 'I'll do that, Ruth, and ... thank you.'

'You've no need to thank me,' she now told him softly. 'It's me that should be thankin' you.'

'I'll pop over to the Hall to see Brigie tomorrow and then I'll get a train to the Midlands and follow up the first lead then.'

'You do that.' She smiled tenderly at him, and once again he wished with all his heart that he could love her as she deserved to be loved.

Before going up to what he still thought of as the nursery floor to see Brigie the next morning, Dan went to see Jonathan, and he was heartened when his son looked towards him when he heard the door opening.

Crossing quickly to where the man was sitting in his usual window seat, Dan dropped down on his hunkers and taking his son's hand in his, he asked softly, 'So how are you feeling, Johnny?'

Although he remained silent, Jonathan's eyes stayed locked with his father's and Dan's heart skipped a beat. He could almost believe that there was recognition there.

Nurse Byng, who had been sitting in a chair reading a book, laid it aside and, crossing to them, placed her hand on Jonathan's arm as she told Dan, 'He's doing splendidly, aren't you, dear? The doctor thinks he might be well enough to go downstairs and spend a little time in the day room soon. It will beat being shut away in here all the time, won't it, sir?'

They both looked into Jonathan's eyes for signs of a reaction and when none was forthcoming, the nurse went on brightly, 'One tiny step at a time. That's the best we can hope for. It's early days yet.'

Dan swallowed the lump in his throat as he nodded and slowly rose. It broke his heart to see his son like this, but then as the nurse had pointed out, it was early days and he could only pray that Jonathan would emerge from the dark world that he currently inhabited, and come back into the light.

'So ... off up to see Mrs Bensham now, are you, sir?'

When Dan nodded, she leaned towards him and said in a low voice, 'She's not too good at the moment, I'm afraid. The doctor had to go into her during the night, apparently.'

'In that case, I had better get up there.' Dan gave his son's shoulder an affectionate squeeze and turned towards the door.

When Dan entered Anna's room some moments later she turned her head on the pillow towards him and he felt as if he had received a thump in the stomach, for suddenly she looked so old and frail that it frightened him. Her hands were lying limply on the eiderdown and her eyes, which had always seemed to be able to see into his very soul, looked dull and glazed.

'Dan, I am so glad you have come.'

The nurse who was sitting in the bedside chair rose and discreetly left the room, saying, 'Just ring the bell when you are ready to leave, sir.'

'Of course.' He waited until the door had closed softly behind her and then perched on the edge of the bed and took Anna's hand in his. Normally she would have scolded him for sitting there but today she made no comment.

'Are you feeling unwell, dear?' he asked gently.

Her head wagged feebly from side to side. 'It is not that I am unwell, Dan. It is just that I slept fitfully last night. My sleep was full of dreams – strange dreams that haunted me even when I awoke.'

'Perhaps you ate something that disagreed with you?' he suggested, but again she shook her head.

'No, no – it was nothing I ate. It was Thomas. He comes to me in my sleep. I think he is impatient for me to join him and ... I think he knows that I gave our child away and is displeased with me. Have you any news of her, Dan?'

'Not yet, Brigie, but as soon as I leave here I am going to resume the search. I will do all I can to find her, I promise you.'

'I know you will, dear. But ... well, I fear it is too late, which is why I am so pleased to see you now. I–'

'Don't say such things,' Dan scolded her, his voice laced with fear. It was not like Brigie to talk thus. 'You know what Harry always used to say, don't you? He said we would have to shoot you; that you would go on for ever.'

'Nothing is for ever,' she told him regretfully. 'And yet I am not afraid of death. My mind is still young and that makes it all the more difficult for it to be trapped in this old body. But never mind that

233

for now. There is something else I must entrust to you, just in case.' She stopped to draw breath before ordering him, 'Feel beneath my mattress ... just here.'

Feeling beneath the sheets and blankets, Dan moved his hand about until it closed around a small key. When he held it up she smiled weakly.

'That is the key to my safe. You will find it behind that picture on the wall over there. Inside is all my jewellery. And it is beautiful jewellery and worth a great deal of money. Harry always bought me a piece for an occasion, although I told him after the first year of being married that I did not need any more. Your father was a good man, Dan. And so was your mother, God rest their souls.'

Dan could not find words to answer, for his throat was full and so he merely nodded as she went on. 'Should you find my daughter, I want you to make sure that it is all passed on to her. It is little enough to give after the wrong I did her when I gave her away, but I hope it will show her that she was in my thoughts. Will you promise to do that for me, Dan?'

'Gladly. But what if I don't find her?'

'I have given that some thought, and if that should prove to be the case, then I want you to divide it between Hannah, Ruth and Constance.'

'Constance?'

'Yes. I know that we have been estranged for some years due to circumstance, but I still have a deep affection for her. At one time, she and her sister, Barbara, were my whole life, you see?'

His chin drooped and now it was her hand that gently squeezed his. 'Do not be sad,' she implored him. 'For there is nothing more sure than the fact that death comes to us all, whether we be peasants or kings. Life is for the living and I want you to promise me that you will live your life to the full from now on. You wasted too many years on Barbara. Will you do that for me, dear?'

'Yes, Brigie, I will try,' he told her, and now the tears rolled unashamedly down his face as he pressed her wrinkled hand to his cheek.

Part Three

The Search

Chapter Seventeen

Rain was lashing against the window of the train as Dan stared out across the rolling Warwickshire countryside. He had visited Nuneaton and found the first address that Meg had given him, and now on the journey home he was deeply perturbed. Mrs Gallimore, the woman he had traced, had told him of her adopted daughter's origins and Dan had realised immediately that this was not the woman he was seeking. But it was not this that was troubling him. It was the fact that another man had come asking the whereabouts of her daughter some short time before Dan's visit. Mr Wolfe, Mrs Gallimore had said his name was, but rack his brains as he would, Dan could not think of anyone else who might be looking for her.

He wondered if Meg had decided to send someone to help him in his search, but dismissed that idea almost immediately. Surely she would have informed him of her intentions if she had planned to do that?

The thought of her brought a hint of colour to his cheeks as he realised that he would now have to visit her again, and he instantly felt guilty. She was a married woman and he was now a married man again. So why then, he wondered, did he feel so strongly attracted to her?

As he strummed his fingers on the small wooden table that separated the seats in the train carriage,

239

his mind ran on. Perhaps he should take Ruth back to London with him, and combine business with pleasure? The more he thought of it, the better the idea seemed. They had not had a honeymoon and he could take her to a show, or to one of the silent movies with Rudolph Valentino in that she was so fond of seeing at the picture-house? Yes, that's what he would do. Ruth had never been to London. In fact, as far as he was aware, she had never ventured further than Newcastle. He could take her on the River Thames and show her some places of interest like the Tower of London and Buckingham Palace. She would like that, he was sure of it. And he knew that she would enjoy staying at the Ritz. She deserved a holiday and it would make a change for her to have someone waiting on her. Feeling somewhat better, he once again stared from the carriage window.

'Word 'as it that old Brigie is on her last legs,' Florrie Harper informed Lily as she slurped at the scalding tea Lily had just placed before her.

'Well, accordin' to gossip she's been about to peg it fer some time,' was Lily's caustic reply.

'Aye, 'tis true, but the doctor's been up an' down to her that many times in the last couple o' days it's a wonder as he ain't worn a hole in the stair-carpet. They reckon she's fadin' fast, so happen she won't be around long enough to find out what happened to her long-lost daughter after all.'

Sarah, who had stopped work in the dairy to join them for a mid-morning tea-break, scowled. If Brigie died before Dan discovered what had become of her daughter, all the cash she was paying Quentin Wolfe and his partner, Mr Peale, would be like money down the drain. She had been into their office earlier in the week, only to be informed that the first of their leads had led to nothing. For the first time she wondered what she would do if they did manage to find Brigie's daughter. She hadn't given it much thought before, but now as she pondered, her face dropped into a deep frown. She was no fool and had guessed that the private detectives were shady characters, to say the least. No doubt they would know of some way to stop the women being reunited. Perhaps Brigie's daughter could meet with a little accident? It would cost her dearly, no doubt – but oh, what sweet revenge it would be for all the heartache that Brigie had caused her. And in Sarah's twisted mind, the loveless marriage she had been forced to endure *was* Brigie's fault. She was quite aware that Brigie had always considered her to be beneath her – and Michael too, if it came to that, which was why she had refused to let Barbara marry him. Had he done so, Sarah would never have lost her leg to that she-witch and would probably be happily married to someone who loved her now; instead of which, she had spent the whole of her married life living in Barbara's shadow. She now asked herself, 'Could I be responsible for murder?' And the answer came back: '*Yes*,' if it concerned anyone to do with that whore living up at the Hall. The whore who had lived in sin with Thomas Mallen for years before tricking Harry Bensham into marrying her, and yet who still had the audacity to look down on *her!*

The anger inside her began to bubble, and

suddenly slamming her cup down onto the table she stood up and, ramming her crutch under her arm, she lurched from the room. Lily and Florrie raised their eyebrows and then their cups, and continued with their gossip.

'Are you feeling unwell again, Hannah? You look a little peaky.'

'I'm fine, dear. I just haven't woken up yet,' Hannah told her husband as she smiled at him across the breakfast-table.

Lawrie's shapeless mouth twisted into a smile as he piped up, 'Will we be going into town today, Hannah? I ... I have another load of carvings all packed up ready for the shop.'

It was Ben who answered him when he said, 'In that case then, I shall take you in. I think Hannah is hoping to go over to the Hall to see Brigie.'

Lawrie's face lit up. Ben had recently found a shopkeeper who had offered to display some of Lawrie's carvings in his window, on the understanding that if any of them sold, he would take a small commission. They had actually sold like hot cakes and now Lawrie seemed to be spending almost all of his time in the outhouse, busily whittling just to keep up with the demand. Ben was delighted for him, for the young man had a purpose in life now and was inordinately proud of his fast-growing savings. Not that he really needed the money, for Katie and Pat Ferrier, his parents, had left him admirably provided for. In fact, he was a very wealthy young man, not that Lawrie really understood the value of money.

Ben's main concern was Lawrie's health, for

lately he seemed to have slowed down somewhat. He had always suffered from a weak heart, which was part of his condition. Katie, Ben's aunt, had been devastated when she had discovered that Lawrie also had a heart condition. 'Mongolian imbecile' was the label the doctors had placed on him, but even so her devotion to him had been unfailing until the day she had died. Ben could remember only too well how she had glowed at his every small achievement, for each step that would be a normal step for the average child was a milestone for Lawrie.

When he rose and shuffled from the room, Ben now asked his wife, 'Do you think we should get the doctor to have a look at Lawrie? He seems to be getting very out of breath lately.'

'I had noticed. And yes, I think we should, but Ben... I hate to say this, for I know how much you love him, but... Well, Lawrie has already lived for far longer than the doctors expected him to. I think you should resign yourself to the fact that he is unlikely to have a long life.'

'I know. I know.' Ben flung himself away from the table and now he began to pace up and down the room. Somehow he could not envisage life without Lawrie. Oh, he knew that there were those who were wary of him, and he had become accustomed to the stares he often attracted when he or Hannah took him out. Not that he was ugly or frightening exactly. Just ... he sought in his mind for the right word to describe him but failed dismally. Lawrie was one on his own somehow, for despite the strangeness of his looks he was capable of giving unconditional love. Lawrie lumbered rather than walked and his eyes were slightly slanted, which gave him a faintly Oriental look. His mouth had a tendency to gape and when he cried, he cried as a child might. Yet even so, most people when they got to know him, grew to love him – all apart from his grandfather, Harry Bensham, that was. He had turned away from him from the first time he had set eyes on him, and refused to believe that his daughter could present him with such a child.

Ben had never understood that, for he had seen his grandfather pass pennies into the hands of beggars on the street in Newcastle. He had seen the look of pity that would light his eyes when he saw legless monstrosities being pushed around in barrows with tin mugs tied about their necks. And yet he had never accepted Lawrie until the day he died, the only saving grace being that Lawrie was not bright enough to realise it, although his daughter had. Her father's response to her only child had nearly broken her heart, for all she had ever heard from him was Ben this, or Harry that, or Jonathan the other...

Ben suddenly stopped his pacing and, with his face stiff and his mouth barely moving, he told her, 'I shall take him into the surgery whilst we are in town. No point in making the doctor travel out here when I am almost on his doorstep.' With that he turned and walked from the room and Hannah's hands clenched at her sides as tears started to her eyes.

She was aware of Ben's devotion to Lawrie and sometimes it frightened her, for how would it affect him when the inevitable happened? Sighing, she began to collect the dirty pots together. The sooner she got back to work, the better. She had too much time on her hands to think at the minute and she certainly had plenty to think about at present, but it was not anything that she could share with Ben. Not yet, at least. Not until she was quite sure.

The newly delivered carvings had all now been duly placed in the window, and Lawrie was hopping from foot to foot in his excitement as the shopkeeper handed him a small bag with the money he had made from the last lot.

'We shall have to take that straight to the bank,' Ben informed him with a twinkle in his eye. 'Then maybe visit the candy shop and choose a treat as you've done so well.'

Lawrie returned his smile and, after saying their goodbyes to the shopkeeper, they then made their way back out onto the street.

After depositing Lawrie's earnings into his bank account, Ben now led him towards the doctor's surgery, assuring him, 'It's only for a check-up, old chap, to make sure that everything is as it should be. And then we'll go straight to the...'

His voice trailed away as he looked across the street and spotted a young boy with striking black hair, through which grew a white streak. He gulped deeply as shock washed over him, for he might have been looking at a photograph of himself at that age.

'W ... what did you say, Cousin Ben?'

Ben glanced briefly at Lawrie and when he next looked across the street, the small boy had vanished as if he had never been.

Dragging his attention back to Lawrie, Ben took his elbow and steered him along. 'Come on,' he urged. 'The time is running on and Hannah will be getting worried about us.' And all the time a picture of the child he had just glimpsed was flashing before his eyes.

'So the long an' the short of it is, this trek to this 'ere Mrs Gallimore was a wasted journey.'

'I would hardly call it that.' Dan was standing in front of the fire and Ruth was laying out the cutlery on a crisp white tablecloth for their evening meal. 'At least I have crossed off one of the names from the list. I dare say it will have to be a process of elimination.'

'So what's the next step?'

'I shall have to go back to Mrs Fellows in London and get the address of the next adoptive parents on the list.'

Ruth now paused to ask him, 'Why didn't you just write down the names an' addresses of *all* of 'em an' be done with it when you were last there?'

'I er ... I suppose I could have done that, couldn't I?' Dan suddenly felt very foolish. Could it be that if he only took one address at a time, he had an excuse to go back and see Meg Fellows again? He puffed hastily on his cigar. Barbara had never allowed him to smoke in the house, other than in his study – but Ruth never objected. In fact, she assured him that she liked the smell of cigars. Not that she said the same when Mary Ann lit up a cigarette, mind. The young woman had informed her that it was fashionable for women to smoke nowadays, but the first time Ruth had seen her puffing on a cigarette in a long holder she had almost hit the roof.

'Fashionable me arse,' she had scolded. 'If someone tells you it's fashionable to throw yourself under a tram, will you do that an' all?' Mary Ann had exchanged an amused glance with her father and then Ruth had tutted her disapproval and stormed from the room.

Now Dan asked her, 'I was wondering if you would like to come to London with me this time? I thought a little break would do you good. We could go to a show and do a bit of sightseeing, and I thought I'd take you to the Hammersmith Palais de Danse. It's only recently been opened and I believe the Dixieland Jazz Band are playing there at present. So, what do you say?'

'*Me* ... go to London?'

'Yes, why not?'

Ruth leaned heavily on the edge of the table before saying, 'Well, I ain't got the right clothes to wear for a start. An' who would look after Mary Ann?'

Dan laughed aloud. 'For a start off I think Mary Ann is quite old enough to look after herself for a few days, and secondly, once we get to London you can treat yourself to as many new clothes as you like. You'll certainly have plenty of choice there.'

He gently took her into his arms. '*Please* say yes, my love. We could treat it as a honeymoon, if you like. And you'd get to meet Pip. You said you would love to meet him, didn't you?' It was suddenly important that she came with him, perhaps because if she did, it would go some way towards salving his conscience for the uncanny feelings that sprang to life every time he thought of Meg Fellows.

Ruth stared up at him indecisively but at that moment Mary Ann walked into the room and asked teasingly, 'What's this then?'

'I was just trying to persuade your mother to come to London with me for a few days but she seems to think you need her here to look after you.'

'Oh *really*, Mam. I'm a grown woman. Get yourself off and enjoy it. I shall be perfectly all right and I doubt very much that the house will fall down if you leave it for a while.'

'Don't be so sarcastic, madam, else I'll skelp your ear,' Ruth told her, but there was a twinkle in her eye and a bubble of excitement forming in the pit of her stomach. 'An' where would we stay if I did come with you?' she asked Dan. 'I'm not sayin' that I will, mind, I'm just askin'.'

'We'd stay at the Ritz,' he told her. 'Just think of it ... wall-to-wall carpets that your feet sink into. Crystal chandeliers that almost blind you ... chambermaids to make your bed, and waiters to serve all your meals. There won't be a pot in sight for you to wash.'

She slapped at him playfully now as she told him, 'All right, I'll think about it.' And with that she disentangled herself from his arms and walked towards the kitchen.

Mary Ann winked at her father before saying, 'I think you can take that as a yes.' They then fell together and smothered their laughter as they looked towards the kitchen.

At that precise moment, up at the Hall, Nurse Byng was screaming, *'Doctor, Doctor!'* as she burst from Jonathan's room and out onto the landing.

Within seconds, footsteps were heard thumping up the stairs and the Matron, closely followed by a red-faced doctor, spilled onto the landing.

'Whatever is the matter, Nurse Byng?' Matron gasped.

Waving her hand in the direction of Jonathan's room, the nurse told them, 'Listen!'

Both the Matron and the doctor took a step towards the door and it was then that they heard it – faintly at first but growing stronger.

'It's a long way to Tipperary...'

'Why, he's singing!'

'Yes, and that isn't all.' Nurse Byng's cheeks were glowing with excitement. 'I was giving him a drink from his beaker when he suddenly took it from my hand, said thank you, and drank it all by himself.'

As one, they all strode into the room and instantly Jonathan's head turned towards them. Flashing them a weary smile, he told them haltingly, 'F ... feel tired.'

'Then let's get you back into bed, young man. Could you but know it, you've just taken a major step forward, but we don't want you overdoing it, now do we?'

Matron tossed back the bedclothes and, approaching Jonathan, she took his elbow and led him towards the bed, where she slid his dressing-gown from his shoulders before telling him, 'Well done, sir.'

Jonathan climbed slowly into bed as Matron settled the blankets across him with a wide grin on her face. Oh, there was no doubt about it; there were times like this when she loved her job. Oh, yes she did.

She now shooed both the nurse and the doctor back out onto the landing and there she told them, 'Give him a couple of weeks and he should be able to come out of there and go into one of the dormitories – if he wants to, that is. I think he's turned the corner and I'm wondering – should we let Mr Bensham know? I've no doubt the news will make his day.'

Nurse Byng, who was due to go off duty in an hour's time, said, 'I shall be passing by Ben and Hannah's cottage when I knock off. I could perhaps call in and tell them, and then no doubt Ben would pass the news on to his father?'

'What a good idea, Nurse.' Matron beamed her approval and then they all went about their business with a smile on their faces. It was nice to think that Jonathan was going to recover, for he was a good lad – a lovely lad, in fact, Matron thought. If only all the officers who had passed through the Hall could have fared as well! Determined not to think of the poor souls who had eventually had to be shipped off to mental asylums, she kept the smile fixed firmly in place and tried hard to hold on to her happier thoughts.

Chapter Eighteen

Lawrie looked from one to another of them with his cavelike mouth gaping loosely open. Everyone was happy and smiling, and that made him happy too. He just wished this pain in his chest would go away. It had been troubling him for some days now, more so for some reason, since Cousin Ben had taken him into Newcastle to see the doctor. The doctor had listened to his chest and then grinned at him as he ruffled his hair before turning away to talk to Cousin Ben. He liked the doctor. He was kind, and he always gave him a sweet whenever he saw him.

He looked drowsily around the room one more time, moving from one smiling face to another. Uncle Dan and Ruthie were there, and so was Mary Ann, and a nice young man she had brought with her. Lawrie had never seen the young man before but he liked him because he had introduced himself to Lawrie and shaken his hand as he told him that his name was Tom. Cousin Ben was refilling everyone's glasses with sherry and port, and Hannah had allowed him to have a sip of hers. He hadn't really liked it. It wasn't half as nice as the lemonade that Nancy made him, and it had burned his throat and brought tears to his eyes as it slid down his throat, which had made everyone laugh. Now he was tired, for as he glanced at the clock he saw that the little hand was pointing to nine, which meant it was way past his bedtime. Everyone was celebrating because Cousin Jonathan was going to get better. Nurse Byng had called in to tell them so earlier on, and since then the house had been filled with laughter. He decided to creep away to the outhouse where he had left the lights burning, and then he would come back and get tucked into his own comfortable little bed. He thought of telling Hannah where he was going, but when he looked across at her, he saw that she was deep in conversation with Mary Ann, whose eyes were sparkling as she showed off a ring that she was wearing on her left hand.

Quietly he slipped into the hall and headed towards the front door, stiffing a yawn as he went. It wouldn't take him many minutes to shut off the lights and then he would go off to bed. He closed the front door behind him and then shuddered as the chilly air hit him like a slap in the face. It had been raining for most of the day and now the moon was struggling from behind the big black clouds overhead and a mist was floating across the ground. The whinnying of a horse made him pause, and looking towards the gate at the end of the garden path, he saw a horse and trap tethered there.

He frowned as he wondered who it could be. Uncle Dan and Ruth had arrived in an automobile taxicab with Mary Ann and Tom, so he reasoned that it could not be theirs. Cautiously he rounded the side of the house that led to the outbuildings. It was dark here save for the light he had left burning, but that did not penetrate this far across the garden. He was walking towards it when a movement from the corner of his eye halted him. There was someone trying to see through the gap in the curtains in the room where all the merriment was taking place.

For all of his life, Lawrie had been surrounded by people who loved him, so he now fearlessly approached them as he said into the darkness, 'Hello, who is there?'

He heard someone curse softly under their breath and swing about but it was too dark to see who it was.

Again he asked, 'Who is there?'

The figure was moving towards him and now as the moon sailed from behind a cloud he found himself face to face with Sarah, Hannah's mother. Lawrie had never liked Sarah, for she always scowled at him and never spoke to him, but now she did as she hissed, *'Get out of me way, you big gormless idiot you.'*

Lawrie's mouth dropped open. Her crutch was swinging from side to side as she lumbered towards him and suddenly he felt afraid.

'Cousin J ... Jonathan is g ... going to get better,' he informed her and his voice came out as a squeak as she glared at him.

'Huh! An' that's a matter for rejoicin', is it? The fact that another Mallen will soon be on the loose again?'

At a loss as to what to do, Lawrie stood there with his hands hanging slackly at his sides.

'I'd come to have a word to Hannah, but no doubt she'll be too took up with that lot in there. It's a pretty kettle o' fish when a daughter puts her in-laws and half-wits like you afore her own mother, ain't it?'

Lawrie now knew real fear for the first time in his whole life and his heart began to pound as she spat, 'Get out o' me way, will you? Or do I have to give you a taste o' this!'

Lifting her crutch, she now swung it towards him threateningly, and as Lawrie ducked to avoid the blow, his feet slipped on the wet grass and he felt himself falling. He landed heavily, but totally ignoring him, Sarah tramped past him and seconds later he heard her clamber into the trap and urge the horse on.

He lay there trying to get his breath back, for the fall had badly winded him. But the pain in his chest was worse now and somehow his legs wouldn't do as they were told.

He opened his mouth to shout for Cousin Ben but no sound came out, and so he lay there until at last his eyelashes fluttered across his eyes and a comforting darkness claimed him.

It was a merry party that trooped from the house late that night. Dan had ordered the taxicab to come back and collect them at midnight, and he had to help Ruth to it, for after two glasses of sherry she was tipsy, much to everyone's amusement. They left with promises of being back the next day so that they could all go and visit Jonathan.

Once Ben and Hannah had waved their party off they went back into the cottage with their arms about each other. In the warmth of the hallway, Ben kicked the door shut behind him and hugging his wife, he smiled down into her face.

'Well, I think we could safely say that was a very good evening. Wouldn't you agree, Mrs Bensham?'

'I certainly would, Mr Bensham.' Her eyes were dancing with merriment and although Hannah had never been known as a beauty, in that moment to Ben she was perfect.

She now gently pushed him aside, however, as she told him, 'I'm just going to go and tell Nancy to leave the dirty pots for tonight. You know what she's like – if I don't, she'll be up till all hours and there's nothing that can't wait till morning.'

'Well, don't be too long about it,' Ben teased. 'I'll go up and get the bed warm.' He strode towards the stairs but then paused to ask, 'Has Lawrie gone up?'

'I should think so. You know what he's like if it goes past his bedtime. Bless him, the last time I looked at him he looked worn out, so don't get going in to him tonight and disturbing him.'

'Yes, Boss.' Dan did a comical salute and then taking the stairs two at a time, he hurried away.

Shortly afterwards, as they lay wrapped in each other's arms, he whispered into the darkness, 'It's been a grand evening, and grand news about Johnny. I have a feeling that things are going to get better for us from now on.'

She sighed heavily as she wrestled with her conscience. There was something she had been keeping from him but now, after such a pleasant evening, she felt the time would never be more right to come out with it.

'As you say, Ben, it is wonderful news about Johnny. And there is something else I have to tell you that is wonderful too. I hadn't intended to for a while. But... Well, the thing is, I think I may be pregnant again. I have made an appointment to see the doctor next week and I wasn't going to say anything until then because of raising your hopes, but–'

Ben startled her when he sat bolt upright in the bed and fumbled with the bedside light, and when it was finally glowing he said, 'Oh darling, that's wonderful – but isn't it too soon after...? I mean, will you be all right?'

She laughed as she pulled herself up onto the pillows and told him, 'Of course I'll be all right. It is a little soon, admittedly, but these things happen. Of course, until I've seen the doctor I can't be absolutely sure, but–'

She had no time to say more, for he had clasped her in his arms, and as he buried his face in her firm breasts he cried like a baby – and they were tears of pure joy.

After stabling the horse Sarah crossed the farmyard and slipped into the darkened room. She was just making her way towards the staircase when a voice from the darkness demanded, 'And where have you been till this time of night?'

She heard someone fumbling with a box of matches and then the oil lamp sputtered into life and she saw Constance staring across at her in the glow it cast.

'I er ... I felt the need for some fresh air.'

'Fresh air at this time of night? And if you only needed fresh air, why did you take the pony and trap?'

Sarah's temper snapped as she shouted furiously, 'Do I have to be accountable to you for my every move? I sometimes feel that I am in a prison!'

Constance's back stiffened and her hands came together at her waist as she looked across at her daughter-in-law. Sarah had changed so much that Constance could scarcely remember the fun-loving girl she had once been; the girl whom she had urged her only son to marry – and what a mistake that had turned out to be! But it was too late to turn back the clock now. What was done was done and now they were all the other had, for it was widely known that Sarah's daughter had little time for her, and secretly, Constance understood why.

'I ... I'm sorry.' The old woman's voice was weary. 'I did not wish to interrogate you. I was merely concerned for your safety. It isn't safe to go riding about on the fells at this time of night, as well you know. But get to your bed now. We can talk more in the morning.'

Sarah's thin lips formed into a straight line as she stalked away, and turning her head towards the fire, Constance stared into the dying flames as despair washed over her.

When Ben and Hannah appeared the next morning they found the table all laid for breakfast. They found this mildly surprising, as Nancy had had more than a tipple or two the night before, and the last they had seen of her, she had been in the kitchen with Fred, and they had been giggling like a pair of youngsters.

The appetising smell of bacon and liver frying

was issuing from the kitchen and Ben rubbed his stomach as he told his wife, 'My – that smells good. I could eat for England today.'

Hannah laughed as she walked towards the kitchen door. 'Then get yourself to the table and I'll see what I can do to hurry it up. I wouldn't want you wasting away, now would I?'

He playfully slapped at her backside as they parted and once in the dining room he looked around for a sign of Lawrie. The room was empty and now his smile broadened. Lawrie was always up with the lark but the impromptu party of the night before must have tired him. Moving back into the hallway he shouted in the direction of the kitchen, 'I'm going to wake Sleeping Beauty up. We must have tired the poor chap out with all that jollity. But you know what he's like for his belly. He'll never forgive me if I let him miss fried liver. I'm surprised the smell of it hasn't woken him.'

Whistling merrily, he mounted the stairs, tapped lightly on Lawrie's bedroom door and shouted, 'Come on, sleepy head! Nancy's cooking you your favourite this morning.' He paused and when there was no reply he inched the door open and peered towards the bed. It was neatly made and of Lawrie there was no sign. He went back downstairs and after entering the kitchen he remarked, 'That's funny. Lawrie must already be up and about. Have you seen him, Nancy?'

'No.' She turned her eyes from the eggs she was frying to comment, 'He must be in the outhouse. You'd best go over there and fetch him in. You know what he's like when he gets whittling. He tends to lose track of time.'

Without further comment, Ben headed to the door and once outside he stared towards the outhouse, where he could see a light shining out from the window into the cold overcast morning. Once inside it, he looked around, but again there was no sign of Lawrie, and now the smile disappeared and a frown took its place.

Ben began to feel worried. It wasn't like Lawrie at all to just go off. Crossing to a carving of a lamb that was almost finished, he raised it to the light. It was absolutely exquisite, from the tip of its nose to the end of its tail, and once again Ben was stunned to realise how talented Lawrie was when it came to carving.

The boy had a gift, as his mother had long ago recognised. She had encouraged him in his hobby, and this beautiful piece of work and the many others that he had made were the result. Ben's eyes softened as he thought of how proud Katie would have been of him now, could she have seen him. But then he pushed the sad thought aside. This was a day for happy thoughts. Jonathan was on the long road to recovery. And added to that was the news that he was about to become a father again. He could hardly dare to believe it after the heartache of the stillbirth just a couple of short months ago, but then as Brigie had always insisted, God moves in mysterious ways.

Turning about, Ben strode out of the workshop, cupped his hands about his mouth and shouted, *'Lawrie!'*

The sound echoed back from the open fells beyond, but other than that there was silence. His face was tight with concern now as he made his way back into the kitchen and asked, 'Is there still no sign of him?'

Hannah was crouched on her knees, holding a long toasting fork with a slice of bread on it towards the fire. She looked up and answered, 'No – isn't he in the workshop?'

She saw the worry settle across Ben's face and rising, she placed the bread down on the table as she said, 'Come on, we'll get our coats on and have a scout round for him. He won't have gone far. Lawrie never ventures further than the garden gate usually.'

They wrapped up warmly in the hallway, and when they bumped into Fred outside, Hannah told him, 'You walk that way up the lane and I'll go towards the Hall with Ben. One of us is sure to find him. I'll guarantee he won't have gone far.'

With a curt nod Fred strode away but when they all met up again almost an hour later, they had still not glimpsed so much as a sight of him and now they were all deeply concerned.

'Perhaps we should get the trap out and see if he's gone into town?' Hannah suggested. It would have been the first time Lawrie had ever done such a thing, but she could think of nothing else.

They now all made their way around the side of the house together as they moved in the direction of the stable – and that was when they saw him. He was lying in the damp grass beneath the parlour window and he was so pale that Hannah feared he was dead.

As one they rushed towards him and dropped to their knees as she and Ben each took one of his cold hands into their own.

'*Oh my God, Oh my God,*'Ben chanted over and over again, and suddenly he was teetering on the edge of a great gaping hole again.

Seeing his deep distress, Hannah said sharply, 'Stop it, Ben and pull yourself together. You will be no good to Lawrie if you fall apart.' She quickly undid the buttons on Lawrie's waistcoat and, plunging her hand beneath it, felt for a heartbeat. She thought that she could detect one, but it was so weak that she could not be sure, and so now she lifted his hand and, gripping his wrist, she felt for a pulse. Again, it was there but it was so weak that it terrified her.

'Right.' She knew that she would have to take control of the situation, for Ben seemed to have gone into shock. 'It's imperative that we get him into the warm immediately. Run and fetch Nancy. It's going to take all of us to lift him.'

Without a word, Ben ran to do as he was told, only to reappear with a white-faced Nancy at his heels seconds later.

'Eeh, me poor little lamb.' Nancy too was deeply upset as she stared down on Lawrie's inert figure, and screwed her apron into a ball at her waist.

'Nancy, you get a leg and I'll get the other.' Hannah began to bark out orders. 'And you, Ben and Fred, lift him under the arms. Between the four of us we should be able to get him into the parlour.'

Loving his food as he did, Lawrie was no lightweight and by the time they had deposited him gently onto the settee in the parlour they were all out of breath.

'Now, Nancy, run and get some blankets and a shelf from the oven. And you get up to the Hall and fetch the doctor, Ben. It will be quicker than going into town. Take the horse, it will save time.'

'I could do that,' Fred offered, but Hannah shook her head.

'No, Fred, thank you, but it would be better if Ben went. The doctor knows us and will come straight away for him.'

Fred nodded, and as they ran to do as they were bid, Hannah began to rub at Lawrie's frozen limbs before beginning to undo his damp clothing.

'We need to get these wet clothes off him,' she told Nancy when she reappeared, clutching a bundle of blankets in one hand and a shelf from the oven in another. Very gently they undressed him and Hannah then wrapped the blankets about his still form and slipped the oven shelf beneath his feet.

'That's about all we can do now until the doctor arrives.' Hannah rose and, glancing towards the clock, she prayed that he would not be too long in coming, for a feeling of dread had wrapped itself around her like a shroud.

It was almost an hour later when the doctor reined the horse to a shuddering halt at the gate. After hastily tying him to the post he snatched his black bag from the saddle and ran the length of the path and burst into the hallway.

'Doctor Stroud, he's in here.' Hannah was glad that it was this doctor who had come, for although she had met him only once before, she had been greatly impressed with his medical knowledge. He had only recently gone to reside at the Hall after spending most of the war on the front line with the men. He was young and had an easygoing manner about him that had already endeared him to both staff and patients alike. The atrocities he had been forced to witness whilst caring for the soldiers in battle had also made him an extremely good listener.

'I rode back on Ben's horse to save time,' he told Hannah. 'Your husband is following on foot. Where is the patient?'

'In here.'

He stepped past her and Nancy rose from her place beside Lawrie and joined Hannah in the hall, closing the parlour door softly behind her.

'I'll get Fred to take the horse round to the stable, lass,' she said to Hannah. 'Meanwhile, why don't you go an' put the kettle on. We'll mash a pot o' tea while the doctor examines him, eh?'

With that she turned about and pottered away as Hannah went to do as she was bid with a heavy heart. It was almost ten minutes later when the door to the parlour opened again and the doctor emerged. Hannah beckoned him into the kitchen and solemn-faced he joined her there as she motioned him to a chair.

Her hand shook as she began to pour him a mug of tea. 'So, how is he?'

Dr Stroud gratefully accepted the tea she pushed towards him and now, staring down into the steaming liquid, he told her, 'His heart is very weak, I'm afraid. Added to that is the fact that Ben thinks he may have lain outdoors in this weather all night. He is now running a dangerously high temperature. I think what we need to do now is get him upstairs into bed and then someone is going to have to stay with him. Until he comes around I really cannot say much more. I'm so sorry.'

A moment later, Ben exploded through the door. He had run all the way from the Hall but still he found the breath to ask, 'Well?'

When the doctor repeated what he had told Hannah, Ben put a hand over his eyes and tears squeezed past them. 'But what could have happened to make him collapse like that?' he asked in a muffled voice.

The doctor shrugged. 'It could be that he had a stroke or even a mild heart-attack. All the signs point that way, but as I said, until he comes round there is not much more I can do.'

It was two hours later; two hours that had seemed to last a lifetime, and now Lawrie was tucked up in his own bed with Hannah and Ben sitting at either side of him as they anxiously watched for a sign of him waking.

Whereas before he had been dangerously pale, his face was now flushed and his breathing was laboured. As instructed by the doctor, Nancy had placed a bowl of cold water at the side of the bed and Hannah constantly rinsed a flannel in it and wiped it about his sweating face in an attempt to bring down his temperature. Dr Stroud had left a short time ago with the promise that he would be back later in the day, and now all they could do was wait.

Nancy had been dispatched to tell Dan what had happened. She arrived at Ruth's little house to find him engrossed in a Hercule Poirot book, a detective novel by a new novelist called Agatha Christie. He immediately laid it aside as Nancy gabbled out to him what had happened, and then he snatched up his coat and together they made the return journey.

The doctor called again later in the afternoon as promised, by which time Lawrie was muttering incoherently as his head wagged from side to side on the pillow. His chest rose and fell alarmingly with each laboured breath he took, and when the doctor had listened to it, he slowly shook his head.

'It sounds to me like he has developed pneumonia.' His voice was grave. 'I'm afraid it could go either way now. I should think the fever will break sometime during the next twenty-four hours and then it is in God's hands. I'm so sorry, but there is nothing more I can do. Keep him cool and try to get some liquids into him.' When he snapped his bag shut the sound was like that of a gunshot in the silence that had settled on the room. He paused in the doorway to tell them, 'The instant there is any change, do not hesitate to fetch me.' He then closed the door softly behind him and they heard his footsteps descending the stairs as they gazed at each other numbly.

It was almost too much to take in. Only last night they had been celebrating Jonathan's first step towards recovery and the house had rung with laughter. And now, less than twenty-four hours later, they were having to face the fact that they might lose Lawrie, who had become an important part of their lives.

Nancy sniffed loudly before saying, 'Right. Let's work out a rota. There's no sense in us all losing sleep, so why don't you two go and have a rest? I'll do the first watch with him and then one of you can come and take over later on.'

'Thank you, Nancy, but no. I think I'd like to stay with him.' This was from Hannah and Ben's head bobbed in agreement.

'So would I, so why don't you take Father down to the kitchen, Nancy, and make him a meal?'

Dan and Nancy trooped sadly from the room and as the young couple looked towards the person lying on the bed, their vigil began.

It was now almost midnight and, as yet, Lawrie had shown no sign of waking although his head was still thrashing from side to side on the sweat-dampened pillows. Every now and again he would call out incoherently, but other than that he showed no sign of knowing that the two people he loved most in the world were there. Dr Stroud had come and gone again, feeling utterly helpless; there was nothing he could do to help the poor soul. He had grave suspicions that Lawrie might have suffered a stroke, for only one side of his body seemed to show movement. He had not as yet commented on it, since it was obvious that Ben and Hannah were distressed enough as it was. There would be time enough to discuss the implications of that, when – or if – Lawrie regained consciousness.

Throughout the long day, Nancy had brought meals up to them on a tray with the warning, 'You have to keep your strength up. You'll be no good to Lawrie when he comes round if you don't, now will you?'

Even so, she had carried each meal away untouched and now she had slipped into a doze at the side of the kitchen fire. Ben had told her to go to bed hours ago, when Dan had left, with promises that he would return first thing in the morning, but she had chosen not to. Hannah too had fallen asleep with her head resting on the side of the bed and Fred had sadly retired to his rooms above the stable-block. But Ben was ever watchful, praying that Lawrie would pull through as he gently washed his face and hands over and over again with cold water. He constantly cursed himself as guilt wrapped itself around him. Why hadn't he checked on Lawrie the evening before, as he usually did? If he had, Lawrie would not have had to lie out in the bitter cold all night, and the condition he was in now might have been avoided. It had become almost a ritual, their goodnights. Ben would go in and tuck the blankets around him as he would have a child and Lawrie would tell him, 'Good night, sleep tight, hope the bed bugs don't bite.' Just as his mother Katie had once told him. And now for this to happen on the one and only night when Ben had not gone into him! He knew that he would carry the guilt of it to his grave.

The long night stretched on, with only the sounds of Hannah's gentle snores to disturb the silence, and still the raging fever showed no signs of breaking. Eventually, Ben too slipped into an uneasy sleep as he held fast to Lawrie's burning hand. It was as the first cold fingers of dawn were streaking the sky that he suddenly started awake and looked towards Lawrie, who had now ceased to thrash about the bed.

He cried out with relief even as he knuckled the

sleep from his eyes when he saw Lawrie silently observing him, and the sound brought Hannah springing awake too.

'Oh, my dear.' She was the first to stroke Lawrie's childlike face. 'You gave us such a terrible fright. How are you feeling?'

Lawrie's mouth worked but no sounds issued from it, so Hannah took up a glass of water and, gently lifting his head from the pillow, she held it to his parched lips. He was still dangerously hot and seemed to be trying to tell her something.

'S ... Sa...'

He dropped back against the pillows exhausted as Ben told him softly, 'Don't try to talk just yet, old chap. God willing you are over the worst now that the fever has broken, so try and sleep, eh? Hannah and I will be right here when you wake up, I promise.'

Lawrie's eyelids closed and just as Ben had advised, he was soon fast asleep.

Ben and Hannah exchanged a relieved glance and she saw that tears of relief had started to Ben's eyes. Moving around the bed, she wrapped him in her arms and told him, 'Why don't you go down to the kitchen and make us both a nice cup of tea? I think I could drink one, now that I know he's over the worst.'

Ben nodded as with a final glance at Lawrie, he walked from the room. When he entered the kitchen, Nancy started awake and asked guiltily, 'Good Lord, what time is it? I must have dropped off. How is he?'

'I think he's turned the corner. At least his fever seems to have broken,' Ben told her and she could hear the relief in his voice. 'And as for what the time is, I thought I told you last night to get yourself off to bed?'

'Happen you did. But I wanted to be at hand should you need anything. Now, how about I make us all a nice hot drink an' a bite to eat?'

Ben nodded gratefully as he sank down into a chair and yawned. 'That sounds wonderful, Nancy. Hannah had sent me down to make a cup of tea as it happens, but if you're offering I won't argue.'

Nancy rose and stretched painfully before pottering away to put the kettle on. Soon she was carrying yet another tray up the stairs with Ben close at her heels. But this time they drank the tea and also ate the hot buttered toast she had made them.

'Poor lamb is wet through with sweat,' she commented as she looked towards the sleeping figure on the bed. 'Perhaps we should change him?'

'Not until he wakes up,' Hannah told her. 'I don't want to disturb him while he is sleeping so peacefully.' Addressing Ben now she said, 'Why don't you go and get washed and changed? I'll stay here and then I'll do the same when you come back.'

Ben nodded and hurried away, and twenty minutes later he was back, looking a lot better. He now took Hannah's seat at the side of the bed as she slipped away. Outside, a cock was crowing and the trees were alive with the sound of birdsong. He had become so immersed in listening to them that it was some seconds before he realised that Lawrie was awake again.

'Hello.' He gently stroked Lawrie's damp palm and for no reason that he could explain, a feeling of dread descended on him as Lawrie flashed him a smile.

'I ... I have to go away, Cousin Ben.'

'You are not going anywhere,' Ben quickly assured him, but Lawrie shook his head.

'Mamma came to see me. Sh ... she is w ... waiting for me. And Papa.'

'*No!*' The word exploded from Ben's lips like a bullet from a gun as panic gripped him. Tears spurted from his eyes and now Lawrie's face became sad as he told him, 'Don't b ... be sad, Cousin Ben. I am not af ... afraid. It is a beautiful place I am g ... going to.'

'Please, Lawrie – you have to stop talking like this.' Ben had now wrapped Lawrie in his arms and was lying beside him on the bed as a sweet smile settled across Lawrie's face. He was looking beyond his cousin's shoulder to a corner of the room, and now he lifted his hand as if he were reaching out to someone.

'Lawrie, *listen to me.*' Ben's words stopped abruptly when Lawrie's head suddenly slipped to one side and his hand fell back onto the counterpane. Almost beside himself with grief, Ben cried, 'Lawrie, *stop it.* Do you hear me? You can't leave me. It was you who brought me back from the brink. I *need* you.' Even as the words were uttered he knew that Lawrie was already gone from him, and now he held him against his chest and sobbed as if his heart would break.

He was still in the same position when Hannah and Nancy entered the room some minutes later.

Realising what had happened, Nancy's hand clapped across her mouth as she made the sign of the cross on her chest with the other.

Lawrie looked so peaceful. In fact, in death he looked almost handsome, with no sign of the imbecile, as he had been labelled, about him.

'May God take his soul,' Nancy muttered, and then lowering her head she too wept as Hannah looked on in shocked disbelief.

It was not until the day before his funeral that Hannah remarked as they all sat in the kitchen, 'I wonder what Lawrie was trying to tell us when he woke up for the first time? He seemed very agitated. Something beginning with *sa*, wasn't it?'

'He were probably trying to tell you that he felt sad,' Nancy said objectively. 'Lawrie always said that he was sad if anything upset his routine, God rest his soul.'

'You're probably right,' Hannah sighed, and once again a silence settled on the room as they all felt his loss.

Chapter Nineteen

Four perfectly matched black horses with high feather plumes dancing above their manes pawed impatiently at the ground as the solid mahogany coffin was carried from the house by four solemn-faced pallbearers. The feathers on their black top hats swayed in the breeze, to match those on the horses' heads. Gently they slid the coffin into the glass hearse, being careful not to disturb the many wreaths that were placed around its sides. There were spring flowers of every colour imaginable, and as Ben leaned heavily on Hannah's arm he thought how much Lawrie would have liked them. Lawrie had always loved flowers. He had loved every living thing, now Ben came to think of it. He recalled an incident when the cat had once come into the kitchen with a dead bird in its mouth, and how Lawrie had openly sobbed before insisting that Ben should give the poor bird a proper burial in the garden. And now here he was, about to bury Lawrie.

It was raining and the sky was heavy and overcast. A row of horses and traps as well as automobiles stretched way back down the Lane as the mourners waited to follow the hearse on Lawrie's final journey. He was to be laid to rest beside his mother and his father in the Ferrier family mausoleum, as his mother had requested before she passed away.

Ben glanced towards the outhouse where the crib that Lawrie had lovingly carved for their baby was housed. Somehow he determined he would get through today, for soon, the child that Hannah was carrying would rest in it, as would all the other children that he hoped would follow. And one day, when they were older, he would tell them about the gentle man who had made it.

As Mr Wolfe passed the bandstand in Southend, he pulled the lapels of his jacket more tightly about him and shuddered. He had no doubt that the holidaymakers who flocked there in the summer would think it a grand place but now at the beginning of March the streets were almost deserted and there was a cold wind blowing in from the sea that had chilled him to the bone. He had not long since passed the Westcliffe Parade where the Royal Family were known to stay, and now he was looking for Wilson Road. He found himself in Alexander Road, and then Cambridge Street, and then at last he saw the sign he was seeking. Wilson Road consisted of three-storey Victorian townhouses that must have been very impressive in their day. Now most of them were displaying bed and breakfast signs in their windows, no doubt to cater for the people who swarmed there in the summer.

When he arrived at the right number, he saw that this too was displaying a Vacancies sign in the window. He rapped at the door and waited. Some moments later, a plump middle-aged woman appeared in the doorway.

'Looking for a room, were you, dearie?' she asked in a friendly manner.

'No, dear lady. Though had I been, I have no doubt that your establishment would have suited my needs perfectly! In actual fact, I am looking for someone and wondered if you could help me.'

'Oh yes, and who would that be then?'

'Well, the family I am seeking lived here some years ago. Their name was...' He paused to scratch his head as if he was trying to remember. 'What was it now...? I'm afraid my memory has a habit of letting me down. It began with R.'

She now told him apologetically, 'I'm afraid I'm

not going to be able to help you then. My husband and I have only lived here for seven years and we bought the house from a lady called Mrs Franks.'

'Oh, I see.' Disappointment clouded his face, and seeing that she was about to close the door, he asked hurriedly, 'Would you happen to know of anyone else in the street who might know of their whereabouts? The couple I am seeking lived here some fifty odd years ago. In truth, I realise that they may not even be alive now.'

'Mm...' She pondered on his question for a moment before telling him, 'The only person I can think of who might be able to help you is Mrs Thederman. She lives in the very end house over there and she's as old as the hills. From what I've heard, she's lived here most of her life. You could try there.'

'Thank you, dear lady. You have been most helpful. I shall do that. Good day to you.'

As he turned away, the landlady thought what a charming man he was, but then she went about her business and in no time at all he was forgotten.

Mr Wolfe, meantime, was making his way towards the house she had pointed out to him. There was a deep scowl on his face. He was cold and hungry, and in two minds to stay in Southend for the night if he had no luck at this address. Yes, that's what he would do, he decided. Even if he found the person he was seeking. He would add the hotel bill to the list of Mrs Radlet's expenses, and he might even throw in a slap-up meal.

In a slightly better frame of mind again he tapped briskly at the door. The windows of this property looked grimy and neglected, and the small front garden was overgrown with weeds. After he had knocked on the door three times and still received no response, Quentin Wolfe turned away and, jamming his hands into his coat pocket, he strode off down the road. He would go and find somewhere decent to stay for the night, not one of these dumps, have a nice meal and try again tomorrow. Humming at the prospect of a full belly and a warm bed, he hurried away on his long legs.

'I can hardly believe it,' Constance said sadly.

As usual, Florrie Harper had come hotfoot from the Hall on her first day off to inform the people at Wolfbur Farm of Lawrie's death.

'From what's bein' said, he lay outside in the cold an' wet all night.' Florrie loved nothing better than having a captive audience and now she was well in her stride. 'They think he might have had a stroke, though God knows what could have brought it on. He were in the best o' spirits earlier in the night, accordin' to form. Mind you, I know I shouldn't say it but the chap always fair gave me the creeps. Ugh, wi' those big starin' eyes an' that slack mouth o' his.'

Constance's back stiffened as she said primly, 'Lawrie was handicapped, Florrie. He could not help being as he was.'

'Happen you're right but all the same you have to wonder if he wouldn't have been best locked away in one o' them institutions, don't you?'

'I don't think that was ever an option. Katie and Pat, his parents, loved him dearly while they were alive.' There was a hard edge to Constance's voice now and for a moment no one said anything.

But then the silence was broken when Sarah suddenly blurted out, 'He had a weak heart, so the stroke could have come about at any time. No doubt Hannah and Ben will be heartbroken. Huh! I bet they wouldn't care a fig if it had been me. They didn't even have the decency to get word to me, did they? Or invite me to the funeral – an' I am family, after all.'

Constance glanced at her disapprovingly. Even at a time like this, Sarah could think only of herself. It suddenly occurred to her that Lawrie must have collapsed on the night that Sarah had taken the pony and trap across the fells, and a cold hand closed around her heart. She dismissed the thought instantly. Sarah might be bitter but she would never harm anyone ... would she?

'So, my dear. What do you think of your first glimpse of London?'

Ruth gulped before saying, 'It's big!'

They had just alighted from the train at King's Cross station after a six-and-a-half-hour journey, and as Ruth gazed about, she was sure she had never seen so many people all in one place before. The smoky platform was crowded with porters, and men and women who were moving so fast it was as if they didn't have a minute to live.

'This is nothing,' Dan informed her with a grin. 'Wait until you get outside.' He nodded to the porter who was waiting behind them with their luggage on a large metal trolley, and taking her arm he led his wife from the station into the crowded streets beyond.

Ruth's eyes almost started from her head. It

was the noise that alarmed her the most, for there were motor-cars everywhere she looked. And the smell of the place; it smelled dirty, nothing at all like it did at home, where you could take in a deep breath of clean fresh air. If she were to do that here she dreaded to think of what she might be inhaling. However, she had no wish to upset Dan so she stood patiently while the porter loaded their bags into the boot of a taxicab.

Dan tipped the man handsomely, upon which the porter touched his cap respectfully and gave Dan a cheeky grin, telling him, 'Fank yer kindly, guv.'

Goodness me! They didn't even sound the same here. They seemed to have a dialect all of their very own.

Seeing Ruth's expression, Dan's grin broadened. 'If you think he was strange, just wait until you meet Pip.' His voice was teasing. 'Now he is a *true* little cockney sparrow.' Leaning towards the driver, he told him, 'The Ritz Hotel, if you please.'

Ruth closed her eyes as the cab driver drove haphazardly into the flow of traffic and she kept them shut for some time, for there seemed to be cars heading towards them from every direction. She had hitherto thought the streets of Newcastle were busy, but they were nothing more than country lanes compared to the streets of London.

She finally dared to open her eyes, flinching as an omnibus hurtled past them and wondering why she had ever agreed to come in the first place. She felt like a fish out of water, but having no wish to hurt Dan's feelings, she simply nodded as she flashed him a weak smile.

When the car finally pulled up outside the Ritz Hotel, Ruth stifled a sigh of relief. The taxi journey following the train ride had made her feel quite queasy, and now all she wanted was a nice strong cup of tea. However, with her first sight of the foyer, her good spirits returned, for she felt as if she was stepping into paradise. A crystal chandelier that would have taken up the whole space of her parlour was suspended in front of a sweeping staircase that would not have looked out of place in a royal palace.

The carpet was so deep that her feet sank into it, and everywhere she looked, men in livery were strutting about with their heads held high.

As she stood there nervously wringing her gloves in her hands, Dan walked towards the counter and told the gentleman standing behind it, 'Mr and Mrs Bensham. I have booked the Honeymoon Suite.'

Ruth felt colour flood into her cheeks as the man smiled. 'Why, of course, sir. We have everything ready for you. I will get a porter to take your luggage up for you, and may I say that I hope you have an enjoyable stay.'

Ruth wished that the ground would open up and swallow her as the man now turned his attention to her and flashed her a polite smile.

He must think I'm mutton dressed as lamb, she thought to herself, suddenly wondering if she had been wise to allow Mary Ann to choose the outfit she had travelled in. The dress was calf-length and, although the shop assistant had assured them that it was the very latest fashion, still Ruth felt vaguely uncomfortable in it and had to keep resisting the urge to pull it down. On top of that she thought she detected an amused twinkle in the man's eye. The Honeymoon Suite indeed! What had Dan been thinking of, at their age? She had never been under the illusion that she was beautiful, or sophisticated if it came to that, and the man must be wondering what Dan had seen in her. Oh, it was all very embarrassing and now she just wanted to run and hide.

Even as these thoughts were chasing through her mind, Dan took her elbow and asked, 'Would you like to take the lift, my dear, or would you prefer the stairs?'

'The stairs,' she snapped without meaning to, and not waiting for an answer, she turned about and hurried towards them.

By the time they had reached their suite of rooms the porter had already carried their cases inside for them, and Ruth crossed to the ornate gilt mirror that hung above the marble fireplace and removed her hat as Dan tipped the porter and closed the door behind him.

'Ruth.' His voice was heavy with concern. 'Do you not like it here? We could always go somewhere else if you prefer.'

'Oh, Dan Bensham.' When she turned towards him he was shocked to see tears glistening on her lashes. 'How could you have brought me to such a place? You must have known I'd be out o' me depth here. I ain't posh, Dan. Nor have I ever pretended to be. I ... I'm afraid I shall let you down.'

Dan immediately went to her and took her in his arms.

'My dear. I am so sorry if I have upset you. I

feel so ashamed about the way I have treated you over the years and I just wanted you to enjoy yourself. You have asked so little of me and I–'

'Shush.' Her finger came up to his lips as she told him, 'You have nothing to feel ashamed of. I came to you willingly all those years ago, and if I could turn the clock back I would do the same again. I were never under any illusions as to where your heart lay. The mistress had that till the day she died. But I knew that you had an affection for me an' that were enough. Still is, if it comes to that. But now I am your wife, an' I still have to pinch meself to believe it. So, if this is where you want us to stay it's all right by me. I'm just feelin' a bit overwhelmed at the minute, that's all. So, you order some tea an' I'll have a look round, eh?'

She was all sunshine again now as she stepped away from him, and once more he thought what a truly remarkable woman she was as he watched her disappear into the bathroom that adjoined their suite.

Later that day, Dan took Ruth on a sightseeing trip. They went for a stroll across Green Park to see Buckingham Palace, and then back along the Mall and through Admiralty Arch to Trafalgar Square and Nelson's Column.

They were on their way back to the hotel when he asked her, 'Would you care to call in and meet Pip and his family this evening, or are you too tired?'

'I'd love to meet Pip,' Ruth declared, and so after a rest and a teatime snack, they took a cab to Bow, to the house where Pip lived.

'I ought to warn you, it isn't very er...'

'Posh?' she finished for him and now he grinned. Ruth could always read his mind. The smell hit them as they entered the building in Adderton Road: an overriding stench of unwashed bodies and stale urine.

'The Beddows family live up here,' he told her as he took her elbow, and side-by-side they climbed the rickety stairs until he drew her to a breathless halt outside the rooms that Pip and his family occupied.

Beyond the door they could hear the sound of children laughing, but the noise stopped abruptly when Dan knocked. It was Pip himself who answered, and when he saw Dan standing there, he launched himself at the man as if he were a long lost friend, and wrapped his skinny arms around his waist.

'*Mr Dan!*' His face was alight as he grabbed Dan's hand and drew him into the room beyond, and Ruth slowly followed. As she looked about her, her heart was filled with pity. To think that people were forced to live like this! It was almost beyond belief – and yet the welcome Dan had received was rapturous. The children were all clambering about him now, but it was not them she was looking at but the woman who was lying in a bed that was piled high with threadbare blankets and coats at the side of the room.

'Thanks fer the 'amper you 'ad sent round,' she heard Pip say. 'Cor, it was lovely, weren't it, Mum? There was that much stuff in it we ate like kings fer a whole week. An' talk about 'eavy! The poor sod wot delivered it was sweatin' like a pig after he'd lumped it up all them apples an' pears.'

When Ruth looked at Dan questioningly, he explained, 'Young Pip means stairs. I did warn you that he has a language all of his own.' He now turned his attention to Pip's mother and asked, 'And how are you, Mrs Beddows?'

'Oh, you know, so so – but I mustn't grumble.'

Dan pulled Ruth forward and told her, 'This is my wife, Ruth.'

'Pleased to meet yer I'm sure, me dear.' Then to Pip: 'Push that kettle onto the fire then, son. Where's yer manners gone again? Offer our guests a cup o' rosie lee at least, can't yer?'

'Oh no really,' Ruth protested. 'Please don't go to any trouble on our account. Dan just wanted to pop in an' say hello to Pip, but we'll be on our way in a minute.'

'So 'ow's yer search goin' on then?' Pip now asked and Dan shook his head.

'Not so good up to now, which is why I am back in London – to get the next address off Mrs Fellows.'

'Why didn't yer just get *all* the addresses, the last time yer went to see her?'

Ruth had asked him exactly the same thing, and Dan awkwardly tried to pass it off by saying, 'Well, if I'd done that I wouldn't have had an excuse to come back and see you, now would I?'

Pip grinned as he scratched furiously at his head, and the next fifteen minutes flew by as they told each other of all that had happened since they had last met. Pip was sad to hear that Dan's nephew, Lawrie, had passed away, but he brightened up as he confided in Dan: 'I've got a job on a market-stall now, three days a week, ain't I, Mum? It's made no end o' difference. I got the two little 'uns some shoes last week wiv me wages, an' we 'ave a proper fire every day now.'

'Well done.' Dan pressed some coins into his hand and a slip of paper on which he had written his home address. 'Be sure to write if ever you're in trouble and need my help. I doubt I'll be coming back to London for a while, but if I do, I'll be sure to call by and see you, if that's all right with your mother?'

Mrs Beddows gave him a tired grin.

'Fanks fer this. You never know, I might come an' see yer one day,' Pip promised as he followed Dan and Ruth to the door. 'You've bin a real gent, Mr Dan. I'll get us all some grub to last us the week wiv wot you've given me.'

They shook hands, and after all the goodbyes had been said, Dan and Ruth went back down the steep staircase and out, through the smog that was now settling across the cobblestones, away from the squalor of the East End to the tram stop and all the luxuries of the West End.

The following day, Dan took Ruth shopping through the Burlington Arcade, and it happened that just as they were passing the tailor's shop, Mrs Fellows appeared at the door. For a moment it would have been hard to say who was the more surprised of the two of them, but it was she who exclaimed, blushingly, 'Why, Mr Bensham! How nice to see you.'

'And you too, Mrs Fellows.'

Ruth had spotted the flush that rose to the

woman's cheeks as suddenly remembering his manners, Dan drew her forward and announced, 'This is my wife, Ruth.'

Meg Fellows smiled warmly as she shook Ruth's hand and told her, 'It's so nice to meet you, Mrs Bensham. I do hope the wedding went well?'

'Oh aye, thank you, it were grand.' Ruth couldn't help but like her, for as well as being very attractive, there was a warmth and sincerity about this woman that was immediately apparent.

Meg Fellows now turned towards Dan again and asked, 'And how is your search going?'

'Slowly, I'm afraid. I travelled to Warwickshire and discovered that the woman near Nuneaton was not the one I was searching for, but then we suffered a family bereavement recently, and that and our wedding sort of held everything up. That is one reason why I am back in London, although I also wanted to take Ruth on a sightseeing tour. I wondered if you would very much mind giving me the next address on the list?'

'Not at all,' she assured him. 'Thankfully I still have the ledger, though many of my bits and pieces were stolen during a recent burglary. It was Sally's day off and the thieves broke in through the back window.'

All the while they were talking, Ruth was watching them closely. She noticed the way Dan's eyes roved across the woman's face and the way they lit up, much as they had once done when he looked at Barbara. But she did not have long to think of it now for she heard Meg Fellows say, 'Why don't you call around to the house this evening? Both of you, of course.'

284

'Thank you. We shall do that, and now I suppose we had better get on with our shopping expedition. Good day, Mrs Fellows.'

'Good day.' Meg flashed a last friendly smile at Ruth before continuing on her way, and Dan now turned his attention back to Ruth.

'She's a pleasant woman, isn't she?' he remarked.

'Oh aye, she's that all right. An' quite charmin' too. I liked her.' And so, it was evident, did her husband, for Dan seemed quite flustered as he took her elbow and steered her in the opposite direction to that which Meg Fellows had taken.

Chapter Twenty

Quentin Wolfe had slept well and now as he strolled along the promenade in Southend he was feeling in high spirits. He had just eaten a full English breakfast, which had tasted all the more enjoyable because Sarah Radlet would be paying for it, as she would also pay for his night in the hotel.

But now he supposed he should continue with his search. Better not push his luck too much, else he would have his partner, Herbert Peale, chewing his ear off when he returned home.

Today the weather was fine, although the wind that was rolling in from the sea was biting. He turned and began the long climb up the hill towards Wilson Road; once at the top he paused to stare out across the terraces at the ships that were bobbing on the ocean.

Before he left, he intended to visit a local pawn-broker's and rid himself of some of the trinkets he had stolen from Meg Fellows's house. They would be worth a pretty penny if he wasn't very much mistaken, particularly the solid silver snuff box, which no doubt belonged to her husband. If he got rid of them here it would be far enough away from London for them not to be traced. He thought back to how easy it had been to break into her home. Not that there were many houses that he couldn't break into. He was also a very nifty pickpocket which, added to the little business he had embarked on with Herbert, meant that he was rarely without a pocketful of cash. In truth, he had not intended to steal anything from Mrs Fellows's home. He had merely wanted a peep at the ledger to take down the addresses of the people he had been employed to find. But then, once inside he had reasoned that it would look strange if someone had gone to the trouble of breaking in without taking anything. And so he had stuffed his pockets with a clear conscience. Only small pieces, mind. Things that could easily be disposed of.

With his head bent against the wind he moved on, his waxed moustache dancing merrily in the breeze, and soon he came to the house on the corner of Wilson Road. Once again there was no response to his knock at the front door although he hammered on it loudly enough to waken the dead. Deciding to try his luck at the back entrance he skirted the house and arrived in a small overgrown yard. Stepping over the weeds, which grew in profusion there, he rapped loudly on the back door and this time his efforts were rewarded when a voice called, 'All right, all right, keep your hair on! I'm comin', ain't I?'

The door creaked open and he was confronted by a woman who looked to be as old as the hills. She was positively tiny and her face was deeply wrinkled. Glaring at him, she demanded, 'Yes? What do you want? Can't a soul be left in peace!'

Quentin knew that it was going to take all his charm to win this one over, so he flashed her his most winning smile before saying apologetically, 'I am so sorry to bother you, madam. I am looking for someone, and a lady who lives further up the street told me that you might be able to help me.'

'Oh yes, an' who might you be lookin' for then?'

He shivered dramatically and taking the hint she grunted, 'You'd best step inside, but be quick about it. I ain't got all day to stand about talkin' to the likes o' you.'

He stepped past her into a kitchen that was so cluttered he barely knew where to look first. Remembering his manners, he quickly removed his hat as he told her, 'The people I am looking for lived further up the road some fifty odd years ago – at number thirty-eight B. Their surname began with an R. Now what was it again? R...'

Once again he went through the pretence of trying to remember, but he had no need to, for almost immediately she told him, 'It would be the Richardsons you're on about.'

He immediately deduced that though her body was old, her mind was still as sharp as a needle.

'That's it!' he declared triumphantly and then, 'You wouldn't happen to know where they are now, would you?'

'Oh, I know all right. They're upstairs.' When she cocked her finger heavenwards, Quentin's heart sank.

'What – you mean they are both dead?'

'That's about the long an' the short of it. He died with liver problems some years since, and the influenza outbreak took the old lady back in 1918.'

He looked so crestfallen that she went on, 'They had a daughter.'

His ears pricked up again now.

'Adopted her when she was just a baby, they did. I couldn't cotton on to her for some time, myself, but to be fair she turned up trumps for 'em. She nursed the pair of 'em till the day they died. Never got married – but then she wouldn't, would she? They treated her like some sort of un-paid skivvy from what I could see of it, and never left her so much as a penny when they passed on. Last I heard of her, she was workin' in the Kardomah Café down on the seafront. Her name is Josephine. Couldn't tell you where she's livin' but you'll find her there, if that's any help to you.'

'Oh, my dear Mrs Thederman, that is *more* than helpful. Thank you very much.' When he began to pump her hand up and down she looked slightly embarrassed, and now he placed his hat back on and turning to the door, flashed her one of his most sickly smiles. 'Until we meet again, dear lady.'

As the door closed behind him the old woman shook her head in bewilderment. Now there was a strange one and no mistake.

Quentin Wolfe was bowling along now and when he reached the bottom of the hill he was breathless. Deciding to turn left at the end of the road, he walked along the seafront until, sure enough, there was a small café to the right of him, a faded sign outside, with the word Kardomah faintly visible on it. Holding tight to his hat, which the wind was trying its best to blow away, he approached the small building and slipped inside.

Two couples and a young woman with a baby in a perambulator were sitting at the tables with pots of tea in front of them, but apart from them, the café was empty. He approached the counter and rang a small bell, and instantly a door opened and a round, red-faced man in a slightly grimy apron appeared.

'Yes, sir. And what can I be getting you?'

'Oh, a pot of tea and perhaps a nice buttered scone, if you please, my good man.'

He watched the man pour the tea, which looked as if it had been standing for hours, into a chipped cup. He then slapped a scone onto a plate, using his grubby hands. Quentin fumbled in his pocket for some change to pay him. He then retreated to a far corner to drink his stewed tea and wait. If the woman he was hoping to find was here, she was obviously in the kitchen at the back – and the way he saw it, she had to appear at some time.

The tea was lukewarm and had a thin film of grease floating on the top of it. The scone was stale, too, but he sat without complaint with his eyes fixed firmly on the door at the back of the counter.

Seconds later, the door to the café opened

289

again and two women appeared and approached the counter.

'A pot of tea for two, please. And *do* see that it is freshly made. I don't want any of that stewed concoction you served us the last time!'

Quentin stifled a smile. Judging by the disgusting mess slopping around in the cup in front of him, the women had obviously used the café before.

The café-owner sniffed then shouted through the door behind him, 'Josephine, a pot of tea for two an' make it snappy.'

Now Quentin was leaning forward in his seat as he waited for Josephine Richardson to appear. When she did, he intended to find some excuse to have a chat to her. The two women who had just entered now took a window seat to wait for their refreshments as Quentin kept his eyes glued to the door. Beyond it, he could hear someone clattering about, and at last it opened and a woman carrying a tray stepped through it. Quentin had been just about to swallow a mouthful of the stale scone, but now it lodged in his throat and threatened to choke him as his eyes bulged with shock. This then was Josephine Richardson. Well, it was a sure thing he would have no need to question her, for the woman now walking towards him had skin that was as black as midnight. Now so many of the comments that Mrs Thederman had made earlier in the morning became clear. *Couldn't cotton on to her. Never married, but then she wouldn't, would she?*

Thick black hair that was so frizzy Quentin wondered how she would ever get a comb through it, stood out from the woman's head like snakes' tails. Her teeth, when she smiled, were startlingly white against the darkness of her skin, and as she looked across at him now he quickly averted his eyes as he rose hurriedly from the table and left the café.

Another wasted journey, he thought irritably, but then what did he care? The longer it took him to find the woman Sarah Radlet was seeking, the more she would pay him. But what a shock this one had been. His hand rested on the trinkets nestling against his thigh in his jacket pocket and he set off back into town. It was time to find a pawnbroker's and do a bit of business before getting the train to Liverpool Street and beginning the long journey home.

They had had a wonderful day but now Ruth was tired. In the afternoon, Dan had taken her to the matinée performance of a new show by Hugh Lofting called *Doctor Doolittle*, and she had laughed until she had cried, for it was all about a man who was able to talk to animals, who then spoke back to him. She was now lying on the elaborate chaise-longue in their room after enjoying a delicious meal in the elegant dining room, and was still getting over the shock of being waited on. Dan seemed slightly on edge as he stood with his hands behind his back at the window, staring down into the street below. Ruth guessed that he was keen to go and get the information he needed from Meg Fellows, so she now told him, 'Why don't you get off to Mrs Fellows, Dan? I'm feelin' a bit tired, to be honest, so if you don't mind I'll just stay here an' put me feet up.'

'But she invited both of us,' he objected, as he turned to look at her.

Ruth straightened her skirt over her knees. 'I know she did, but you can make apologies for me, can't you?'

'You aren't feeling unwell, are you?'

Ignoring the edge of fear in his voice, she sighed. 'No, Dan. As I told you, I'm just a bit tired, that's all.'

'But it doesn't seem right to go off and leave you here on your own.'

Her laughter bounced off the walls as she spread her hands to encompass the luxurious surroundings. 'Oh, it's goin' to be a real hardship to be left to me own devices in a place like this, ain't it?'

Ignoring the teasing note in her voice, he looked into her eyes. She was staring back at him, and as her eyes locked with his, her face became straight and he had the strangest feeling that she could see right into his very soul.

'Go on, you daft ha'porth. I'm goin' to go an' have a long soak in that lovely bathroom an' then I'm goin' to tuck down in that big comfortable bed there. Take as long as you like. Happen I'll be asleep the minute me head hits the pillow, so you've no need to rush back.'

He collected his hat and coat, and at the door he paused to look back at her before saying, 'I'll see you later then.'

'Aye lad, you will that.'

The minute that the door had closed behind him, Ruth's clenched fist found her mouth and she had to squeeze her eyes tight shut against the emotions that were raging through her. Today, when Dan had looked at Meg Fellows, she had seen the look in his eyes that he had always reserved for Barbara alone.

Never once in all the long years they had been together had he ever looked at her like that. But then she had never expected him to, for he had never made promises that he could not keep. That was one of the wonderful things about Dan. You always knew where you stood with him. Perhaps that's why it had come as such a shock when he had asked her to marry him. But now she knew for sure that he had done it merely out of a sense of duty and pity because her time was short.

Sniffing loudly, Ruth drew herself up to her full height. Well, she could live with that for now, and she would continue to love him just as she had always done. Nothing could have come of his feelings for Meg Fellows even had he not married her, for wasn't Meg married to the man that owned the tailor's shop?

Crossing to the window, she stared beyond the heavy swags and tails and was just in time to see Dan emerge onto the street below before being swallowed up in the crowds. The tears ran down her cheeks unheeded, and yet strangely she was not crying for herself but for Dan. Why does he always have to fall in love with the wrong woman, she asked herself, for she was sure that he was falling in love with Meg Fellows, even if he had not yet allowed himself to admit it. Turning towards the bathroom, she shook her head sadly and wondered at the unfairness of life.

Sally answered the door following Dan's first

knock and smiling, she took his hat and coat before leading him towards the parlour where Meg Fellows was waiting for him.

'Ah, Dan. Do come in.' She rose from her seat to shake his hand before looking across his shoulder and asking, 'Is your wife not with you?'

'No. I'm afraid I have tired her out with all the sightseeing. She sends her apologies.'

He settled in the chair she motioned him to and she told him, 'I asked Sally to get us a tray of tea ready for when you arrived. Or would you prefer something a little stronger? The March winds are quite bitter, are they not? A glass of sherry or port would warm you through.'

'Thank you. That would be very nice. Port, if you don't mind.'

She lifted a cut-glass decanter and poured him a generous measure of port before pouring herself a slightly smaller glass of sherry, and then when she was seated again she asked, 'So tell me, what happened when you visited Warwickshire?'

Dan now told her of his visit and when he had finished she said thoughtfully, 'That leaves three possibilities now. One in Southend-on-Sea and one in Manchester, if I remember rightly. If the person you are looking for turns out to be at neither of these places, then I'm afraid you may be facing a very long trek to America.'

He nodded in agreement but then looking on the bright side again he said jokingly, 'Let's hope that it won't come to that, eh? I don't think I could persuade Ruth to go on a boat. To be honest, I'm not even sure if she is enjoying this trip. Ruth is a home bird, and between you and me, I don't think she'll be sorry to get home.' As an afterthought he then asked, 'Do you and your husband do much travelling, Meg?'

She lowered her eyes and for a moment he thought that she was going to ignore the question but then she said quietly, 'I am a widow, Dan.'

'Oh... I'm so sorry.' The shock on his face was so transparent that she instantly smiled at him.

'Please don't be. You had no way of knowing. It's been some years since George died and I can cope with talking about it now.'

'Was he er ... ill?'

'No, not at all. George always joked that he was as fit as a butcher's dog, despite the fact that he was almost eighteen years my senior. He was a good man, Dan. I feel that you and he would have liked each other. He was also an excellent tailor. Men from all over the country came to be fitted for a suit made by George, and inadvertently it was this that was his downfall.' She now paused to sip at her sherry before going on, 'George had interest from abroad in his suits and so he decided to follow it up and take some samples over there – to New York, that is. He had always dreamed of owning a string of tailor's shops and so this seemed like the perfect opportunity. It was 1912 and the newspapers were full of the *Titanic*, the so-called unsinkable ship. I persuaded George that he should travel to New York on her, on her maiden voyage and he was so excited about it. I can remember waving him off... He looked so happy, but then... Well, it is common knowledge what happened, isn't it? George went down with the ship and I have blamed myself for it ever since. If only he had gone on some other ship, things might have been so very different now. But then our whole lives are made up of if only's, aren't they? The dear man left me very comfortably provided for. In truth, I only keep the shop on because it gives me something to keep me occupied. I really cannot think of anything worse than sitting about all day and doing nothing, can you?'

As Dan looked into her sapphire-blue eyes he was filled with admiration. This woman had spirit and he had a feeling that she and Mary Ann would have got on like a house on fire. The conversation moved on and soon they were talking as if they had known each other for years, about everything from the state of the country to politics. Dan realised that as well as being very beautiful, Meg was also a highly intelligent woman with opinions of her own that she was not afraid to voice. It was just like the first time: the hours ticked by until suddenly he glanced at the clock on the mantelshelf and started.

'My goodness me, it is gone ten o'clock.'

Following his gaze she smiled, and as the firelight played on her pale hair a thousand butterflies fluttered to life in his stomach and he had to resist the urge to reach out and touch it.

'And we haven't even looked at the next address on the list yet.' Her eyes were sparkling and he found himself returning her smile. He had intended to take all the addresses with him, but now he decided he would once again take just the next one on the list. He did not allow himself to admit that in doing this, he would have an excuse to come back yet again.

After fetching her aunt's ledger, Meg duly wrote it out for him and he thanked her before tucking it away in his breast pocket. He then hurriedly scribbled down his own address and handing it to her, he told her, 'Just in case you should ever need me. I was concerned when you mentioned to Ruth and I earlier on that you had been burgled.'

She shrugged. 'Surprisingly enough, they didn't take an awful lot, although some of the things that were taken were worth quite a bit, and some had great sentimental value for me. Still, it isn't the end of the world. At least no one was hurt. I would never have forgiven myself if they had tried to come in whilst Sally was here alone and anything had happened to her.'

'Quite.' He shook her hand and she then accompanied him to the door.

Once there she told him, 'I've really enjoyed our chat. It's so nice to have company. You and your wife are more than welcome to call around if you have time before you return home. I do hope that she won't be angry because I have kept you out so late?'

'Not at all,' he assured her. 'Ruth is a very easy-going woman. And now I will wish you a very good night, Meg.'

She inclined her head and closed the door softly behind him. For a time Dan stood there staring at the lighted window and then he slowly descended the steps and made his way back to Piccadilly with a preoccupied expression on his face.

It was late the following afternoon when Sarah called into the office of Wolfe & Peale to demand,

297

'Well? Have you had any success yet?'

Mr Wolfe, who had not long since stepped through the door, shook his head. 'I am afraid not, dear lady, though I have only just returned from Southend where I followed up the second of the leads. Would you believe that this particular lady was as black as pitch when I finally managed to track her down! Needless to say, I did not even waste my time in questioning her, for I am sure you will agree that your Mrs Bensham and Thomas Mallen would not have produced such a child?'

Sarah's mouth pursed into a grim line as he coughed discreetly and went on, 'Sadly, the trip proved to be a little expensive. I was forced to stay overnight in a hotel and–'

'What you are trying to say is that you will need more money. Is that it, Mr Wolfe?'

'Well, train fares and such are expensive, as I am sure you are aware, and–'

With a face that would have done justice to the thunderclouds that were scudding across the sky outside, Sarah snatched a small bundle of notes from her bag and slammed them onto the table. 'I sincerely hope your *next* journey will prove to be more successful, sir,' she hissed, 'for my savings are now becoming sadly depleted.'

'I understand,' he simpered. 'And rest assured I shall do all I can to bring this investigation to a hasty conclusion.'

'You'd better!' Jamming her crutch beneath her armpit, Sarah turned about and flounced from the room. When he heard her stumping away down the stairs, the smile disappeared from

Quentin Wolfe's face. She was a nasty piece of work if ever he'd seen one. No wonder her old man had kept a piece on the side for years. A face like that could curdle the milk.

Lifting the bundle of notes, he slipped them into his inside breast pocket. He would treat this payment as a little bonus. After all, as Herbert was out, what he didn't know wouldn't hurt him. And as for the last address he had to try in Manchester... As far as he was concerned, that could wait for a couple of weeks. It would not pay to let her think that it was *too* easy. Humming merrily now, he lifted the newspaper and soon became absorbed in it.

Chapter Twenty-One

The atmosphere in the cottage was still gloomy following Lawrie's funeral, and each and every one of them was feeling his loss. It was as if a light had gone from their lives. Ben had taken it harder than the women, which was why Hannah had not mentioned the griping pain in her side. She had had her pregnancy confirmed two weeks ago, and the joy of knowing they were to be blessed with a child following her stillbirth had kept them going through the dark days following Lawrie's death. But now the pain was becoming unbearable and Hannah knew that she would not be able to keep it from Ben for much longer.

First though, she would ask Nancy's advice.

Seeing that Ben was settled with a newspaper in the parlour she made her way into the kitchen, where she found Nancy stuffing a chicken prior to putting it in the oven.

Nancy smiled but then seeing the pallor of Hannah's face she asked, 'What's wrong? You look a bit peaky.'

'It's this pain in my side,' Hannah told her as she slid onto one of the hard-backed kitchen chairs that stood against the table. 'I don't think it's anything to do with the baby because the pain is here.'

She rubbed the area as Nancy chewed on her lip thoughtfully before saying, 'I hope you ain't coming down with appendicitis. Happen you should get yourself into town and have it checked out by the doctor. Ben would run you in, I'm sure.'

'No, I don't want to mention it to Ben just yet,' Hannah told her hastily. 'He's got enough on his plate grieving for Lawrie at the minute without having to start worrying about me. It's probably just something and nothing.'

'And how long have you had it?'

Hannah shrugged. 'Right from the first to be honest; though it seems to be getting worse.'

'In that case you shouldn't mess about,' Nancy stated wisely. 'God knows, we've gone through enough heartache lately without anythin' else goin' wrong. The thought o' this baby is keepin' Ben goin', God bless him.'

Hannah wished now that she had never mentioned it, and standing up she flashed Nancy a false smile. 'I'll tell you what I'll do, I'll give it today and if it hasn't eased off by tomorrow then I'll go and see the doctor.'

'Hmm, well, meantime I suggest you go an' put your feet up till dinner's ready. You're always doin' somethin' or another. You should rest more.'

Hannah's lips twitched into a genuinely amused smile as she informed her, 'I'm only pregnant, Nancy. I'm not ill. Lots of women work almost up until the time their babies are due.'

'That's as maybe, but happen they have a need to. You don't – so get yourself away and do as you're told for a change else you'll have me to answer to!'

'Yes, ma'am,' Hannah said obediently before heading back towards the hall. But once the door had closed between them, the pain suddenly came again and she clutched at her side. Perhaps she would go and have a lie-down, after all. Once in their bedroom she limped to the window and stared out, her hand still pressed to the nagging ache in her side. The sky was lying low and heavy over the hills and there was a promise of rain in the air.

She and Ben now occupied the room that had once been Thomas Mallen's. And of all the rooms in the cottage, this was the one that still remained much as it had been back then. The same four-poster bed that he had once slept in stood against one wall, flanked by the same sturdy wardrobe that had once housed his clothes on one side, and the dressing-table on the other. Only the decor had changed, for Hannah had had the walls repainted in a soft cream, which complemented the curtains and carpets that were all in matching autumn colours. It was the view that had made them decide to take this room, for it boasted a huge window that looked out upon the foothills and mountains beyond. From this window they could watch the changing seasons and Hannah never tired of staring from it. Today, however, it was not the view she was thinking of but the child that was growing inside her. Could it be that the sharp pain she was experiencing was a warning that something was about to go wrong again? She shuddered to think of how Ben would react, should this happen to be the case. It was only the thought of this little life that had kept him going during the last sad weeks.

She shook herself mentally. She was probably just thinking the worst because her spirits were low. Moving to the bed, she clambered onto it and curled herself into a tight ball, praying that the pain would go away and take her misgivings with it, for if she were to lose this baby too she did not know how she would be able to bear it.

As Ruth threw her coat over the bottom of the banister she stifled a sigh of relief. She and Dan had just returned from their trip to London and she was so pleased to be back that she almost felt like crying. An expression that her mother had been fond of using sprang to mind: *There's no place like home!* Ruth now knew without a shadow of a doubt that it was true. Oh, she felt ungrateful for feeling as she did, for she knew full well that Dan had taken her to London out of the goodness of his heart. But even so, within a very short time of being there, Ruth had begun to feel like a fish out of water. The hotel had been truly magnificent and the sights she had seen would stay with her for ever. But at heart, Ruth was still the same girl who had once worked in the nursery with Ben and Jonathan and Harry as their nursery nurse. She was not a lady, nor would she ever be, even if she was now Mrs Dan Bensham.

Dan was close behind her, and as he carried the cases into the hallway and placed them at the foot of the stairs, she asked him, 'Would you like a cup of tea?'

'I certainly would.' He began to take off his coat, his eyes following Ruth as she moved towards the kitchen. She had no need to tell him that she was pleased to be home, for her every action in London had shown that she was feeling uncomfortable. He had lost count of how many shops they had entered where he would point out an outfit that caught his eye, only to be told, 'What would I want that for? And where would I *ever* go to wear it? 'Twould be a bit posh for trailin' round the market in!'

He had finally given up, and so they had ended up coming home with more presents for Mary Ann than treats for Ruth herself.

Dan decided that he might go back to Brook House later in the day after he had spent some time with Mary Ann. Ada and Betty had seen little of him since his marriage to Ruth, and he needed to check that all was well there. He'd pop over to the Hall as well, and look in on Brigie and Jonathan before calling in to see how Ben and Hannah were doing.

As if thoughts of his daughter had conjured her up from thin air, he now heard a key in the lock and Mary Ann walked in with a large bunch of flowers across her arm.

'Hello, Dad.' Her smile expressed her surprise and pleasure at seeing him. 'I wasn't expecting you back until this evening. I'd just popped out to get these to brighten the place up a bit.'

'It was your mother's idea to come back early.' He nodded at the kitchen and then leaning towards her, he told her conspiratorially, 'I'm not sure that she altogether enjoyed the trip. Between you and me, I don't think she could wait to get home.'

Mary Ann smiled broadly. 'That doesn't surprise me. Mam has always been a home bird. Still, it's been an experience for her, if nothing else... But how is she?'

'Very well, I'm pleased to say.'

A look of relief flitted across the girl's face as she said, 'I'm glad you're back because there's something I was wanting to talk to you both about.'

'Oh yes, and what would that be then?'

Taking his elbow, she steered him towards the kitchen and when they walked in Ruth flew across to her and hugged her daughter tightly as if she hadn't seen her for a month.

'Eeh, lass. I missed you, so I did. Have you been all right on your own?'

'Of course I have,' Mary Ann told her in exasperation. 'I *am* a grown woman, you know, Mam, and quite able to take care of myself. But now will you *please* put me down before you squash these flowers?'

Ruth laughed as Mary Ann laid the flowers on the table. 'I was just saying to Dad that there's something I want to talk to you about, but tell me all about your trip first.'

Ruth lifted the kettle and poured the boiling water into the teapot before saying, 'Never mind about the trip for now. What was it on your mind?'

'Well...' They were all seated at the table and Mary Ann looked from one to the other of them and took a deep breath as a flush sprang to her cheeks. 'The thing is, Tom and I want to get married – as soon as possible.'

'Why, that's wonderful news, but why the sudden rush?' Ruth stopped talking abruptly as a possibility occurred to her – and now Mary Ann's cheeks were not only flushed, they were positively burning.

'Is there anything else you were wanting to tell us, lass?'

'Well, I don't think there's really any need to, is there, Mam? Being you, I think you've already guessed.'

'You're going to have a bairn? Is that it?'

Mary Ann nodded before declaring, 'I'm not going to apologise for my behaviour. Tom and I love each other and planned to wed in due course anyway. The way we see it, this has just made us move things on a little quicker than we intended to.'

'Aw, hinny.' Ruth had now sprung from her seat to take her daughter's hand, and her eyes were full as she told her, 'I am the last person you should think of apologising to – isn't that so, Dan? And just think on it – we're going to be grandparents! Who would ever have thought it, eh?'

Being the more practical of the two, Dan asked,

'When were you hoping to get married, my dear? And have you given any thought as to where you might live?'

For the first time, Ruth's face fell at the prospect of Mary Ann leaving home. But then, their daughter was now well into her twenties and deep down Ruth had always known that she would fly the nest at some stage. It was a natural progression, after all.

'We thought we might be married quietly as soon as possible. We really don't want any fuss. And as to where we might live...Well, I was rather hoping that we could stay here.'

Ruth clapped her hands together with glee. 'Why, that's a fine idea! There's more than enough room, and I would be at hand to help out wi' the little one when it came along.' She did not allow herself to think that she might not be there to see the child, for it wasn't every day that you discovered you were about to become a grandma.

Dan, however, was more cautious as he replied, 'There is another option. I could buy you and Tom a house. It could be my wedding present to you both. And of course, I shall pay for the wedding and it will be my pleasure.'

'Thanks, Dad.' As Mary Ann looked from one to the other of these dear people, her heart was full to bursting. Her upbringing had been unconventional to say the very least, and yet she had never wanted for anything, least of all love. 'I appreciate that. But to be honest, Tom and I have talked about it and we would both prefer to live here with Mam, if you don't mind? Though I'll take you up on your offer of paying for the wedding gladly.'

'That's settled then.' Ruth was beaming. 'If truth be told, I never thought I'd see the day when you settled down. Tom must be some man to snare *you.*'

'Oh, he is.' The blush was back on her cheeks now as her parents laughed.

Then Ruth suddenly declared, 'Oh damn and blast! I should have bought that nice lilac costume you wanted me to have in London after all, Dan.'

'Well, I dare say we'll find you something suitable.' As he looked from one to the other of them he remembered back to the time of Barbara's death when he had thought that he would lose the will to live. But Ruth and Mary Ann had given him the strength to carry on without her. For no reason that he could explain, a picture of Meg Fellows's smiling face suddenly flashed before his eyes and angrily he blinked it away. He had chosen the direction his life was taking, and it was here with his new wife and his daughter. Meg could never be anything more than a friend.

'That's it! I think this has gone on for quite long enough!' Ben paused in his pacing to stare at Hannah who was huddled on the bed. 'I'm going to send for the doctor right now, whether you like it or not.'

Hannah had been in bed for three days now. Three long days during which time she had been in so much pain that she had barely known what to do with herself.

For the first two days she had managed to hide the truth from both Ben and Nancy, but now the pain was so bad that she didn't care any more.

'Nancy, ask Fred if he would ride into town and get the doctor for me, would you?'

'He's already gone into town wi' the cart to get some feed for the horses,' she told Ben fearfully.

'Very well then. Stay with her, will you? I'll saddle Major and fetch him myself.'

His voice brooked no argument and Nancy nodded as he strode towards the door where he paused to look back at his wife, whose face was whiter than the linen on the bed. He then hurried away as Nancy crossed to the bed and took Hannah's feverish hand in her own.

Two hours later, as the doctor rose from examining Hannah, Ben and Nancy saw the concern written clearly on his face.

He stood tapping thoughtfully at his chin for some seconds before informing them, 'I think it might be wise to have her taken to the infirmary. There is a definite swelling in her side and it may be that we shall need to operate so that we can have a look at what is going on in there.'

When he saw the panic cloud Ben's face, he smiled at him kindly. 'It may be that it is something or nothing, so don't go working yourself into a lather just yet. But better safe than sorry, eh? We don't want to risk another tragedy so soon after the first, so I would feel better if your wife is somewhere where we can keep her under observation until we decide what is best to do.' He turned to Nancy. 'Perhaps you could prepare a bag for Mrs Bensham to take in with her? As soon as I get back into town I shall order an ambulance to come and fetch her to Newcastle

General Infirmary.'

'Of course. It will be ready, sir.' Nancy nervously twisted the front of her apron.

'Try not to worry, my dear,' the doctor told Hannah as he departed. 'We should have you as good as new in no time if you do as you're told.'

An hour later, an ambulance drew to a stop in front of the gate and two orderlies gently loaded Hannah onto a stretcher.

'I'll come in with you, shall I?' Ben said.

The men shook their heads regretfully at him. 'There would be no point, sir. The Matron at the Infirmary is like a bloody Sergeant Major. She wouldn't allow you in outside of visiting hours even if you'd travelled halfway round the world, so you'd be best to come in this evening between six or seven.'

'Very well.' Ben kissed Hannah tenderly and then began the long wait until he would be allowed to see her again.

That evening he was shown into a long ward with beds running the length of each wall with only a small bedside cabinet and a hard-backed wooden chair to separate them. Hannah was lying in one about halfway along, and when she saw him striding towards her with an enormous bunch of flowers in his hand she smiled wearily.

He pulled the chair as close to the bed as it would go and then, doing his best to keep the fear from his voice, he took her hand and asked, 'How are you feeling now?'

'Better. They've given me something for the pain but they still don't know what is wrong yet. I've had so many doctors poking and prodding me since I came in that I've lost count of them.'

Ben grinned, knowing that he must try to keep up her morale as he passed the flowers to a nurse who had come to hover at the end of the bed.

'I'll just go and put them in water, sir.'

Ben smiled his thanks before turning his attention back to his wife. 'So, have they told you how long you might be in for?'

'No, not yet. I suppose it will all depend on what it turns out to be. They're not ruling out the possibility that it could be appendicitis, but we will know more in the morning. They are sending the surgeon to see me.'

'I see.' Ben could feel himself breaking out in a sweat. Hospitals had always had this effect on him ever since he had been confined to a hospital tent after being injured in the war. Just the thought of it could still make him shudder, for that had been nothing like this orderly ward. The hospital tent had been like something out of a nightmare and he knew he would never forget it for as long as he lived. He could still hear the screams of the wounded when he closed his eyes. Smell the sickly-sweet scent of blood as doctors hacked off some poor soul's limb there and then in the tent with nothing to divide the person in torment from the rest of them but a thin curtain. And then there were the deaths. They would come and take a corpse away on a stretcher and before the bed had even had time to go cold there would be someone else in it.

Knowing his fear, Hannah told him, 'You don't have to come in every day, Ben.'

'Huh! Do you really think I could leave you

here without visiting you? I know hospitals are not my favourite places but I would lie in the next bed if it meant being near you.'

Seeing that he was becoming upset she now asked him, 'How is everything at home?'

'Everything's fine and I've got some good news to tell you. Father called round later this afternoon and it seems that we have another wedding to look forward to.'

When she raised her eyebrows quizzically he told her, 'It's Mary Ann and Tom, and apparently it's going to be some time within the next month or so. So, Mrs Bensham, I want you to make a concerted effort to get better so that I can take you out and treat you to a nice new outfit!'

'Well, after an offer like that, how can I refuse? It's wonderful news. I liked Tom as soon as I met him. They make a nice couple, don't they?'

Ben nodded in agreement. He had always been very close to Mary Ann and liked the thought of seeing her happily settled. Content with being together, a comfortable silence now settled between man and wife until the bell heralding the end of visiting sounded.

Rising reluctantly, Ben bent to kiss Hannah softly on the lips before running his hand gently across her stomach. 'You just look out for your mother now, do you hear?' he told their unborn child, and then with a final wave he made his way from the ward feeling for all the world as if he had left his right hand behind him.

That night and the whole of the next day passed painfully slowly and Ben was relieved when at last he found himself in amongst the

311

throng of visitors who were waiting to be admitted to the ward the next evening.

Through the glass in the top of the doors that opened onto the ward, he could see the Ward Sister with her eyes tight on the wall clock. Exactly on the stroke of seven o'clock she opened the doors and the visitors, who were loaded down with fruit and flowers, poured through them.

His eyes instantly swept the length of the ward and, when Ben saw the curtains drawn around Hannah's bed, his heart plummeted into his boots.

'Mr Bensham?'

Turning about, Ben came face to face with the Sister. He nodded solemnly and she now asked, 'Would you mind stepping into the office, sir? The doctor would like a word with you.'

Ben followed her back the way he had come until they reached a small room at the end of the ward. Opening the door, she ushered him inside where a tall gaunt-faced doctor was sitting at a desk writing up notes.

'Doctor Bone, Mr Bensham to see you.'

At any other time, Ben would have found the doctor's name highly amusing, considering the profession he was in. But for now all he could think of was what the man was about to tell him. Had something happened to Hannah?

'Ah, thank you, Sister. Mr Bensham, do take a seat.'

As Ben did as he was told, the doctor laid down his pen and peered at him over the top of the gold pince-nez spectacles that were perched on the end of his red, bulbous nose.

'I'm afraid I have some rather bad news for you, Mr Bensham.'

The words brought Ben back to the brink of the edge of the world and his heart started to pound painfully. The doctor was going to tell him that Hannah had died, he was sure of it – but even so, he could not utter so much as a single word. It was as if he had been struck dumb.

'During the night, your wife took a turn for the worse and so we had no choice but to take her down to theatre to perform an exploratory operation. It's a good thing we did too, for if we hadn't, I think I can safely say she might not have survived the night.'

Relief washed over Ben in a wave. Hannah was alive. No matter what the doctor told him now, he could bear it just so long as he didn't lose her.

'Unfortunately, when we opened her up we discovered that your wife was having an ectopic pregnancy.'

When Ben stared back at the man uncomprehendingly, he went on, 'To explain as simply as I can, an ectopic pregnancy occurs when the fertilised egg attaches itself outside of the cavity of the womb. In your wife's case, the baby was growing inside the Fallopian tube, hence all the pain she was suffering. Thankfully, we managed to remove the tube before it ruptured. Had we not, it could have been very serious indeed. However, we also discovered that the other tube was also badly infected, so we had to remove that too.'

'So, we've lost the baby then?' Ben now asked falteringly.

'Yes, I'm afraid so, and I have to tell you that

now we have had to remove your wife's tubes there is no possibility of her ever having another child. I am so very sorry, Mr Bensham.'

The blood was pounding in Ben's ears as the doctor's words echoed around and around in his head. *No possibility of her ever having another child. No possibility of her ever having another child!*

But he had to be mistaken! Hannah was one of the healthiest people he knew ... and they had planned to have lots of children. A houseful of them, in fact. The crib that Lawrie had carved was all ready and waiting for them back at the cottage.

He swallowed, and forced himself to ask, 'Does Hannah know?'

'Yes, Mr Bensham. We told her when she first came round from the operation earlier on. Are there any questions you would like to ask?'

Ben shook his head as he rose unsteadily from his seat, and now the Sister was smiling at him sadly as she told him, 'Come along, Mr Bensham. I think you and your wife need a little time alone.' She took his arm and Ben allowed her to lead him back into the ward. When they reached Hannah's bed she twitched the curtains aside and gently pushed him through them and then she was gone and all Ben could do was look helplessly down on his wife, who seemed to have shrunk overnight. She was lying on her side, but when she heard the movement of the curtain she turned to him and now the tears exploded from her eyes as she told him brokenly, 'Oh Ben. I'm *so* very sorry. I've let you down. I...'

'Shhh...' Ben had her in his arms now and he was kissing the tears away as he held her tight to

314

his heart and told her, 'We will get through this, my love. As long as I have you, nothing else matters.'

But deep inside he was crying for their lost dreams and all the children that they would now never know.

Suddenly he knew why this had happened and he was back in the nursery again and his mother was telling him, *You are bad, you are a Mallen through and through.*

And he *was* a Mallen. The streak in his hair told of his heritage, and it was a well-known fact that all the Mallens were cursed.

Chapter Twenty-Two

Ruth was in her element as she planned the wedding and so Dan decided to stay at Brook House for a few days before setting off to Southend. It was now early in April and finally the weather had taken a turn for the better. The garden of Brook House, which amounted to a little over two acres, was now coming slowly back to life after the long cold winter. Crocuses and daffodils were peeping from beneath the hedgerows, and the buds on the trees were a delicate green. Once again, birds had come to nest in the trees and now as Dan strolled about the grounds, the sound of their singing filled the air.

It was a little over two weeks to go now until Mary Ann's wedding, and Ruth had delighted him with her choice of venue for the wedding reception, which was to be held in a small but select hotel in Allendale. They had chosen everything for the wedding together and Dan found that he was looking forward to it.

Brigie's health had slightly improved with the weather and Jonathan was also making progress, although Dan had been devastated to learn that his son's eyesight had been badly affected by the gas he had been exposed to on the battlefield. It had not been apparent whilst he had been confined to his chair in the window, locked away in his own private hell. But as soon as he became able to walk about a bit, the way he held his hands falteringly out in front of him had made it apparent.

Dan had decided that, as soon as Jonathan was well enough to travel, he would take him to see a Harley Street eye specialist, but the doctor at the Hall had urged him not to raise his hopes. As he pointed out, he had seen many such cases, and usually the damage done by the gas was irreversible.

Still, until a few short months ago, Dan had believed that his son was dead and so even the fact that he was partially blind could not stop him giving thanks that Johnny had been returned to them alive.

His thoughts now moved on to Ben and Hannah, and his heart ached as it always did as he thought of their plight. They would have made such excellent parents – he had no doubt about it. Especially Ben, for after being deprived of his own mother's love as a child, he had so much love trapped inside him to give. Hannah was still recovering at their home, although she had already spoken to the Matron at the Hall about returning to work there when she was well enough. Dan had feared for a time that losing their second baby, as well as any hope of another, so soon after Lawrie's death, would destroy them. But thankfully the couple's deep love for one another seemed to be pulling them through.

And Mary Ann; the smile returned to his face as he thought of his only daughter. She had positively bloomed during the last few weeks, and he knew that in Tom she had finally found her soulmate.

'Master Dan. Master Dan!'

He turned to see Betty hurrying across the grass towards him, waving an envelope in her hand.

'The postman just brought this an' it's got a London postmark on it,' she told him breathlessly as she drew abreast of him and pressed it into his hand.

'Thank you, Betty.'

'You're welcome. But don't be too long out here, mind. Ada has cooked you a steak and kidney pudden an' it should be ready to serve up in half an hour or so. She'll have your guts for garters if you let it spoil, so she will.'

He flashed her a smile as he took the letter to a wooden bench that was set beneath the spreading branches of an enormous oak tree, where he carefully opened it and extracted a single sheet of paper.

As his eyes settled on the address that was neatly written on the right-hand side of the page, he realised that it was from Meg Fellows and now he sat straight as he began to read.

Dear Dan,

I trust this note finds both you and your wife well? I hope you will not think it too forward of me for writing to you at home, but I have some information that I thought would be of interest to you. Yesterday, I happened to spot your little friend, Pip, hanging around outside my shop, and so I went out to have a word with him.

It seems that the poor soul's mother passed away last week, and as you can imagine, he was utterly devastated. I think he had nowhere else to turn, and so he came to me. Knowing that you had a fondness for the child, I felt that I should inform you, particularly as he asked me if I had seen you. I know you gave him your address, but clever though Pip is, I do not believe he can read and write well enough to send you a letter.

With kind regards,
Meg Fellows

Dan sighed. Just as Meg had said, he *had* grown fond of the child. But what could *he* do for him? There was a whole rook of Beddows, from what he could remember of it. But how would they cope now without their mother? He had no doubt that the older boys would be more than capable of fending for themselves, but what of Pip and his two younger brothers? What would become of them? Would they be taken into an orphanage?

Rising slowly, he made his way up the lawn, and seeing the despondent look on his face, Betty

318

said, 'Lord love us – whatever has happened now? You've got a face on you like a wet weekend.'

He passed her the sheet of paper without a word and once she had read it she asked, 'So who is this 'ere Pip then?'

He quickly explained about his meeting with the boy in London's East End, and of how fond he had become of him, and Betty said, 'So why don't you bring him back here? Me an' Ada rattle about like two peas in a pod when you ain't here. An' even when you are there's spare bedrooms lyin' empty.'

'It isn't as simple as that,' Dan told her regretfully. 'There is quite a large family of them, two of them even younger than Pip. I've no doubt the older boys could survive, but I can't see how they would be able to provide for the three younger ones. And knowing how loyal and devoted to his family Pip is, I really can't envisage him leaving the little ones to fend for themselves.'

'You won't know until you ask, will you?' Betty told him. 'It would be wonderful to have a child in the house again. Just like it was when the young masters were little. We could set him small jobs to do, gardening and suchlike if he felt so inclined.'

Dan nodded thoughtfully. 'I suppose Pip might agree to that if he thought he was earning his keep. But of course, I would have to discuss it with Ruth first and see how she felt about it.'

'O' course you would. But now, come along an' have your dinner. There ain't nothin' goin' to spoil in the time it takes you to eat it, is there?'

'I don't suppose there is.' Dan folded the sheet of paper and tucked it into his pocket before following Betty obediently to the small but elaborate dining room.

He arrived at Ruth's house later that afternoon to find Mary Ann standing on a chair whilst her mother pinned up the hem of her wedding dress. It was a shop-bought dress, for there had been no time to have one custom-made. Even so, it fitted perfectly, apart from the length. Ruth smiled up at him through a mouthful of pins before asking, 'So what do you think then?'

'I think she looks absolutely beautiful,' Dan replied proudly as he stared up at his daughter, and she did.

'That should do it,' Ruth told her a moment later, and Mary Ann hopped lightly off the chair to hug her father.

''Ere, that's enough o' that,' Ruth scolded. 'You don't want it all creased up, do you? Go on, get off with you an' hang it up while I make your dad a cup o' tea.' Rising slowly, she told Dan, 'Come through to the kitchen. I'll be glad of a break.'

Once there she put the kettle on and then, as he sat staring off into space, she said, 'Come on then. Spit it out. I can see that you've somethin' on your mind. What is it?'

Without a word he handed her the letter, and as she read it a frown creased her brow. 'Why, the poor little mite. But what does Meg Fellows expect you to do about it?'

'Actually, when I was back at Brook House, Betty suggested that perhaps he could go to live there. Betty and Ada are both getting on a bit now and as she pointed out, he could do little jobs about the house and garden to help out. What do you think of the idea?'

Ruth rubbed her face before answering. 'Well, you have no need to tell me that your heart is in the right place. But it's a lot to take on a young boy at your age. No disrespect intended, o' course.'

'You're right,' Dan admitted. 'But what other option is there? I'm not offering to adopt him; but more to employ him as a help for Betty and Ada. I just hate the thought of the poor little mite ending up in an orphanage.'

'Well, if I weren't goin' to be so full up here what wi' Tom an' the baby that's on the way, I'd take him on.' Ruth had only met Pip the once on her visit to London, but like Dan, she had taken to him too and hated to think of him as an orphan.

'I dare say it wouldn't hurt if you were to go an' see him an' put the idea to him,' she went on. 'Though I wouldn't hold me breath on him takin' you up on the offer. From what I could see of it, despite havin' very little, they were a close-knit family.'

Dan nodded in agreement. Ruth was his wife now, for better or for worse, and he had not wanted to do anything without speaking to her first.

'If you're goin' I dare say you'd better make it soon,' she advised him. 'The weddin' is drawin' near an' you need to be here for that, so why don't you get yourself off tomorrow?'

A wave of guilt flooded through him. He had intended to travel to Southend tomorrow and continue his search for Brigie's daughter, but surely she would understand the delay if he explained the circumstances to her?

'I think I might well do that, if you're quite sure you don't mind,' he replied, then they settled down to talk of the wedding and enjoy their tea. He would sleep on it, he decided, and then he would know the best course of action to take.

The sun was riding high in a cloudless blue sky as Ben strode through the marketplace. He had taken to coming here at least twice a week in the hope of seeing the child he had once glimpsed with the streak in his hair, but as yet, each time, he had gone away sadly disappointed. Today looked set to be no different, for he was now loaded down with the shopping Nancy had asked him to get, and soon he would be setting off for home again.

He could not explain why it was suddenly so important to find the child and discover to whom he belonged. But somehow the need to find him was gnawing away at his insides.

Back at the cottage, Hannah was recovering well from her ordeal, though the brightness seemed to have gone from her smile and she was much quieter now. There was a silent pact between them that they did not speak of the fact that they could no longer have children, for it was still far too raw for either of them to address.

In the very near future, Hannah was intending to return to her nursing and Ben had decided that he would spend more time at the mill in Manchester, in which he had part shares. His Uncle John, who had the main share in the business along with Dan, was bedridden now and so was more than grateful that Ben intended to put in more time there. But still Ben's heart was heavy, for when he had looked into the future, he had always imagined himself and Hannah surrounded by children. Children who would be loved unreservedly as his mother had failed to love him. The running of the mill would merely be a way of filling his time, as would Hannah's nursing.

Even now that he was a grown man, the way his mother had treated him still rankled. Still filled him with anger that would bubble up at the most unexpected times. It could be triggered merely by the sight of a mother on the street holding the hand of a little one. His mother had *never* held his hand! In truth, she had rarely taken any of them out. But on the rare occasions when she had, it had always been Jonathan and Harry who walked at her side whilst Ben was told to walk in front of them. And all because he was the only one of the triplets who had borne the Mallen streak, which was a constant reminder of where she herself had sprung from.

Pulling his thoughts back to the present, he moved on amongst the market stalls. He would have a jug of ale before returning home, he decided, and had just turned in the direction of the Horse and Jockey Inn when he saw him – the child with the Mallen streak! He was some distance up the street and going at a merry trot. Oblivious of the shopping bags that were now banging against the sides of his legs, Ben began to hurry towards him, pushing his way rudely through the shoppers as he ran. He had almost caught up with him when the boy suddenly turned into a side street and disappeared. Determined not to lose him, Ben raced after him, and as he turned the corner, he saw the boy some way ahead of him.

'Hey, you – BOY!!'

The shout brought the boy to a shuddering halt and now as he turned to see Ben bearing down on him, his small mouth fell into a gape. The man who was approaching him had hair the same colour as his own with the same white streak running through it.

Ben was breathless by the time he caught up with him but he forced a smile to his face as, bending to the child's level, he said, 'Hello, what's your name?'

The child, who was slightly built, stared at him solemnly for a moment before replying, 'My name is William.'

'That's a fine name.' Ben's heart was hammering so loudly that he was sure the child must be able to hear it, but his voice betrayed none of his inner turmoil when he then asked, 'And where do you live, William?'

The child thumbed back across his shoulder and told him solemnly, 'In there with my mother.'

'I see.' Ben noticed that the child was reasonably dressed, and clean, unlike many of the urchins who lived in the back streets hereabouts. Most of them were crawling with head lice and could be smelled a mile off.

'And does your father live with you too?' he now asked.

The child shook his head. 'No, sir. I don't have a father. He was killed during the war.'

'Then I am very sorry to hear it.'

Suddenly the child, whose eyes had been tight

on Ben's hair, tentatively raised his hand and traced down the streak. 'You have the same hair as me,' he stated wonderingly. 'I've never seen anyone with hair like mine before.'

'It is very uncommon,' Ben told him softly. 'In my family, it is called the Mallen streak. What is your surname, William?'

'Cartwright, sir. William Cartwright.'

Cartwright, Cartwright, Cartwright! The shock of the child's words made the colour drain from Ben's cheeks.

This child must be the son of Felicity Cartwright! He had enjoyed her company many a time before he went away to war … therefore, this child must be the result of their liaison. There could be no other explanation for it.

He slowly rose now and, doing his best to compose himself, he asked, 'Do you think that your mother would mind very much if I called around to see her, William? I have reason to believe that your mother and I were friends before I went away to fight in the war. Is your mother's name Felicity?'

'Yes, sir, it is. And if you and she were friends, then no, I don't think she would mind you calling to see her. Mother says that it is important to have friends. Mother doesn't have many though. She works very long hours to keep us and rarely goes outdoors.'

'Does she now? And what work does she do?'

'She does sewing, sir. She's very good at it too.'

'I'm sure she is. But come, William. There is no time like the present. I shall walk with you back to your home and if it is convenient, I shall call to see your mother this very day.'

'Very well, sir.'

It was all Ben could do not to snatch the child trotting beside him into his arms and bury his face in his shoulder there and then, for a million emotions were coming to life inside him. This was *his* child! The child that he had thought he would never have. But why hadn't Felicity told him that she was pregnant before he went away? And what was she doing, living in these grimy back streets? She had come from a good family. So why had they allowed her to sink to living in such a place?

Shame washed over him as he thought of how his own flesh and blood had been forced to live for the first part of his young life.

And then he suddenly wondered how he was going to explain all of this to Hannah. How would she feel when he told her that he had a child he had never known existed, when she had just been told that she could never have any? It was sure to come as a shock to her, to say the very least. He pushed the thought firmly to the back of his mind.

First, he must talk to Felicity. He would worry about what Hannah would make of it all later. What was it Lawrie had used to say to him? *Just one small step at a time* ... that was it. Dear dead Lawrie.

The further into the back streets they got, the darker it became, for here the houses, which amounted to little more than hovels, were built very close together. So close that there was barely room to walk between them, and the overhanging roofs blocked out the light of the sun. And the smell! Ugh! Ben tried hard to keep his smile in place for the sake of the child as they picked their way across the rubbish-strewn cobblestones.

Eventually, William paused in front of a doorway to tell him, 'This is where my mother and I live.'

Ben noticed that the step to this house was clean, as were the windows, which was more than could be said for the neighbouring dwellings.

William now lifted the latch and as he stepped into the room beyond, he said across his shoulder, 'Come in. Mother will be working.'

Ben found himself in one of the tiniest rooms he had ever entered. There was an oak sideboard standing against one wall and two easy chairs to either side of an empty fireplace. In the centre of the room was a small table and two hard-backed wooden chairs. Everywhere he looked were partly sewn garments and reels of cotton of all the colours of the rainbow, but apart from that, the room was bare.

Through a small door that led off from this room he could hear the sound of pots clattering but this stopped abruptly when William called, 'Mother, it's me. And I have someone here who would like to see you.'

'Oh, yes, dear, and who would that be then?'

He heard footsteps on the flagstoned floor and then Felicity was in the doorway, wiping her hands on an apron as she looked towards them. As her eyes settled on Ben, the colour drained from her face and she leaned heavily against the door as she exclaimed, 'BEN!'

He was shocked to see how changed she was,

for she seemed to have aged prematurely. The weight had dropped off her and her fair hair, which she had always teased into elaborate curls that would peep from beneath her bonnet, was now scraped back into a severe bun at the back of her head.

As William looked from one to the other of them in total confusion she told him, 'William, go to your room and read for a while, would you?'

He obediently crossed the room to a small staircase in the far corner, and forcing a smile to her face she said softly, 'There's a good boy.'

At the foot of the stairs he paused to look back at Ben and tell him, 'Goodbye, Mr Mallen.'

'Goodbye, William.'

The two adults stood staring at each other until the sound of a door closing upstairs reached them.

And then, glaring across the room at him, she asked, 'What are *you* doing here?'

There was no warmth or greeting in her voice and now Ben slowly placed his shopping bags on the floor before telling her, 'I should think that is fairly obvious, Felicity. Can you imagine what a shock I had when I saw William walking through the marketplace! Why didn't you tell me that you were going to have a child?'

'Why *should* I tell you?'

Ben glared back at her, his temper now matching her own. 'If you *had* told me, you would never have been reduced to living in a place like this!' He spread his hands as he glanced around the room with contempt writ clear on his face. 'I would have looked after you. Married you, if it came to that. And what of your parents? How could they see you living here?'

'My parents disowned me when they discovered that I was pregnant,' she snapped back. 'Though what business it is of yours, I fail to see.'

'*You fail to see?* Are you completely mad, woman? It's obvious that I am William's father! And as such, I should at least have a say in his upbringing!'

'You are *not* William's father and so now, if you don't mind, I would like you to leave. We have managed quite well up to now without you poking your nose in where it isn't wanted.'

Ben's mouth fell into a gape. He had not come here looking for a fight but this was fast developing into one.

'How can you stand there and deny the fact that I am William's father? Look at him ... he's like the spit out of my mouth. How many more are walking about with the Mallen streak, I ask you?'

'Well, if I remember rightly, there could be quite a few. You were never one for tying yourself down to one woman, were you, Ben? Now get out this instant.' She was advancing upon him now and there was an air of menace about her. Lifting his bags she opened the door and tossed them into the street before hissing, 'Just *go,* can't you, and leave us in peace? We do not want or need you here.'

Ben stumbled blindly through the doorway into the dark alley as the door banged to resoundingly behind him.

Slowly he shook his head as he tried to take in all that had happened within the last hour. Now he would have to go and confess the latest developments to Hannah, for they had never had any secrets between them and he had no intention of it being otherwise. And then somehow he must devise a way of at least having some say in his son's life. For one thing he was sure of the child he had just left in that god-forsaken hovel was a Mallen through and through.

Chapter Twenty-Three

The rhythmic chug of the steam engine had lulled Dan into a doze, but now as the train drew to a juddering halt in King's Cross station, he started awake and knuckled the sleep from his eyes.

He had not been looking forward to this trip, and as far as he was concerned, the sooner it was over and done with, the better. As he clambered down onto the platform, he shuddered to think what state he would find Pip in. There was no doubt that the child had worshipped his mother, and Dan could only imagine that he would find him devastated at her loss.

Heading for the main exit, he stared out across the busy streets. In case Pip agreed to come home with him, Dan decided that it might be better if he found a room for them tonight in a more modest place than the Ritz. His sombre face creased into a smile as he imagined the reaction if he were to turn up in the Ritz's luxurious foyer with a little street urchin whose head was alive with lice!

He chose to walk until eventually he came to a small hotel in a street behind Euston station. It would suit his purpose admirably, he decided, so without a qualm, he walked in and booked a room for the night.

Once he had unpacked his small overnight valise, he then had a meal in the hotel's dining room before setting off to Adderton Street, wondering what he would find when he got there. It was mid-afternoon by the time he arrived, and once again he grimaced with distaste as he opened the front door of Pip's building. Now that the weather had improved, the smell was even worse than it had been – if that were possible. A huddle of raggy-arsed children who were playing in a corner raced towards him with expectant faces and out-stretched hands.

'Spare a penny, mister?'

Dan rummaged in his pockets for change, and once it had been distributed, the youngsters skipped away to disappear into various doorways with cries of glee.

Dan smiled sadly. It always hurt him to see how these people were forced to live. But then he couldn't take the worries of the whole world on his shoulders, could he? He could help Pip, though – if the boy would allow him to, that was!

He began the long climb to the second floor and by the time he had arrived there, he was breathless. Taking a moment to compose himself and get his breath back, he then approached the right door and rapped on it sharply. From within he could hear the loud howling of a baby, which he thought rather strange, for if he remembered rightly, Pip's youngest brother had been about five years old. He was further confused when a

331

toothless woman of indeterminate age opened the door and barked, 'Yes? Whadda yer want?'

'I er ... I'm so sorry to bother you, madam. I was looking for the Beddows family?'

'Huh! Well, yer won't find 'em 'ere, matey. They got chucked out on their arses fer not payin' the rent last week. Me an' my family live 'ere now.'

'Oh.' Dan was shocked, but as she began to close the door on him he pulled himself together enough to ask hastily, 'Would you happen to know where they have gone?'

'Ain't got a clue. The ma snuffed it so I expect they'd 'ave been sent to the orphanage. The younger ones, at least.' With that she closed the door smartly in his face and Dan stood there for some minutes as if rooted to the spot with shock. Poor Pip. What could have become of him?

As he slowly began to descend the stairs, his mind worked overtime. There must be dozens of orphanages in London, so how was he ever to find him?

Once outside, he looked despondently up and down the length of the street, then with heavy tread he began the journey back to the hotel, feeling for all the world as if he had let the poor child down.

That evening, he pushed his meal about the plate, for his appetite seemed to have fled. Where could Pip be?

Suddenly remembering Meg's letter, he drew it from his pocket and quickly re-read it. Would it be worth visiting her to find out if Pip had mentioned where he might be going? Deciding that this was better than doing nothing at all, he darted up to his room, collected his coat and headed towards the Underground.

Half an hour later, he was standing outside Meg's home. A thousand butterflies seemed to be flying around in his stomach, but he put this down to the anxiety he was feeling about Pip.

He tapped lightly on the door, and when Sally's now familiar face appeared, she smiled at him broadly before saying, 'Evening, Mr Bensham. I've got a funny feelin' you'll be a right welcome sight!'

Dan raised an enquiring eyebrow. 'Oh yes – and why would that be?'

'You'll see.' Sally now ushered him inside, took his coat and then led him towards the sitting room, where there seemed to a party going on.

The second she opened the door, Dan's eyes fell on Pip who was sitting next to Meg on the settee and his mouth gaped in surprise.

'Mr Dan!' Pip launched himself at him, and as his skinny arms slid around his waist, Dan looked at Meg quizzically.

'So, what exactly is going on here then?' It seemed to be the day for shocks.

'Come and sit down,' she invited, and as he went to do so, his mouth opened even wider as his eyes now settled on Pip's two younger brothers.

'I think you'd better make another pot of tea, Sally,' Meg grinned, 'and I dare say these boys wouldn't say no to a biscuit or two to go with it.'

'But I just gave 'em a dinner that would 'ave fed an army!' Sally exclaimed in exasperation.

'Even so, I'm sure they'd find room for a little more, wouldn't you, boys?'

Three little heads now nodded eagerly, and Sally sighed as she ushered them all towards the door.

'Come on then, you lot. I reckon you must have hollow legs, the way you put it away.'

As the door closed behind them, Dan sank onto the nearest chair and gazed at Meg.

Folding her hands sedately in her lap, she explained, 'I saw Pip last week, as I told you in my letter. That was when I learned that his mother had passed away, the poor little chap. Anyway, the weather was so nice today that I decided to take a stroll along the Embankment – and that is when I spotted Pip and his brothers. They had made a makeshift shelter out of the oldest, dirtiest blanket you have ever seen, and when I approached him and asked why he was there, he told me that the landlord had turned them out because they were unable to pay their rent. They had actually been sleeping there! It seems that any money they had got had been spent on burying their mother the cheapest way they could. There were four older boys there too, who introduced themselves as Pip's brothers. Two of them had found jobs on a farm. The other two were planning to travel until they found jobs too, but they didn't feel that they could leave the younger ones. Bless them. The oldest could have only been about fourteen. Anyway, the outcome of it was that I'm afraid I... Well, the long and the short of it is, I rather impulsively offered to bring the three little ones home with me. I know what you're going to say...' She held up her hand as if to ward off a blow before going on, 'It was a stupid thing to do and I have no idea what I'm going to do with them now. But anything must be better than the way they were being forced to live.'

'You are quite right,' Dan assured her. 'And I have to say that I think you are a very remarkable lady. Many people would have closed their eyes to the children's plight. But now ... I rather think I should take over the responsibility of them. After all, it is only through me that you met Pip in the first place. To be honest, I discussed the situation with Ruth after receiving your letter and we decided that Pip should come and stay at my house – if he would agree to it, that is. I have to say though that I hadn't reckoned on three of them.'

'So you're telling me that you might take *all three* of them home with you?' Meg's voice was incredulous. 'But what will Ruth say when you turn up with them all in tow?'

Deciding that it was time he was honest with her, Dan explained, 'The thing is, I still have my own house and I would be taking them there. I don't actually live with Ruth *all* the time. You see...' Slowly now he began to tell her of how and why he and Ruth had come together, as Meg listened attentively. When at last the tale was told she leaned across the space that divided them and gently squeezed his hand.

'Oh Dan. I had no idea. I'm so very sorry.'

'It's just one of those things.' He stared off into space. 'I thought when Barbara and I were first married, that she would come to love me in time, but she could only ever love one man and that man was not me. She married me merely to get away from Brigie, whose birth daughter I am

335

now trying to trace. And Ruth ... well, she was so good to me, so when I discovered a short time ago how ill she was I felt it was only right to marry her. Not that I don't care about her, you understand? I have a great fondness for her...'

Meg's eyes were full of tears, and she was sure that she had never heard such a sad story in the whole of her life. However, Dan was smiling now as he told her, 'I shall take the children back to Brook House with me. They'll certainly keep Ada and Betty on their toes. The problem is, I don't think there are any trains back to Newcastle tonight...'

'Oh, please don't worry about that,' she told him quickly. 'The boys can stay here.'

'Are you quite sure?'

'Absolutely. But now shouldn't you be telling them and see how they feel about it?'

He nodded. 'I dare say I should.'

Some minutes later Sally marched the children back into the room and Dan called Pip to his side. 'Pip, how would you feel about coming back to my house to live with me?' he asked.

Pip stared at him guardedly. 'Why would you want to take me back there?'

'Well, where else are you going to go?'

Pip shrugged. 'I don't rightly know. All I *do* know is I ain't goin' nowhere wivout Simon an' David. They're only babies an' I 'ave to look out fer 'em. Mum made me promise that I would.'

Tears trembled on his lashes as he thought of his mother, and Dan's heart went out to him, even as he wondered what the hell he was doing. He must be stark, staring mad to think of taking

336

on three little boys at his age, but then, what other option did he have? He would never be able to live with himself if he left them to fend for themselves.

'So how would you feel if I were to tell you I intend to take all three of you home? For now, at least, until we can come up with a better solution.'

Pip stared at him as if he could hardly believe his ears. 'What ... you mean we'd 'ave somewhere to stay? You wouldn't try stickin' us in an orphanage?'

'I wouldn't dream of it, so what do you say? I'm not saying you wouldn't have to help out about the house and garden, mind. Ada and Betty aren't as young as they used to be, so they wouldn't be able to run about after you all. What I can say though is that you would have a warm bed to sleep in, food on the table, and you would be properly clothed for as long as you were in my care. The bedrooms on the nursery floor where my sons used to sleep are ready and waiting, and I think you'd like Brook House.'

Suddenly, the brash front that Pip presented to the world slipped away and his bony young shoulders began to shake with the strength of his emotions as he thanked the Lord for the day he had met this kind man. And Mr Dan *was* kind, Pip had known it from the moment he had first met him. And now here he was, offering him a home. But not just him ... a home for his brothers too – for now, at least. They were going to sleep in *real* beds and live in a *real* home for the first time in their lives. It was almost too much to take in.

'N ... Nurse? I th ... think I would like to go up

337

and see … B … Brigie.'

'Of course, sir.' The nurse laid aside the cardigan she was knitting and crossing to Jonathan, she helped him from his chair and led him towards the door. He was making remarkable progress now; she had heard the doctor telling Matron so, only that very morning. In truth, there was no need for him to be in this room now, but she supposed as he was the brother of Ben Bensham, who would own the Hall when Mrs Bensham passed away, he could stay in whichever room he liked.

Shame about his eyesight though; he was quite handsome in his own way, though nothing like Ben in looks. It was hard to believe that they had made up two parts of a set of triplets. The nurse, who had only recently started at the Hall, had heard that the third triplet, Harry, had been killed in action and she thought that was a shame too.

Out on the landing, they went slowly towards the lift that would take them to the top floor where Mrs Bensham resided. Nurse Hoffman had only ever seen the woman once, and a right wizened-up little thing she was, though word had it that at one time she had ruled this house with a rod of iron. The 'Goddess of the Nursery Floor' they had used to call her by all accounts. Still, that was what age did to you – although they reckoned that the old lady's mind was still as sharp as a whip.

When they came to the lift, Jonathan fumbled blindly into it and stood silently at the nurse's side as it slowly rose to the top floor. Nurse Hoffman then led him to the door of Mrs Bensham's room, where she asked, 'Would you like me to wait out here for you, sir?'

'N ... no, Nurse. Thank you, but I shall b ... be perfectly all right. I will r ... ring when I wish to go back to my r ... room.'

'Very well, sir.' She watched him tap at the door and enter the room before turning about and taking the stairs two at a time. If she was lucky she would have time to squeeze in a quick tea break – if Matron wasn't about, that was.

'B ... Brigie.'

The old lady, who was in bed today, turned and, holding out her hand, she said, 'Why, Jonathan – what a lovely surprise. Come and sit here by me and tell me how you are doing.'

'I ... I am doing fine,' he said, sitting in the chair by her bedside.

'Good, I am pleased to hear it. You were in a pretty bad way when you arrived here, apparently.'

'Yes, I believe I was, but then it was no more than I deserved.'

'What do you mean, my dear?'

His head wagged from side to side and she saw the distress on his face as he said in a low voice, 'I once did a terrible thing, Brigie.'

'We all do terrible things from time to time, Jonathan. Believe me, I should know, for I too once did a terrible thing and now I pay for it every single day. But is it something that you would care to talk about? Sometimes it helps to share your concerns with someone else.'

'N ... no – but thank you.'

A silence now settled over them until Brigie broke it when she said, 'So, have you planned what you are going to do when you are well enough to leave here?'

'Not yet. Although now m ... my eyesight is restricted, I sh ... shall be limited in what I can do anyway. No doubt, F ... Father will give me a share in the mill and set me up in a nice little house somewhere.'

'I can think of worse things to happen to one.'

'Oh, I wasn't m ... meaning to sound ungrateful. It's just ... I suppose now, I shall have to spend the rest of my life a ... alone. Who will want someone who is almost blind?'

'I should think there would be any number of smart young women out there who would jump at the chance of taking up with a handsome young man like you.'

He laughed softly 'The problem is, B ... Brigie, there is only one young w ... woman I want.'

'Really?' There was a teasing quality to her voice now. 'I had no idea you were seeing anyone.'

'I haven't. Not for years. She will probably be married to someone else by now.'

'Well, there is only one way to find out, is there not? When you are well enough to be allowed out of the Hall, you must go and see this mysterious young lady and state your intentions.'

He looked towards the shape of her lying in the great brass bed and smiled sadly. 'Do you know something, Brigie?' he said. 'You could always make me feel b ... better, even when I w ... was a child. But I'm afraid that this time, even you cannot help me.'

'I am sure that is not true, Jonathan.' Brigie's voice was that of the governess now, and he found himself thinking, She is still the same Brigie; she will never change. And strangely, the thought brought him comfort, for everything else in his life had changed and right now she was someone stable and reliable to whom he could cling.

Hoping to lighten the mood now, she turned slowly in the bed and asked, 'Do you think you will be well enough to attend Mary Ann's wedding?'

'I am hoping so.' His relationship with his half-sister was one that he treasured, for they had been close since childhood.

Brigie sighed. She too was fond of Mary Ann and regretted the fact that she would not be able to see her be married. Lately, the bed she was lying in had taken the form of a prison cell, for she was now trapped in it, with no hope of ever getting out unless someone helped her. And she was tired, oh, so tired; often, now, the thought of death was something to embrace. But not just yet. First she must give Dan time to finish his search for her daughter. The daughter of whom she had refused to let herself think, through the long years since her birth. In her mind, she saw again the tiny body Mary Peel had taken from her arms following the birth. She had been a tiny little thing with soft brown hair and eyes as blue as bluebells. She remembered thinking at the time how glad she was that the child did not bear the same black hair as her father, Thomas, that would mark her out as a Mallen. But what would she look like now, she wondered. Would she be portly as her father had been, or slim like herself?

God willing, if Dan was successful in his search

she might soon set eyes on her. But it must be soon. For each day was becoming an effort now and she longed to be at peace.

Chapter Twenty-Four

'Good Lord above. Whatever have we here then?' As Betty stared at the little party assembled at the kitchen door, three pairs of eyes stared fearfully back at her.

Looking very sheepish and apologetic, Dan explained: 'Things didn't work out quite as I had planned, Betty. So for the foreseeable future, the lads will be staying here.' He pushed them forward one at a time as he introduced them.

'This is Pip, this is Simon, and this is David.'

Ada had come to stand in the doorway of the kitchen and her eyes now stretched wide too as she looked at the state of the little ragamuffins standing with the master. Even as she eyed them, David, the youngest, began to scratch furiously at his head.

Crossing to him, she parted his hair and then threw up her hands in horror. 'Good God above. You're crawlin' wi' dickies, so you are, laddie. It's into the bath an' then the nit comb for you.'

When Pip dared to grin she wagged a plump finger in his face. 'An' you needn't grin neither, young fellow me lad, 'cos you're next! Now come upstairs the lot o' you, while Betty here has a word to Mister Dan.'

'I'm so sorry, Betty.' Now that they were alone again, Dan was keen to explain what had happened, and by the time he had finished, Betty's kind heart was won over.

'Well, all I can say is, you did right to bring the poor little mites here. Though I warn you, it's goin' to cost you. We can't possibly let 'em walk about in the rags they're wearin'. The only decent things I could see atween the three of 'em were the coat the middle one was wearin' an' one decent pair o' shoes on Pip's feet. An' I don't mind bettin' you bought them an' all.'

When he lowered his eyes she said, 'I thought as much. But come on, give me some money an' I'll pop into town an' see if I can't get 'em a decent outfit each for when Ada has got 'em scrubbed clean. An' don't look so worried. It will be nice to have children about the house again. I dare say we'll manage between us, one way or another.'

Dan delved into his wallet and when he had handed her four large £5 notes, she whipped off her apron and snatched up her coat, telling him, 'I shouldn't be gone for too long. I'll just get 'em what's necessary for now. I've an idea there are still some o' the triplets' clothes in the trunk up in the nursery. No doubt they'll be a bit dated, but they'll be better than what they're wearin' now, an' they'll do for about the house. I'll sort through 'em when I get back.' With that, she grinned and slipped away.

Dan found himself smiling. The boys had already experienced the excitement of going on a train for the first time; he had grave doubts whether any of them had ever had a bath before,

343

and he had the strangest feeling that they weren't going to be too happy about it...

At that moment, Pip was standing naked with a large towel wrapped around him eyeing the tub of hot water cautiously.

'What yer sayin' is, I 'ave to get in there an' *sit* in it?' His voice was incredulous.

'That's about the long an' the short of it,' Ada told him bluntly. 'Now come on, lad. The two little 'uns will be goin' in next an' you don't want to set 'em a bad example now, do you?'

Pip frowned as he tentatively dangled his foot over the side of the large roll-top bath. The only time he had ever been totally immersed in water before was on the few occasions when he had swum in the murky waters of the River Thames. Other than that, he and his brothers had all taken turns at washing as best they could in a big tin bowl at the sink.

Feeling that the water was at least warm, he now dropped the towel and sat down in the bath very slowly. His backside had barely hit the bottom when Ada tipped a large jug full of water over his head and began to vigorously rub at his hair with carbolic soap.

'*Ouch!* What yer tryin' to do? Drown me?' he objected loudly as he coughed and spluttered.

Downstairs, a smile lifted the corners of Dan's mouth. It didn't sound as if Pip was enjoying his first experience in the bathtub too much at all. Chuckling now, he lifted his bag and carried it to his room with the sounds of Pip's cries ringing in his ears.

Much later that evening, as they all sat around the dining-room table, Dan could hardly take his eyes off the children. They were totally unrecognisable now from the little waifs he had arrived home with earlier in the day.

Ada and Betty had spent hours going through their hair with a fine nit comb and now, their newly washed hair floated around their heads in soft, dark, shining waves.

'You could have started a colony wi' all the dickies we got off them heads,' Betty had told him.

They were now each wearing the new trousers and shirts that Betty had been out to buy for them. She had had to guess at the sizes so admittedly they were all on the large side, but as Betty had pointed out, 'Better too big than too small. You'll soon grow into 'em.'

Dan could hardly believe how excited Betty and Ada were. He had been deeply concerned about what their reaction would be when he arrived home with three small boys in tow. But he needn't have worried, for they were clucking around them like mother hens and seemed to be in their element.

David, the youngest, who was five years old, was already following Betty around like a puppy, and Simon, who was six, had attached himself to Ada's side, much to her delight.

The beds that the triplets had once slept in up in the nursery had been made up with fresh sheets and blankets, and a fire had been lit in the grate to air the room.

The boys' eyes had stretched wide when they

were shown where they were to sleep. Back in London, they had slept five in a bed, and the thought of having a bed each to themselves was almost more than they could comprehend.

But now, as they sat greedily eyeing the large leg of roast pork that Betty had just placed in the centre of the table, they were so shocked that they had been rendered temporarily speechless. They gawped even more when Ada pottered in behind her with a large dish of roast potatoes in one hand and a steaming bowl of fresh vegetables in the other.

Apart from the hamper that Dan had had delivered to them at Christmas and the food they had enjoyed at Meg Fellows's, they had never seen so much food on one table all at the same time.

Now, as Betty hurried away to fetch the gravy boat, Ada began to pile their plates as she told them, 'Come on then, lads. Stick in. There's nowt worse than to stand cookin' an' see it go to waste. I want to see clean plates, do you hear?'

The meal was a light-hearted affair, although Dan did notice that whilst the boy ate everything that was put in front of him, Pip was rather quiet. Dan tactfully did not remark on it, putting it down to the fact that Pip was probably just feeling a little overawed with all that had happened. It had been a very long day for the three children.

The main course was followed by one of Ada's home-made Spotted Dick puddings, served with cream so thick that it stuck to their spoons.

Since Barbara's death, Dan had tended to have a tray in his study, or eat in the kitchen with Betty and Ada, for as he had pointed out, there was no point in going to the trouble of laying the dining room just for him. Now he thought how nice it was to see the room in use again.

As soon as the meal was over, Betty took the children up to the nursery floor, where they changed into the pyjamas she had bought for them earlier in the day. This too was a first for them, for previously they had always slept in their underclothes.

One at a time, she tucked them into the little beds that stood in a neat row along one wall. And then, taking what had once been one of Ben's favourite books from the bookshelf, she settled down in a chair to read them a bedtime story. It was Charles Kingsley's *The Water Babies*, and Simon and David were enthralled with it. Only Pip seemed to be uninterested as he stared towards the window that overlooked the grounds.

Betty had already read some pages when there came a tap at the door and Dan stuck his head around it.

'Am I interrupting anything? I just thought I'd pop in and say goodnight.'

'Not at all, I was just about to finish for tonight anyway. Come on in.'

As Dan approached the beds, Betty snapped the book shut and laid it aside.

'Are you quite comfortable, David?' Dan smiled as the child nodded vigorously. 'And you, Simon?'

Another nod, so he now approached Pip's bed. 'And how about you, young man? Have you got everything you need?'

He was saddened to see tears glistening on Pip's long dark lashes so, lowering himself onto the side of the bed, he took his small hand in his and asked softly, 'Is something troubling you, Pip? You can tell me if there is.'

Pip bravely blinked back the tears as he shook his head. 'There ain't nuffink wrong exactly, an' I'm more than grateful fer what yer doin' fer us, Mr Dan. It's just...' Suddenly, he could hold back the tears no longer and they spurted from his eyes, as he turned to bury his face in the pillow.

'Hey now! Come on, old chap. Tell me what's wrong.' Dan placed his arm about the child's trembling shoulders and a muttered little voice came back to him.

'I ... I miss me ma, Mr Dan... I miss 'er *so* much!'

'Of course you do. That is only to be expected, so have a good cry, Pip. There is no shame in showing your emotions.' Pip was now in his arms and Dan could feel the child's tears damping his shirtfront. He rocked him to and fro, just as he had once rocked his sons, as he whispered soothing words into the child's clean-smelling hair.

'It will get easier with time,' he told him, and he of all people should know.

'You mean to tell me you have brought *three* children back to Brook House?' Ben asked incredulously.

Dan lowered his eyes as he muttered, 'Yes, that's exactly what I have done. I could hardly leave them there, could I?'

Ben and Hannah exchanged a glance, but it was Hannah who now said, 'Well, for what my opinion is worth, I think you did the right thing,

Dan. Poor little mites. What would have become of them, if you had not taken charge? It doesn't sound as if Sally and Mrs Fellows could have coped with them all. But the question is ... what are you going to do with them now?'

'I admit I haven't thought that far ahead.'

Dan was saved from saying any more when Nancy appeared carrying a large tray of tea and hot buttered scones fresh from the oven.

When she had left the room, Hannah began to spoon sugar into the cups as she asked, 'How are Betty and Ada coping with three little ones rampaging about the place?'

She passed Dan a scone and taking it from her, he answered, 'Actually, the pair of them seem to be in their elements. They said it's like having the triplets back at home again. They've certainly livened the place up, I can assure you.'

'That's all well and good, but what about schooling? Have you even thought of things like that?' Ben was totally exasperated and it sounded in his voice. He had always known that his father was a kind man, but to go off and return with three orphans just like that! Whatever had he been thinking of?

Suddenly thinking of William, he became silent. He had still not spoken to Hannah about it. He had intended to, but somehow up to now the right moment had not presented itself. Or, he wondered, was it deep down that he was afraid of how she would react to the news? After all, it wasn't every day your husband informed you that he had a little flyblow running about, was it? He could hardly expect her to be happy about the fact. Even so, he would have to tell her – and soon – for the thought of William living in that grimy back street was eating away at him. Then he would go and see Felicity again and demand his rights as a father – and *this* time he would not take no for an answer!

He now took the cup and saucer she was offering to him and asked his father, 'Have you told Ruth about the children yet?'

'No. I only got home yesterday, remember. But after I've popped up to the Hall to see Jonathan and Brigie, I shall be going to stay at Ruth's. I'm off back down to London and then to Southend the next day, to follow this other lead about Brigie's daughter.'

Hannah's head wagged from side to side. 'I still can't take in the fact that there's another Brigie out there somewhere! Or another Mallen – whichever way you want to look at it. Fancy keeping a secret like that, all these years! Let's just pray that she doesn't find out it is now common knowledge.'

'Thankfully, I think there is little chance of that. She never leaves her room now, so she's hardly likely to find out that someone has spread the word. But what do you think your chances of finding this long-lost daughter of hers are, Dad?'

Dan shrugged as he sipped at his tea. 'To be truthful, there are only two more leads to follow up now. Other than the child who was adopted by an American couple, that is. I'm praying that she wasn't Brigie's child. I had fully intended to have visited the other two by now, but what with Lawrie and then Hannah...'

'It's all right, Dan,' Hannah assured him as the colour rushed to his cheeks. 'You are allowed to mention what happened.'

Dan bowed his head as he watched the pain wash across Ben's face. Him and his big mouth. He knew full well how much Ben had wanted a family, so why hadn't he been more careful about what he was saying? The irony of the situation suddenly struck him. Here was this lovely couple who wanted a child more than anything in the world, and there was he, stuck with three back at home, whom nobody wanted! Life could be a funny old thing, there was no doubt about it.

Hoping to lighten the mood now, Hannah asked, 'And how are the plans for the wedding coming along?'

'Oh! Don't even ask.' Dan was laughing now. 'It's pandemonium round at Ruth's. She's flapping over everything. I have an awful feeling she'll be a nervous wreck by the time the big day arrives. She practically frogmarched me into town and even chose my outfit for me. I don't know what she thought I was going to turn up in, I'm sure. She wouldn't let me wear my own wedding suit for some reason. Between you and me, I shall sigh with relief when it's all over. It's nice to see her and Mary Ann looking so happy though.'

'Well, I'm really pleased for her, and I can't wait,' Hannah said gaily. 'I'm off into town for my own outfit tomorrow. You know what we women are like, any excuse.'

She winked at her father-in-law and they then talked of everyday things until it was time for Dan to leave.

His good mood was restored even further some time later when he arrived at the Hall to find Jonathan looking much more like his old self. Unless Dan was very much mistaken, there was even a little colour back in his cheeks now.

'Hello, son.'

Jonathan fumbled his way across to his father, who shook his hand warmly before telling him, 'I have to say, you're looking brighter. How do you feel?'

'Much better, though it's hard to get about with not being able to see so well.'

'Try not to worry about that, old chap. As soon as Matron says you're up to the journey, I intend to take you down to London to see an eye specialist.'

Jonathan shook his head. 'It would be a waste of money, Father. It's a known fact that damage done to the eyes through exposure to gas is irreversible. You'd just be wasting your money, I'm afraid. I'm just going to have to learn to live with it.'

Dan was silent for a moment before saying softly, 'But at least you are alive. For a long time, we thought you were dead. Your mother took it very badly.'

They had spoken little of Barbara since Jonathan's return, but now his son told him, 'I'm so sorry about the way things turned out. And for her to die as she did...'

'She died as she chose to.' Dan's lips set in a grim line, but then he said more calmly, 'I did not really lose her when she died, Jonathan. I think you are old enough to realise that she was never

352

really mine from the day we wed. Her heart and soul always belonged to Michael. The only good thing to come from the marriage was you boys, so for that fact alone I would not have had it otherwise. But come ... let's not be sad. Matron tells me that you will be well enough to attend the wedding. It will do you good to get out and about for a while. For now though, let's go up and see Brigie, eh?'

His son hesitated; there had been something he had wanted to discuss with his father. Something that was keeping him awake at night. But still, now was not perhaps the right time. It could wait.

Threading his arm through his father's, they turned about and side-by-side they left the room together.

'So, another wasted journey then?'

'I'm afraid so.' Dan moved a packet of pins from the seat of the chair and sat down as Ruth filled the kettle at the sink. He had just returned from Southend and his search had once again led him to a dead end.

'The strange thing is though, that the lady I spoke to said that I was the *second* person to be looking for Josephine Richardson within days. That happened in Nuneaton as well, if you remember rightly. It's all very peculiar, isn't it?'

When Ruth nodded he went on regretfully, 'That only leaves one other possibility in this country now. And if this one in Manchester *isn't* Brigie's daughter, then it will mean travelling to America. Between you and me, I think I'm on a fool's errand. I mean, what are the chances of finding her after all these years? She might be dead by now.'

'And she might not be, so for Brigie's sake you have to at least try. Not that I want you doin' a disappearin' act again just now afore the weddin'. There are a million an' one last-minute things left to see to, so I could do with you bein' at hand. An' what about the boys? If Ada and Betty are comin' to the weddin', who will look after them?'

'I was rather hoping they could come too?' Dan suggested hopefully.

Ruth beamed; she had been hoping he would say that. She had taken the news far more calmly than Hannah and Ben, almost as if it was an everyday occurrence for her husband to visit London and arrive home with three little orphans in tow. She was only sorry that there wasn't room for them to live here. But once Tom had moved in after the wedding and the baby had arrived, they would have been squashed in like sardines in a can. Still, from what Dan had told her, the boys had given Betty and Ada a new lease of life, so perhaps things had worked out for the best, after all.

Humming merrily, she turned back to the kettle with her mind full of flowers and all the other important matters that she still had to arrange before her daughter's big day.

Chapter Twenty-Five

It was the day before the wedding, and as Betty hurried to answer the door, she was muttering under her breath. She was busy pressing the outfits the three boys would be wearing the next day and had been hoping that she would have no more interruptions. Hannah and Ben had left not an hour since, and now here was yet another visitor – no doubt someone come to deliver a wedding present. It was funny, now that she came to think about it. Hannah and Ben had called in some days ago, and since then they had called in almost every day. She suspected that the boys were the reason for their visits, for they had both taken to them immediately, as the boys had to them. So much so, in fact, that today, little David had sobbed when Hannah stood up to leave.

Outside on the lawn, Dan and the boys were kicking a football about and the sound of their laughter was floating around the house as she opened the door.

She found herself face-to-face with an attractive blonde-haired lady who smiled at her charmingly as she said, 'I am so sorry to disturb you, but I am looking for Mr Dan Bensham. Have I come to the right house?'

'You have that. He's outside at present, but do come in. I'll give him a shout for you. Who should I say is callin'?'

'Mrs Fellows. Mrs Meg Fellows.'

Betty nodded, and once the visitor was inside she motioned her to a chair and told her, 'Sit yourself down. I'll not be a minute.'

Meg smiled and watched the woman potter away before looking around her. The house was far bigger than she had expected it to be and tastefully furnished too. But then she should have expected that, for Dan had told her that his first wife was a lady, and being such she would have had good taste.

The sound of laughter was wafting through an open door, but it stopped abruptly and seconds later, Dan breezed into the hallway closely followed by the boys, who shrieked with delight when they saw her.

'Why, Meg! What a pleasant surprise.' Dan extended his hand but before she could take it, the two smaller children had launched themselves at her and as she bent to their level she could only smile up at him apologetically.

Hands on hips, Betty watched with a look of astonishment on her face. Dan's cheeks were as red as a beetroot and he was smiling from ear to ear. But it was not this that shocked her. It was the look in his eyes. The look he had saved for Barbara, on the rare occasions when she had chosen to be nice to him. The look that seemed to say that all his birthdays and Christmases had come at once.

'Shall I er ... put the kettle on then?' she asked for want of something to say, and now Dan suddenly sprang forward as if remembering his manners.

'Oh, I'm so sorry. How remiss of me. Betty, this is Mrs Fellows, the lady I told you about who has been helping me in my search for Brigie's daughter. And Meg, this is Betty. She's been with me for years and quite frankly I don't know what I would do without her.'

Betty blushed becomingly as she smiled at the woman who seemed to have Mr Dan in a tizzy. She was very easy to look upon and her nature seemed to match her looks, for her eyes were smiling as well as her lips. But saying that, there was no edge to her and Betty found herself liking her.

'Come on, you lot.' She gathered the children to her and ushered them towards the kitchen. 'Let's go and see if we can't find you a bit o' that fruit cake you're so fond of, eh? And Mr Dan – why don't you take your visitor through to the parlour? I'll bring you a nice tray o' tea through shortly.'

'Thank you, Betty. That would be lovely.' Taking Meg's elbow he steered her in the direction of the parlour as Betty ushered the excited children away.

Once through the door she told him, 'I'm so sorry to turn up like this unannounced, but I think you must have left this behind on your last visit.' She took from her handbag a pen with a solid gold nib, and as Dan's eyes settled on it he laughed.

'Well, I'll be. I wondered where that had got to! It must have slipped out of my pocket during my last visit. But you really shouldn't have come all this way to return it.'

She blushed now and, suddenly lowering her eyes, she told him truthfully, 'I didn't come just for that, to be honest. I've been worrying about the

357

boys and wondering how you were coping with them, so I suppose I used the pen as an excuse to come and see for myself. I do hope you don't mind?'

'Not at all. It's wonderful to see you, but now, won't you sit down and I'll tell you all about what happened when I went to Southend.'

Once he had described his fruitless visit she then asked, 'And the children, how are they settling?'

'Simon and David are fine. In fact, as you probably noticed, they have Betty and Ada wrapped around their little fingers. But Pip ... well, he misses his mother terribly, although being the brave little chap that he is, he tries not to show it.'

'And have you given any thought as yet to their longterm future?'

Dan sighed. 'To be honest, it's been so hectic, what with my daughter's wedding plans and one thing and another that I'm afraid I haven't as yet. But they are all right here, for now at least. Obviously I can't keep them here forever. I'm a little long in the tooth to be taking on three youngsters, but ... well, I couldn't see them out on the street. Once the wedding is behind us I'll have to think of something, of course. I suppose a boarding school would be the ideal solution, although I think the two little ones are a bit young to be sent away.'

She nodded in agreement, and when Betty entered the room with their tea some minutes later she found them with their heads bent close together, deep in conversation. For no reason that she could explain, she found herself thinking of Ruth and suddenly felt decidedly uncomfortable and something of an intruder as she asked,

'Would you like me to pour for you, Mr Dan?'

'What? Oh, no thank you, Betty. Just leave it there, would you, and I'll see to it.'

'As you will.' She left the room, closing the door quietly behind her, and once in the kitchen she raised her eyes at Ada. 'They seem to be getting on like a house on fire in there,' she remarked.

Ada shrugged before replying, 'Then let's just hope as he remembers he's a married man.'

'Ada, really! What a thing to say.' But even as the words were being uttered she saw again in her mind's eye the look in Dan's eyes when he had first seen the woman sitting there. And what she was thinking was, eeh, life can be a cruel bugger at times! For never in her life had she ever seen Dan look at anyone like that except Barbara, and now here he was, married to Ruth.

It was almost an hour later when Dan escorted Meg back into the hallway. Betty ran from the kitchen and asked, 'Will your visitor not be stayin' for dinner, Mr Dan? There's more than enough to go round, even wi' them little scally-wags back there eatin' us out o' house an' home.'

It was Meg who replied when she smiled at her warmly and told her, 'Thank you for the offer, Betty, but I have a train to catch. And anyway, I would not like to impose on the eve of the wedding. I'm sure you all must have a hundred and one things left to do.'

Betty returned her smile before hurrying away back to the kitchen as Dan now turned back to Meg.

'Well, once again, many thanks for returning the pen. And also for bringing the last address. I shall follow it up as soon as I have time.'

They were both very aware that there was no reason now why they should ever meet again, and a silence settled on them as Dan opened the door for her. He walked with her to the gate, and suddenly he said, 'Look, you have my address, so ... do keep in touch from time to time.'

He could have sworn that her smile held a trace of the sadness he was feeling now as she told him, 'Thank you, but I don't really think that would be such a good idea, do you? But good luck with the wedding – and with the boys, of course. And do give my regards to Ruth. She really is a lovely woman.'

'Thank you, I will. And yes, as you say, she *is* a lovely woman.'

She held out her hand and when he shook it warmly he held on to it for a fraction longer than was necessary as he savoured the feel of her slim fingers in his.

'Goodbye, Dan.'

'Goodbye, Meg.' She was walking away and he stood and watched her until she turned a bend in the road and was lost to sight. Only then did he slowly turn about and make his way back into the house.

Had they ordered the weather they could not have wished for a more perfect day; the sun was riding high in a cloudless blue sky and the little church was packed to capacity. As Dan walked down the aisle with his daughter on his arm his heart was overflowing with love for her and he felt as if he must surely be the proudest man on earth, for she looked absolutely beautiful. And it was nothing to do with the clothes she was wearing, but more to do with the glow that seemed to be radiating from her.

He could see Ruth sitting in the front pew, with a handkerchief dabbing away at the tears that were slowly rolling down her cheeks, and then the young couple were standing before the altar and the vicar was asking, 'Who giveth this woman to this man?'

Dan solemnly placed Mary Ann's hand in that of Tom, and as he saw the love shining from the young man's eyes he knew that he need never worry about his daughter again. She had finally found her soulmate.

Immediately after the wedding, they all enjoyed a sumptuous meal in a smart hotel in Allendale before returning to Ruth's where the wedding reception continued. It was a lively affair. No expense had been spared and the wine was flowing like water. Everyone was in fine spirits, although Dan was concerned to see that as the day wore on, Ruth looked totally exhausted.

When she made one of the numerous trips to the kitchen to load the table with yet more food he discreetly followed her, and once the door had closed behind them he asked, 'Are you feeling all right, dear?'

She turned wearily to look him in the eye. 'Oh aye, I'm fine. Tired, admittedly, but fine. It's been a grand day, hasn't it, lad?'

'Yes, it has.'

They were both smiling at each other, and suddenly taking his hand she whispered, 'Do you

361

know something, Dan? Should the good Lord decide to take me tonight, I would die a happy woman.'

'Don't say that, my dear.' His brow creased into a deep frown. 'You have years ahead of you. *Years*, I tell you!'

'No.' She was still smiling but he saw now that there were tears shining on her lashes. 'I never thought that I would see Mary Ann happy and settled, for until she met Tom there seemed to be no one who could hold her attention for long. And added to that, I am now Mrs Dan Bensham. But ... I want you to promise me something.'

'Anything.'

'We will have no need to worry about those two, for they have each other now, and they are kindred spirits. But you... Well, when I go I want you to promise me that you won't grieve. Somewhere out there is *your* kindred spirit. You will know when you meet, as I knew when I first set eyes on you. And when you find her, I want you to be happy. *Really* happy. Will you promise me that you'll do that?'

'I can't believe you are talking like this, today of all days.' Dan ran his hand distractedly through his hair. 'You are my wife, Ruth. Why would I want anyone else?'

She was saved from having to answer when the door was suddenly flung open and Simon appeared, closely followed by Hannah, who was as red in the face as the child was.

'Oops, sorry,' Hannah called over her shoulder as she chased the child out into the small back garden. The sombre mood was broken now as

Ruth laughed aloud.

'Seems to me that Hannah and Ben have taken a right shine to them little boys,' she commented. 'Makes you realise what wonderful parents they would have made, don't it? I wonder if they've ever given any thought to adoptin'?'

The seed had been planted and she watched Dan's eyes as Ben now joined in the chase, with Pip and David on his heels.

Ruth was quite right. Now he came to think of it, his son and his wife had been frequent visitors to Brook House since he had taken the children in, and just as Ruth had pointed out, they *did* seem very taken with them.

He strolled to the window and as he stood with his arms folded, thoughtfully watching the antics that were taking place in the garden, Ruth smiled with satisfaction. All in all, the day had been just about as good as it could have been all round.

As Ben and Hannah were making their way home that evening in the new car that Ben had recently purchased, Hannah was smiling. Really smiling for the first time since the terrible day when the doctor had gravely informed her that she would never bear children following her operation.

'They're a handful, aren't they?'

'Who are?'

'The boys your father has taken in, of course.'

'Oh yes, yes, I suppose they are.' Ben suddenly drew the car into the side of the road and gazed at her solemnly. The time he and Hannah had spent with the boys had made him think of William – not that he had stopped thinking of the

363

child in the previous days. He had been longing to tell Hannah about him, and now he could hold it back no longer. Swallowing nervously, he said, 'Hannah, I have something I need to tell you.'

'Oh yes, and what would that be then?'

He stared up at the crescent moon that was suspended in the sky above. How did you tell your wife that you had an illegitimate child?

'I er ... well, the thing is, when I was in town the other day I saw a child in the marketplace. A child that bore the Mallen streak.'

The smile was gone from her face now but he forced himself to go on. 'I was so full of curiosity that I followed him, and when I caught up with him I asked him what his name was. He told me that it was William. William Cartwright.'

'So?'

'Before I went away to war I had a casual relationship with a woman. Her name was Felicity Cartwright.'

'So?'

A silence descended on them for what to Ben felt like an eternity until Hannah said falteringly, 'I had heard of your association with her. But what are you saying? Do you think that William might be *your* child?'

'I ... I'm sure of it. You see, I went home with him – if you could call the hovel he is forced to live in a home. And I saw Felicity and asked her straight out if the child was mine.'

'And what did she say?'

'Oh, she flatly denied it and ordered me out of the house. But it speaks for itself, doesn't it? How many men do you know who bear this?' He yanked at the streak in his hair and now he told her, 'I am *so* sorry, Hannah. I know this must have come as a dreadful shock to you. But if you will allow it, I want the child in my care and I will fight Felicity for custody of him, if that is what it takes.'

He held his breath as he waited for her reaction, but when it came it was not what he had been hoping for, for what she said was, 'Is Felicity a bad mother then?'

'Well, it rather speaks for itself if she is forcing him to live in squalor, doesn't it?'

'No, Ben, I'm afraid it doesn't.'

His eyes almost started from his head as she went on, 'If she is being forced to provide for the child on her own, then she is probably having to live in what she can afford. And it says something that she kept the child, doesn't it? What I mean is, many ladies of breeding would have farmed him out after the birth and forgotten all about him. But she kept him, and to me that speaks volumes. You cannot just turn up out of the blue and expect her to hand him over to you without so much as a qualm.'

'But I thought that we could perhaps–'

'You thought that we could take him and bring him up as our own ... is that it?'

When he nodded and lowered his eyes, she sighed into the darkness. 'Should she wish to give him up, then yes, of course I would take him if he is half yours, Ben. But you can't just go and tear him away from his mother if they have a genuine affection for one another. It would be cruel. You have to do this properly.'

'And how do you suggest I do that?'

365

'I suggest that you let me go to see her. It's obvious that you have upset her, especially if she thinks that you are going to try and take the child away from her.'

Ben thought this through, then said, 'I suppose you are right.' His hand groped in the darkness until it found hers, and he said shamefacedly, 'I am so sorry to drop this on you. It must have come as a terrible shock.'

'Not really. I too have seen the child – and so did Lawrie, and I think from the moment I set eyes on him I knew deep down that he was yours. To be honest, I have been thinking of putting a suggestion to you since we discovered that we could not have children of our own. But we haven't spoken of what happened. Probably because it was so soon after losing Lawrie and the baby that it was too painful to do so. But I was going to suggest that we could perhaps adopt a child.'

'*What?* One that isn't ours?' Ben was shocked. 'No, I don't think I could do that.'

'Why not? I have seen you with the boys your father has taken in. You seem to have taken to them all right.'

'That is because they are nice children. But they are not *mine*, Hannah. Try to understand. William *is* mine and therefore he should be with me. Felicity should have got in touch somehow and told me that she was going to have a child.'

Disappointment clouded Hannah's face before she asked, 'And just how was she supposed to do that, when you had gone off to war? Were you in a serious relationship?'

'Well, no, not really. She seemed to cool to-

366

wards me for some weeks before I went away.'

'Then there is your answer. But now I would like to go home. I ... I have a lot to think about.'

There was a hardness to her voice now and, grim-faced, Ben started the car and they continued their journey in silence.

Nancy was waiting for them when they got home but Hannah politely refused the hot drink she had ready for them and swept away to bed as Ben parked the new car in the outbuilding that Lawrie had once used as his workshop.

Alone in the sanctuary of their bedroom, Hannah flung her hat into a far corner and sank onto the edge of the bed as despair washed over her. She knew that she had no right to feel as she did. After all, what had gone on between Felicity Cartwright and Ben had happened long before she and Ben had fallen in love. So why then did the knowledge that he had a child to another woman hurt her so? Was it because she herself could never now give him one? But then, she reasoned, that was no cause to take it out on the child, William. *William* ... she rolled the name around on her tongue and saw him again in her mind's eye as she had that day in the marketplace. He was a Mallen, all right. In fact, he was a mirror image of Ben. And if what Ben had said was true – and she had no reason to doubt him – then they could not just ignore the fact that he existed.

An image of the babies she had lost flashed in front of her eyes. Would they have looked like Ben, with the same coal-black hair and the white streak running through it? Somehow over the last weeks she had managed to shut the agony away, but now it was as if a floodgate had opened and suddenly the tears were gushing from her eyes, as grief poured out of her. She would never now hold her own child in her arms or lay it in the crib that poor dear Lawrie had so lovingly carved. She would never see Ben playing ball with their children as she had seen him playing only that very afternoon with Pip and his little brothers, or sit with them at night and read them a bedtime story. Her babies were gone but William was alive, and although at the moment her heart felt as if it were breaking, she knew that she would have to do right by him. He was, after all, an extension of her husband, and she loved Ben with all her heart.

Long into the night she lay staring sightlessly up at the ceiling as Ben's gentle snores echoed around the room. And finally, as the birds started their morning chorus, she reached a decision. Today she would go and see Felicity Cartwright.

Part Four

The End of an Era

Chapter Twenty-Six

Jim Waite had carried a chair into the yard of Wolf-bur Farm and Constance was sitting there enjoying the feel of the sun on her face. Chickens were clucking at her feet and up on the fells to the side of the barn she could see the sheep grazing. In the dairy she could hear Lily clattering about, and to all intents and purposes, everything was as it should be. So why then, she wondered, had this sense of foreboding settled around her like a mist? It had been growing stronger for days, to the point that she could no longer sleep easy in her bed. Sarah had long since left in the trap, telling Constance that she was away to do a bit of shopping in Newcastle. That in itself was strange, for Sarah had never been one for just up and taking off when the fancy took her, until the last few months. But now... Constance sighed. She sometimes felt that she did not know Sarah any more, for the bitter-ness she had harboured since Michael's death seemed to have robbed her of all reason. She was full of hatred, and now that Barbara was dead, most of it seemed to be directed at Brigie.

Constance stared away over the hills in the direc-tion of High Banks Hall, as if the staring would somehow transport her onto the terrace that ran along the front of it. So often of late she'd almost asked Jim to take her there, but each time she had stopped herself. Only yesterday, Florrie Harper'd informed them on her visit that Brigie had come down with a summer cold and was very poorly.

Strangely, Constance had realised that Brigie was all she had left of her past, now that Michael was gone. But then he had never really been hers since the day Hannah drew breath, for from that moment on, it had seemed to be him and the child against herself and Sarah.

Despite the heat of the day she drew the shawl that was draped across her shoulders more tightly about her. If she was to make her peace with Brigie then it would have to be soon, for she had the strangest feeling that time was running out for both of them, even though Brigie was so much older than herself.

Brigie had had something and someone to live for following her marriage to Harry Bensham but now, like Constance, she had no one. Sometimes the thought of death was welcoming, for Constance did not know how much longer she could stand Sarah's harsh words. A picture of her old governess floated in front of her eyes and making a hasty decision, she suddenly shouted, 'Lily!'

The woman came running through the dairy, wiping her hands on her apron as she asked, 'Aye, missus?'

'Where is your father?'

'Up in the top field, last I heard. One o' the sheep is havin' trouble lambin'.'

'Well, when he comes back, would you tell him I would like to see him?'

'Aye, missus. I'll do that.' Lily watched as Constance rose painfully from the chair. She then took up the walking stick that was propped against the farmhouse wall and limped away into the shade of the kitchen.

Lily sighed heavily. She'd be glad to get away from this place and that was a fact, for everyone seemed to be walking about with a face that could have curdled the milk! Swiping the sweat from her brow with the back of her hand, she returned to the dairy with a deep frown on her face.

Constance meanwhile was preparing for her visit. First of all she made her way to her room, where she tipped some water from the jug into a bowl and washed every inch of herself. She then brushed her hair and secured it tightly on the back of her head, and she then settled down to wait.

It was almost two hours later when Jim Waite tapped at the kitchen door.

'Come in.'

He entered the room, blinking as his eyes adjusted to the shade, and muttered, 'Our Lily's just informed me as you wanted to see me, missus.'

She was sitting at the table and he saw at a glance that she had changed from the clothes she usually wore about the farm into a smart day dress and bonnet.

'Yes, Jim, I do,' she told him stiffly. 'I wish to visit High Banks Hall.'

A look of utter astonishment crossed his features as he muttered, 'But, missus, our Sarah has taken the trap into Newcastle.'

'I am quite aware of that fact, Jim. But we have a cart, do we not? Prepare that.'

'*The cart?*'he gasped incredulously. 'Why, seven miles across the fells in that will rattle the teeth out o' your head.'

Since Michael's death, Jim had more or less seen to all the outdoor running of the farm and Constance had been happy to let him, but now she left him in no doubt as to whom the boss was as she barked, 'The cart, Jim! Go and prepare it *now!*'

He fled from the kitchen so quickly that he almost stumbled in his haste with a look of utter amazement on his face. It had been many a long year since the missus had talked to him like that, and he didn't like it. No, he decided, he didn't like it one little bit!

Twenty minutes later, he was helping her up onto the hard wooden seat. Constance stared ahead, her hands folded neatly in her lap, and as Jim urged the horse into a trot and out of the farmyard she looked to neither left nor right, for all her thoughts were focused on what she was about to do. Every instinct that she had was screaming that time was short and she must make peace with the woman who had once been like a mother to her.

It so happened that, as Constance was crossing the wild fells, Hannah was passing through the marketplace in Newcastle. She had gone past several stalls when she saw a familiar figure ahead of her, and paused. She could only see the back of the figure, but the crutch that was jammed tight beneath the woman's arm told her immediately that it was her mother. Hannah paused as a frown flitted across her face. What would her mother be doing in Newcastle again? Until recently, she had lived an almost reclusive life on the farm, and yet the last time Hannah had visited her grandmother, Constance had informed her that her mother was a regular visitor to the town now. She hesitated. Should she catch up with her mother, or find the address that Ben had given her? Deciding on the first option, she began to hurry along in Sarah's footsteps. She would pass the time of day and then go on with her errand. Hannah had almost caught up with her, when Sarah suddenly turned and began to pick her way across the cobblestones through the back streets.

Hannah had been just about to shout out to her, but now she frowned. What possible business could her mother have there? She had intended to simply have a word before going on her way but now she was consumed with curiosity, and slowly she began to follow, keeping well back in the shadows.

After a time, she saw her mother turn into a doorway and as she grew nearer, she heard the clump of Sarah's crutch as it mounted a staircase.

After approaching the dilapidated building, Hannah stared at the rusting sign that was screwed to the wall. *Private Detectives, Wolfe & Peale, 39 Dock Street.*

Hannah's eyes almost started from her head. What possible need could her mother have for the services of private detectives? Unless... Hadn't Dan informed them that, on each of his journeys to try and discover the whereabouts of Brigie's daughter, someone had already got there before him? No, she pushed the thought away. Her mother could be bitter – but why would she wish to find Brigie's daughter? She looked around her and shuddered. An old man who was obviously blind was tapping his way towards her on a stick with a tin mug held out piteously in front of him. As she fumbled in her bag for some change she found that her hands were shaking. Quickly dropping some coins into the mug she then turned about and fled back to the marketplace.

Once there, she leaned heavily against a wall and took a deep breath. She supposed that she should have waited for her mother and questioned her, but for some reason her nerves had failed her.

Deciding that she would raise the point the next time they met, she pulled herself away from the wall and, after smoothing her dropped-waist dress over her slim hips, she continued on her way.

She soon found herself in a labyrinth of dark, foul-smelling back streets, this time on the opposite side of the marketplace. Children were rolling glass marbles and empty tin cans along the cobbles, their skinny arms and legs bare, as were their feet. Others sat listlessly on doorsteps. Their eyes when they glanced up at her were dull and lacklustre, and Hannah had to stifle the urge that came upon her to cry. The smell of urine was overpowering and she saw with horror that raw sewage was visible in a rough channel that ran along one side of the street. Now she began to understand why Ben was so averse to his child living in such a place, for never in her worst nightmares had she imagined that such conditions existed.

After a while, she approached a grubby little boy to ask, 'Could you tell me where Wharf Street is, please?'

''Tis that way, missus,' he said, pointing and sniffing.

When Hannah dropped a shining sixpence into his hand, his thin little face was transformed. It broke into a smile revealing blackened teeth.

'Ta, missus. Ta!' As she watched him scamper away, the unfairness of life hit her full force. So much poverty and so many children who looked unloved and unkempt. And yet she and Ben, who would have adored their offspring, had been denied the chance of ever having any.

Moving on, she took the direction the child had pointed out and soon found herself in Wharf Street. After fumbling in the pocket of her jacket she removed the address that Ben had reluctantly written down for her. She could still hear his loud objections ringing in her ears.

'But Hannah, I wish to come too!'

She had stood her ground, had insisted on coming alone. After all, as she had pointed out, he had already upset the child's mother, and a further visit so soon after the first could surely only make the situation worse? Now she was wondering if she had made a mistake. One thing was for sure: she was not looking forward to the confrontation ahead one little bit.

Unfortunately, many of the houses were not numbered, but when at last she came to the door of number 13, she paused. Unlike the houses adjoining it, she saw at a glance that the curtains that hung at the windows, although of a very poor quality, were clean, as was the doorstep, showing that whoever lived there had made an effort at least. Gathering together every ounce of courage she possessed, she raised her hand and rapped at the door.

'So *why* have you not yet followed up the lead in Manchester?' Leaning heavily across the desk that separated them, Sarah glared at Quentin Wolfe.

'I sincerely apologise for the delay, Mrs Radlet. But as you can see, I met with an unfortunate accident and have been unfit to travel.' Quentin Wolfe grimaced with pain as he slightly raised his left arm, which was bound tightly in a grubby piece of rag that was serving as a sling.

'Huh! So could your partner not have followed it up, then?' Had Sarah known that Quentin had met with his 'unfortunate little accident' as he termed it, whilst trying to pick someone's pocket, she would have been yet more incensed.

Mr Wolfe now dripped charm as motioning her to a chair he told her, 'Mr Peale tends to deal with investigations that are closer to home, but never fear, my dear lady. I shall be following on with my enquiries within the week. You have my assurance on that.' He had been tempted to ask for a further fee at this meeting but now, seeing that she was already in a towering rage, he decided to wait until after the next journey. After all, this investigation was proving to be a good little money-spinner and he had no wish to spoil it.

Turning about, Sarah limped to the doorway, where she paused to tell him, 'I shall be back on the same day next week. And I assure you, should you *not* have some news for me, be it good, bad or indifferent, you will find yourself facing a very irate client! Good day, Mr Wolfe!'

With that, she clumped away down the steep narrow staircase, leaving him in no doubt what-

378

soever exactly where he stood.

Once he had heard her emerge onto the street below, he moved to the window and watched her progress as she swung her crutch across the cobbles. No wonder her husband had taken himself a mistress! Wolfe thought, twirling his moustaches for comfort. He should have been awarded a medal for ever taking on the sour-faced bitch in the first place!

It was mid-afternoon when Jim drew the cart to a halt in front of High Banks Hall. For a while, Constance sat motionless as her mind slipped back in time to when she and Barbara had lived here with their Uncle Thomas. They had been just small children then, with their whole lives before them. The future had looked bright, and yet each of them had gone on to live a life of misery.

'Are yer ready then, missus?'

Pulling her thoughts sharply back to the present, she looked down to see Jim Waite standing at the side of the cart.

'Oh, sorry, Jim.'

She placed her hand in his and he helped her to the ground where she took a moment to adjust her bonnet and straighten her skirts. She then told him with a note of authority in her voice, 'Take the cart round to the stables, Jim, and see that the horse has a drink. I should not be too long but I'm sure they will find you some refreshment if you go to the kitchen.'

'Aye, I'll do that.' His voice was surly and as she turned to look beyond the topiary trees he took the reins and led the horse away.

Constance was pleased to see that the grounds had been maintained. In fact, they had scarcely changed and were just as she had remembered them. She looked to the south where lay Nine Banks Peel and then north to the little West Allen village of Whitfield. Finally she trained her eyes straight ahead to the mountains that today were washed with sunshine, and just as it always had, the sight filled her with wonder, for it seemed from here, that she had a view of the whole world.

'May I help you?'

Constance turned to see a young nurse standing at the top of the steps smiling down at her.

'Oh yes. I am here to see Mrs Bensham.'

'How wonderful. Mrs Bensham doesn't have too many visitors, so I am sure she will be delighted to see you. Won't you come in?'

Constance slowly climbed the steps, and once at the young woman's side she again turned to stare at the panoramic view before saying, 'It's a lovely sight, isn't it?'

The nurse nodded. 'It certainly is. Have you ever visited the Hall before?'

With a wry smile, Constance admitted, 'I used to live here once, but that was a very, very long time ago.'

'Really?' The young woman was intrigued. 'In that case, I'll have no need to show you up to the nursery floor then, will I? That's where Mrs Bensham's quarters are.'

As they made their way into the house, Constance experienced the weirdest feeling. It was almost as if she was coming home. She had been just two years old when she first came here, and her earliest recollections were of living in this house. Now as she glanced around she had the uncanniest feeling that her Uncle Thomas might walk out of one of the rooms leading off from the hall at any minute.

'We have had a lift installed for the officers who have problems with the stairs,' the nurse told her. 'It's down at the end of the passage if you would care to take it?'

'Thank you, but no. I will use the stairs.'

The nurse watched the woman approach the staircase with a wry smile on her face. She had no idea at all who this visitor was, but she somehow put her in mind of Mrs Bensham. It was something about her erect posture and the way she walked, graceful and tall.

At that moment, one of the officers appeared from the day room and the young nurse hurried towards him and soon forgot all about the visitor.

Constance felt as if she were stepping back in time as she slowly mounted the sweeping staircase. The banisters were still highly polished, just as they had been when she and Barbara had slid down them – when Brigie was not there to scold them for being unladylike. When she reached the galleried landing she paused to look first one way then another. She knew that many of the rooms on this floor had been turned into dormitories for the officers who were recuperating from their ordeals. The landing, however, remained unchanged and once again she was transported back to her childhood. She and Barbara had often played on this landing when the weather was too inclement for them to take the air outside, as

Brigie had termed it.

Brigie. Soon she would be face-to-face with her again after long years apart, and the thought caused the first worm of uncertainty to wriggle its way around her innards. Would Brigie be pleased to see her? Or would she send her away with a flea in her ear?

Well, there was only one way to find out. She had taken no more than two steps along the staircase that led up to the nursery floor when Florrie Harper came round the corner, carrying a mop and bucket. Constance silently cursed. The woman was a gossip, and Constance had no doubt that Florrie would now break her neck to tell Sarah that she had been there – that's if Jim Waite didn't inform her first, of course.

Inclining her head she moved on, ignoring the fact that Florrie was staring after her open-mouthed. Once at the door that she suspected would be Brigie's bedroom, she drew herself up to her full height, smoothed her hair behind her ears and tapped.

'Come in.'

Constance's heart began to beat wildly. That was Brigie's voice. Even after all these years she would have recognised it anywhere. After slowly pushing the door inwards she stepped into the room and instantly her eyes were drawn to the huge brass bed. But the woman lying there could not be Brigie, surely? Brigie had always carried herself proudly, with her head held high, whilst the woman in the bed was a wizened-up little creature with snow-white hair.

Her doubts were dispelled when the woman

turned her head to stare at her, for it was Brigie's eyes that were looking back at her, and for a moment it would have been difficult to say who looked the more shocked of the two of them.

The old woman's gnarled hand now flew to her throat as she stared at her visitor as if she could hardly believe her eyes, and then after what seemed an eternity she whispered, 'Constance ... is it really you?'

'Yes. It is me, Brigie, I...' Sudden tears sprang to her eyes, and she could not go on. During all the long years they had been estranged, Constance had kept a picture of the Brigie she had known and loved in her mind. And now to be confronted by this poor pathetic invalid was more than she could bear.

'Constance ... don't cry, my dear. Come here to me.'

Of their own volition, her feet took her to the side of the bed and now the old woman's hand came out and grasped hers. 'I have prayed for this moment,' she muttered softly. 'I ... I wanted to see you one last time before I died. And to tell you how sorry I am for the grave injustice I once did you. But I want you to know, when I persuaded you to marry Donald, knowing that it was Matthew whom you really loved, I thought I was doing right by you. I swear I did.'

As Constance stared back at her, she found that the strangest sensation was overwhelming her. There was a constriction in her throat that was threatening to choke her and a tightness in her chest. And suddenly, in her mind's eye she again saw the wreck of a woman before her as she had once been. The Goddess of the Nursery Floor. A lady whose word was law, and who insisted that etiquette must be observed at all times. And now the words that had been trapped inside her finally found relief as she sobbed brokenly, 'Oh Brigie, I have missed you so.' And even as they were being uttered, Constance knew that it was true, for whilst at times she had hated this woman with a vengeance, almost to the point of wishing her dead, she yet still recognised that Brigie had been the nearest thing to a mother she had ever known, and her love for her had never died.

And then suddenly she was leaning towards her and their arms were entwined as the tears on their cheeks joined and fell to dampen the fine lawn pillowcase.

'Come, sit beside me and tell me how you are.' The old hint of command was still there and now Constance perched obediently on the edge of the bed, thinking to herself, Imagine it! Brigie has a child somewhere! A child that she thinks no one except Dan knows about. Not that she would ever mention it, of course. Oh no, she hadn't come here to cause pain but to mend bridges that had been broken and impassable for far too long.

The entrance of a nurse with a tea tray disturbed them almost an hour later. She smiled when she saw that Brigie had a visitor and asked Constance, 'Will you be staying for tea, ma'am? I could soon slip away and get another cup?'

'Oh no. Thank you, but no. I have already stayed far longer than I intended to. I don't want to tire Mrs Bensham out.' Her eyes were full of affection now as she stood up and stared down on her old governess.

'Well, from what I can see, I'd have to say that your visit has had quite the opposite effect,' the nurse told her. 'I haven't seen Mrs Bensham looking quite so bright for many a long day. You appear to have done her more good than all the tonics we have been pouring down her throat.'

Brigie was clinging tightly to Constance's hand and now she asked, 'Will you be coming again, my dear?'

Constance's head wagged slowly from side-to-side. 'No, Brigie. It might be for the best if I didn't. I just wanted us to make our peace.' Her heart was racing and she could feel the heat burning up through her whole being before it came to rest in her cheeks.

Brigie nodded slowly. She knew that this was Constance's way of saying goodbye. She would never see her again. Not in this life at least – but that was all right. They *had* made their peace.

'Thank you.' An unspoken message seemed to pass between them until Brigie then said softly, 'Goodbye, my dear.' The old Brigie was evident again now as she formally held out her hand and, smiling through her tears, Constance took it and shook it before whispering, 'Goodbye, Brigie.'

She then turned and left the room.

Chapter Twenty-Seven

'Yes?'

Hannah found herself confronted by a tall fair-haired woman who was nothing at all as she had imagined her to be.

She gulped deep in her throat before saying, 'Mrs Cartwright?'

The woman frowned before replying, 'May I ask who you are?'

'I am Mrs Hannah Bensham, Ben's wife – and I wondered ... would it be possible for us to have a chat?' There, it was said, and now she saw the hostility light up in the woman's eyes as she shook her head and began to close the door on her.

'I have nothing to say to you, or him for that matter. Now go away and leave me in peace.'

'*Please...*' Hannah's hand shot out and stopped the door from closing just in time as she pleaded, 'I haven't come here to cause any trouble, I promise you. Please, I beg you, can't you spare me just a few minutes?'

The woman paused uncertainly, but then eventually she opened the door a fraction and muttered, 'You'd better come in, but only for a few minutes, mind.'

'Of course.' Hannah heaved a sigh of relief and stepped past the woman into a room that was surprisingly clean and tidy, apart from the many garments that were strewn about. She saw that many of them were in the process of being made, and on a table in the far window were spools of cotton in every colour of the rainbow, along with an assortment of pins and needles.

'Well?' The woman stared at her coldly.

'I know that Ben upset you when he came to see you the other day, which is why I am here,' Hannah said softly.

'I said everything that needed to be said then, so I hardly see the purpose of your visit.'

Despite the woman's icy attitude, Hannah could sense that she was deeply distressed. She was well-spoken and her clothes, though of poor quality, were washed and pressed. As Hannah stared back at her, she glimpsed the beauty she must once have been and understood why Ben would have been drawn to her.

A silence stretched between them as they surveyed each other, but then the woman suddenly flung herself about and leaning heavily on the edge of the table, she snapped, 'If you have come here to try and persuade me to part with William, then you are wasting your time. He is *my* son and we need no one apart from each other.'

'Of course he is yours. No one is disputing that. And I have no wish to take him away from you, I assure you. But the thing is, Ben is his father and as such he would like to contribute towards his upkeep.'

'I do not need Ben's money. I am more than capable of earning us a living and I take charity from no one.' The woman's eyes were starting from her head now. 'And furthermore, Ben is *not* William's father as I told him quite clearly the other day.'

'But ... the streak?' breathed Hannah. 'How can you dispute his parentage when it is displayed for all to see?'

'Ben was not the only Mallen born, in case you had forgotten. He was one of triplets, was he not?'

'What are you saying?' Hannah was now deeply shocked and suddenly the fight seemed to leave the woman in front of her and her shoulders sagged as she sank onto a chair.

'If I tell you something, will you promise to leave us in peace?'

Wide-eyed, Hannah nodded and now the woman went on slowly, 'I did have a brief affair with Ben, although it was a very on-and-off thing. And then I met Jonathan and I... Well, the long and the short of it is, I fell in love with him. He was terrified of Ben finding out about how we felt about each other. He was concerned that Ben might see it as a betrayal of him, and so we chose to keep our relationship a secret. I had ended my liaison with Ben by then, anyway. And then, of course, Johnny, Ben and Harry all went away to war and shortly afterwards I discovered that I was pregnant. My family threw me out; disowned me. I wasn't overly concerned, for I knew that when Jonathan came home we would be married. And then I heard that he had been killed...'

She paused here, and now Hannah saw the raw pain in her eyes as she gasped, 'So, what you are telling me is that William is *Jonathan's* child and not Ben's?'

'Yes. Although Jonathan never bore the Mallen streak it was there in him just the same, and the streak was passed on to our child.'

Now it was Hannah who sank onto a chair as reaction set in. How was Ben going to take this news, she wondered. He had been so convinced that William was his. But more importantly – what about this poor woman? She obviously had no idea whatsoever that Jonathan was still alive. Should she tell her?

As she looked across at her now she realised with a little shock that, had they met under other circumstances, they might have been friends. And so now she took a deep breath and told her, 'Felicity, I am grateful to you for being so honest with me, and now I think I should be honest with you. You see, Jonathan *isn't* dead. He was presumed to be so for some time, but then he was found in a hospital tent and sent home. At present he is convalescing up at the Hall–' She had no time to say more, for the colour suddenly drained from the other woman's face and to Hannah's horror she slid from her chair and fell in a dead faint at her feet.

Hannah glanced around the room, then hurrying to the sink she snatched up a cloth and wet it. Sinking to her knees, she gently wiped the cloth around the woman's face and she was still in this position with Felicity's head in her lap when the door suddenly opened and a child appeared.

'What is wrong with my mother?' he burst out.

The little boy looked terrified and Hannah told him gently, 'It's all right, William. I'm afraid your mother has had a bit of a shock, but she'll be fine in a minute, I promise.'

With the door still flapping open behind him he

stood wringing his hands, and seconds later his mother's eyes fluttered open. Hannah helped her back onto the chair as Felicity asked, 'Is what you have told me true? Is Johnny *really* alive?' Her face was chalk-white and her hands were shaking uncontrollably as Hannah solemnly nodded. And then the tears came spurting from her eyes to run in rivers down her cheeks as she stared at Hannah incredulously.

William came straight to her side and she caught him to her, burying her face in his shoulder for comfort as the child looked on in bewilderment.

Hannah rose. 'I am going to leave now,' she said. 'You need time to take in what I have told you. But I shall be back. In the meantime, would you like me to tell Jonathan that I have spoken to you?'

Raising her tear-drenched face, Felicity stared at her for a while, trying to make up her mind. 'Yes, I would like that,' she whispered eventually. 'And then you could perhaps tell me what his reaction was. It could be that after all this time, he will no longer wish to see me. But please, don't tell him about...'

Hannah glanced at William before replying, 'I understand. But before I go, there is one more thing that you should know.' She braced herself, then went on quietly, 'Jonathan has been very ill. In fact, for some time he did not even know who he was and recognised no one. Thankfully he is over the worst now and making steady progress, but the thing is... Well, I have to tell you that he was exposed to gas and he is now almost blind.'

As Felicity's hand flew to her mouth, a sob escaped her lips.

Hannah waited for a moment and then asked, 'Do you still want him to know that we have spoken?'

Felicity nodded. 'Yes, of course I want him to know. You see, I have never stopped loving him. It would make no difference to me if he had lost *all* his limbs, just so long as he was still alive.' Her eyes grew dreamy and her voice softened as she thought back to the all-too-brief time they had shared together. 'I had been seeing Ben on and off for some time when he took me to visit Brook House one day. That was where I met Jonathan. I had never believed in love at first sight till then, but from the second I set eyes on him I knew that he was the man for me. And strangely, when we finally came together, he told me that he had felt the same way also, but was too afraid of Ben's reaction to do anything about it. So yes, I do want him to know that we have spoken.'

'Very well. Goodbye, Felicity. Goodbye, William. It was lovely to meet you, and I will call again soon.' Hannah let herself out, feeling overwhelmed by emotion. Taking a deep breath, she leaned wearily against the outside wall. How was Ben going to take the news that William was not his child? Worse still, how was he going to react when he knew that the child was Jonathan's? With her head bent, she turned in the direction of the marketplace. What a rare old twenty-four hours this had turned out to be! First to discover that her husband had a son, then to catch her mother visiting a private detective ... and then to meet Felicity and learn the truth about William ... it was almost more than she could take in.

Ben was pacing up and down the room like a caged animal when Hannah entered the parlour back at the cottage some time later. Normally, at sight of her he would hurry over and kiss her, but today he rapped out, 'Well? Did you see her?'

'Yes, I saw her.' Hannah's heart was hammering and her tongue felt thick as she went on, 'I think you had better sit down. What I have to tell you may come as a shock.'

Never taking his eyes from her face he sank down onto the settee, and now she took his hand and unable to look him in the eyes, she began to relay the tale that Felicity had told her. Throughout the telling, Ben never uttered so much as a single word, and when the story was told, a silence settled between them that seemed to stretch on for ever.

Eventually, she dared to raise her eyes and look at him. He was staring towards the empty grate and wearing a look of such desolation that it tore at her heart.

Finally he broke the silence. *'Felicity and Johnny,'* he muttered. 'But why didn't he tell me that he had feelings for her? In truth, there was never anything serious between us. I would have given them my blessing.'

'But he was not to know that, was he?' Hannah pointed out softly. 'He probably felt that you would think he had gone behind your back, and loving you as he did, he didn't want to hurt you.'

'And she is *quite* sure that William is Jonathan's child?'

'Absolutely.'

'Then we must tell him.'

Hannah stifled the urge to cry. Knowing Ben as she did, she knew that deep down he had wanted William to be his, for she could never give him children now. Yet even so, he was man enough to put his brother's feelings before his own.

Slowly rising, and looking down on her, he said, 'There's no time like the present, so they say. I think we should go up to the Hall right now. Jonathan is doing well, but this might be just the push he needs to put all the bad behind him. Did you tell Felicity that he was now almost blind?'

'Yes, I told her.'

'And?'

'She said that it would make no difference. She still loves him.'

'I see. Come, Hannah. We should go to see Johnny as soon as possible.' His mouth set in a grim line, Ben started towards the door and Hannah followed behind him.

'Why, all these visitors in one day,' Matron beamed as Ben and Hannah stepped into the hallway. 'There was a lady here to see Mrs Bensham earlier on, though I can't say for sure that the visit did her any good. According to the nurse, she hasn't stopped crying since the woman left.'

'Oh, and who was that then?'

'The older of the Mrs Radlets, by all accounts.'

'*What?* Grandmother came to see Brigie?' Hannah's voice was shocked.

'She certainly did, and I have to say after seeing her that you look nothing like her, my dear. You must take after your father.'

Hannah's mind was reeling as she wondered what other surprises this day might have in store for her. But now was not the time for thinking of her grandmother, or Brigie for that matter. Ben was impatient to see Jonathan and so now she asked, 'Is it all right if we go up to see Jonathan?'

'Well, it wouldn't do you much good if you did. He's sitting out in the garden at present. Why don't you go and join him? I'd like him to come in soon, mind. It will go chilly soon, and I don't want him catching a cold now that he is on the mend at last.'

Hannah promised, and taking Ben's hand, she led him back out of the entrance doors and around the house until the back lawn was in sight. Jonathan was sitting on a wooden bench beneath the branches of an enormous oak tree, and they were relieved to see that he was alone.

They exchanged a glance before setting off across the emerald-green grass towards him. They had almost reached him when his head turned in their direction and he asked, 'Who's there?'

'It's Ben, Jonathan, and Hannah.'

'Ah, then come and join me. It's so peaceful out here, I was just about to drop off.'

They took a seat on either side of him and after a minute had passed, Ben nodded at Hannah and she licked her lips and began, 'Jonathan, I have something to tell you. I went into Newcastle today and whilst I was there I saw someone who was not aware that you had returned from the war. They were so relieved to hear that you had been found alive.'

'Oh yes, and who would that be then?'

'It ... it was Felicity Cartwright.'

Jonathan's mouth fell into a gape and had it not been for Ben's hand on his arm, he would have risen from his seat as he babbled, 'Ben, please let me explain. I never intended–'

'Oh *shush*, man. You have no need to explain anything to me. Felicity and I were never in a serious relationship. Why didn't you tell me that you were seeing each other?'

Shame-faced, Jonathan admitted in a low voice, 'I was afraid of how you would react. Afraid that you might think I had done the dirty across you.'

'Never, but now listen, for Hannah has more to tell you.'

'Well, the thing is, it seems that Felicity still has very strong feelings for you,' Hannah continued. 'She would like to come and see you – but only if you wish to see her, of course.'

Jonathan looked wretched as he muttered, 'What would be the point? She would hardly want me now, would she?'

Sighing, Ben asked him, 'Answer me one question. Do you still love her?'

Jonathan remained motionless for some time but then his head slowly nodded up and down. 'Yes, I still love her – I have never stopped loving her. But why would she want to tie herself to someone who is almost blind?'

'Oh, for God's sake, man!' Ben snapped impatiently. 'Have you forgotten who you are? You are the grandson of Harry Bensham. He left you more than comfortably provided for – a wealthy man. When you leave here, you could live anywhere you liked and have servants to wait on you hand and foot for the rest of your life, if that's what you wanted. Why should the fact that your vision is now impaired stop you from being happy? Would you not rather be blind with the woman you love beside you, or will you choose to be blind and alone, so that you can wallow in self-pity?'

Ben knew that his words were harsh, yet they seemed to have the desired effect, for now Jonathan said, more strongly, 'And you would not hold it against me? The fact that you and Felicity knew each other first?'

The mood was lightened now as Ben chuckled. 'In case you hadn't noticed,' he said, 'I am now a very happily married man. In fact, I have the best wife in the world. The only cross we have to bear is the fact that we cannot have children. Your cross will be the loss of your eyesight.'

Jonathan's hand now groped in front of him until he found Ben's, and suddenly he was laughing and crying all at the same time.

'Oh Ben, you will never know how many times I have come close to telling you about Felicity and me,' he told him, 'but each time, shame stopped me from doing so. I feel as if a great weight has been lifted from my shoulders. And yes, I would love to see her. Would she really come here, do you think?'

'I know she would,' Hannah assured him. 'And the sooner the better.'

'Is ... is she still beautiful?'

As Hannah heard the wistful note in his voice, a picture of Felicity's work-worn face and shabby clothes flashed in front of her eyes, but what she told him was, 'Oh yes, Jonathan. She is still beautiful, very much so. So – shall I arrange for her to visit?'

When he nodded, she and Ben exchanged a smile. Suddenly Jonathan's future looked bright again, and it would be brighter still when he discovered that he was the father of a beautiful little boy.

After seeing Jonathan safely back to his room, hand-in-hand they began the mile-long walk back to the cottage. Early evening was casting a cloak of colours across the hills and fells, and Hannah was relieved to see that Ben was calm.

As if reading her mind he said softly, 'I wonder how he will react when he knows that he has a son?'

'I should think that he will be delighted,' she answered, and they went on their way in contented silence.

Chapter Twenty-Eight

'How are you, Betty?' As Dan stepped into the kitchen, Betty sighed with frustration. She was sitting with her leg, which was plastered from the knee to her ankle, resting on a stool.

'Mad at meself,' she muttered. 'Fancy goin' me length like that. They reckon at the hospital that this cast will have to be on fer at least six weeks. *Six weeks*, I ask yer! How is Ada goin' to see to the cookin' an' the cleanin' an' lookin' after the lads all on her own?'

Dan acknowledged that she did have a point. Ada was no spring chicken now, and as lovely as the boys were, they had created a lot more work for the women. He had hoped to set off for Manchester tomorrow to continue his search for Brigie's daughter, but there was no chance of that now. Not with Betty laid up as she was.

'Don't worry, I shall be around to help,' he told her, and at that moment a whoop of delight sounded from the direction of the hallway and Hannah appeared with David already seated on her hip and the other two following close on Ben's heels.

'So what have you been up to then?' Hannah asked Betty with a twinkle in her eye.

'Eeh, I went me length on a potato peelin' of all things.' Betty clucked her tongue in annoyance. 'You'd think I'd be more careful at my age, now wouldn't you?'

'Well, sadly, accidents do happen,' Ben replied philosophically. 'But how are you going to manage with this little lot?' As he spoke he ruffled Pip's hair and the boy grinned up at him. He had put on weight, and his cheeks were rosy from the fresh air and healthy way of life.

'I were just sayin' the same thing to Mister Dan,' Betty told him fretfully. 'Ada would rather die than admit it 'cos she worships these children, but I think she's strugglin' a bit at present. Particularly now she has me to pander to an' all!'

'In that case, I think we just might have the solution to all your problems, because Hannah and I have come to offer to take the boys back to the cottage with us until you can get about again.'

'B ... but I couldn't ask you to do that!' This was from Dan, who was staring at Ben as if he had taken leave of his senses.

'Why not?' His son stared steadily back at him. 'We have more than enough room and I'm sure the children wouldn't object, would you?'

Three little heads nodded eagerly. Dan thought it over. He supposed if Ben and Hannah were offering it would be foolish to turn them down. And the children did seem to be more than happy with the idea.

'Very well then. If you are quite sure it won't be too much of an imposition I shall take you up on the offer,' Dan agreed, and the children grinned broadly before scuttling away with Hannah to pack their things.

Deep down, Dan felt a sense of relief, for although the Beddows boys were a delight to have about the place, he knew that he could only offer them a temporary home. Since their arrival he had spent far less time with Ruth, and although she was putting a brave face on things, he had seen a change in her since the wedding. She seemed to have slowed down, and had taken to having a rest during the afternoon – something he had never known her to do in all the time they had been together. Sometimes he felt as if he were torn between the boys and Brook House, on one hand, and Ruth and Mary Ann on the other. Not that Mary Ann really needed him any more. Since marrying Tom she had had eyes only for him, and Dan felt that this was just as it should be.

Taking advantage of the fact that the children were out of earshot, Ben decided to confide in his father about Jonathan and Felicity Cartwright. When he had done, Dan shook his head in disbelief. There seemed to be so much going on around him that sometimes he felt as if he were struggling to keep up with it all. The visit to Manchester was also weighing heavily on his mind, for Brigie was sinking fast now and he felt as if he had let her down. Now that the boys were sorted, he wondered if he should go to spend some time with Ruth or set off for Manchester?

He had no time to think on it, for at that moment, the boys burst back into the kitchen like a breath of fresh air to say their goodbyes.

Ada and Betty kissed them all soundly then watched with amusement as Hannah herded them out to the car that Ben had recently purchased. Dan waved them off from the gate and pensively watched them drive away. Perhaps while they were gone he could make enquiries about a boarding school? Pip's two brothers were a little young to be sent away to school, admittedly, but at least that way they could be sure of having a good education. One thing was certain, things could not go on as they were. Betty and Ada could not be expected to cope with three energetic youngsters indefinitely. Sighing deeply, Dan turned and made his way back into the house.

As the car pulled up at the bottom of the steps leading up to the Hall, Hannah squeezed Felicity's hand reassuringly. The woman was shaking like a leaf in the wind, and William, who was sitting next to her, looked totally bewildered by his first journey in a car and all that was happening.

His mother had merely told him that these people were taking him to visit someone very special, and with that he had had to be content for now, for his mother had closed up like a clam when he had tried to question her.

'Perhaps I could take William for a stroll around the grounds whilst you go up to Jonathan with Ben?' Hannah suggested and gulping deeply, Felicity nodded.

'Yes, that might be best ... thank you.' It had only been a few days since she had learned that Jonathan was still alive, and although she was thrilled, she was still reeling from the shock of it.

Ben came around to the other side of the car and after helping the ladies down from it he smiled as he then held his hand out to William. He was a fine boy, there was no doubt about it, and deep inside Ben regretted the fact that the child was not his, for he would have been proud to call him his son. But then, the way he saw it, Jonathan was overdue a little happiness after all he had endured, and if he and Felicity could make their peace, then they might soon become a family unit, and he would see his brother happily settled.

As he walked with Felicity up the steps, he looked across the lawn to where Hannah was leading William by the hand towards the topiary trees. She looked happy – in fact, he realised with a little shock that she looked happier than he had seen her for some long time.

Since Lawrie's death, followed so closely by the loss of their second baby, she seemed to have lost some of the sparkle that went to make up the person she was. Yet since having the boys to stay with them, she had blossomed again. A smile lifted the corners of his mouth as he thought of the little rogues. They had left them in Nancy's charge, and no doubt she would be running around after them like a cat that had lost its tail by now. Not that she would mind in the least, for Nancy seemed as taken with the youngsters as Hannah did. So did Fred, if it came to that. Only the day before, Fred had taken them fishing in the burn with little nets and they had come home as proud as punch with jars full of tadpoles. Ben grudgingly admitted to himself that he too was enjoying having them scampering about the place, though he would never admit it to the womenfolk, of course.

He was holding Felicity's elbow and he flashed her a reassuring smile as they entered the Hall. Sweat was standing out on her brow and she was as white as a sheet, but she managed to smile weakly back at him all the same.

'Come on,' he said kindly. 'Let's go and get it over with, eh? I've no doubt Jonathan will have chewed his fingernails down to the quick by now. He is so looking forward to seeing you.'

Felicity nodded, but deep down inside she was almost dreading their reunion, for she knew without doubt that neither of them were still the same people they had been when they parted, near six years ago. Too much had happened to both of them. She had suffered the shame of being disowned by her family and the birth of an illegitimate child, whilst Jonathan must have seen sights that no man should see on a bloody battlefield. She had lain awake the whole of the night wondering how they would react to each other. Would the love still be there – that wonderful tingly feeling that used to start in the pit of her stomach every time she so much as looked at him?

As if he were able to read her thoughts, Ben told her quietly, 'Things will pan out fine, you'll see.'

They were standing on the landing outside Jonathan's bedroom door now and suddenly she turned to Ben and blurted out, 'I'm so sorry for all that has happened, Ben. And also for the way I shouted at you the other day. I suppose it was guilt.'

Pain briefly lit his eyes but then he told her solemnly, 'It's me who should be apologising to *you*. Looking back, I don't know why you ever bothered with me in the first place. I had a chip on my shoulder and realise now that I treated you very badly.'

'No,' she said fairly, 'you never forced me into doing anything that I did not want to do, and I always knew exactly where I stood with you. I'm just sorry that I wasn't honest with you when I met and fell in love with Jonathan. Can you ever forgive me?'

'I already have,' he told her affectionately, and now he tapped at the door and pushed it open.

'Go on – in you go,' he encouraged. 'I shall be in the garden with Hannah and William, but take as long as you like. Your boy will be perfectly all right with us, and you and Jonathan have a lot of catching up to do.' His hand now resting gently in the small of her back, he eased her into the room and then closed the door and tiptoed away.

The second he heard the sound of the door opening, Jonathan turned towards it with his heart in his mouth. He had worked himself into a sweat but now as he saw the silhouette by the door he asked, 'Is ... is that you, Felicity?'

'Yes – yes, it's me.' Tears had started to her eyes as she looked towards him, for he was almost unrecognisable. The memory she had held dear was nothing like the man who stood before her now. The weight seemed to have dropped off him and there were streaks of premature grey in his hair. His eyes had also changed, for now they had a glazed look about them – but then she supposed that was due to his partial blindness.

They stood as if they had been cast in stone for long seconds that seemed like an eternity, but then he was fumbling towards her with his hands outstretched and she seemed to almost spring towards him as she sobbed, 'Oh my dear. To think what you must have suffered.'

And then she was in his arms and he was kissing the tears that were raining down her cheeks as he gasped, 'I ... I wanted to let you know that I was home, but... Well, so many things stopped me. Firstly, I was sure that you would be married and would have forgotten all about me by now. Secondly, I was afraid that you would not want to see me when you learned that I was now partially sighted, and thirdly ... I was too ashamed to tell Ben that you and I had come together before I went away. I was afraid that he would think I had done the dirty across him.' Tears were wet on his lashes too now, and as she looked into his beloved face, the years fell away and he was once again the man she had fallen in love with.

'Shush,' she murmured. 'None of that matters now. All that matters is that you are safe. I told you once that if I could not marry you I would never marry anyone, and I meant it. But come, we will sit down.' Taking his elbow, she steered him towards the two chairs that were positioned by the open window and soon they were seated opposite to each other although their hands remained tightly joined.

'So,' Jonathan pulled himself together with a great effort and asked, 'how are you? And your family – your mother and father – are they well?'

Her teeth bit down on her lip as she slowly replied, 'My family and I are estranged, Johnny, and have been for some years.'

'But ... but why?'

This was the moment she had been dreading, but there was no avoiding it so now she told him, 'After you left, I er ... I discovered that I was to have a child. When my mother and father found out and I would not name the father, they disowned me.'

'You ... you have a *child?*' he asked incredulously.

There was a slight pause before she told him, 'Yes. His name is William and since the moment he drew breath he has been the light of my life. I ... I think you will like him.'

'But ... how have you managed? Where do you live?'

'I live in Newcastle and I manage very well. As you know, I have always been very adept with a needle and I now earn my living by sewing.'

'Oh my dear, it must have been so very hard for you.' The question he was longing to ask had been lodging in his throat but now it burst from him when he asked, 'Is ... is William *my* son, Felicity?'

The silence stretched until he began to fear that she would not answer him, but then she whispered, 'Yes, William is your son.'

She held her breath as she waited for his reaction, but when it came it was nothing like she had hoped it would be, for he suddenly sprang from the chair, overturning the small table that was placed between them in the process.

'Then from now on you will not have to work. I shall support you both. That is the very least I can do.'

Shock anchored her to her seat. She had hoped to hear words of love and endearments. Instead, Jonathan was standing there telling her that he would support her and their child financially. Her back stiffened and now her voice was cold as she replied, 'There will be no need for that. I did not come here looking for charity.'

'Then why did you come?'

She rose slowly and after smoothing down her skirt she made to walk past him as she said in a voice that shook, 'I came hoping to find the man I love, hoping that he would still love me. But I see I had a wasted journey.'

His hand grasped her arm and brought her to a shuddering halt as he whispered brokenly, 'You *did* find the man who still loves you – but how could I expect you to take me on now? Look at me, Felicity, and tell me what you see. Or better still, I will tell you what I am now. I am blind, or as near as damn it – do you hear me? *Blind!* What use would I be to you now? Or to our child, if it came to that?'

She looked him straight in the eye and her voice was loaded with sadness and regret as she told him, 'I would have taken you, had you been without limbs *and* sight, just so long as I could be near you.'

He stared at the blurred shape of her for long minutes as if he could scarcely believe what he was hearing, and then suddenly his arms went about her and their lips were pressed together, and for now they were the only two people in the world, and that was fine, for they needed no one but each other. When at last they broke apart she saw a glimpse of the man Jonathan had once been when he laughingly told her, 'In that case, you leave me no choice but to make an honest woman of you, Miss Cartwright. So ... I ask you now: will you marry me, Felicity?'

'Yes, Mr Bensham, I will marry you.' She laughed through her tears and then they were clasped together and she was sure that he would squeeze the breath from her body, so tightly did he hold her.

When she at last stepped back from him he said, 'Well, come on then. We must go and tell Ben and Hannah the good news, not to mention our son. I think it's about time I met him, don't you?'

A feeling of unreality settled on her as he took her hand and began to drag her towards the door. The sad man she had seen when she first entered the room seemed to have vanished into thin air, to be replaced by a man who now had something to live for. And as they clattered down the stairs side-by-side she was praying, 'Please God, let us always be as happy as we are now right at this minute.'

When they burst onto the terrace some minutes later, after passing a startled Matron in the hallway, he asked her, 'Where are they? Can you see them?'

Her eyes flitted around the grounds and then she saw them down by the ornamental pond beyond the topiary trees. Taking his hand, she began to lead him down the steps and now he was shouting, *'Hey!* Ben ... Hannah!'

The small party assembled at the side of the lake swung about and looked towards them, and now a smile settled on Hannah's face as she told Ben, 'I think we may be just about to have another happy-ever-after ending, if I'm not very much mistaken.'

William was staring at the woman coming towards him as if he could not recognise her. His mother's face was glowing and the child thought he had never seen her look so happy, but who was the man who was holding her hand? And why were they laughing so?

When they eventually came abreast of them, Ben discreetly put his arm about Hannah's shoulders and whispered, 'How about we pop up to have a word with Brigie? I think they need a little privacy, don't you?'

She nodded numbly and taking her husband's hand, she walked with him in the direction of the Hall. At the bottom of the steps she paused to look back across her shoulder and the sight she saw warmed her heart, for Felicity and Jonathan were sitting on the grass with William between them, and even from here she could see the look of wonder on the child's face as he was introduced to the father he had thought he would never meet.

Chapter Twenty-Nine

Quentin Wolfe sighed as he stepped down from the train. The journey to Manchester had been most uncomfortable with his arm troubling him as it was, and he was relieved that he had finally arrived at his destination. Glancing through the smoke that floated around the platform, he spotted the exit and started towards it.

Once through the soot-blackened doors, he had his first view of the town – and was not favourably impressed. Like the station, it looked dirty and neglected. Fumbling in his pocket for the address with his good hand, he frowned. Southall Street. From enquiries he had made, he knew that Strangeways Prison was situated in the same street, and even from here, the high tower of the prison that provided the heating and the ventilation for the place was visible, standing out above the rooftops like a scar on the skyline. He shuddered. Since the closure of Salford Prison, Strangeways had become a place of execution. It had its own execution shed and condemned cell, as well as a permanent gallows, and as he thought of it now, the sweat stood out on Quentin Wolfe's brow. Twenty-eight men and one woman had been hanged there during the period between 1869 and 1899, and it suddenly occurred to him that for all he knew, some other poor soul might be getting ready for the noose right this very minute.

Loosening his cravat but trying to make his resolve as stiff as his moustache points, he set out in the general direction of the tower. It was not difficult to find Southall Street, for even when he entered a labyrinth of back streets, still the tower hung above him, growing closer with every step he took.

In no time at all he found himself passing the imposing entrance gates to the prison, and without even being aware of it, his footsteps quickened as if he was afraid that some great hand might suddenly plunge through them and drag him into the godforsaken place. Some way further along the road he stopped and frowned; the houses seemed to end abruptly at number 19 and the one he was seeking was number 26. He cursed softly beneath his breath. All that stretched beyond the remaining houses was a wasteland. Dwellings had obviously once stood here, but now there was nothing but grass and weeds, through which the remains of buildings leaned like drunken gravestones.

Spotting a group of children who were rolling a hoop along the road he called to them, 'Here, what happened to the houses that used to stand here?'

'Couldn't tell yer, mister,' a raggy-arsed little urchin shouted back. 'They were gone afore my time. But why don't yer call into the Dog an' Duck further along aways? Me mam reckons that Dougie, who keeps it, is as old as the 'ills. Happen

410

he'll know.'

'Thank you, young man.' Quentin Wolfe took a penny from his pocket and tossed it to the child, who caught it expertly.

The lad waited until the man was some way away before muttering, 'Tight-arsed old sod.' What was he supposed to do with a penny? It wouldn't even buy him a twist of aniseed bullets! Still, he supposed it was better than nothing so, whistling merrily, now he turned in the direction of the shop.

Just as the boy had told him, Quentin Wolfe eventually came to a dilapidated old public house. A sign hanging from a rusting chain announced that this was the Dog and Duck. He stared at the façade of the place. It was hardly prepossessing. In fact, it looked a real spit and sawdust sort of dump where you might get your throat cut for sixpence if you didn't keep your wits about you. Still, he decided, the sooner he followed up his enquiries the sooner he could get home, and seeing as he had an assignation lined up for that very evening with a certain lady of dubious reputation who was singing at the local music hall in Newcastle, Quentin decided to risk it. His policy had always been: nothing ventured, nothing gained – and he saw no reason why today should be any different.

Pushing open a door from which the paint was peeling, he found himself in a bar-room that looked more like a cattle shed. In fact, he was convinced that the majority of cattle sheds would probably be cleaner than this place. A rough wooden bar ran the length of the room, and he approached it through a haze of foul-smelling blue smoke. Men of various shapes, sizes and ages were sitting at trestle tables, drinking jugs of ale and smoking pipes as they curiously followed his progress across the room.

Once at the bar, Quentin flashed the elderly landlord his most dazzling smile as he said, 'I'll have a tankard of ale, my good man, if you please.'

The landlord turned to hawk into a spittoon that was standing at the side of the bar and then began to fill a none too clean tankard with ale, saying not a word. When it was full, he slapped it unceremoniously onto the bar. After pushing some loose change across to him, Quentin asked conversationally, 'Lived around here for long, have you?'

'Long enough.'

Quentin decided to try again. 'Then I dare say you will have seen many changes in the area?'

'Aye.'

This was proving to be hard work, but Quentin had never been one for giving up easily so now he said, 'I was actually looking for number twenty-six, but the houses seem to stop at number nineteen?'

'Aye.'

'Have the houses that have been knocked down been gone for long?'

'Aye.'

Thankfully, just then an old man with a long white beard who put Quentin in mind of Father Christmas piped up. 'They was pulled down years since. We 'ad a fever epidemic 'ereabouts an' they was demolished shortly after that. Terrible thing it were, terrible! Folks were droppin' like ninepins, so they were.'

Lifting his tankard, Quentin now joined him at his table and asked charmingly, 'May I get you a refill?'

'Happen I wouldn't say no.'

Once he had had the old man's tankard filled to the brim, Quentin rejoined him and probed, 'So, did you know any of the people who lived in those houses?'

'Every last one of 'em, God rest their souls,' his elderly companion said piously as he slurped noisily at his beer.

'And would you happen to know who lived at number twenty-six? They had a daughter, I believe.'

'They did that, an' thank the Lord she survived the outbreak. Bonny little lass she were, if me memory serves me right.'

'Do you know what became of her?'

'Well, I knows where she went, if that would be of any 'elp to you. But all this rememberin' is thirsty work, so it is.'

Lifting the tankard, which the old man had drained in record time, Quentin took it to the bar and filled it yet again before returning to his companion and placing it in front of him.

The old man once again raised it to his lips and took a long drink, then wrinkling his brows he scratched at his beard as he said thoughtfully, 'Now, let me see. Number twenty-six...'

When Quentin Wolfe left the inn some time later he was almost reeling from the shock of what the old man had told him. What a turn-up for the books, eh? He could hardly wait to get home and give Mrs Radlet the news. In fact, he was so excited that he had even forgotten all about the little floozy he had lined up for that evening. If he wasn't very much mistaken, this piece of news was going to warrant a hefty bonus in his pocket. Oh yes, a very hefty bonus indeed!

Dan woke to the sound of birdsong and stretched lazily. Downstairs he could hear Ruth and Mary Ann pottering about the kitchen, and the smell of bacon frying was wafting up the stairs to him. Being a Sunday there was no rush for anything, and for a moment he lay there letting the peace of the place wash over him. Since taking the boys, he had become used to being woken by the sound of laughter or squabbling, and it was nice to just lie there and listen to his family downstairs.

Looking towards the window, he saw that it was going to be another fine day. Ruth had suggested they might take a picnic up onto the fells in the afternoon, and Dan decided that it might be pleasant to do just that. It would give Mary Ann and Tom a little time alone in the house too.

At that moment he heard the sound of footsteps on the stairs and then Ruth pressed the door open, saying, 'Here, sleepyhead. I thought you'd like a cup o' tea in bed.'

'You spoil me,' he told her with a wide grin on his face and she flapped her hand at him and laughed gaily as she placed the cup and saucer on the small bedside table.

'Well, ain't that what wives are supposed to do?'

Leaning up on his elbow, he took a sip of tea before telling her, 'That idea of yours about a picnic – I think we ought to go. The weather certainly seems as if it's going to be in our favour.'

'We'll do that then.' She straightened the eiderdown before turning about and making for the door, but there she paused to tell him, 'Do you know somethin', Dan? I never dreamed that I could be this happy.' With that she turned and walked from the room. Dan stared after her, with the usual stirrings of guilt. If only he could love her as she deserved to be loved.

At lunchtime, the four of them sat down to a saddle of lamb that had been cooked to perfection, and crispy roast potatoes that Ruth had done just as Dan liked them.

As he loaded his plate for the second time he noticed that Ruth had barely eaten anything. Through a mouthful of broccoli he asked, 'Aren't you hungry, dear?'

'I've got a bit of indigestion,' she informed him jovially as she thumped at her ample chest. 'Too much bacon at breakfast, no doubt. Still, it'll mean that I'm all the more ready fer me picnic, won't it?'

'Oh, Mam,' Mary Ann teased. 'If you went more than a couple of hours without getting food inside you, I reckon you'd pass out.'

'Happen you're right,' Ruth agreed affably. 'But there ain't nothin' wrong wi' havin' a healthy appetite, hinny. I'll pile a bit more into the hamper to make up for what I ain't eatin' now'

The meal ended in laughter and soon after, Dan and Ruth set off. Before they left, Ruth paused to kiss Mary Ann soundly, and taking her face in her two hands she told her, 'You enjoy havin' the place to yourselves for a while now, do you hear me? I love you, lass.'

'I love you too, Mam,' Mary Ann replied affectionately, and now Dan lifted the hamper and they went on their way. Ruth was dressed in her Sunday best, wearing a new hat that Dan had recently bought her, and as they strolled along she was feeling the bee's knees as she hung onto his arm.

They headed for the outskirts of the village and soon came to the open fells. Presently they climbed a small hill and it was there that Ruth told her husband, 'Eeh, happen that's far enough, lad. I ain't as young as I used to be, you know. Let's stop here, eh? The view couldn't be bettered.'

She was right, for the landscape that stretched before them was breathtaking. Dan happily spread out the blanket and she sat down and carefully removed her hat, gazing around her. 'Happen you couldn't be much closer to God than up here.'

Dan looked at her questioningly, before remarking, 'That's a bit sombre, isn't it?'

'Not at all. We all 'ave to go sometime, an' bein' up here gives you a little taste o' what heaven is goin' to be like.'

Dan was unpacking the hamper, and once the feast was spread out he joined her on the blanket and they began their meal as they stared at the panoramic view in silence.

After a while, he remarked, 'You're very quiet today, Mrs Bensham.'

She turned to stroke his face. 'I was just thinking how lucky I've been. Do you know something? If I had me life to live all over again, I wouldn't change a single thing.'

Ruth meant every word she said, for the only regret in her life was the fact that Dan had never once told her he loved her. But then, she supposed, she couldn't have everything so she was quite content with her lot.

She lay back on the blanket, enjoying the feel of the sun on her face as Dan rose and stretched, and shook the crumbs from his trousers. 'I think I might take a little stroll down to the brook,' he said. 'Do you fancy coming along?'

'No, lad. I've still got a touch of that dratted indigestion. I think I'll stay here and have a little rest. You go on.'

He bent to kiss her gently on the lips before striding away across the heather, and when he returned half an hour later, he saw that she was fast asleep. There was a smile on her face and she looked so peaceful that he decided not to wake her. Not for a while, at least. The way he saw it, it would do her good to have a rest; she was always running around after one or another of them. He sat beside her and the time slipped by as he watched the sun's progress across the hills.

Eventually he reached across the blanket to gently shake her arm. 'Ruth, come on. We ought to be thinking of getting back. We don't want to be caught up here in the dark, do we? You'll have slept the clock round at this rate.'

When there was no response he lifted her hand, and it was then that fear snaked its way up his spine. Her hand was cold.

'Ruth, do you hear me? Wake up, I say!' Panic was setting in now but still she lay silent and unmoving.

He now crawled across the blanket and touched her cheek and as he did so, her head fell to the side and in that moment he knew that she had gone from him for ever and his heart was so full of pain that he didn't know how he would bear it.

'*Noooooooooo!*' His cry echoed across the fells, startling the birds from the trees as he gathered her lifeless body into his arms. And there he sat rocking her to and fro until at last he placed her gently down on the blanket and grim-faced, walked down into the village. He would need help in getting her back home where she belonged.

'So what will happen to the boys now?' Hannah asked. Ada had just visited them to tell them of Ruth's death, and neither Ben nor Hannah could take it in. They could not remember a time when Ruth had not been a part of their lives and were still reeling from the news.

'They can stay here until Father has had time to come to terms with it,' Ben told her. 'He's going to have his hands full, what with organising the funeral and one thing and another. And the boys aren't really any trouble, are they?'

'Not at all,' Hannah agreed. 'As far as I am concerned, they can stay here indefinitely.' Secretly she was already dreading the day when Dan would take them home, but now was not the time to dwell on her own feelings.

'Just think,' she mused. 'Here we are, and already within months of each other we have heard of a wedding, a death and soon a christening.'

'That's life's progression, I'm afraid.' Crossing to

the open window, Ben gazed out on the boys, who at that moment were trying to climb the large oak tree that stood in the far corner of the garden. They had changed almost beyond recognition from the pallid, stick-thin urchins that Dan had brought home from London, for now they were filling out and fitting their clothes due to all the good food they were eating. His thoughts turned to his father who, according to Ada, had taken Ruth's death very badly. But then he supposed that was to be expected, for even whilst his mother had been alive, Ruth had been Dan's rock.

Hannah now interrupted his thoughts when she said, 'Do you think we should go over there? I don't like to think of your father all on his own.'

'Well, he won't be on his own, will he?' Ben pointed out. 'He will have Mary Ann and Tom there, but yes, perhaps I should go. You can stay here with the boys if you like.'

As he strode from the room, Hannah sank down onto the settee. To think that Ruth was gone – just like that! And she had seemed so very happy since she and Dan had been married. It just didn't seem fair, but then as Hannah had discovered, life rarely was.

Ben returned some hours later just as Hannah had finished tucking the boys into bed and reading them a bedtime story. She was descending the stairs as he came in at the front door and she immediately asked, 'How is he?'

Ben ran his hand through his coal-black hair, a habit he always adopted when he was upset or worried about something.

'Not good, but then we could hardly expect

him to be, could we? Ruth is laid out in her coffin in the parlour, and he refuses to leave her side. He wouldn't even contemplate her lying in the chapel of rest.'

'Well, if it gives him comfort to have her there, that is not a bad thing. And how is Mary Ann taking it?'

'Very upset, as you can imagine. Apparently, Father has already told her that the house is to be signed over to her and Tom after the funeral.'

Hannah ran softly down the stairs and took her husband's elbow. She steered him towards the parlour, telling him, 'You go and sit down. You look all in. I'll get us a nice hot drink, eh?'

Ben nodded absently as he entered the room, and once alone he crossed to lean on the mantel-shelf and stared down into the empty fire-grate. There was something weighing heavily on his mind; he had intended to talk to Hannah about it this very night. It was an idea that had been growing there for some days, but now that Ruth was gone he felt the time was not right to put it to her, and so he pushed it to the back of his mind.

They chose to have a light supper on a tray that night, for neither of them were very hungry after the sad news they had received earlier in the day. Hannah was picking at a ham sandwich when Ben said, 'Oh, I forgot to mention. I called in at the Hall after my visit to Father's. I thought Brigie and Jonathan ought to be made aware of what has happened.'

'And how are they both?'

'Well, Johnny is like a different fellow; full of the joys of spring. But then he would be, wouldn't he?

He and Felicity had decided to be married by special licence as soon as possible, but he says that as a mark of respect to Ruth, they might postpone it for a while now. Felicity and William were there, as a matter of fact, and Johnny and William are getting on famously. You would hardly believe they have only recently known about each other. It's quite touching to see them together, to be honest, but Brigie... Well, I have to say I don't like the look of her. She seems to be failing fast.'

'People have been saying that for years, but Brigie is a fighter,' Hannah stated optimistically.

Ben smiled wearily; it had been a long day and he was ready for his bed. 'Let's hope you are right,' he said. 'God knows we have enough grief to cope with, what with losing Ruth so unexpectedly.'

Hannah nodded in agreement and then, hand-in-hand, they left the supper tray where it was and slowly climbed the stairs. Once on the landing they inched open the bedroom door where the children were sleeping, and as they looked down on the three contented little faces, they smiled at each other before moving on to their own room.

Chapter Thirty

'For goodness sake, Sarah. Will you *please* stop clumping up and down? You are making me quite dizzy!'

Sarah's lips drew back from her teeth in a snarl as she rounded on Constance and spat, 'Why *should* I? I *hate* this house now! Do you hear me? *I hate it!* And you ... whatever were you thinking of, going off to see Brigie like that after all she has done to this family?'

'Oh, not that again,' Constance's voice was weary, for ever since the day of her visit to the Hall, Sarah had nagged her relentlessly. Jim Waite had almost broken his neck in his haste to tell Sarah about it, but then Constance supposed that this was because of the way she had spoken to him. Jim had been strutting about the farm like the Lord of the Manor ever since Michael's death, and when, every once in a while she tried to put him in his place, he always acted like a spoiled child.

Now she tried to placate her daughter-in-law as she said softly, 'I am getting old, Sarah, and I have finally realised that to bear malice does no good at all. It simply makes you twisted inside. I merely wanted to make my peace with her. Brigie was once like a mother to me.'

'Huh! Just as she tried to be a mother to that bitch who stole my husband,' Sarah retorted. She now leaned heavily against the table and, raising her crutch, she wagged it menacingly in Constance's direction. 'It's unbelievable when you come to think on it, ain't it? She gave her own flesh and blood away, yet spent her life trying to dominate other people's children.'

'I'm sure she had her reasons for doing such a thing. And knowing her as I do, I believe she is suffering for it now. Why else would she appoint Dan to try and find her daughter? She obviously wishes to make amends.'

It was as Constance was speaking that Sarah's hatred of the woman lying up at the Hall got the better of her and an idea began to form in her mind. The old witch was obviously only holding on in the hope that she would get to see her daughter before she died. But deep inside she was still the same Miss Brigmore who had ruled the nursery floor. Sarah had no doubt at all that, should she ever discover that her secret was out, the shame would kill her.

Flouncing about, she now made for the stairs as Constance watched her with a worried feeling. She had seen that sly look on Sarah's face before and knew it did not bode well. Just what could she be planning now, she wondered.

Ten minutes later, Sarah reappeared, wearing her Sunday-best dress and hat.

'And where are you thinking of going?' Constance asked.

Sarah smiled cunningly. 'Let's just say that I have a bit of business to attend to.' With that she clumped from the room and the next instant, Constance heard her cry, 'Jim! Jim, get the trap ready for me, would you?'

Constance bit her lip in consternation. She just knew that Sarah was up to no good. But what could she do about it? The woman was a law unto herself these days and Constance was tired of battling with her.

She heard the horse pull up in the yard some minutes later and the sound of a startled chicken as Sarah kicked it out of her way, and then through the small leaded window she watched the crippled woman hoisting herself up onto the wooden seat of the trap, and all the time the feeling of foreboding was growing inside her.

Sarah was now high up on the fells, and as she passed an old derelict house she scowled. Within those ruins was where it had all started. Oh, she knew all about it, for Jim Waite had told her of how Constance had once lain on that filthy floor and made love to the brother of the man she was about to marry. And it seemed that the whole lot of them had been cursed ever since, the way she looked at it. Had Brigie allowed Constance to marry Matthew instead of Donald, things might have been different. But no, the woman had been too afraid of repercussions, should Constance have fallen for a child and so she had forced her into a loveless marriage.

Well, now it was time for revenge! Mrs Anna Bensham would soon know that the whole world knew of her shameful secret. Sarah looked out across the wild hills and the hatred inside her grew like a great boil that was soon to burst. And now she whipped the horse into a gallop, heedless of the fact that the trap was swaying wildly from side-to-side on the uneven track.

By the time she reined the horse to a shuddering halt at the steps of the Hall she had worked herself into a frenzy and the horse was frothing at the mouth. She flung herself down onto the ground and after snatching up her crutch she allowed the reins to dangle free and dragged herself towards the large black oak doors. She was in the hall and making for the staircase when Matron hurried towards her, exclaiming, 'Why ... it's Mrs Radlet, isn't it! Are you all right?'

Ignoring her, Sarah moved on towards the staircase as the Matron watched in consternation. The poor woman seemed to be quite demented. But what could she be doing here? Deciding that she might need some assistance, she rushed away to find the doctor.

When Sarah reached the nursery floor, she was panting, and her damaged leg was paining her, but in the red mist of her rage, she barely felt it. She was standing at the door now; only a piece of wood separated her from the woman who, as she saw it, had wrecked her life. She flung it open and it bounced back against the wall before dancing on its hinges as she burst into the room. The old woman lying in the bed turned startled eyes towards her and suddenly Sarah was a child again, cringing beneath Miss Brigmore's openly hostile gaze.

The hurt and hate that had built up in her now found release as Sarah hissed, 'You sanctimonious *old bitch!* Lying there pretending to be the Lady of the Manor. Well, I know different! You never thought I was good enough to lick your precious Barbara's boots, did you? But do you know somethin'? I'm *clean* compared to you and her. At least my Hannah was born in wedlock to the man I married. But you ... huh! You are no better than a *slut*. The whole county knows that you gave birth to an illegitimate child. *A bastard!* The prim and proper Miss Brigmore bore a bastard child to Thomas Mallen, an' all the while you *dared* to look down on me an' mine as if we were no better than a dirty smell under your nose. Well, you'll not play the lady again because everyone is laughin' at you. *Everyone* knows what you really are now! Do you know that? They *all know* what you are!

'*No!*' Anna's blue-veined hand was pressed tight across her lips and now, as her head wagged in denial and tears sprang to her eyes, the Matron burst into the room with the doctor close on her heels.

Taking in the situation at a glance, they charged towards Sarah and grabbed an elbow each, which sent her crutch skidding across the floor as she screamed, 'Get off me! Get off me – *do you hear!*'

They were pulling her back towards the door as spittle slid down her chin and her eyes flashed fire, but now she was out on the landing and suddenly the fight went out of her and she became limp in their grasp as she asked, 'Will you get me crutch, please? I've done what I came to do.'

Matron scuttled back into the bedroom and retrieved the crutch from beneath Brigie's bed then hurried back onto the landing. She handed it to Sarah without a word and watched as the woman slid it beneath her arm and negotiated the stairs as cool as you like.

She and the doctor then exchanged a puzzled glance before hurrying in to Brigie, who they could hear sobbing broken-heartedly.

By the time Sarah drove back into the yard of Wolfbur Farm, the sky was awash with the lilacs and purples that heralded the coming of evening. She was feeling strangely calm. So much so, that even the sight of a motor car parked in front of the barn did nothing to arouse her curiosity. Until she entered the kitchen, that was, and then the sight of Quentin Wolfe seated at the table brought her hand clasping in a fist to her heart.

'Wh ... what are you doing here?' Her face had paled alarmingly and she was aware of Constance watching her every move. 'I thought I had given you strict instructions never to come to the farm!'

'So you did, Mrs Radlet. But I have some information that I felt you should hear right away.'

Glancing towards Constance, Sarah told him, 'You had better follow me.'

Rising from his seat, he bowed to Constance then followed Sarah back out into the yard where she rounded on him.

'Well?' she demanded.

'I have discovered who the daughter of Mrs Anna Bensham is.'

Sarah could feel the ground rising up to meet her, and she had to lean heavily on a wall as she tried to compose herself.

'I see,' she gulped. 'Then in that case you had better tell me who she is and how you came by this knowledge.'

He began to tell her of his journey to Manchester and how he had found that the house he had been seeking was now no more than a ruin. He spoke of his conversation with the old man in the pub, and then hesitated as he glanced towards the open kitchen window.

'Well, go on then!' Sarah snapped impatiently. It no longer mattered that Constance might be able to hear his every word.

'It er ... appeared that the people who adopted

this little girl were a couple by the name of Waite.
They called her Sarah. But then, when she was
still quite small, both of the parents died of the
fever. It seems that the child was then taken on by
the man's brother, who lived on a farm. Wolfbur
Farm.'

Everything began to sway now as Sarah felt her
leg buckling beneath her.

'You ... you must be mistaken!'

When he shook his head from side to side she
drew in a deep breath. He was telling her that
Anna Bensham was *her* birth mother. But it
couldn't be true! He must have got it wrong! The
thought of being born to that witch and Thomas
Mallen was more than she could bear. The
woman had always hated her. Had always placed
Mallen's other bastard before her.

His voice seemed to be coming from a long way
away now as he took her elbow and asked, 'Are
you all right, Mrs Radlet? I realise that this must
have come as a great shock to you.'

A shock! That word hardly covered her feelings.
She stared back at him vacantly, and all the while
her mind was rebelling against what he had told
her.

At that moment, Constance appeared in the
doorway and the man saw that she too was
deeply shocked. Crossing to Sarah, she took her
arm and then, turning towards him, she told him,
'I think you had better leave now, sir.'

'Yes. Yes, of course.' He had been wringing his
hat in his hands but now he placed it firmly back
on his head and strode towards the motor car as
Constance led Sarah, unresisting, back into the

kitchen. Pressing her down onto a chair, she then hurried away to push the kettle into the heart of the fire. She would make her a good strong cup of tea with plenty of sugar in it. It was good for shock.

The room was silent save for the sound of Constance arranging the crockery and the chickens pecking in the dust outside.

It was not until Constance had placed a steaming mug on the table that she said quietly, 'Whatever possessed you to hire a private detective, Sarah? You knew that Brigie had set Dan the task of finding her daughter.'

Sarah stared at her unspeaking for a moment but when she finally answered, her voice held such venom that it made Constance's blood run cold.

'I hired him because I hate her. Do you hear me? I *hate* her! And if I could have done one single thing to cause her pain, then I would have done it. But I never dreamed that *I*...' Her words now faded away as she shook her head in disbelief. To think that she had once lain in that woman's womb... It was unbelievable.

Suddenly, another thought occurred to her and she sat straight in her seat.

'If *I* am Brigie's daughter, then that means that *I* am now legally her next-of-kin!'

Constance frowned as she realised the way Sarah's mind was working. 'But you know that Harry Bensham wished the Hall to pass to Ben after Brigie's death. Surely you would not deny your own daughter the chance to live there?'

'Why not? Hannah has never had any time for me, has she? She was always hand in glove with her father when he was alive, and since his death she has hardly bothered with me – so why should I consider her? I could be a lady of means. Think of it – *me* the Lady of the Manor!'

There was a pain in Constance's heart as it suddenly struck her that the woman's mind was unhinged. Sarah was rising from the table and Constance asked her, 'What are you planning to do?'

'Go over there and tell her, o' course!' A maniacal laugh now escaped from Sarah's lips. 'Can you just imagine how she will take it? No doubt the shock will ensure that I claim my inheritance all the sooner.'

Panic was setting in as Constance watched the woman hobbling towards the door, and in desperation she blurted out, 'Why don't you wait until the morning? If you try to cross the fells in the dark, you will likely get lost. Wait until then, I beg you.'

Sarah paused as she looked towards the window. Constance was quite right. Even people who knew the fells like the back of their hand had been known to get lost on them after dark.

Seeing her hesitation, Constance quickly continued, 'Come and sit back down, lass. You have a lot to think about. I will make us a meal and then you can rest, and in the morning you can go over there first thing if you still have a mind to.'

Sarah now moved hesitantly back to the chair, and once she was again seated, she stared unseeingly towards the fire with overly bright eyes as Constance began to prepare their evening meal.

Some time later, she placed a dish of fried liver

and onions in front of her daughter-in-law and whilst Sarah was eating it she crossed to the mug of tea she had just poured out for her and with her back to Sarah, she took a small bottle of laudanum from her pocket and tipped a generous measure into the steaming liquid. This was followed by three heaped spoonfuls of sugar, which would mask the taste of it. Her hand was trembling slightly as she carried it back to the table and placed it at Sarah's right hand.

'There you are, my dear.' Her voice was gentle as she stared at this woman whom she had once loved as her own. This woman who had just discovered that she had Mallen blood running through her veins.

Sarah stared at her suspiciously for a moment but then she lifted the mug and took a great swallow from it as Constance looked on.

Once the meal was over, Sarah began to yawn as Constance cleared the dirty pots into the sink. The lamps had been lit now and cast a cosy glow about the room.

'I think I'll just have five minutes in the chair,' she said drowsily.

Moving to the fireside chair, Sarah leaned her crutch against the arm of it and laid her head on the cushion, and within seconds she was fast asleep. Now as Constance looked down on her, tears began to roll from her eyes.

Sarah was going to destroy Brigie and she could not allow it. She took up the tin of paraffin that she used for lighting the lamps, and after bolting the door and closing the windows securely, she began to sprinkle it about the room.

When she had done, she slowly climbed the stairs to her room and after rummaging about in the drawer where she kept her handkerchiefs, she withdrew a faded photograph. It was of Matthew, the man she had loved for all of her life. Kissing his smiling features she then calmly made her way back downstairs and taking up a spill, she held it out to the fire. Once it was alight she paused to stare down on Sarah's slumbering features as she whispered brokenly, 'Forgive me, my dear. But it is time for all this misery to end.' She then held the burning spill to the curtains: within seconds, they had burst into flames. The flames then began to spread and within minutes, the whole room was ablaze. After the heat of the sun the timbers of the place went up like kindling and soon the flames were licking all around her as they consumed everything in their path.

Taking a seat opposite Sarah, and folding her hands sedately in her lap, Constance closed her eyes tightly against the intense heat. Very soon now, it would all be over.

Chapter Thirty-One

'Doctor, I am sorry to disturb you but I think you should come. It's Mrs Bensham. Her nurse has just informed me that she seems to be having trouble breathing.'

'Very well, Matron. I shall be there presently. Just allow me time to get dressed, would you?'

'Of course.' The Matron left the doctor's room, and hurried back to the nursery.

The old lady's eyes were feverishly bright and every breath she took seemed to be an effort now. She had declined ever since the visit from Mrs Radlet earlier in the day, and Matron blamed herself for that. If only she had realised that the woman was there to cause trouble she would *never* have allowed her access to Brigie's room.

Taking up a damp cloth, she wiped it around the old woman's face as she told her soothingly, 'There, there, my dear. The doctor will be here soon. Just try to rest.'

Brigie flapped her hand at her and tried to lift her head from the pillow as she gasped in great agitation, 'I ... *must* tell you. Thomas ... my beloved Thomas. It all began here ... in this house. We must be together again. I ... I wish to be buried next to him. He is waiting for ... me. Will you promise me that it will be done as I ask?'

'Of course. But you mustn't give up, Mrs Bensham. Just lie back and rest until the doctor arrives.'

'And Dan – tell him ... tell him that the search is over. He ... will know what you mean. Wherever she is, I wish her to be left in peace. Tell him to look no more...'

As the old woman fell back against the pillows, her mouth worked although no words issued from her lips as her bony hands picked at the counterpane. And then of a sudden they became still and she looked towards the corner of the room. The years seemed to slide from her face as a smile lit her lips, and she held her hand out toward the unseen presence. The Matron shuddered as she exchanged a glance with the nurse who was standing at the other side of the bed. They both then simultaneously looked towards the corner that seemed to be attracting their patient's attention. Apart from deep shadows, there was nothing there.

They turned back to the woman lying in the bed and now tears stung at the back of the Matron's eyes. 'She has gone,' she said softly. 'May God bless her soul.'

Brigie's lips were curved in a smile and there was a look of such peace on her face that it was all the Matron could do not to burst into tears. Moving her hand across the eyes that were still trained towards the corner, she gently closed them for the last time. Then, after drawing the sheet across Brigie's face, she and the nurse quietly left the room.

Dan seemed to have gone into shock, for so very much had happened during the last few days that he could barely take it in. First he had lost Ruth, then the very next day he had been informed that a fire at Wolfbur Farm had claimed the lives of both Constance and Sarah. And then for Brigie to go too ... well, it was too much to bear, and he had never even found her daughter for her.

Word had it that the Waite family were distraught, for despite their best efforts to douse the fire, they had failed. For some strange reason, Constance had chosen to lock and bolt the doors and windows that night, otherwise, as Jim had pointed out, he might at least have been able to get in there and drag them out, even if he could not have saved the farmhouse. They had managed to retrieve the bodies, or what was left of them, early the next morning, but the farmhouse was burned to the ground.

The surrounding villages were a hotbed of gossip. 'Well, if yer were to ask me, it's the best thing that could have happened,' the villagers were heard to say in hushed voices. 'It were a well-known fact that Wolfbur were never a happy place since the day Donald Radlet first drew breath there. Cursed, they reckon. Sad though too in a way. It's the end of an era, ain't it? Especially wi' the old governess passin' away on the very same night. Still, it's no more than should be expected. Everyone knows that the Mallens an' anyone connected to 'em always come to a sticky end. An' that lot were entwined as close as could be fer as long as there's been Mallens up at High Banks Hall.'

Ruth's funeral was so well attended that the mourners were forced to spill out of the little church where Mary Ann had only recently been married, into the churchyard. The same glass hearse that had carried Lawrie to his resting-place now took Ruth on her final journey, and the flowers... There were so many of them that after the gravediggers had filled in the grave it was rumoured that they covered five other graves as well as Ruth's, and the scent of them wafted all around the churchyard. The sun was riding high in a blue sky, across which powder-puff clouds were lazily drifting. And throughout the whole of the service and the burial, Dan shed not so much as a single tear, for the pain he was feeling this day went beyond tears. In fact, there were those who whispered that he might as well have been dead himself, so expressionless did he look.

The following day, Brigie and Constance were buried in two separate graves next to that of Thomas Mallen. Unlike Ruth's funeral, there were few mourners attending these burials, with only Mary Ann and Tom, Hannah and Ben, and Dan present.

Lastly, the remains of Sarah Radlet were interred next to the grave of her husband, Michael, and as the coffin was lowered into the grave, Hannah prayed that her mother might at last find the peace in death that she had lacked in life.

Chapter Thirty-Two

It was New Year's Eve and the whole family had assembled at the beautiful house that Dan had bought for Jonathan and Felicity as a wedding present. They had now been married for a little over four months, though no one would have guessed it to see them together. For they were still, as Hannah jokingly referred to them, like a couple of lovebirds.

Situated on the outskirts of Nine Banks Peel, Squirrel Lodge was a fine big house boasting six bedrooms and two bathrooms. It had formerly belonged to a mill owner, who had now retired to a house in London. The downstairs was of generous proportions too. There was a large entrance hall, from which an ornate staircase led to the first floor and a small galleried landing. Five doors led off from the hallway downstairs. The first being a good-sized parlour, the second a library – followed by a dining room, an enormous kitchen and finally a day room that William had adopted as his toy room.

The grounds surrounding it amounted to a little over two acres, and this included an orchard and a small copse to the side of it that William never tired of playing in.

Even today, when the snow lay thick on the ground, Ben was amused to see the boy's eyes straying towards it through the window. His own three boys were no better, he noted, and the thought brought a smile to his lips. *His own three boys.* The phrase had a nice ring to it. It was two months since he had approached his father and suggested that perhaps he and Hannah could offer the boys a permanent home. The idea had taken little persuasion, for Dan was still withdrawn from all of them, as he had been since the day of Ruth's death. And so, Ben and Hannah had now enrolled the boys in a local school and were in the process of legally adopting them. It sometimes seemed that their lives had changed almost beyond recognition, for it was not every day that you gained a ready-made family of three mischievous brothers.

Mary Ann and Tom were there too, Mary Ann

jiggling her baby daughter up and down on her knee as her husband looked proudly on. She and Tom had chosen to call the baby Ruth, in honour of Mary Ann's mother, and there was no doubt at all that she was a beautiful child, much adored by the whole family. She had eyes that were a deep periwinkle blue and already her head was covered in a thatch of thick, coal-black hair.

All in all, as Dan looked around at the smiling faces of his family, he knew that he should be feeling happy. After all, they were all well and settled, were they not? So why then, he wondered, did this terrible empty feeling in the pit of his stomach still exist – as if a part of him was missing?

He was no longer a young man and sometimes, just to get out of his empty bed back in Brook House each day seemed to take an enormous effort. After all, what did he have to get up for?

The door to the parlour suddenly opened and Nancy, who had come to help with the preparations for dinner, declared, 'Come on then, you lot. Let's have you all into the dining room now. Maggie and I haven't slaved over a hot stove all day just to see it go cold.'

Maggie was a local woman who came in each day to help Felicity see to the running of the house. Jonathan had begged Felicity to have a live-in servant but being a modern sort of woman, she would not hear of it. As she had pointed out, they were almost into 1921 and she had kept her own house in the years before she and Jonathan were married, so why should things be different now?

The children charged ahead of the adults and soon they were all seated around the shining mahogany table. This had been a wedding present from Hannah and Ben and was Felicity's pride and joy. Only the day before, her husband had teased her, 'You'll wipe it away if you keep polishing it!'

To which she had flicked her duster at him and retorted, 'Get off with you! I have certain standards to maintain now that I am the Lady of the Manor, even if it is only a small manor.' They had then fallen together in a giggling heap and as Jonathan thought back to the incident, a smile lifted the corners of his mouth. Not that this was the only thing he had to smile about, but the other good news could wait until after dinner when the children had retired to the playroom.

The meal was a jolly affair with much bantering amongst the boys and much conversation amongst the adults. By the time they were barely halfway through it the women had covered everything, from Dr Marie Stopes's first birth-control clinic that was due to open in London, to Charlie Chaplin's latest picture.

The men's theme of conversation seemed to be aimed at the new Austin Seven motor car that Ben had ordered for the New Year. When at last each delicious course had been devoured, Ben sat back in his chair and groaned.

'Oh dear, I don't think I should have eaten that syrup pudding after all that turkey and cranberry sauce.'

Hannah eyed him with amusement. 'Well, perhaps the fact that you had double helpings of everything hasn't helped,' she scolded. 'Don't go waking me up in the middle of the night if you end up with chronic indigestion. You have only yourself to blame.'

A ripple of laughter passed through the party as one by one they left the table and began to make their way towards the parlour. The children meanwhile scampered away to the playroom to play with some of the toys they had had for Christmas.

Felicity filled their glasses with sherry and port, and now the mood amongst the people assembled around the fire became sombre as she said, 'I would like to propose a toast, firstly to absent friends and loved ones.' They all solemnly sipped at their drinks as they thought back over the last few months, but the mood lightened somewhat when she went on: 'Secondly, to the New Year ahead. May 1921 be a good one for all of us. And lastly...'

A blush now stained her cheeks and Jonathan felt his way across to her and placed his arm about her waist as she continued, 'And lastly, I would ask you all to raise your glasses to the baby that Jonathan and I are expecting sometime in June.'

For a moment there was silence but then suddenly she and Jonathan were being caught in loving embraces as everyone tripped over themselves to congratulate them.

Dan pumped his son's hand up and down proudly. 'Congratulations, son. A little brother or sister for William, eh? What better way to start the New Year! Well done, I couldn't be more pleased for you.'

Ben teased, 'It's just as well you have a house with six bedrooms. At this rate you'll fill them in no time.' He playfully punched his brother in the shoulder.

It was then that Nancy made her announcement as she looked towards Fred. 'Happen this is a good time to tell you our news too. You see, the thing is ... well, Fred an' I have decided to get wed!'

Ben chuckled as he again raised his glass and exclaimed, 'Well, thank God for that! We were wondering when you were finally going to get around to it. Congratulations.'

Suddenly, for no reason that he could rationally explain, Dan felt the need to get away. Glancing towards the window, he saw that the snow was still coming down thick and fast, so choosing his moment he said, 'Well, that was a wonderful dinner, Felicity. And wonderful news to start the New Year. But now I really ought to be going. If I don't leave very soon, it looks as if I'll have no choice in the matter.'

'Oh, must you? Can't I persuade you to stay here and see the New Year in with us?' she implored.

He shook his head. 'Thank you, my dear, I appreciate the offer but I promised Betty and Ada I'd be back to see the New Year in with them. Besides, you youngsters don't want an old man like me spoiling the party for you.'

'Rubbish! We would love you to stay, but all the same if you have promised Betty and Ada then I won't press you.' She hurried away to get his hat and coat as he went about the room saying his goodbyes to everyone. Lastly he went into the playroom, where the children all kissed him soundly before waving him off.

Once at the door, Felicity looked towards Dan's

car and said with a note of concern in her voice, 'Are you quite sure that you will be all right, travelling in this? It's turning into a blizzard from what I can see of it.'

'I shall be absolutely fine,' he assured her. 'Now you get back to your guests and I will see you sometime next week. Goodbye, my dear, and a very Happy New Year to you.'

'The same to you,' she rejoined, as she hugged him, and then he ushered her back inside before striding away towards his car. The journey home took twice as long as it should have done, for the roads in places were almost impassable, and it was dark by the time Dan drove the car into the garage he had had built at the side of Brook House.

Turning off the engine, he sat for a moment letting the peace of the place wash over him before wading through the deep snow towards the kitchen door. Just as he had thought, he found Betty and Ada sitting either side of a roaring fire.

'Eeh, lad, you look frozen to the bone, so you do!' Betty declared as she hurried towards him and began to drag his coat from his shoulders. 'Go an' warm your hands by the fire an' then I'll get your meal set out for you.'

'Oh, no more food, *please*,' Dan groaned. 'I couldn't eat another thing after what I put away at dinnertime, but I wouldn't say no to one of your lovely cups of tea.'

'Comin' up.'

'I'll have it in here with you two, if you don't mind, and then I think I'll get myself away for an early night.'

'What – yer mean you ain't stayin' up to see the

New Year in?' Betty was appalled but Dan was adamant, and after drinking his tea he wished them both a very good night and made his way to his lonely bed.

Once the door had closed behind him, Betty sighed deeply. 'I don't mind tellin' yer, that one is givin' me cause fer concern,' she remarked to Ada. 'That's the first time he's set foot out o' the house fer weeks an' it ain't healthy for him to shut hisself away as he is doin', if you was to ask me.'

'I know what yer mean,' Ada agreed. 'He ain't been himself since Ruth went, God rest her soul. He's lost weight an' all, have yer noticed?'

'Aye, I've noticed. You'd have to be a blind man on a gallopin' donkey not to.' Then a sudden thought occurred to Betty. Should she ... or shouldn't she? Was it the right thing to do? But then, after all, she reasoned, what had she to lose?

It was almost four weeks later when Dan finally ventured from the house again – and that was only because Betty and Ada had hounded him to go and see his sons and their families.

It was early evening when he arrived home and just as she always did, Betty met him in the hallway and helped him off with his coat as she asked, 'And how did you find them all then?'

'Very well, thank you, Betty. I swear Pip has shot up at least another two inches. The boys seem to be growing like weeds.'

'Good, and have you eaten?'

'Yes, thank you, I have.'

Ada had come to join them now and as he stamped the snow from his shoes it was she who told him, 'Get yerself away into the parlour then.'

'Aye, get yourself away an' I'll bring you a nice tray o' tea in,' Betty piped up.

He saw her wink at Ada and frowned. Just what was she up to? Now that he came to think about it, she had been acting strangely ever since she had come back after taking a few days off earlier in the week. That in itself had been strange, for never in all the time that she had worked for him had she ever asked for leave before. Not that he minded, of course. It was just a little strange, to say the very least – particularly as when he had asked her conversationally if she was going somewhere nice, she had almost snapped his head off.

Now she was nudging him towards the door as she told him, 'Well, *go on* then, go through an' get yourself comfortable. I'll bring your tea through shortly.'

As he walked away, Dan was thinking, Women are funny creatures, there's no doubt about it. Should I live to be a hundred, I doubt I'll ever get to figure out how their minds work.

He slipped into the cosy parlour and glanced about. The lamps were lit and a fire was crackling brightly in the grate. Through the high bay windows he could see the snow falling in thick white flakes that were clinging to the glass, and it was then that loneliness engulfed him and he had to fight the urge that was on him to cry. He felt so utterly alone. But then, he reasoned, had he not always been alone? For, looking back, he realised that throughout the long years he had spent with Barbara they had never *really* been together. Her heart had always been elsewhere and the love had been all on his side. And Ruth – dear faithful Ruth. He had loved her, no doubt, but not with the passion that he had once felt for his wife. The passion that had slowly died with every lonely year that passed.

Crossing to the window, he pressed his forehead against the glass and screwed his eyes tight shut. Some minutes later he heard the door open softly and, thinking it to be Betty with his tea, he told her quietly, 'Just put it on the small table, would you, Betty? I will pour it presently.'

He waited for a reply and when none was forthcoming, he turned and looked towards the door – and the sight he saw made the breath catch in his throat, and for the most awful moment he was afraid that he might be dreaming.

'Hello, Dan.'

'*Meg!* What brings you here?' He was afraid to blink in case she vanished into thin air.

Laughing, she crossed to him and now she took his hand and led him towards a small sofa to the side of the fire before saying, 'Well, actually it was a visit from Betty earlier in the week. She told me about Ruth and of all the other terrible things that have happened to you and so... Well, I thought you might be glad of a friendly face, so here I am.'

'B ... but how did she know how to find you?'

'In a word – Pip,' she answered brightly, but then a frown crossed her face as she said, 'I do hope I am not intruding?'

'*Never.*' There was a great pressure building inside him, and as he looked into her blue eyes he could feel it slowly climbing from his stomach into his throat, where it lodged and threatened to choke him.

Seeing his distress, she stroked his hand, and the feel of her fingers set his pulse racing. 'I am so sorry about all you have had to endure.' The words were said with such sincerity that suddenly the tears he had held back for so very long exploded from him and he was in her arms and she was rocking him back and forth as if he were a child.

'That's it, my dear. Let it all out.' He was basking in the feel of her arms about him, and in that moment he was forced to admit what he had known deep down since the moment he set eyes on her. He loved her. Loved her with all his heart. But the realisation brought him no joy, for he better than anyone knew that love brought pain. And he had suffered so very much pain that he didn't know if he could bear to love again.

Her next words brought his head snapping around on his shoulders when she told him, 'I have a confession to make to you, Dan. You see, my reasons for coming here are not purely unselfish.'

When he raised a questioning eyebrow she flushed and lowered her eyes as she went on softly, 'My husband was a wonderful man; a good man in all ways. But as you know, he was somewhat older than me and our marriage was ... well, shall I say ... comfortable? I suspect much as yours to Ruth's was. That is perhaps why, when I met you, I could not understand my feelings. And then as time passed and your face stayed fresh in my mind, I realised that I had fallen in love with you and–'

He jerked away from her so quickly that she

almost slipped from her chair as she bowed her head in shame. 'I ... I'm so sorry, Dan. I should never have come here. It was a mistake.'

'Shush!' Snatching her hands, he drew her to her feet and now they were looking into each other's eyes and he had the weirdest feeling that he was coming back to life after a long, long sleep.

He had loved two other women in his life, but now it hit him like a blow to the stomach that he had loved neither of them with the force of the love he felt for this woman standing before him now. For this woman was returning his love with all her heart and he could feel their souls joining, and so now he told her, 'Oh Meg, I think I too fell in love with you the moment I set eyes on you, but I never thought that you could feel the same.'

They were both laughing and crying all at the same time now, and then, as he lowered his head and their lips met, Daniel Bensham knew that he had come home at last.

Dan had always been conscious of his slight stature, but in that moment he felt ten feet tall, and suddenly it did not matter that he had Mallen blood running through his veins, for he had the strangest feeling that he would be the first of his line who would one day die peacefully in his bed with this wonderful woman at his side, and it was all that he could wish for.

The curse of The Mallens had finally been laid to rest.